THE DARKENING

STEPHEN M IRWIN

D1343665

sphere

SPHERE

First published in Australia and New Zealand in 2009 by Hachette Australia,
an imprint of Hachette Australia Pty Limited
First published in Great Britain as a paperback original in 2009 by Sphere

A CIP catalogue record for this book
is available from the British Library.

ISBN 978-0-7515-4396-4

Printed and bound in Great Britain by
Clays Ltd, St Ives plc

Papers used by Sphere are natural, renewable and
recyclable products sourced from well-managed forests and certified
in accordance with the rules of the Forest Stewardship Council.

Mixed Sources
Product group from well-managed
forests and other controlled sources
www.fsc.org Cert no. SGS-COC-004081
© 1996 Forest Stewardship Council
FSC

Sphere
An imprint of
Little, Brown Book Group
100 Victoria Embankment
London EC4Y 0DY

An Hachette UK Company
www.hachette.co.uk

www.littlebrown.co.uk

For Ross

1

Snow fell.

It drifted down slow as morning mist, settling white on brown, white on silver, white on white. It fell so thickly that Nicholas could see no more than a metre or so ahead. His hair, normally the colour of dry grass, was white with it. His hands on his hips, flecked coral, blood red and indigo, grew steadily paler as he stood in the steady downward wash of white. His eyes, the darkest part of him, were all that moved as he watched the figure above him. A ghost, swaying its arms to the milky sky, waving. Or a summoning angel. A spectral thing, unmindful of him.

He stared a long moment, then pulled off his earmuffs.

The snowfall thundered down, driven by the roar of an orbital sander. The machine's electric hornet buzz so amplified by the soundbox of the ceiling that it seemed some lunatic was on the roof rolling an endless stream of rocks down the tiles. A stepladder was perched half-in and half-out of the bath, and atop it Cate strained upward as she sanded around the vent in the bathroom ceiling. Plaster dust was everywhere, making the small room a blizzard world of indeterminable size.

She imagined herself unseen, and the thought that he was watching her unedited self, her true self, pleased him. She attacked the ceiling in broad strokes that belied her size, swooping mightily over the plaster filler like a chef spreading dough or a shipwright planing planks. He watched the way her arm muscles moved

1

under their geisha patina, the way her calves stretched. Her energy warmed him.

It was a gloomy Saturday afternoon. While Cate prepped the bathroom, Nicholas had been chiselling up tiles in the minuscule laundry. Because they worked in separate rooms, it was all the more enjoyable to come together, picking their ways through the battlefield of paint cans, balled drop sheets, takeaway curry containers holding limey water and soaking brushes, to find some clean little beachhead in the madness, wipe the dust off each other, kiss and encourage themselves that the renovations would indeed end and this would soon – God, please, soon! – be the sexiest little flat in Ealing.

The dumb sky outside grumbled darkly, making the small bathroom in false winter seem even cheerier.

A tearing sound, and Cate switched off the sander.

'You effing . . . shit.' Her lips pursed tight, as if fighting to dam a wild ocean of obscenities.

Nicholas tutted. 'The language. It never fails to shock me.'

She turned to him – an albino alien, goggled and masked.

'Funny boy. How long have you been skiving off there, pervert?'

Nicholas shrugged. 'Why the foul mouth?'

Cate preferred not to swear, but that didn't mean she wouldn't. At a dinner party eighteen months ago, the host had asked Nicholas what date his and Cate's wedding anniversary fell on and he had momentarily drawn a blank. In the car on the way home, Cate had described the moment as 'fucking humiliating'. Delivered quietly in her round, wholesome vowels, the words cut with surprising efficacy. Less, for Cate, was more.

'A nail head tore the sandpaper. Again. Last sheet.'

She lowered her dust mask and lifted her goggles, revealing skin almost as pale as the plaster dust. She climbed down off the ladder, over the bath, to the floor. She was small. She spread her arms wide. Without thinking, he stepped into them – a beautiful trap. She slapped her arms around his waist – thup! – releasing a huge cloud of white dust.

'Sucka!' she cackled, and stepped back to survey her handiwork: a huge white patch on his front and a belt of white powder around his waist. She grinned.

Nicholas shook his head in mock disgust. 'You lured me. You used your body as bait and lured me.'

'Sucka!' she repeated, grinning more broadly. And opened her arms again.

This time she closed them around him slowly, and they talked through their kiss.

'How are you going?'

'Good. Bored.'

'Lazy slag.' Cate slapped his bum. 'Get back to it. I'll drive in and get some sandpaper.'

'I'll go. You're dirty. A dirty, filthy girl.'

He felt her lips smile under his.

'And now you're a dirty, filthy boy.'

It was four years ago, in a flat like this on a rainy evening, that he'd met her. They'd talked for an hour, danced drunkenly and badly for ten minutes, and kissed – smiling and clicking teeth – until the hosts called them a cab and, with no small relief, sent them home together. Maybe that was why he so liked their little apartment: because it felt like Cate. New love, and lovely at it.

'Be careful, bear,' she said. 'It sounds like rain outside.' She patted his backside again and clambered up the ladder.

•

She was right: rain fell steady and chill.

Nicholas shoved his hands in his pockets and stumped towards the kerb. Their flat might end up being the sexiest in Ealing, but it would still be one without off-street parking.

He stopped and swore under his breath.

Their '03 Peugeot was neatly trapped between a Yaris and the new neighbour's newer Land Rover. Again. *He owns a truck capable of climbing Kilimanjaro*, thought Nicholas, *but still catches cabs to get to Hounslow*. But he was in a good mood and didn't want it ruined by 'having words'. He'd take the bike.

A minute later, Nicholas pulled on his helmet, twisted the throttle, and his BMW let out a baritone rumble as it eased out from its stable behind the dustbins onto the street. He'd be soaking wet before he got to the hardware, and thoroughly dissolved by the time he got home, but he couldn't be arsed going back inside to fetch his slick or facing Cate's insistence that the urban adventurer next door get a talking-to. The lumpy side panniers would keep the sandpaper dry.

The world was painted from a palette of greys. There was next to no traffic. The rain on his face stung lightly enough to be pleasant, and the bike rumbled contentedly. As he turned down past Walpole Park, Nicholas resolved to enjoy the icy wet. He would be cold and happy with it: a pasha on his mount, a cavalier on royal duty; a man with an excuse to become naked before his beautiful wife in a quarter of an hour. He smiled to himself and glanced at the green park flashing past.

The grove always drew his eye. It was tucked in the corner of the park, its old trees cloistered together, huddled close as old soldiers under grim umbrellas. Neglected and conspiring. Secretive. Their trunks were dark as tar in the late light and the grey rain, and their tops were huge inverted bowls of sea black – thick green and rambling and restless.

Between the dark trunks was a face.

A man's face . . . yet not human. Larger. Older. In the instant before it retreated into the night-black shadows of the grove, Nicholas saw that from the corners of its mouth grew –

SLAM! A sharp, sick symphony of collapsing metal and shattering plastic, then he was arcing through the air. For a long moment, his eyes were filled with cloud-bruised acres of sky and telephone lines and silence. Then a small cracking sound and his lungs filled with mercury. Pain as hard as ice jolted through him like electricity. He was still moving: not flying now, but sliding on his back along the wet tarmac, frozen in a breathless world of insane agony. Sliding. Slowing. Stopped.

Grey rain and dark leaves. Silence.

And pain so solid that he felt carved from it – lungs spasming, wanting to work but unable to, more winded than he'd ever been during high school rugby or behind-the-shed fisticuffs. He could do nothing but lie there and will his burning lungs to please, please, please inhale!

A face loomed over him. Brown teeth behind thin fish lips. Wide eyes, deep frowns. Two faces. Then, like a tide returning and bringing waves with it, the world's noise returned with his breath – with a rattle, he sucked in cold, wet, beautiful air.

'. . . ring 999!'

'Don't move him!'

He let out a whistling breath and tried to sit up, but the movement brought fresh icicles of pain.

'He's okay!'

'Oh, Terry, he's okay!'

Nicholas, wanting to contribute to the optimistic mood, tried to whisper, 'I'm okay,' but it came out as a weak sigh.

A man and a woman stood above him, their details vague through tears of wretched pain.

Words spilled out of the woman like marbles from a split sack. 'We just backed out and didn't look and we're so, so sorry —'

'Don't say you're sorry!' hiss-whispered her husband.

'I didn't say sorry.'

'You did!'

'Phone?' wheezed Nicholas.

The couple clarified: a horse-faced pair in matching tweed, looking down at this wounded, talking marvel.

'Of course.' The man handed over his mobile. Nicholas's thumb shook as he dialled. He loosened his helmet as the LCD screen blinked: *Calling*.

'My bike?' he whispered.

The man lifted his chin and peered between the top of his glasses and the brim of his tweed driver's cap.

'Pretty well buggered. You know you're bleeding?'

'Oh, God! He's bleeding?!'

5

Nicholas held up a hand for silence. A click as the other end picked up.

'Hello?'

Cate. Nicholas's heart slowed. Relief as warm as sunlight washed through him.

'Cate.'

'Hello, bear. What's up?'

'Cate.' He was so happy to hear her. Why? He'd only left her a moment ago . . .

'Nicky? Where are you? Are you on the road?' Concern in her voice now. 'I heard the motorbike and – oh, God, have you had an accident?'

Her voice was growing fainter.

'I'm fine, nothing. A little bingle. You, though. Are you all right?'

He was so happy. Happy and amazed. She was fine. Why had he worried so?

Evening seemed to be falling fast. The equestrian couple was darkening in shadow, their faces growing as lean and hidden as the evening trees themselves. The rain was a steady hiss.

'I'm worried about *you*! Where are you? Nicky? Nicholas?' Her voice was thin and distant, words from the bottom of a well.

'I'm here . . . but you're all right!'

'Nicholas?'

Bump.

A grey pall fell over the world, rapidly making everything dimmer and darker. Grey became black. Evening became night.

'You're all right . . .' he whispered.

Bump.

•

Bump.

Just a little nudge, stirring a tinkle of ice. Bump. A flick of paper somewhere.

6

Nicholas opened one eye a fraction. It was night. Well, dark, certainly. And his face was cold and damp; chill hissed down on him. Was it still raining? His vision was swimmy.

Bump.

He opened the other eye, and blinked.

The aircraft cabin was as dark as a cinema. Hard plastic window shades were pulled down. The cool air was loosely laced with body odour and cologne. Passengers lay motionless with blankets drawn to necks, mouths agape, sleeping. Most lights were out, but a few private oases of yellow or blue peppered the gloom, a woman reading here, a man wearing headphones watching a small screen there. Up the aisle, a flight attendant checked on her wards, walking between passengers as silently as a benevolent spirit.

Someone behind Nicholas was drinking: ice ticked on glass. Across the aisle from him, a girl of six or seven sat awake, colouring a picture.

'Oh, God . . .'

Nicholas turned at the desperate whisper, before realising it was his own. His nose was blocked by mucus. He touched his face. His cheeks were wet and cold under the air hissing from the vent above.

He'd been crying in his sleep.

If I shut my eyes now and go to sleep, he thought, *I can go back.* Back to the beautiful lie that Cate was on the phone, worried, but alive.

But it was too late. The truth of things rushed through spill-gates, dousing him wide awake. He was alive and leaving Britain. Cate was dead: three utterly dreadful months in the ground. She'd fallen getting down the ladder to answer his telephone call after the motorbike crash, splintering her neck on the bath edge.

The cold weight of the realisation sank Nicholas deeper into his seat. He swallowed back bile and wiped his nose. The little girl across the aisle glanced at him disapprovingly. The flight was an eternity. He angled his watch to catch what little light there was.

'Are you all right, sir?'

He blinked.

A flight attendant looked down at him, brows drawn in tight concern. Her face was pale but her cheeks were pink and her nose freckled. Young.

'Excuse me?'

The flight attendant leaned closer, whispered again, 'Are you all right, sir? You . . . made some noise in your sleep.' She held a tissue towards him.

'Oh.' Not knowing what else to do, he took the tissue. 'I'm fine.' A lie to send her on her way.

'Bad dream?'

'Yes.' Another lie. So, now she could go.

But she lingered. The little girl across the aisle had stopped colouring and was sitting upright.

'That's no good. We like our passengers to sleep well.' The flight attendant's white smile was disconcertingly bright in the darkness.

'How considerate.' *So, please go.*

'We hate to see our passengers upset.'

The little girl was shaking. Nicholas tried not to look at her. He dragged his eyes back to the woman and forced a smile that must have been horrific.

'You really don't have to charm me. I'm already on the plane.'

The woman's smile faltered, but Nicholas really couldn't give a toss. The little girl was convulsing now, her legs jack-hammering and her hands clawing at her tiny neck. Her face was sharp red and her mouth was opening and closing like a hooked fish's.

The flight attendant recovered and cocked a smile at Nicholas – his frown could be turned upside-down. 'But we'd like you to come back. Another blanket? Pillow?'

He nodded, then shook his head. The little girl was turning blue, her eyes so wide they showed a finger's width of reddening white around the irises. *Don't look. Say nothing.* She fell to the floor right at the attendant's comfortable flats. Invisible fingers tore her top open, exposing her fluttering little chest and ribs.

Nicholas tried not to watch. His voice was a sandy whisper. 'No, really. I'm awake now.'

8

The little girl's back arched, and her head wrenched back at a hideous angle. She jerked mightily, a landed trout flopping with horrible, drowning violence. Then, like a sandcastle undermined by a wave, she collapsed on herself and grew still.

'Tea? Or coffee?'

The little girl's dead eyes stared at the cabin ceiling for a long moment . . . then rolled to fix on Nicholas's.

Nicholas shut his, then opened them on the attendant. 'What did the little girl die of?' he whispered.

The woman blinked. 'I beg your pardon?'

The girl was suddenly in her seat again. Her blouse was whole. She watched Nicholas, eyes unreadable. Her hands, as if with minds of their own, picked up the colouring book and crayon and recommenced their childish business.

Nicholas knew he should just shut up. But he wanted to wipe the smile off British Airways' face.

'A little girl died just here, didn't she?'

The woman stared at Nicholas, her mouth working as she made some decisions. He knew the look: the how-did-he-know-that-is-he-a-reporter-is-he-mental-is-he-*dangerous* look.

'How do you —' Her words were clipped. No politeness now.

He'd managed to strip her smile away. It didn't cheer him at all.

The little girl was colouring her book with tedious slowness. Her face was in shadow. The passenger beside her rolled in his sleep and put his arm right through her head.

The flight attendant straightened her skirt. 'I have no idea, sir. Information like that is kept by the airline. I must ask you not to talk about . . . such things on the flight, sir.'

She glanced once at the empty seat opposite Nicholas, then moved away, ghostly silent and a little too fast, up the dark aisle.

Nicholas looked over. The girl's hands stopped colouring. Her gaze was on his as she started shaking and turning blue again.

He rolled away from her and closed his eyes.

2

The air was cold. Yet this chill was light and fragile, ephemeral. Nothing like the entrenched and leaden cold of a British winter.

Nicholas walked across the car park to the rows of white and silver hire cars, reading the space numbers stencilled on the tarmac. He carried just one small suitcase. He found his car, pressed the remote, popped the boot.

Overhead, the sky was salted with tiny lights.

Stars. I've come back to a city where you can still see the stars.

He turned slowly, scanning the constellations. There it was: the Southern Cross. He had expected the sight of it after so many years would inject a warm tequila rush of nostalgia or a defibrillating jolt of hope. Instead: nothing. The cold July breeze tugged at his hair. The five stars of the cross seemed unimpressed. *We've guided campers, warmed lovers, drawn the fingers of fathers and the eyes of nodding children. What have you done? Killed your wife. Top job. Welcome home.*

Nicholas got inside and twisted the car alive.

•

The bones of a city don't change. Perhaps its skin grows tight or flaccid as suburbs grow fashionable or become déclassé; crow's feet spread from pockets – new streets, new arteries into fresh corpulence. But the skeleton of its founding roads, the blood of its river, the skull of the low mountain that looms over it with its thorny crown of television towers like its own blinking Calvary . . . these things hadn't changed.

It was nearly eleven. Nicholas drove the almost empty streets, amazed to be moving so swiftly and surely: a tardy San Juan Capistrano swallow in a white Hyundai. He had become so conditioned to London crush that to see inner-city streets so quiet made him shiver and wonder if everyone else knew some secret apocalypse was about to occur; some rapture to which he wasn't privy.

In the seventeen years since he'd last seen it, Coronation Drive had grown an extra couple of lanes and tidal flow traffic signals. But as he glanced across the wide, black waters of the river, the doppelgänger lights of factories and apartments winking on its wind-worried surface were so familiar that he could have been a child again, in the back-seat of his mother's Falcon, little Suzette snoring lightly beside him, tucked inside a pile of brightly coloured sample bags from the Royal National Show.

Parallel with the river drive ran the train line, its pylons winking into occasional view between new glass office towers and nineteenth-century townhouses resurrected as boutique law firms and restaurants. As he passed them, he said aloud the names of the railway stations, the same he'd rattled through each day returning from art college, each one closer to home and a hurried meal followed by hours in the garage riveting together a chair from coffee cans or weaving a fabric wall from speaker wire – ambitious, excited, even then dreaming of designing in London.

But London had proved nothing to be excited about. At the end of the eighties, it had seemed an endless expanse of dour faces pinched above colourful wide-shouldered jackets; a loud and falsely jolly bustle on a hurtling train heading nowhere in particular. No gymnasia back then, but a pub every twenty metres. The endless knock-backs. The bad bosses. The worse bosses. The dull twist of panic every time you looked in your wallet to pay for a shitty Marks & Spencer's sandwich and wondered how the fuck you were going to pay next week's scandalous rent. Too many Australians. No sunshine. No work.

But he was nothing if not creative. He found a niche and jumped for it like a busker at a twenty. A mate of a mate told him to look into a mob riding the wave of love for all things Eire and building 'authentic' Irish pubs across the south-west.

He rode to their sawdusty workshop in Streatham; after a coffee mug interview, a squint at his résumé and a test of his handshake, he got the job of decorating the pubs' interiors. It sounded easy. But it took less than an hour strolling through London's Davies Street antique shops to realise that if he bought his knick-knacks in the city, he had the budget to dress perhaps one shelf. It was motoring through little villages in the Midlands, Bedfordshire and Sussex that Nicholas discovered he had charmed luck sniffing out old curios, furniture and bric-a-brac. He'd leave London in a hire van on a Monday and potter without a plan, letting the front wheels find their own ways onto increasingly narrow roads flanked by dry-stone walls and watched by edgy sheep and unblinking blackbirds. For the first few months of this unlikely treasure hunting, Nicholas actively appraised the buildings in the villages to calculate which would be most likely to house an elderly soul ready to part with old junk. But experience taught him not to think; simply to let the solid feeling of surety in his midriff tell him which barn, which leaning Tudor, which locked presbytery would yield the rusty lamps, the worn shillelaghs, the dry-wattled accordions and beaten valises that London paid a fortune for. Without fail, he was guided to homes where owners, daughters, new tenants, disgruntled landlords, weary widows and forgetful widowers cheerfully divested themselves of odds and sods they were happy to see the arse-end of.

He would return to London on a Friday, poorly shaved with a sore back and bowels clotted by the stodge of fry-up breakfasts, in a van filled with old crap that cost perhaps three hundred quid yet was worth twenty times that to his employers and customers. He became Nicholas Close, Master of Old Shit. Need some tattered books, a rusty shotgun and decrepit fishing gear with a distinctly Gaelic twist? Call Nicholas Close. He's shameless, mildly charming, and he'll find it cheap. Oh, and did you hear? He used to be a designer or something.

London had finally, shyly, revealed her lucrative teat. One job alone had paid the deposit on the flat. And that contract had led to a permanent consultancy with a firm that opened Irish pubs in Kuala Lumpur, Dubai and Santiago. Nicholas had been charged with the dubious task of vivifying new spaces with objects whose original owners were long dead. It was tolerable and various, and the travel was good. He intended to get back to design next month, next financial year, after Christmas.

He met and married Cate. The mortgage had been reduced at a good clip. But the amusing collectables, the money, the diminishing loan statements, everything, lost its value the instant he walked into the flat in his wet and scraped motorcycle jacket and found why Cate hadn't answered his call.

You killed her.

'Shh,' he told himself.

Because you just had to take the bike.

'Shut up.'

There, said the voice in his head, *arguing with yourself. The slippery slope to madness. No wonder you couldn't keep a job.*

No. Not true. He was never fired. He quit.

And why was that?

Because the old shit he sought for a living tended to be found in old places. And the older the place, the more chance it had of being . . .

He didn't want to think the word.

Go on. Say it. It doesn't bite. Not any more.

'Haunted,' he whispered.

The word hung in the air like despair in a dying man's bedroom. It was still hanging, as if it were itself a ghost, when Nicholas sucked it back in with a gasp.

•

Time had frozen here.

While his mind had dragged through the thorny brambles of his last few months in London, his hands had steered him by dormant habit onto Carmichael Road and the suburb of his childhood.

Tallong.

For eighteen years it had been his home suburb. Earth was broken here not twenty years after the city was founded in the mid-1800s. Then the rolling hills of Tallong had been cleared of dense native forest, dotted with farmhouses and infected with Friesian cows and sheep. But the town became a city, and as it breathed in and its chest pushed out, the paddocks of Tallong were striped with gravel streets. Distinctive homes of chamferboard with one window glinting from under a corrugated iron gable and a cheeky wink for a side veranda began to spread along the new roads – avenues with names occasionally Aboriginal but mostly Anglo, as breezy as open sulkies and jauntily optimistic as the residents who built there. Pennyworth Street. Wool Street. Harts Avenue. Princess Street.

Tramlines were laid. Gas lines went in. Tarmac covered the gravel. Tramlines were ripped up. Telephone poles were sunk between yawning jacarandas and festive red-frosted bottlebrush.

In the sixties, when memories of the privations of war and rationing had lost their sting, the wood and iron houses were viewed with eyes now brought to a critical sharpness by the sight of rockets streaking skyward from Kennedy and Baikonur and Woomera. Some houses were torn down and replaced with monolithic hulks of pale brick and yellow glass. Septic tanks were drained and sealed. Sewer lines were dug in. The suburb grew green and fat and settled, a contented dame lounging by a slow loop of river; the fat queen of a well-made hive. Her only wildness was a wide corner of untouched native forest at her edge. Two square kilometres of rippling hillocks thick with trees, ripe for razing and selling and sprinkling with a thousand new houses.

It was the sight of the woods that made Nicholas suck in his breath and step on the brake. They were still there.

He stared out the side window. He was on Carmichael Road, the street he'd walked almost every day to and from school until something happened when he was ten, something that made him change his route. But even then he'd passed the woods each week; in buses on his way to high school, on foot on his way to the train station and college.

Seventeen years he'd been gone. In that time, the value of the houses here must have tripled. Yet this huge tract of densely wooded land sat at the edge of the suburb, unassailed. The moon was up now, furbishing the pelt of the treetops silver. The forest's bulk glowered below, black as shadowed eyes under a severe brow, watching . . .

He opened the door and stepped into the crisp night air. He walked across the crackling grass of the no-man's-land between Carmichael Road and the dark-toothed edge of the woods.

How could they still be here? Some developer should have snapped up the huge block, cleared it, slashed it, veined it with new streets with bromidic names like Spinnaker Court and Mahogany Place, and salted it thickly with pastel-rendered McMansions. Yet here they were, extant and untouched. Was it crown land, fiercely guarded by some cleverly written covenant? Maybe a park was planned? Perhaps the developers were just waiting till house prices boomed again?

Nicholas's feet crunched on gravel, and he stopped.

He stood on the same path he used to take home from school, a path that once yielded all sorts of treasures. A path on which he'd found something small and disturbing, something silently awful and strange and offensive . . .

His nostrils flared and his heart – as if having heard its own starter's pistol – began thudding in his chest. The memory of a hot November day a quarter-century ago reached out of the woods, put its sly hands inside him and knotted his stomach. He'd been ten. He was with his best friend, Tristram. Running. Terrified. Chased. Soon after, Tristram was dead.

Apart from the silvery whisper of the chill air in the leaves, the night was silent.

Nicholas realised he was avoiding looking at the tree line. He dragged his eyes from the electrum crowns of the trees down to the dark trunks. They stood like a row of black teeth, endlessly huge, stretching left and right into the night. The maw of some undersea thing, some behemoth, sentient and unquiet. Waking as it scented prey.

Something's coming.

The woods were alive. His heart hammered behind his sternum. Something inside the trees had sensed him, tasted him on the cold air. Recognised him.

It was coming.

Go! he yelled in his head. *Run!*

But his body was frozen. His feet would not move. His fingers sat cold and still as icicles. His eyes were locked on the darkly grinning trees, waiting for them to open and for whatever they held to reach from their damp innards and take him and consume him and leave him slit and empty and drained as Tristram's little body had been so many years ago. And part of him welcomed that fate.

Nicholas flinched. A raindrop hit his scalp. Another, his cheek. And another. His head, as if released from some dark spell, jerked upward.

The sky that had been clear and starry at the airport was now an eyelid half-closed; clouds as black and inscrutable as the woods before him had consumed the sky to its zenith and were marching further overhead, already dropping their ordnance of cold, heavy drops.

A whisper of white flickered at the corner of his eye. He turned, catching a glimpse. Something small and pale flickered away between the dark trunks, as if devoured by the trees.

His galloping heart was shaking his whole body. He again told himself to turn; this time his body listened, and he put his back to the biding woods and strode through the matchstick grass to his car.

It took all his willpower not to run.

•

Rain rioted on the tin roof.

Nicholas watched his mother pour steaming water into a teapot, glumly mesmerised by the billowing clouds of steam. The sight of her making tea was so familiar that it could have been transposed, with just a little loosening around the edges, from two decades ago. The kitchen had been freshened with new benchtops and a stainless-steel fridge, and his mother was a bit heavier and just a little shorter, but nothing significant was different. Seventeen years, and nothing had changed. The thought made him tired.

'Your sister is coming up from Sydney tomorrow.'

Katharine Close's voice had a singsong matter-of-factness that suggested schoolteacher or marriage counsellor. In the early seventies, she had been a weather girl at a local television station – a shapely lodestone for the discussion of meteorological events in service station garages and on fairways. Katharine had just been offered the upward move to reading the six o'clock news when she fell pregnant with Nicholas. Motherhood then separation then widowhood conspired to pretty well put a bullet behind the ear of her fledgling television career. She raised her two children alone. When they were both old enough for school, she cleaned houses until she had squirrelled away sufficient to buy herself a kiln and wheel. Then she sheeted up a small studio between the stumps under the house and taught herself the secrets of clay and flux and glaze. She paid for her habit by selling her pots and platters at farmers' markets and teaching a handful of students when the mood took her. On the kitchen dresser, Nicholas saw berthed a small armada of perhaps twenty teapots.

Katharine handed him a steaming cup.

'Suzette's coming up,' he said. 'Why?'

'I have no idea. To see her brother?'

'I only just arrived.'

His mother tapped her spoon sharply on her cup. 'Yes. Selfish bitch.'

They drank in silence a while. Above the surf-like rataplan on the roof, Nicholas could hear the house ticking around them as it cooled. He felt his mother's eyes crawling over his face.

'You look awful,' she said.

'Cheers, Mum.'

In his memories, his mother's hair was perpetually chestnut, worn tight as a fiercely guarded nest. Now it was grey and loose.

He took a biscuit from a plate, scrutinised it, and put it back. Katharine tutted and whisked it up, then dunked it in her tea. It was a gesture Nicholas remembered from a frugal childhood – nothing wasted. Nothing, except time. Even after his father died, some two or three years after he left them, Nicholas never saw Katharine with another man.

'Seeing anyone?' he asked.

She scowled at him over the rim of her cup. 'I see lots of people. None worth talking to.'

'Having a thing with the clay man? Dalliances with horny delft pedlars?'

'No.'

'You'll get a reputation.'

'As what? A cranky old dyke?'

Nicholas shrugged.

'Grand.'

They ate and drank in silence.

'You know they offered me five hundred thousand for the house?'

'Who?'

'People.' She waved the word away. 'Not bad, though, for an old girl.'

'Not bad,' he agreed.

Rain gurgled in the downpipe outside, a visceral rush of cold water in dark places. He thought about mentioning the Carmichael Road woods, asking his mother how they could still be there, asking if she thought, too, that they lurked with the menace of a group of shadowed men on an otherwise empty street, men whose silhouettes were drawn taut with latent trouble. But he felt foolish trying to catch the words, and so let them swim away into the ocean-like patter outside.

'I'm sorry I couldn't make Cate's funeral.' Katharine said it boldly, but the silence that followed bled the words dry.

Nicholas ran his tongue around his teeth, as if hunting for a civil thing to say that might be caught there.

'No airline would have carried you, you were sick as a dog,' he said finally. 'She liked you.'

Katharine smiled. It bloomed and died on her lips. 'Poor man.'

He looked up. She was watching him carefully, wearing the same owlish look he knew from thirty years ago, when he was five and thinking of raiding the biscuit jar. A look that warned him against doing something he might regret.

'It was an accident, Cate's death. You do know that, Nicky.'

Nicholas drained his tea, stood, and kissed the top of his mother's head. She looked old.

'I'll see you in the morning.'

•

Katharine dried Nicholas's teacup and put it quietly back on the shelf. *Well*, she thought, *the day has come. He's here at last.* She flicked the kettle on and sat as it started to sigh.

How did she feel? It had been three weeks since Nicholas rang to say he was leaving England and coming home. Every day since, she'd wondered how she'd feel when he arrived. And every day she'd been forced to admit she was dreading his return. Then she saw him as he stepped from the car – a thin, long-legged man with a shock of dirty blond hair – and her heart had leapt like a pebble on water. *Donald!* Then she chastised herself. Donald had been dead thirty years. But, my God, didn't he look like his father?

She'd watched him step through the shadows cast by the yellow streetlight, saw how unwell he looked. Like that painting by Sargent of Robert Louis Stevenson. Thin-limbed and long, pale and dark-eyed. Harried into long strides by silent things in dark corners. Bright-eyed with something that could be fever or genius or madness. When the doorbell rang, she'd had to fight the temptation to turn off the lights, burrow into a corner and pretend she wasn't home. Why? Why did she want to avoid her own son?

Because he's bad luck.

She'd fairly slapped herself for thinking that, and threw open the door and threw her arms around him before they'd both realised a nod and a kiss would do.

The kettle rumbled discontentedly and switched itself off. Katharine popped a teabag into her cup and drowned it in scalding water.

Bad luck. *Just like Donald.*

She snorted, angry with herself, and sat.

Nonsense. She was unsettled because her boy was coming home after such a long time, and he'd want to be part of a life that she'd made very comfortable without him. Suzette in Sydney, Nicholas in London, a phone call each week and that was fine. Her life was hers, and her children were loved well from a distance. A visit every six months from Suze and the kids. A flight to London every second year to see Nicky and Cate . . .

Ah.

Katharine sipped her tea. Cate was dead, and Nicky was home.

She'd almost wanted to see him burst into tears at the sight of his mother. It would have meant he wasn't coping. She'd coped, when Donald left, and later when he died. She'd had to. She had two kids to raise. If Nicky had cried tonight, well, that would have proved something, wouldn't it?

He looked so ill. Had she been drawn that thin when she made Donald leave? No: she'd known it was a war then, a war against time and the world, a war to be fought and won; and in war one ate what and when one could. She'd kept her strength. It was Donald who'd faded. Donald who'd grown thin and haunted . . .

She shrugged off the thought. Past. All in the past.

She took one more sip then poured the rest down the sink. Her boy was home, and he needed looking after. It had been a long time, but she'd at least *try* to be a mother again.

•

'I don't see why he can't come here.'

Suzette ignored Bryan. She was up to her arse in the spare-room cupboard looking for her second hairdryer, the small one.

'I mean, honestly, it's just him, right? Couple of days with your mum, then he can fly down here —'

'Bryan,' called Suzette in a sweet voice. 'Come here a minute, darling.'

There was a moment's silence – long enough for Suzette to imagine Bryan realising he'd really pissed his wife off. Then she heard reluctant footsteps in the room behind her. Aha! There was the dryer, in the Country Road bag. She wiggled out of the cupboard and turned to face Bryan.

'What?' he asked in a quiet tone that said he knew very well what.

'Are you going to keep harping on about this?'

She realised she was holding the hairdryer like a pistol, and so started rewinding the cord. She wasn't really angry with Bryan; he was a good bloke. A funny bloke. A fabulous father. And it was always his business that played second fiddle when things needed to be done. He was a hydrology consultant and a reasonably successful one, but it was Suzette's business that brought in the big bucks that allowed them to live in this beautifully renovated stable-house so close to the centre of Sydney that there were times she felt almost obliged to apologise to their friends for their good fortune. Once again, she would fly out of town, and Bryan would have to put his appointments on hold to look after the kids. Normally, he was so easygoing she wondered if he'd taken up smoking pot. But he had a real bee in his bonnet about this trip.

'I'm not harping. I just don't see why your brother can't spend a couple of days with your mum, then fly down here. I mean, it's not like he has any ties or anything —'

'Now his wife's dead?' asked Suzette.

'You know that's not what I mean,' said Bryan. 'Forget it. Forget it . . .'

'No. What do you mean?' She could hear the curtness in her voice, and it reminded her of her mother. Now *that* was depressing.

Bryan sighed and put his big hands in his pockets.

'Why have you got to go straightaway? He's hardly back in the country. And I really don't see why he can't come here. I mean, we flew all the way to bloody England for his wedding —'

'He did pay for our hotel.'

'— and he's back for . . . I don't know, for good, I guess. So . . .' Bryan shrugged. 'Why have you got to leave us?'

Suzette looked at him. He was like a panda bear, and she felt a sudden wave of love for him. She put her hands around his waist and kissed the spot on his chest just below his neck.

'I'm going *because* he's come back,' she explained. 'Mum's not going to be much of a comfort, they're like dogs and cats those two.'

'I like your mum.'

'Well, you're a member of an elite minority. Nicholas . . .'

Suzette pulled away from her husband. How could she explain this? She looked up into his glum, handsome face.

'I just think Nicholas is going to need a bit of an eye on him. Just for a couple of days.'

Bryan took in a long, slow breath, then nodded. He kissed the top of her head.

'Quincy's going to miss you. You were going to make apple pancakes Sunday.'

'You can make them.'

'I really can't.'

They smiled at each other.

'You'll be fine,' said Suzette. She paddled his bum with the dryer. 'Now, go get me the blue suitcase.'

•

The rain on the roof grew louder until it was as steady and manic as applause at a rock concert.

Nicholas lay staring at the ceiling boards. This had been Suzette's bedroom – lying in his own old room would have made the image of a failed artist too complete.

His mother was wrong. *No one* had regarded Cate's death as an accident. Certainly, Cate's brother, her parents, her friends, their mutual friends, even his own London friends, had all said the word 'accident' aloud, but the silences that followed debased its currency. An undertow of quiet blame dragged the time along whenever he met his in-laws. They *knew* he could have taken the car, if only he'd bothered to speak with the neighbour. They *knew* he'd already dropped his bike once in the rain, on a roundabout in

22

Wembley. They knew that *he* knew Cate would be up the ladder when he telephoned. Their daughter's death may have been an accident, but it had been an avoidable one. Cate's had been a cruelly swift ending, and the blame for it would roost forever darkly on Nicholas's shoulders.

The Nicholas Close 'Welcome to Widowerhood' freeze-out had been choreographed with a subtlety that was a credit to London society. It began with a dwindling of phone calls, ratcheted to a sharp decline in dinner invitations, and climaxed complete as a solid, glacial wall of quiet.

Nicholas had tried to keep working. But it was hard to be productive and persuasive when one kept seeing things that, logically, shouldn't be there.

The motorcycle accident had left him almost unscratched but not without injury. After the crash, headaches came as unbidden and unwelcome as evening crows. After hitting the car and sailing through brisk London air, the bolt-of-pain landing had rammed his teeth together (slicing out a nice chunk of inside cheek) and jarred his brain like stewed tomatoes in a tin thrown against a brick wall. His growing panic that Cate wasn't answering the phone shoved the bright headache to the wings. The gutting despair and the hollow business of the funeral preparations kept the nagging pain in the background, but as sad days spun out to sad weeks, he was forced to acknowledge that headaches had made permanent nests for themselves in the dark eaves of his skull.

The decision to sell the Ealing flat was the only easy one he took in those lead-lined weeks. He listed it with a tall and jolly estate agent, found a room to rent in nearby Greenford, and began excising his life from the rooms he'd planned to share for years with Cate.

The one mercy was that Cate's brother and his girlfriend had volunteered to box up Cate's and Nicholas's belongings. Nicholas knew this wasn't to spare him more grief, but rather so that almost everything of Cate's could be taken back to the family home in Winchmore Hill without the need for a scene. He didn't argue. The idea of packing make-up brushes that would never again touch

Cate's skin and dresses he would never again pull from her shoulders had been filling his chest with a cold and stultifying mud, so he was grateful to find the small hillock of boxes marked 'N' packed in the front hallway.

He'd been carrying a last and cumbersome pile of boxes, topped with a framed photograph of him and Cate on their honeymoon in the Orkneys, down the front outside stairs when he stepped on a discarded Boots carrier bag. His feet snapped out from under him. He felt a brief and quite lovely sensation of weightlessness before the concrete steps seemed to fly up and hit him brutally hard in the small of his back and the rear of his skull. The world skipped forward a few seconds – moments lost in an inverted lightning flash of darkness.

When his eyes fluttered open, his headache was gone.

True, it had been supplanted by a severe slug of hurt between his hipbones and a burning gravel-rash throb on his scalp, but the black worms inside his skull had suddenly been exorcised. He lay motionless staring at the slate sky, enjoying the sensation of feeling – at least for a moment – that pain for once was all on the outside. The sky was as grey as an old headstone, and a small flock of starlings hurried across it.

Then a young man in a stained corduroy jacket stepped into his vision.

Nicholas realised he must look like a drunkard, and hoped this might grant him licence to remain lying there a while longer. 'I'm fine,' he said.

The boy looked down at him, unblinking. He had heavy bags under his eyes, and his skin was as pale as herring scales. His hands fidgeted like spring moles in his pockets.

Shit, Nicholas thought. *Maybe I'm not making sense.* He reluctantly rose to his feet, wincing in anticipation of the flurry of black claws into his brain. But the headache stayed away.

'I slipped,' he said.

The boy pulled his hand from his jacket pocket. It held a screwdriver. Nicholas's brain just had time to register it was a Phillips head when the boy shoved the chromed shaft hard into Nicholas's chest. Nicholas jerked reflexively, waiting for the wave of agony that was sure to come. The boy withdrew the screwdriver, then shoved it in a sweeping underhand into Nicholas's stomach.

Nicholas braced himself. But no pain came.

The boy watched him, jaw tight, red eyes glistening with tears. Then he took one step back, another . . .

Nicholas looked down at his chest and stomach. His T-shirt was unmarked. No punctures. No blood. No pain.

The boy took a step backwards off the gutter onto the road. A blue Vauxhall was racing towards him, only twenty, fifteen, ten metres away.

'You're going to —'

The car sped right into the boy, sending him flying. It kept going, accelerating.

'Jesus, Jesus!'

Nicholas took one, two, three jerky strides down the stairs and across the footpath. The boy lay prone on the road, a twisted swastika. *Christ*, he thought. *The car didn't even slow.*

He stared.

In fact, you didn't even hear it hit him . . .

Then the boy was up. He was walking on the weedy footpath towards the flats. As he passed, he rolled his gloomy eyes to Nicholas. Hands in pockets, he climbed the flat's front stairs to the buzzer panel, pressed it, waited, pulled the screwdriver from his pocket and stabbed an invisible victim twice, then retreated back, back, back and onto the road again before being struck by an invisible car and flying through the air, landing once more in a crippled heap. Then he vanished from the road, was walking on the footpath, and did it all again.

Nicholas was rooted to the spot, transfixed by the macabre loop. A woman with a blue anodised aluminium walking frame trundled right through the boy as he backed across the footpath. *She didn't see him.*

Nicholas waited till the boy had backed off the stairs, then scurried up, grabbed the boxes and shattered photograph, and ran to his car, shaking hard, not looking back.

A CAT scan – booked on the pretext of solving the now-vanished headaches – revealed his brain to be perhaps two per cent smaller than average, but otherwise normal.

But nothing was normal.

He was seeing the dead.

After his vision of the boy with the screwdriver, Nicholas drove home to his new and humbly tiny Greenford flat, took three Nytols and slid into a thick and dreamless sleep. The next day, he'd been able to dismiss the boy as a *Fata Morgana* brought on by the bash to the back of the skull, but the CAT scan results were a mixed blessing.

'Seeing things?' the radiologist asked. 'What kind of things?'

The look on the woman's face made Nicholas whip out the first lie he could think of, like an under-rehearsed magician pulling out a badly hidden bouquet. 'Freckles. All over people. Dark, join-the-dot kinds of freckles . . .'

She'd explained that there was no physical reason she could see for him to be having hallucinations.

Not ten minutes later, waiting for a bus on New Cavendish Street, he saw a portly middle-aged woman gag on a sandwich and fall to her knees. 'You all right?' he called, leaping to help her up. His hands passed through her and he landed painfully on all fours on the gum-sticky concrete, shaving skin off his palms. He scrambled up, aware that a small crowd of commuters had taken careful steps backwards, trying not to look at him. The choking woman rolled on her back, sausage fingers to her throat, heaving and turning blue until she fell still . . . and vanished.

Nicholas found himself apologising to the crowd, and stalked away on shaking knees to find another bus stop.

He saw them every day after that. Curled broken in space, the invisible wrecks of crashed cars around their suspended bodies. Falling from buildings. Screaming silently as long gone flames turned their splitting skin red and black.

He was sure he was going mad.

And that feeling grew worse when he went back to work.

The 'you-all-right?' winks and 'lovely service' pats on the back lasted a day or two but felt an eternity, so he was glad to get in a van and leave London. But the gladness was short-lived.

His canny hunts led him into wet-throated cellars, dust-cauled attics, lean-boned garages, weed-choked caravans. Grey places, rich and still. Places that were disturbing to stand alone in when the light was fading from the damp sky outside. These gloomy rooms where he found his booty left such a harrowed feeling in him that he was never tempted to keep any of his finds for himself. Not one old Smithwick's sign, not one dented Royal typewriter, Hignett cigarette card, Ekco bakelite wireless or Meerschaum pipe. Nothing. They were all strangely tainted. It was only after his fall down the steps and thump on the back of the head that Nicholas understood at last why those grim, quiet places where he found his dusty curios gave him the willies.

They were haunted.

Now, in those silent attics, garages, basements and back rooms, behind boarded windows or under musty eaves or paused on damp cellar stairs, he watched empty-eyed men throw ropes over rafters, thin farmers ease their yellow teeth over shotgun barrels, tight-jawed mothers stir rat poison into tea, young men slip hosing over car exhaust pipes . . . over and over and over. To make the horrors worse, he was invariably accompanied by the home's new owner or executor, who couldn't see the ghost and chattered about the charming virtues of the world's love affair with all things old, about the latest foot-and-mouth scare, about the weather, unaware that lonely death was being silently repeated right before their florid faces. And the ghosts, in return, took no notice of their living landlords, spouses, children, enemies . . . yet they all watched Nicholas. Their dead eyes rolled to him. They knew he could see them.

Nicholas stuck with his job for three weeks. Then, shaking and sleepless, he quit.

•

He had felt perpetually like crying. The dead were everywhere. He had to tell someone.

In the end, he confided in just three people.

The first was his workmate Toby, a full-faced cabinet-maker who headed the team that prefabricated the stalls and bars of the Irish pubs that Nicholas would later line with books, rods, copper kettles and Box Brownies. Toby was a bit of a tree-hugger, often talking about how the wood under his hands felt alive, always reading his horoscope in the *Daily Star*. He seemed the sort of chap who might listen to a story about hauntings. Nicholas was most of the way through explaining his fall on the stairs, the attack by the dead boy with the screwdriver, his consequent calls to police and hunts through newspaper microfiche files to discover that in 1988 a Keith Yerwood had stabbed his girlfriend, Veronica Roy, nearly to death on the stairs of her flat – *my flat!* – when he noticed the expression on Toby's face. It had been hard for Nicholas to place; he'd never seen anyone regard him that way before: it looked a little like confusion, a bit like scepticism, somewhat like anxiety . . . and yet it was something completely different, something solid and primal. Then he placed it. It was fear. Toby was afraid of him. The chat ended there. Very soon after, Toby began avoiding him on the shop floor and stopped returning his calls.

Nicholas finally found the courage to make an appointment to see a psychologist. He told the bird-fingered, beak-nosed doctor about Cate's death, about the headaches, the fall on the stairs and the haunted places. She nodded, took notes. He told her that other people thought he was a bit crazy, but he wasn't. From the small amount of research he'd done, the ghosts he saw correlated with records of deaths. The ghosts were *real*.

She nodded some more, and looked up from her notes. 'Do you think you're unwell?'

The question irritated him.

'I'm seeing the dead. It certainly doesn't feel fucking healthy.'

She nodded again and propped her head on an avian fist.

'Do you miss your wife?'

Nicholas hesitated. Was that a trick question? 'Yes.'

She pursed her thin lips. 'And do you think you could be inventing these "ghosts" in the hope that you might, at least for yourself, bring your wife back?'

The question struck like a cricket bat.

He'd been seeing strangers' ghosts for nearly a month, but had never thought about the possibility of seeing Cate again.

He hurried home to Greenford, heart racing, and grabbed the spare key for the as yet unsold Ealing flat.

The sun had dropped below the city's grey skyline when he hurried past the 'For Sale' sign around to the back of the complex (he studiously avoided the front stairs) and up the rear stairwell to their little place. The flat was clean and empty as a robbed tomb. His heart was throbbing in his chest so hard that his fingers shook. He strode through the echoing kitchen, past the still lounge room, to the bathroom. It was clean now – the long line through the dust where Cate's heel had slid as her neck swung down on its fatal parabola to the bath edge was long gone, the plaster dust all swept away. The shower curtain that had popped from the rail as she'd fruitlessly grabbed to save herself had been replaced. The ceiling remained unpainted.

And she was there.

Straining high on an invisible ladder.

'Cate?'

She turned at the sound of his voice. Put one foot down to a step in the air, another . . . then one foot slipped and kicked out from under her. One plaster-dusted hand struck out, grabbing at empty space. The other closed around a shower curtain that wouldn't hold her. She fell. Her mouth opened in a small 'O' of surprise. One heel hit the floor, and slid out – much as his own must have done finding the Boots bag – and she arced backwards. Nicholas dived to catch her, and his fingers smacked painfully into the tiles. Right under his face, her neck struck the hard, tooth-white edge of the bath and her hair tossed backwards. The goggles wrenched off. And her eyes stared up at nothing, dusting white under a phantom mist of powder. Her chest deflated slowly and didn't rise again.

Nicholas felt his throat twist and tighten. His wide eyes stung.

She looked so small. This was how he had found her the afternoon of the crash: sprawled as if exhausted, painfully arched, eyes open to nothing.

Then her eyes rolled towards his. Just for a moment. It was a look that could mean a million things or nothing. A look as empty as a dusty glass found forgotten on a window sill. Then she was back up the invisible ladder, floating, sanding, about to die again, and again, and again.

Nicholas stayed until midnight, watching her fall and die, until his eyes were so red and his throat so wretched he could hardly see or breathe. He willed his heart to burst and fail, but it kept squeezing, disconnected from his grief. Then he closed the bathroom door, locked the flat, and drove very slowly away.

He stayed in bed for three days.

The third and last person he told about his visions worked out of a small shop off High Street in between a discount luggage store and a bakery. A hinged shingle proclaimed 'Madam Sydel – Readings, Seeings'.

She was a wizened lady, brown and twisted as the trunk of some hardy Mediterranean tree, her wildly dyed hair sown with glazed beads. When she reached under her scalp and scratched purposefully, Nicholas realised it was a wig. Still scratching, she led him into a parlour lined with tasselled silks and smelling of incense and burnt hair. She sat him down and took his hand.

He jumped straight into business: 'I see ghosts.'

'Oh? How much do you charge?'

Nicholas went home, picked up the phone, and bought his airline ticket out of Britain.

•

The day before he stepped in the cab for Heathrow, he had woken to a rain as light as steam drifting from the sky. By mid-morning, when he reached the cemetery in Newham, the sun was having a tug-of-war with the clouds and was creating small diamonds on the roses and willows.

Nicholas sat heavily beside Cate's grave.

He looked at her headstone and a felt a swirl of guilt. It was black and angular and Cate would have hated it. 'Like something by Albert Speer,' she'd have said. Her parents had done the choosing. Nicholas remembered the typed, formally worded letter asking him for nine thousand pounds for the funeral, grave lease and a 'lovely service where the council plants spring and summer flowers on the grave'. He read the gold-lettered epitaph for the hundredth time.

In God's loving arms.

Was it true? There was no sense of her here. No feeling that she lay below him. No feeling that she watched from above. The air was cool for summer, and, with the rain drying, felt empty and fleeting. Was she trapped in the silent playback going on and on in the echoing little bathroom in Ealing? Was she gone completely, the spark in her brain extinguished and her with it?

In God's loving arms.

'I'm going,' he whispered.

He waited. For a sign. For a whisper of wind. For anything that said she heard him and wanted him to stay.

The willows held themselves silent. A car with a sports muffler rutted past on the North Boundary Road. Nothing.

Nicholas got to his feet and left.

•

Three days later, a hemisphere away, he lay on his little sister's child-hood bed, listening to rain crash down in an endless, dark wave.

And now he was home.

But home with what? A ring wedding him to a dead woman. A few thousand pounds. A couple of niceish Ben Sherman shirts.

Seventeen years. Nothing.

And his mother, what had happened there? No new man. Same house. Twenty new teapots. Nothing.

Rain. Faces. The dead. Trees.

DANG DONG.

The doorbell: a bakelite mechanical thing that rang two tuneless notes, one as you pressed in the smooth worn button, the other as you released it.

Nicholas blinked and picked up his watch from the pink bedside table. It was nearly two in the morning.

DANG DONG.

'Mum?' he called.

He swung his legs out of bed, sat up.

DANG DONG.

'Coming!'

As he passed his mother's bedroom door, he heard hefty snores befitting a circus strong man.

'Why don't I get it?' he suggested to no one.

Down the hall. By old habit his fingers found and clicked the switch for the outside light. He swung open the front door.

Two police officers in slicks waited on the stoop. One was big and dark-haired and stood closest to do the talking. The other, bigger and with fair hair, waited behind, ready to bend the cast-iron handrail or uproot a tree to prevent escape.

'Good evening, sir,' said the dark-haired officer. Nicholas dubbed him 'Fossey' in his mind. 'Sorry to disturb your sleep. We're going door to door seeking information about a young boy who's gone missing.'

On cue, gorilla-man behind held up a laminated colour photocopy of a blond seven year old beaming at the camera. Nicholas jolted.

It's Tristram. But Tristram's been dead twenty-five years.

He leaned in to look more closely.

The photograph was recent. In the background was an LCD TV. The boy wore a *Spiderman 3* T-shirt. Nevertheless, he looked eerily similar to Nicholas's childhood friend.

Who was murdered, Nicholas reminded himself.

His heart was pumping hard. He shook his head. 'No.'

But the officers had seen the frisson of recognition. They exchanged a glance, then returned their steady gazes to Nicholas.

'Are you sure, sir?' asked Fossey.

'Yep. Really. I just got in from overseas tonight.'

'Tonight, sir? What time was that?'

'Half past ten or so.'

Nicholas licked his lips. The police weren't moving.

'Did you come straight home, sir?'

'Yep.'

'Did you stop anywhere?' asked gorilla-man.

Yes, thought Nicholas. *The woods.* He'd stopped at the woods, amazed to see them still as potent and thick as ever. He'd walked halfway to their edge. Had been drawn to them. But why? He couldn't explain that to himself, let alone the police. Randomly scoping out dark woods in the middle of the rainy night when a boy happens to go missing? *God, you're acting like a guilty man! They don't need to know that.* Snap out *of it!*

'No.'

Officer Fossey reached for his notebook. Gorilla-man's right hand casually slipped down to hang straight beside his leg, closer to his service pistol.

'What's your name, sir?'

'Nicholas Close. Look —'

The officer wrote in his notebook, asked, 'C-L-O-S-E?'

'What's going on, Nicky?' Katharine arrived silently behind her son, fumbling with her dressing gown's sash.

The policemen exchanged a glance.

'A young boy has been reported missing, ma'am.'

Silverback held the picture up for Katharine.

'Oh dear.' Nicholas, who knew her voice so well, could just detect a quiver. 'Local boy?'

'Yes, ma'am. This gentleman told us he returned from overseas tonight?'

Nicholas saw his mother's eyes narrow just the slightest margin.

'My son. That's right.'

'What time did he arrive?'

'Just after eleven thirty. His flight touched down at nine fifty, which means he made excellent time getting through customs, hiring a car and getting home here.' Her words came clipped and fast, the shake replaced by something harder. 'We talked in our kitchen till quarter past twelve and both went to bed, and it certainly is tragic that a boy's got himself lost in this rain but I'm not sure I quite understand where this is going.'

The two big men shifted back an almost imperceptible amount. Nicholas sagged a little. He was in his mid-thirties and still needed his mother to keep him out of trouble.

'Ma'am, we're just asking questions,' said Fossey.

'I do understand that. Have you got any more?'

The officers exchanged a glance.

'No, ma'am. Catherine with a C?'

'With a K and two As. Best of luck, Constables. I hope and pray the young lad turns up safe.'

Fossey led Silverback into the rain.

Katharine shut the door. She wrapped her arms around herself. 'I just hate the fact that if you're a man you're automatically a potential sex fiend. Women do it too, you know.'

Nicholas nodded. He felt awfully tired, but sleep seemed a huge ocean away. As they started back down the hall, he saw veins like purple worms crawling on her ankles.

'What woke you up, Mum?'

Katharine looked at him, opened her mouth to lie. But she hesitated. And in that moment, Nicholas saw again the tally of years on his mother's face.

We're getting old.

'I had a bad dream. About you when you were small. You and your friend up the road.'

'Tristram Boye. Did you see how much that boy . . .'

She nodded. 'Only in the dream, it was you . . .'

Her voice trailed off to nothing.

Who died.

The rumble of the rain was as solid as the darkness outside. He kissed her cheek. It felt dry and thin as paper.

'I'm sure they'll find him,' he said.

They returned to their beds.

•

The police did find the child, three days later.

During the first two days, they had searched public toilets and overgrown railway sidings and mossy culverts, but the deluge had made the hunt difficult. A team of police divers sat ready to strap themselves to cables and search the river and storm-water drains through which water thundered like rapids, but the task was deemed too dangerous. A group of State Emergency Service volunteers waited in the Tallong High School hall to start their search of the Carmichael Road woods, but the rain kept falling, heavy as theatre curtains, so they stayed indoors drinking instant coffee from Styrofoam cups and playing Trivial Pursuit. The low sea of dark cloud seemed immoveable in the bloated sky.

The boy's mother was named Mrs Thomas – an ineloquent woman, though by all accounts a gifted tyre-fitter and a regular at the local Uniting Church. She appeared on the evening news, begging through a tight throat for anyone who had seen her boy to help. But in the end, the boy, whose name was Dylan (the press showed unusual good taste in making no sport of the child's mother unwittingly naming him after that doomed alcoholic), had been beyond help for all of those three days. His body was found hooked in mangrove trees some six kilometres downriver from Tallong. A squad of high school rowers – who trained come rain, hail or shine and would *win* the state championship ribbon this year, GO TERRACE! – caught sight of Dylan's red tracksuit pants bobbing in the shoreline shadows. A police spokesman said the boy's throat had been cut. There were no clear signs of sexual assault; however, time in the water made that difficult to confirm. They wished to question a man of Middle Eastern appearance seen in the vicinity of a nearby bus station three nights ago.

Nicholas and Katharine muddled around the house, keeping out of each other's way. When the television news reported the discovery of Dylan's body, they watched silently from the sofa. Neither needed to remark how eerily like 1982 this was, when Tristram's body was found three suburbs from Tallong in a cleared housing block, one pale leg poking out from under a pile of demolished timber, tree roots and tin. His throat, like Dylan's, had been slit wide.

Nicholas switched off the television.

Outside, the rain was finally easing.

'I'll make some tea,' Katharine said quietly.

3

It was the afternoon of a very bad day.

At ten years, Nicholas was slight, with a hint of the tight wiriness he'd keep as a man. His thin legs swung slow arcs through the dull, hot afternoon air, avoiding carefully the dry, severe edges of the sword grass that tissed discontentedly in the weak breeze. He walked along the narrow, gravel path that divided lengthways the long, grassy strip that sat uneasily beside Carmichael Road. The straps of his school port ate into his shoulders, and the sun dug at his eyes from a sky that was the light, hard blue of Roman glass.

He was sweating lightly, but the sharp sunlight was okay with him. It helped bake away the memories of the day's shame, allowed room for idle imaginings that he was a Desert Rat of Tobruk, or a skulking Arab – someone brown and fearless who squinted at shimmering dunes for signs of determined but doomed Jerries.

There was no hurry to get home. Suzette was in bed with the mumps so she would be even more of a bore. Mum would be peeling vegetables with sharp strokes or attacking school uniforms with the iron and wondering how a boy could eat so many biscuits and stay so thin. His friend Tristram had remained at school for trumpet practice, so there would be no visiting his place to play Battleship or Demolition Derby. No, there was no hurry.

It was nearing four o'clock and the heat was rotten – *stinking hot*, his mum would describe it – and in this limbo between school finishing and knock-off time, it seemed no one but Nicholas was on Tallong's streets. No cars broke the snaky heat haze wriggling above the black tar. Weatherboard and fibro houses shrugged against the bashing sunlight under red or green corrugated iron. Opposite them, to his right, were the woods.

The woods. Hectares so thick with rainforest scrub and scribbly gums and trumpet vine and lantana that, from here on Carmichael Road, he couldn't see more than ten metres into their interior. Certainly on some council map they must have a proper name, but he called them 'the woods' because his mother called them that, and so did Tristram's parents and Tristram's older brother, Gavin, and Mrs Ferguson the fruit lady. Nicholas knew, from looking at his father's old street directory, that the woods stretched all the way from here on Carmichael Road back to the looping brown river – maybe a kilometre and a half, though he'd never gone in even a third of that. They were simply too scary, though he could never admit that to Tris. Even now, outside them, Nicholas felt how deep they were, as if he were walking past a bottomless lake of shadowy water rather than a forest. Last week he'd found a book in the school library called *Space* with a chapter about main sequence stars and dying supergiants and fading white dwarfs . . . and black holes. Things so dense and with so much gravity that they drew light even from far away, and anything too close to them was trapped by their gravity and sucked into oblivion.

He found he was staring at the dark trunks, and pulled his eyes away and concentrated on the baked gravel at his feet.

He always slowed here, about halfway along his three-kilometre walk home from school. People dropped things on the path, and he was good at finding them. Lesser finds included a marble, tweezers, half a yo-yo, the ripcord from an SSP racer, a torn two-dollar note, and a pencil with its red paint shaved off just below the rubber and the name 'Hill' written there in ballpoint pen. Once, he picked up a pair of rusted pliers – snubby, alligator-nosed things that he took into the garage and cleaned carefully with machine oil he found in a white can under Dad's old bench. When the jaws opened and closed easily, he hung them on a nail next to Dad's other tools. It made him happy and sad at the same time, so he left them there.

Nicholas knew his mother preferred that he and Suzette walk the long way home through the prim, geranium-gardened backstreets rather than past the woods. 'Why?' he'd ask. 'Don't be difficult,' she'd reply, and a crisp silence would hang there like uncollected washing. On most days, he respected her wishes. But on days like today, when Suzette wasn't with him, he'd come home along Carmichael Road. The lure of strange jetsam was too strong.

He shifted his narrow shoulders. His school port was heavier today, weighted with a damp towel and wet swimming togs. *I got in the pool anyway*, he told himself encouragingly. But that thought wobbled on the top edge of the slippery dip back to this morning and its awful shame. He found his bottom lip tightening and his eyes getting stingy. He grew angry with himself. *Crybaby*, he said. *Sook*. He tried to think about something else – about the new space shuttle or the Mitchell-Hedges crystal skull or why Rommel lost, but it was too late: his thoughts tumbled down that slick slide into dark and unhappy waters.

Around eleven that morning, all the kids in his class had lined up under pandanus palms outside the school swimming-pool changing rooms, clasping swimming togs in plastic bags in hands or cloth duffels over shoulders. Nicholas was near the front of the queue because it was alphabetical and his surname started with C. He was trying so hard – as he tried every swimming lesson – to shrink, to become invisible, to attract no attention. He looked hopefully around for something – anything! – to get him out of this, but saw none. He was dreading the inevitable words that came next.

Miss Aspinall, with a voice like bells and a body like a medicine ball, called, 'Okay, everyone. Sit down.'

Nicholas and his classmates sat.

'Shoes off.'

The light grunting and groaning of piglets as boys and girls reached at their feet.

The smell of chlorine bit and the chug of the filter was loud as he pulled off his left shoe, left sock, right shoe . . . he looked around, and slowly, carefully . . . right sock . . . and there it was.

A pale toe the size of his second smallest, only not aligned with the others, growing out the top of his foot and lying atop the other five like some showboat seal above a striated beach.

He'd become quite good at covering his foot with his bag as soon as the sock was off. He was good at hiding. Perhaps, if no one looked . . .

A silvery tinkle-trundle of a coin dropped and rolling.

'Oh!'

The twenty-cent piece rolled past Eric Daniels, looped in a lazy, diminishing circle, and tingled to a stop right in front of Nicholas. He looked up just as Ursula Gazelle stooped over him to pick up her dropped money. He was frozen, horrified and powerless, as Ursula's eyes slid from her coin to his shoes to his foot . . . to his showboat-seal freak sixth toe.

'Oh,' said the prettiest girl in class, eyes fixed on Nicholas's foot. 'Yuck.'

She scooped up her coin and hurried back in line.

And Nicholas started crying.

He remembered pulling out his hanky, telling Steven Chan nothing was wrong, telling Miss Aspinall nothing was wrong, trying to cover his foot with his bag, hearing people whispering, *His toe. She saw his toe. What about his toe? His extra toe* . . . Cried. Like a pooftah. Nicholas knew what pooftahs were: boys who sobbed like girls.

He'd cried then, and remembering the red-hot shame of it was making him cry like a pooftah again now. He sniffed back mucus as hot as the oven air around him.

And so it was through tears, alone in the thudding heat on a narrow gravel path beside Carmichael Road, that Nicholas saw the bird.

It could have been anything or nothing, a tiny thing at the edge of the path tucked mostly into the whispering grass. Black and white feathers. Was it a magpie? Nicholas leaned closer. No, it was smaller. A peewee.

He wiped his nose with the back of his hand, wondering what to do with it. Dead things, he knew, were dirty (*riddled with germs*, his mother would say), and so he considered simply kicking it completely into the grass and walking on. But as he peered closer, he saw something that made him stop, shuck off his port and kneel.

The dead bird had no feet.

Its legs, no thicker than twigs, had been neatly snipped off below its backwards-facing knees, revealing sections of brown-black marrow ringed inside white bone as fine as porcelain, wrapped in grey, leathery skin.

Nicholas closed his mouth to avoid breathing in the poachy whiff of it. Who would cut off a bird's feet? He scoured the dirt around the bird but couldn't see the severed claws. He did find a short stick, chewed in the middle by someone's dog. Delicately, aware only of the iron sun baking the back of his neck and the high electric singing of insects, he poked the stick under the dead bird and pulled the limp, swollen little body out from the grass. Then his stomach lurched.

Like its feet, the bird's head had been removed. In its place, skewered to the body with a sharpened stick, was a spherical knot of woven twigs. The bird's severed feet were stuck into the knot by the shins and protruded from it like tiny, knurled antlers.

Nicholas felt his fingers pulsing as his heartbeats thupped harder. Carefully, he turned the bird over. Something was painted in rust red on the false head: a vertical downstroke with an arrowhead like a 'greater than' symbol on its right-hand side:

Nicholas felt a swoop between his navel and his testicles. His skin was suddenly cold, and the edges of his vision were tinged with silver.

He stood, heart racing, and was struck by the silence.

No car passed on the road. Not a person moved behind the dark windows of the distant houses. The breeze had died and the blade grass had lost its lizard hiss. The crickets no longer chirruped, as if even they were afraid to announce their hiding places. The sky was as pale and hot as a kiln.

Nicholas suddenly felt dreadfully alive in all this stillness. Brilliantly alive with something so very dead beside him. He felt his heartbeats were as loud as drums, travelling for miles. He was alive and small and terrifyingly alone.

With the woods just a few feet away.

He knew he had to go – now. He kicked the bird and its strange woven head into the grass, and grabbed his port. He shoved his arm into the loop, missed, shoved again, missed again. His vision was edged with glutinous, dizzy stars. Finally, he got his arm through the strap, and straightened just as the silence was broken.

The grass crunched behind him.

Deep slices through the dry grass. Heavy, deliberate footfalls. Stealthy and close. The stagnant air had suddenly thickened with the odour of sweet rot, alive as the cloying whiff around the top of an old septic tank. Tangy and ugly. Something was coming up behind him. Something from the woods.

Bright white terror filled him. His adrenal gland poured its juice into his blood and his heart galloped and his small legs tensed and sprang . . . *Run!*

Without turning, he flew.

4

2007

On the fourth morning after Nicholas returned home from London, the rain had gone. The cloudless morning sky was the brittle blue of artic ice, and abberant winds dragged the temperature down to three degrees. The chill whispered its way between the VJ boards and the loose casement windows of Suzette's bedroom.

Nicholas woke feeling more buoyant than he had for a long time. The slope-shouldered weariness that always arrived a moment after waking – when he confirmed that he was alive and Cate was dead and London was muddling grey and busy regardless – didn't come. He sat up. The sun was still below the horizon, but he could see how the cold winds had scrubbed the sky clean and the day would be beautiful and bright. He felt, he realised, the best he had since Cate died.

Knowing this delicate feeling of warm neutrality could easily slip away like a wriggling, diamond-scaled fish into abysmal waters, he decided to prolong the pleasantness as long as he could. He quickly pulled on his jeans, hooded cardigan and yesterday's socks. He would walk the streets of his childhood suburb and drum up a breakfast appetite.

The Closes' house at 68 Lambeth Street was a bulldog of a building with beige weatherboard flanks hunched on stumps and scowling down the hill at its neighbours. The wrought-iron gate opened silently, its hinge spikes still damp from last night's rain.

43

Nicholas set out into the brisk wind. The walking felt good and easy. He was tall and lean; striding down the hill and forcing his enervated blood to move seemed to improve his already fair mood. He'd been away and, yes, terrible things had happened, but now he was home. New choices were possible. He could get fit. He could get a job. He could start again.

As he walked, he saw that his impression last night that his childhood suburb had been locked in time was wrong. Some things *had* changed during his absence. Sentences of chamferboard Queenslanders were punctuated by malapropos Tuscan-styled villas. The Sheehans' house was gone, replaced by a two-storey block of flats. A tiny roundabout, its axis a bright fountain of yellow verbena, had been installed where Lambeth and Crittendon Streets crossed. But most of the original houses remained, refreshed dames under new paint seated coyly behind neat gardens.

The sun crested the horizon, and treetops were lit a mild gold. Nicholas breathed deeply. The stiff breeze brought fragrant snatches of wisteria. This was good. Life had gone on without him. Things did change. People survived.

He turned the corner into Myrtle Street. Halfway along, a small row of shops sat huddled under the long fingers of a massive poinciana.

Nicholas felt a tripwire in his gut twang, and he slowed his pace. Something about the sight of the shops disturbed him, though he couldn't say what. Determined not to let anything spoil his walk, he picked up his pace and strode towards them.

One building housed four shops in a row that faced Myrtle Street from under a wide, bull-nosed awning. The area under the awning was raised half a metre off the ground; it was tiled and its front was separated from the footpath by a galvanised steel rail and a row of potted topiary trees. In his childhood, the shops had been a convenience store, Mrs Ferguson's greengrocery, The Magill Fruitbowl, a butcher and a haberdashery.

He stopped at the two steps leading up to the shop porch. Jay Jay's, he remembered the haberdashery had been called. Again, the taut, sly wire inside hummed uncomfortably. And again, he shook off the ill feeling. It was not yet six thirty and the shops were closed. The convenience store was still there, but under a new name and with window stickers proclaiming 'Phone Cards: 9 cents/min, Anywhere in the World!'; the fruit shop's most recent incarnation was as a Tibetan takeaway restaurant, the owners of which had clearly overestimated the willingness of locals to enjoy some good Kongpo Shaptak (it was now 'For Lease'); the butcher's had become the storefront for a computer repairer; the haberdashery (an old woman ran it; what was her name? He couldn't recall) was now a health food shop.

Nicholas's footsteps echoed on the cold tiles. The shop windows were dark eyes reflecting sourly the brightness of the new day outside their heavy lid. Quill, he remembered. The old woman's name was Quill. And with the remembering, into his mind's eye flashed an image of being eight or nine, holding Suzette's tiny hand in his, and walking home from school past the shop and looking inside . . . and dark eyes set in a pale, wrinkled face looking back. Then Suzette started crying.

Nicholas stepped out into the early sunlight and felt a small flutter of relief. A long time ago, he thought. Childhood would prove to hold much nastier things than a dour-faced old woman in a dark shop. He picked up his pace again.

Laidlaw Street. Madeglass Street. Roads that to his younger eyes had been so long and languorous now seemed cramped and quaint. Jacarandas and liquidambars poked bare fingers into the crisp air. The leaves of callistemons and grevilleas whispered benignly. A Labrador watched him from a porch, its tail lethargically thumping the hardwood boards.

Nicholas put cold hands in his cardigan pockets and stepped into the narrow, pleasantly shadowed throat of Ithaca Lane. He realised he was looking not at his feet, or a few steps ahead, but to the crest of the steep lane fifty metres up. He was scanning horizons, looking for ghosts. But there were none. No fractured businessmen stepping in front of lorries, no sad-eyed women swallowing eleven, twelve, thirteen pills. He was a long way from London and its ghosts – as far as one could get, really. His memory caught scent of Cate, but

45

he quashed the familiar urge to run and sit by her gravestone, and turned his thoughts to what he might do for work. Buying props for TV commercials? Building sets for the state theatre company? He could volunteer at the arts college until he found his feet and made some contacts. Shit, he could go back to university and get his Master's. There was money in the bank, so why not take the year and start something new? Study illustration? Write and illustrate a children's book? The possibilities pleased him, driving the uneasiness about the Myrtle Street shops from his mind.

Winter sunlight winked in the crystal dew on the ridge caps of houses and rippled silver in gutter puddles. The air was raw and clean and things felt . . . good. Nicholas nodded to himself: yes, things felt *quite* good. He topped the crest of Ithaca Lane and glanced downhill.

He stopped, rock still. His good mood blew away in an instant, as if stolen like smoke by the wind.

At the bottom of the lane was Carmichael Road and, beyond it, the woods and their dark, countless trees.

Just turn around, he thought. But he didn't move. The woods held his eye, a broad and gently rippling lure. From here, even on this low rise, he could sense their size. A huge lopsided square of silver green, emerald green, olive green and chalcedony treetops, each side more than a kilometre, rising and falling back to the distant glimpses of brown river. Why were they still so disturbing? Gazing upon their inscrutable surface, Nicholas had the feeling that the trees were merely a veneer; a cloak over some dark creature, the shape of which remained hidden and the heart of which was as cold as deep earth.

I'm not going past them. Not today. He shifted to return home the way he'd come. But as he turned, movement caught his eye.

On the path through the grass strip that hemmed the woods, a boy was kneeling.

Nicholas's blood seemed to slow to a syrupy stop. He felt as if twenty-five years of life had suddenly fallen away and he was ten again.

The boy was bending to peer at the spot where, so many years ago, young Nicholas had found the dead bird with the woven head.

Nicholas felt ill. *It's Tristram.*

Then the boy looked up and around, and Nicholas could see it wasn't his childhood friend. Yet he recognised the boy's face. The huge policeman had held up a photo of him four nights ago. It was the dead Thomas boy.

The child leaned closer to touch something on the path.

Nicholas felt his stomach fill with cold. *Turn around*, he thought. *Go home. Forget it. He's dead. He's a dream. Like Cate, he's not really there, he can't be there. He's gone . . .*

But he couldn't turn. A wave of disgust rolled through him. He wanted to see what happened next.

The dead child rose on milkstraw legs, dropped with horror something offensive and spoiled, wiped his hands on his pants. Then he stiffened like a cat hearing thunder and his face turned to the woods. His mouth opened in a silent scream, and suddenly one arm jerked straight, as if grabbed by someone invisible and strong, and Dylan Thomas flew backwards into the trees.

Nicholas's heart suddenly remembered to pump. Without thinking, he ran down the hill, across Carmichael Road, through the tall, damp grass and into the woods.

•

Dylan Thomas was being dragged by an impalpable force, his fair hair streaming over his pale face as he flew between tree trunks. Where the sun hit him, he glowed brighter, like a dust mote caught in a spotlight.

Nicholas strained to keep up. Already, the sharp brass pain of a stitch blared in his side and his breaths were raggedly insufficient. When was the last time he'd run like this? Years. He should stop, turn around, go home . . . but the sight of the dead boy flickering between the trees ahead kept him running.

The woods quickly grew thicker, the moist ground between the trunks of brush box and devil's apple crowded with saplings and

47

lantana, lush vines, fallen branches and spider webs glistening coldly with droplets.

Ahead, the boy's arm pointed straight as a compass, and his body whipped behind it, flailing hopelessly. Yet his dark eyes were resigned. They were locked on Nicholas.

Nicholas's breaths came fast and hard. He was running as fast as he could. His heavy feet churned through an ankle-deep gruel of wet, rotting leaves. His shins fouled on moss-thick roots. Scrabbling branches scratched his face and slapped him with dark, prickling leaves. Parasitic vines, as thick as wrists and mottled with grey fungus, looped like fallen question marks, lurking and ready to strangle. The wide, striated trunks of native elms and ancient figs were only arm spans apart, and the canopy overhead grew closer and tighter until it was almost solid and only tiny sapphires of sky winked into the thick emerald gloom below. It was as dark as dusk. The damp air was cold enough to burn the back of Nicholas's throat.

The distance between him and the boy was growing. Nicholas ran harder.

The Thomas boy's face was a bobbing flurry. His small free arm scrabbled at trees, reaching silently at damp, green-flecked trunks. He flew up a steep, shaly slope.

Nicholas's lungs burned as he strained to follow. What would he see when the boy finally stopped? Him struggling? Pleading? Crying for his mother as his invisible killer made him kneel and his white throat opened up? Would he find Tristram, his face set hard as a knife came from behind?

Would he find the murderer himself?

Nicholas suddenly felt sick. He had no plan. What if he ran into some makeshift camp in the middle of the woods, straight into a cold-eyed man with a knife on his belt and a gun in his hands?

You'll end up as dead as the Thomas boy. Dead as Tristram.

That thought in mind, Nicholas crested the rise – and the ground beneath fell away into space.

He barely stopped himself going over into a sharp gully. His arms pinwheeled a moment, then he found his balance and took a careful step back from the brink. Beyond, the ground fell sharply several metres to a narrow, stony creek bed. He caught his breath and looked around.

The Thomas boy had vanished.

He felt disappointment riding a wave of guilty relief that he wouldn't need to see the boy die. He could leave, able to tell himself he *did* try. And at home, with time and distance between him and these sunless trees, he could convince himself never to come here again.

Traitor. Coward.

'Shut up,' he whispered.

He turned to go.

But as he did, his foot hit a sly rock wet with moss and shot from under him, out over space. His body followed an instant later . . . and he fell. He tumbled down the steep gully face, arms flailing, trying to stay upright. Angry branched saplings slapped him for his clumsiness. He hit the gully floor with a sodden crunch, his impact blunted by a wet and tangy clump of native ginger.

His panting breaths were loud in the silence. He awkwardly got to his feet. Both his palms were scratched and bleeding. His upper lip was wet – his fingers came away red. A little blood, but nothing broken.

The air down here seemed even colder, and even denser with trees. The narrow creek bed was the only place where no plants grew. In the half-light, the rocks and stones of the dry stream stood out like bones protruding through flesh. The gully was suddenly familiar. Nicholas nodded. It had been a quarter-century, but he knew where he was. He knew what lay ahead if he followed the uneven creek bed.

The pale, rounded stones clacked nervously underfoot. The larger ones looked like skullcaps, as if this were a road of the dead.

And that's just what it is.

The shadows behind the trees here seemed deeper, more solid, as if something lurked there, something waiting and patient. Hungry.

We were running. Tristram and I were running for our lives. This is where we parted. This is . . .

Then Nicholas saw it.

Almost masked by the mossy trunks of booyong and red ash was the huge water pipe. It was almost three metres in diameter; its steel flanks were rusted to a dark red and it sat on a green patinated concrete footing half a metre thick. It ran perpendicular to the creek bed, maybe seven or eight metres in each direction, before it was swallowed by blood vine and silver-furred star nightshade. If he were to tap its dark, rusty curve, it would ring hollow and mournful as an oubliette.

This is where we left each other, he thought. *Tristram and I.* His mouth was dry. The remembered taste of terror was as strong as alum.

Where the hulking pipe crossed the rocky stream bed, its ancient concrete foundation was deeper. Two parallel tunnels, each almost a metre wide, pierced the concrete foundation like dark nostrils.

Nicholas stopped, lungs still working hard to reclaim the oxygen he'd spent in the frantic chase. His panting was the only sound. No wind shifted leaves. No bird called. No insect chirped.

The pipe, he could see, was too high to climb. It ran who-knew-how-far into the woods in each direction. The only way to pass beyond it was to go under, through the narrow tunnels.

He walked up the creek bed closer to the pipe, and his footsteps castaneted stones together; the sound echoed in the shotgun tunnels like the cavernous clicking of some dead giant's teeth.

He knelt.

The twin tunnels ran right through the concrete base of the pipe, four metres or more. They were as dark as night, but he could just make out circles of light at their far ends. But those circles were dimly shrouded and imperfect. Black shapes moved across them, roughening their edges and peppering them with little shifting silhouettes.

Spiders.

Both tunnels were thick with webs and spiders. And whatever happened to the dead boys happened on the other side.

Nicholas got to his feet, turned around, and started back down the creek towards the gully cliff, heading back to Carmichael Road.

For the second time in his life, the spiders had beaten him.

5

It was Sunday morning, and Nicholas and Tristram were deep in concentration, hunkered in patches of sunlight on the hardwood boards of the Boyes' front veranda. They had set up two enormous opposing ramps made from Tristram's seemingly inexhaustible supply of orange Hot Wheels racetrack. Every so often, the boys would look up from their labours and grin at one another. They were getting ready for one hell of a car crash.

Tristram and his family lived in the street behind the Closes, in (if you asked Katharine Close) a palace of a house. Nicholas would jump the Closes' back fence (a rickety line of perennially damp hardwood palings held together by a thick crest of trumpet vine), run through Mrs Giles's yard, then up Airlie Crescent to the enormous house at number seven.

The Boyes had moved in two and a half years ago.

Nicholas and Tristram became friends. Tristram would short-cut through Mrs Giles's at a quarter to eight every school morning, and he and Nicholas would begrudgingly escort Suzette to school. Imagining that he and Tristram were her bodyguards, ready to pounce on would-be attackers or leap in front of assassins' bullets, compensated for her girlish chatter about love spells and how smart bees were and bar graphs.

After school when homework was done, and at weekends, Nicholas would visit the Boyes' house. This was better, because their place *was* a palace compared with 68 Lambeth Street. The Boyes had four bedrooms as well as Mr and Mrs Boyes' 'master bedroom', which had its own bathroom (Tristram snuck Nicholas in for a look one Saturday when his parents had left them home alone and Gavin was at some football final), another *two* bathrooms (Tristram called them 'dunny cans'), and wide verandas on three sides. Best of all, the entire house was on stumps, so there was a palace-worth of cool, dark dirt underneath for racing scooters, conducting experiments with bleach and sundry garage chemicals, building Owen guns, and torturing ants by dropping them in conical ant lion pits and watching them taken from below like hapless sailors by hungry kraken.

Nicholas sometimes had Tristram over to his house, but there was less to do. The Closes' house was small, its underneath exposed and useless for private things like making army IDs and shanghais and plans of conquest. The only place that was dark and away from his mother's scowl and Suzette's curiosity was the garage. But Nicholas didn't like taking anyone else in there. It was Dad's space. His tools were there. His old ports were there. Being in the garage made him feel weird – angry and sad and a bit lonely. He could hardly remember his father, but stepping into the dark garage with its smell of grease and sawdust brought a flash of the only enduring image of him: a scarecrow-thin man leaning over the white-washed garage bench as he sharpened a saw with one hand while drinking from a squat bottle of amber liquid with the other; then, hearing Nicholas, he looked down and smiled – half of his face bright with yellow light through the dusty window, half as dark as the cobwebbed shadows in the garage's far corners – and slid the bottle away into the bench drawer. No, the garage was not a place for games.

This Sunday morning, Nicholas had come over straight from church (the Boyes didn't go to church – further evidence of their grand good fortune). Suzette had changed into shorts and T-shirt to tend her little garden patch. She'd found an old book somewhere that had belonged to their dad, and had become excited about planting tiny seeds and urging them up into curling green things. After a spat over TV channels, Nicholas had once threatened to dig up Suze's garden and she'd gone totally spack, hitting him and screaming that he'd better not *dare*! The one male in a house with two females, he was wise enough not to. As Suzette screwed on her sunhat, Nicholas had pulled on his gym boots, kissed his mother's cheek, and jumped the back fence.

He and Tristram had eased into the day's play with a hunt through the Boyes' games cupboard. While Nicholas and Suzette had an incomplete chess set and a deck of cards, the Boyes had an Aladdin's cave of entertainment: Bermuda Triangle, Payday, Microdot (complete with cool plastic Lugers, stiletto knives and wirecutters), Mastermind, Grand Mastermind, Squatter, The Game of Life, Mouse Trap, Cluedo, Chinese Checkers, Monopoly (British *and* American versions), several decks of cards, and a roulette wheel that Tristram said came from a P&O steamer. But this was too bright a day for the lethargy of board games. The sunlight had a tart sting, the jacarandas were dropping sweet blizzards of lavender flowers, nasturtiums blazed between roses . . . no, today called for violence. So they set up the killer jumps for their Matchbox cars.

'We're going to Fraser at Christmas,' said Tristram, slotting an orange plastic tongue into the end of a section of track. The boys had appropriated the whole front veranda and had nearly finished the two ramps, each facing the other. At the farthest ends were kitchen chairs for height. The tracks swooped down to the floorboards, ran two metres, then swept up ramp stays of phone books and atlases. If they timed their releases right, two cars should collide spectacularly in midair.

'Oh?'

'You don't know where Fraser Island is, do you?'

Nicholas shrugged. 'Up your fat arse?'

Tristram chuckled. The boys had just discovered the joy of insults, and Nicholas was the acknowledged master. Not knowing what or where Fraser was didn't upset him, but news of the Boyes' trip did: if Tristram went away, the Christmas break would be really boring.

Tristram pulled out his ace. 'Dad's going to hire a Land Rover.'

'A Land Rover? Really?' Nicholas couldn't disguise his excitement. Land Rovers were what the SAS sped to battle in. They had aluminium bodies and wouldn't rust. 'Wow. Will your dad let you drive it?'

Tristram shook his head and grinned. That was one thing Nicholas liked about him: he might be rich, but he was honest. 'I reckon he'll let Gavin drive it, though. He's thirteen now. Dad learned to drive on Pop's tractor when he was thirteen, so . . .' His ramp finished, Tristram squatted back on his heels and looked at Nicholas. 'What were you going to tell me?'

'About what?'

Tristram came to Nicholas's ramp to help him finish.

'You said you found something on the way home from school on Wednesday, then you went all funny and shut up.'

Nicholas felt some warmth go out of the morning. The dead bird outside the woods. The bird with no head . . . or with a strange head of woven sticks and its own scrawny legs. He had wanted to tell Tristram about it on the way home from school Thursday and Friday, but Suzette had been with them and he didn't want to freak her out with gory talk about birds with legs cut off and the weirdos who did such things. She was really easy to upset right now; for instance, she hated walking home past the shops, but wouldn't explain why. And, to be honest, he didn't know how to phrase the story about the bird. He wanted to sound cool about it, matter-of-fact. But he also wanted his best friend to know how creepy it was, how the sight of it – not just limp and dead, but so helpless and mutilated – had made his stomach grip tight with unexplainable fear.

'I found a dead bird down near the woods.'

Tristram tore the sticky tape off with his teeth and secured track to the telephone books. 'So?'

'It had its head and legs cut off.'

He watched for Tristram's reaction. This would be the decider: if Tris's expression was serious, Nicholas could finish the tale with its bizarre ending. But if he wore his 'what bullshit' look, he would shrug the story off and change the subject to a cool book about Tiger tanks he'd found in the library. Tristram looked up, and Nicholas felt a wave of warmth for his friend: his expression was both serious and inquisitive.

'Yeah? Cut off like by a mower cut off? They mow that grass out front.'

Nicholas shook his head. 'Cut off, cut off. On purpose.'

He described how the bird's head was gone and replaced with a handmade sphere of woven twigs, the poor creature's legs as horns and the strange symbol painted there in what *had* to be blood. By the time he'd finished, Nicholas's voice had dropped to a whisper and his heart was thudding in his chest.

'And?' asked Tristram. They knew each other well enough to know when things were still unsaid.

'And I think . . .' Nicholas bit his lip and frowned. 'I think something came up behind me.' *From the woods.* He shook his head. 'But I don't remember. I remember smelling something bad, and then I ran home.'

'Was it . . . was it a grown-up?'

Nicholas thought about that. 'I don't know. I think so. Whatever it was, it felt . . . it felt big. And old.'

Tristram nodded, chewed his lip. 'Did I tell you I found a cat down there? When we first moved in, before we were friends. A dead cat on the gravel path.'

Nicholas shook his head.

'It was just bones really,' said Tristram. His voice dropped steadily to a whisper. 'Dead for ages. Orange fur, all dried up like a mummy. But it was a mess. Its paws were cut off.'

Nicholas stared. He didn't mind being trumped – cat beat bird hands down. Besides, Tristram wasn't showing off, not this time. In fact, this was the first time he could ever remember Tristram looking . . . well, so worried.

'Did you tell your parents?'

'Tell your parents what?' asked Mrs Boye, emerging from the shadows of the hallway carrying two fruit cordials and a plate of TeeVee Snacks. She was what Nicholas would describe in later years as a stately woman: well-dressed, well-spoken, well-educated. Utterly humourless.

'That we're going to make some noise,' said Tristram without missing a beat.

He turned to Nicholas and shot him a wink that Mrs Boye couldn't see. Nicholas smiled to himself – Tris was one smooth bastard.

'Well, we'd rather you didn't,' said Mrs Boye, surveying the ramps. 'Your father's had a big week and we're going to have a rest.'

Mr Boye was a Businessman who worked for an Investment Company and often had to Extend Himself on Behalf of the Firm on evenings and at weekends, so if he and Mrs Boye wanted a rest, then total silence was expected of the Boye boys.

'Why don't you go to Nicholas's house?' she asked Tristram.

Never mind asking me, thought Nicholas. But Tristram looked over at him and winked again, slyly.

'Sure,' said Nicholas.

'Have some morning tea then,' said Mrs Boye, and left for the darkened master bedroom.

The boys drank and surveyed their handiwork. 'It would have been good,' said Nicholas. He looked over at Tristram. His fair-haired friend was grinning. 'What?'

'Let's check it out.'

Nicholas knew what he meant. The bird. A sudden fear galloped through his stomach, but he swallowed it down and grinned back. 'Tommy guns?'

'Of course.'

They sculled their drinks and flew.

•

They moved like shadows, quiet and slow, hunched to stay below the grass line. The dry fronds chattered around them in the warm air, hissing a constant warning to *beware*. They gripped the stocks of their submachine guns. Tristram led; there was never a question about that – he was bigger and tougher, and if he had to go down to a Jap bullet, goddammit, he would. Nicholas saw him raise his left hand and they both dropped like stones. Nicholas crawled up.

'What is it?'

'Got any grenades?' hissed Tristram.

Nicholas looked around him. His fingers fell on a lumpy rock peppered with pink quartz. 'Only one.'

'Well, hell,' whispered Tristram, and he looked at Nicholas with narrowed eyes. He cocked his head and grinned crookedly. 'You better make it count then.' He pointed.

Nicholas carefully raised his eyes above the grass line. About four metres ahead was the pillbox (disguised cleverly as a council garbage bin). He lowered again and pulled an imaginary pin from the gibber.

'Cover me,' he said, then counted silently: three, two, one . . .

They both leapt to their feet. Tristram aimed his tommy gun (a wooden chair leg with a nail for a trigger and a crosspiece screwed below for a magazine) and fired: 'Ach-ach-ach-ach-ach!!', while Nicholas drew back the rock and hurled it in an overarm cricket bowl. Then they both hit the ground.

CLANG-rattle-rattle-clunk. The sound of rock falling inside the metal drum.

Tristram grinned. 'Good throw!'

Nicholas beamed. The sun was high and hot, they were dusty and dirty and totally happy. Life was grand. 'We got 'em that time,' he agreed.

'That, my friend, calls for a Lucky,' said Tristram, and he pulled out a packet of white lolly cigarettes. He shucked the box at Nicholas, who drew one and put it in the corner of his mouth. Tristram drew another. Nicholas thumbed an invisible Zippo and lit them. They puffed and sucked, stood and walked.

They were on the gravel path, wood guns slung around their thin shoulders. To their right, Carmichael Road ran like a lazy, tarmac canal. To their left was the crowding mass of the woods. *You can just* feel *them*, thought Nicholas. *Even with your eyes shut, you'd know they were there. Alive. Shadowed and watching. Waiting to breathe you in and in, to draw you deep inside, warm and moist and dark and smelling of secrets, where strange hands would lift you and take you . . .*

'. . . around here?' asked Tristram.

Nicholas shook his head, clearing it. 'What?'

'I beg your pardon,' said Tristram.

'Fuck off,' said Nicholas.

Tristram looked at him, shocked for a moment – then he burst out laughing at the bold use of the King of Swear Words. 'You fuck off!'

Nicholas joined in giggling, and Tristram's laughter redoubled.

Tears rolled down their faces, an innocent baptismal to mark the last time the F-word would offend either of them. Nicholas stood and wiped his face. He saw a car pull up on the far side of Carmichael Road: an unremarkable olive green sedan.

'So, guttersnipe,' said Tristram, pointing, 'here's about where I found the dead cat.' The last two words vanished the humour from the air. 'Where'd you find the bird?'

Nicholas looked around, getting his bearings, and pointed. They moved up the path twenty paces or so.

'Here somewhere . . .' He stopped on the track. 'Jeez.'

It was still there. Tucked into the grass, invisible to a casual glance, the bird's little body had swollen in the heat, its feathered skin now a round balloon. Legs snipped off clean exposed matchstick sections of bone. It would be many years later when Nicholas found the right word to describe it: talismanic. The death-tightened claws for horns. The sharply dangerous lines painted in rust-brown blood. The dumb, alien head. There was nothing accidental or joking about it. The bird was murdered, and its corpse twisted and changed into a thing that felt . . . *evil*.

Yes. Evil.

Nicholas looked at Tristram.

Tristram was staring at the dead bird. His jaw was slack and his eyes were wide. A smile curled his lips. 'It's beautiful,' he whispered. Without hesitation, he knelt and gingerly took hold of the woven head. It was still securely spiked to the body and he lifted the tiny carcass out. As he did, white fluid began to drip from the bird. No, not fluid, but pale, wriggling pupae. Maggots.

'Wow . . .' The delighted smile grew wider on Tristram's face.

Nicholas felt his stomach roll sickly, the way it did when he had the runs, weak and afraid. 'You shouldn't touch it, Tris. Tris!'

He bumped Tristram's arm and Tristram dropped the desecrated creature on the path. The swollen body popped open with a bright whiff of rot and maggots started worming out from their nest.

Tristram stared at the infested thing, suddenly horrified. 'Oh, yuck.'

Despite the drop, the round woven head was still attached to the tiny corpse, as if determined to see a job through.

'I can't believe you picked it up,' said Nicholas.

As he rocked back on his feet, movement across Carmichael Road caught his eye. The driver's door of the green car opened. A man was alighting: a large man in a dark suit. In the harsh overhead sun, his face was cast into binary tones of sharp light and dense shadow, yet it seemed he was looking at the boys.

He is looking at us, thought Nicholas. *I can feel it.*

'Tris. We should go home.'

Tristram was wiping his hands on his shorts, staring at the dead bird. 'I thought it was —'

'Let's go,' hissed Nicholas. Tristram looked up.

The man strode across the road towards them, straight at them through the grass. He was even bigger than Nicholas had thought: solid as a rugby player, but older, in his forties. Somehow, middle age made him even scarier. The man turned his head left then right with deliberate slowness, calibrating the surrounds. He wasn't looking for other adults to join him in chastising these boys for throwing stones and carrying toy guns.

He's checking for witnesses.

There were none, and the man hastened his pace.

Nicholas and Tristram looked at each other. They couldn't run to the road. If they tried to dart left or right up the path, the stranger could cut them off without even trying. There was only one way to flee.

They ran into the woods.

•

In his ten years, Nicholas had been afraid many times. But this was his first taste of terror. Adrenaline on his tongue was bitter. Low branches and tough shrubs tore at his face and bare legs. Beside him, Tristram's eyes were wide and his fair hair flew out behind. They ran like men in snow, having to take exhausting, high-kneed steps to clear the thick, ancient knots of vine and undergrowth. From behind them came the steady CRACH-crunch CRACH-crunch of heavier footsteps. Nicholas dared a look back. The suited man was a rhino between the trees, his heavy strides smashing through the stems that would trip the boys.

He was gaining.

Nicholas could see the fear on his friend's face. Neither of them needed to ask why a strange man was chasing them. They both knew – *everyone* knew – that there were men who took children.

'Which way?' he whispered. His cheeks were wet; he realised he was crying.

'We should . . .' gasped Tristram '. . . split up.'

The thought of being alone with the man after him sent a shock of new terror through Nicholas. 'No way!'

'That way . . . he can't . . . get us both.'

The woods were becoming denser and darker as all but the tiniest chips of sky remained visible overhead. Wide trunks and buttressed roots grew closer together, forming a shadowed and slippery maze. Flinty rocks peeked sharply from under wet brows of rotten leaves.

The boys scrambled up a steep slope, grazing knees and palms on spiny vines and hidden shale. The man was just a dozen steps behind them. Nicholas's ears were ringing as his blood thudded, but over that he could hear the man's breath pistoning in and out with horrid monotony. *He could keep this pace up all day!* But it wouldn't take all day to catch them. Just minutes. Moments.

The prospect of seeing Tristram disappear between the trees and being alone with that huge, unstoppable man after him made his bowels watery. But Tris was right.

'Okay,' Nicholas gasped. 'Over the ridge. We'll split.'

Tristram nodded.

Nicholas stole a glance back, and let out a yelp. The man was only two body-lengths behind, striding up the sharp rise, arms stretched out for balance. Years later, he would be watching Karloff in Whale's *Frankenstein*, and the image of the monster lumbering, arms out wide, made him suddenly lose control of his bladder. The most terrible thing of all was the man's face. It was slack and expressionless. There was no anger, no lust. He was as emotionless as a crocodile. And he would catch them.

Nicholas felt fresh hot tears sting his eyes. Lungs burning, he drew the deepest breath he could and yelled: 'Help!!'

The word died without an echo, swallowed by the trees. *What idiots! Why didn't we yell when we were near the street?* Their stupidity made Nicholas cry harder.

'Help us!' yelled Tristram. Again, the words were held tight by the greedy trunks of black figs, the dark ferns, the endless leaves.

They were nearly at the top of the slope. Nicholas looked at Tristram. No tears, but his face was tight and pale. A wave of jealous love went through him. Tristram pointed at himself, then left. Nicholas nodded – he'd go right. They crested the hill.

Their plan fell apart as Tristram suddenly vanished.

Nicholas, a step or two behind, saw him simply drop away into nothing. He slowed a second, just enough to brake his momentum so he, too, didn't fall over the steep edge. CRASH! Tristram hit the gully floor three metres down.

'Oh.' The small sound was much worse and packed more pain than a scream.

Nicholas swung to look behind. The man was only a few steps away, powering up the last of the slope – close enough for Nicholas to smell him: a mist of sweat and cigarette smoke and Old Spice.

Without another thought, he jumped.

He dropped through the air for what seemed an endless moment, waiting for huge hands to snatch him back . . . then hit the moist, leafy gully floor. Tristram was rolling onto his feet, nursing his right arm; his wrist was bent at the wrong angle.

'Your arm —'

Tristram shook his head and looked up.

The man had reached the cliff edge above. His massive chest, thick as a horse's, swelled and sank with huge breaths. He regarded carefully the boys, the drop, the cliff that diminished as it ran left. Then he cocked his head as if listening to something far off, some distant siren song only he could hear.

'Come on!' hissed Nicholas.

He and Tristram ran up the creek bed at the bottom of the gully, their feet rocking on the smooth stones, risking sprains for speed.

Tristram stopped. 'Oh, no.'

Ahead, a huge shape had appeared behind the trees. Horrible despair returned like a forgotten nightmare. 'The pipe.'

They'd rarely come this far in, and only once down here to the gully and the huge, old water pipe that crossed it.

The man was clambering down the cliff face, hands neatly grasping the wild quince and cudgerie saplings growing stubbornly from the rocks. He moved with the speed of a gorilla born to the forest.

There was no splitting up. The woods to the right were choked so thick they were impenetrable. The very air seemed dark green – not a glimmer of sunlight, just ancient shadow. Nor could they go back: their pursuer was less than thirty paces away. Left was the only course, unless . . .

Tristram peered at the base of the pipe. Two tunnels, like barrels of a giant shotgun, penetrated the concrete. Nicholas knelt to look in. The circles of light at the far ends were thickly dotted with familiar shapes. Spiders. Hundreds of them.

His heart seemed to stop in his chest and his eyes watered. The thought of a single spider made his testicles crawl. The sight of these long, dark nests turned his terror into panic. The world grew silver at its edges – he was going to faint.

'Tris, I can't . . .'

'Get help.' And without another word, Tristram dropped to his knees and crawled into the closest tunnel.

Nicholas looked around. The man was striding towards him. His hands were huge. For the first time he noticed the bulge at the man's crotch.

'Fuck you!' he yelled. He turned and ran.

Smack into a branch.

He had just enough time to stagger back and see the man's silhouette fill his vision . . . then everything fell away to instant, coal-black night.

•

He woke to the whisper of leaves.

His eyes flickered open. The trees surrounding him were so deep and dark that he could have been a drowned sailor on the cold floor of the sea. No wind moved the ocean of black branches above him, yet leaves still rustled somewhere out of sight. He turned his head.

The movement made nausea flood through him. He opened his mouth and a pitiful stream of half-digested biscuits and cordial spilled out. But now the sound of movement was louder. His vision rolled like a poorly-tuned television, lurched, rolled, then steadied.

A small distance away, white flesh drifted above the ground. Limbs drooped like the necks of dead swans. Everything was so dark. Nicholas raised his head and strained to focus.

Tristram was being carried past, cradled in large, dark hands. The boy's naked limbs were starkly white in the stygian gloom, swaying loosely. His head lolled back too far, his fulvous hair streaked with something darker. A wedge of darkness divided the white of his throat. Then Nicholas caught a glimpse of bone.

He tilted his head to see who carried Tristram, but the world slipped off its axis, heeled and fell . . . He retched again, and his eyes rolled back in his head.

•

He woke a second time to feel tears on his cheeks.

No. Not tears. Rain. Drops clattered on the canopy of leaves overhead, coalesced, and fell in heavy, cold dollops.

Nicholas rose to unsteady feet, and, arms outstretched in a pose that, had he been able to see himself, would have reminded him horribly of the man who had pursued them and, hours later, had carried Tristram dead from the woods, began shuffling his way home.

•

Four hours later, he was wrapped in his mother's arms. After seeing her brother was home safe, Suzette had curled on the sofa and fallen asleep. Police cars were parked out front, their blue lights coruscating sapphires in the downpour. A bath, and a policewoman with his mother inspecting his head, his neck, his penis, his bottom. Questions, questions, questions. Did he know the man who chased them? What colour was his car? Did he say anything while he chased them? Was he bearded or clean-shaven? Tris's parents sat with Gavin in the next room. Mrs Boye sent hollow glances through the doorway at Nicholas, as if by the intensity of her concentration he might suddenly transform into her youngest son.

The Boyes left. The police left. The kettle boiled. Sweet tea. Bed. And, through it all, rain.

•

The search of the woods for Tristram Hamilton Boye was postponed due to the unseasonably heavy rain. As it turned out, a search was unnecessary: the Frankenstein's monster man told police where to find the child.

Nicholas sat rigid beside his mother watching the news. A television reporter described how Winston Teale, second-generation owner of furniture retailer Teale & Nephew, had presented himself at Milton Police Station and told the desk sergeant where they could find the body of the missing Tallong child, Tristram Boye. The television flashed images of a small lump covered in a sheet being wheeled away from a demolition site not a kilometre from the police station, two suburbs from Tallong.

A week later, Katharine Close made Nicholas wear a tie for his court appearance. All through the hearing – including when the prosecutor asked Nicholas to point out the man who had chased him and Tristram on 1 November – Nicholas watched Winston Teale. The man no longer looked terrifying. He seemed smaller. His eyes shifted like caught mice in a cage, as if he couldn't quite believe that he was in the docks of the Magistrates' Court. And when Teale looked at Nicholas, there wasn't a gram of recognition. He seemed even more confused by his own words during questioning.

'You killed Tristram Boye?'

'Yes.' Teale's voice was that of a smaller man.

'How?'

'I . . . I believe I cut his throat.' He explained that he had used a carpet knife from his warehouse.

'Why did you kill him?'

Teale blinked, frowning. The courtroom was so silent that Nicholas heard a train horn sound at the distant railway station.

'Mr Teale?' urged the magistrate.

'I don't remember.'

'And transported him to the lot on the corner of Myner Road and Currawong Street?'

'Yes.' Teale's voice was unconvincing.

'How?'

Again, Teale shook his head. 'My car. The boot of my car, I think. Yes . . .' Teale shrugged and gave an apologetic smile.

Nicholas felt eyes on his neck, and looked behind.

His mother was watching him, a frown line dividing the brow between her eyes. Her lips smiled, but her eyes kept watching.

•

Winston Teale was convicted of murder and deprivation of liberty, but hanged himself with his shirt the night before he was due to be sentenced.

Nicholas had no more cause to jump the back fence and run past Mrs Giles on his way to visit the Boyes.

Cyclone season came and its hail-teeth winds blew away newspapers carrying the photo of his murdered friend.

One school year finished. The river flowed brown. The city sighed a mournful puff of car fumes and stale perfume and electric train ozone, then shrugged her steel shoulders and braced for her footpaths to be stamped upon by New Year's drunks and her spiry hair stained bright by fireworks.

Time ticked on.

Katharine Close forbade her two children from ever again walking past the Carmichael Road woods.

6

2007

Nicholas watched his younger sister alight from the taxi, her chatty, white smile winking at the cabbie unloading her bags. He let the blinds fall and sank on the bed. Suzette hadn't brought her husband on this trip to see her sad widower brother, nor her children. *I'll be nice*, he decided. *Answer her questions. Accept her sympathy. Send her home tomorrow.*

'Your sister's here!' called Katharine brightly.

'I know!' called Nicholas in matching tone.

Rattling of the latch, the birdsong of greetings and compliments, rustling of plastic bags, the friendly thump of footsteps. Then Suzette was in the doorway, arms folded.

'Get out of my room.'

The last time he'd seen her was at his wedding in Osterley Park. Her hair was longer, but she was still tall and pale and pretty, with a stance like a bouncer.

'No.'

'It's my room.'

'Not any more.'

'I'll tell Mum.'

'Then you'd be a dirty little dob artist.'

'MUUUM!' she yelled, as brutally as a cheated fishwife. 'Tell Nicholas to get out of my room!'

'Nicholas, let your sister have her room back,' called Katharine. The smile in her voice suggested she enjoyed this old game.

Nicholas sighed and got to his feet. He walked up to his sister. She grinned. He kissed her cheek. She grabbed him and squeezed him. He found himself sinking into the hug. She rubbed his back.

'Dear, oh dear,' she said.

•

Suzette felt him gently release himself from her hug, watched him turn his face away and suggest that while she unpacked he might 'make some fucking tea or some shit?', then he was down the hall. The room felt hardly emptier without him. She hadn't expected him to look so . . . gone.

She stood in her old bedroom a moment, trying to reconcile the thin, insubstantial man with the voice she'd heard on the phone just a week ago. He had sounded so fine, so balanced and normal, that no alarm bells had rung. Suzette chastised herself. She prided herself on being sensitive to people, to being good at reading faces, decrypting moods and deciphering subtle expressions – yet this huge lapse had occurred and she'd missed her own brother slipping over that twilit border into a dark and alien place. How? He'd sounded so reasonable on the phone from London. *No, don't come to the funeral. She's gone. Thanks, but Nelson and Quincy need you there. Cate's folks are looking after me. I'll be fine.* Was he that good a liar? Or did he just say what she wanted to hear, absolving her of the need for that exhausting flight and the eviscerating drain of a funeral?

She lifted her suitcases onto the single bed. The springs let out a familiar squawk, recognising their old sleeping mate. She unzipped the larger case and pulled out her toiletry bag and make-up purse.

She'd failed. She and her mother both. Even before Cate's accident, he'd had enough death for one lifetime. Now he looked like death himself.

'Tea's made!' called Katharine from the kitchen, amid the staccato ticking of cutlery on china.

'Okay!'

All this brightness. Pleasant voices and biscuits and tea. No wonder Nicholas was a mess. This was how they'd been taught to deal with grief and heartache: a cup of tea, then back to the washing or into work or on to the bills. Keep busy, don't worry others, the world's got enough problems of its own without yours. That was the Lambeth Street motto. Totally fucked.

'Oy!' called Nicholas.

'Coming! Christ . . .'

Maybe it wasn't too late. She was here, wasn't she? She must have sensed something was wrong, because . . .

She pulled from her suitcase a small parcel wrapped in tissue paper. This might help. She slipped it into her pocket.

'I don't have sugar any more!' she yelled sunnily, and hurried down the hall.

•

Katharine let her children wash up the dishes, casting her ear into their conversation like an angler who doesn't really care if he catches a bite. Nicholas asked about his nephew and niece. Nelson was fine. His sixth birthday had a pirate theme and he got too many presents so Suze and Bryan returned half to the stores. Quincy was enjoying her pre-school and had taken to looking through Bryan's old telescope at the moon, which pleased Suzette for some reason.

Katharine went and folded laundry. Her family was together again. Well, as much as it could be.

What was she supposed to do now? She was out of practice. Was she supposed to be wise? Was she supposed to explain how she'd coped when Don left? Was it time to tell them how her heart had risen to her throat when she saw two policemen at the door a few nights ago; that she'd had the helpless feeling of being wrenched back through time to a night thirty-odd years ago when two policemen knocked at the same door to tell her that there'd been a car accident and Don had been at the wheel? Was she supposed to make things right?

She folded the last towel, smoothing down a sharp crease. No. Her grief was her own, and Nicholas's was his. He'd have to cope.

And the dead boy? *A child goes missing the night Nicholas returns. What does that mean?* Nicholas had lost a father, a friend, a wife . . . and now he was back and more death. What sort of a grim harbinger was he? She remembered the night he was born. It was a Sunday. Don's smiles were peppered with frowns. 'Funny day,' he kept saying. Was it her bad luck passed on to him? Was it Don's? Or was there something darker still?

'Hey.'

Katharine jumped at Suzette's voice at her shoulder.

'Hay makes the bull fat,' she replied, trying to disguise her racing heart. What had she been thinking? Such nonsense. Old wives' tales and rubbish. 'What are you up to?'

'We're going for a walk. Need anything?'

Katharine nearly blurted, *I need you to stay here.* She bit her tongue. Where had that come from? 'Can you pick up some milk?'

A minute later, she was in Suzette's bedroom, watching her children close the front gate behind them. They walked down towards Myrtle Street, just as they used to twenty-five years ago – her daughter, still with the mop of brown hair she'd had as a child, and her son, tall and fair but with a crane frame so familiar that Katharine could swear it was Donald walking away. The hairs on the back of her neck rose. She had a sudden urge to fling open the window and shout to her little girl, 'Get away from him! He'll get himself killed and you with him!'

She smoothed her dress to wipe the stupid thought away, then went to the lounge room and turned the TV on loud.

•

Nasturtiums blazed cold orange fire on the sloping banks that led down to the train tracks. Two pairs of silver rails curved like giant calligraphy around a far bend. They'd come from the nearby 7-Eleven and let themselves under a rusted chain-link fence to sit on mossy rocks at the top of the bank. From here they could look along to

Tallong railway station and its sixty-year-old wooden walkway that crossed above the tracks. Beyond, red roofs and green roofs were peppered among the trees, marching up the suburb's hills. They reminded Nicholas of pieces in a Monopoly set, playthings in some larger game. He chewed fruit pastilles. Suzette ate caramel corn from a brightly coloured bag. Overhead, clouds the colour of pigeon wings tumbled in loose ranks. Evening was coming.

The small talk was done. Nicholas had asked after Bryan (he was well, recovering from a cold), about the kids' teachers (capable, but a bit soft with such wilful little blisters), about Suzette's work as an investment advisor (going very nicely, thank you: two new corporate clients this month). As he finished his last sweet, the conversation fell into quiet and he braced himself for the turn of the tide. Suzette would start asking about him. She'd ask how he was holding up. She'd see if he'd visited a counsellor. She'd tell him it was okay to cry.

But Suzette remained silent. She simply sat beside him, licking her fingers and retrieving the last sugary crumbs from the bottom of the popcorn bag. She seemed content to do so for another hour.

'I don't like your hair that colour,' he said to break the silence.

She licked her fingers. 'Fuck you. Bryan does.'

She looked at him. Her eyes were a steely blue, her gaze as solid as granite. He could see why her financial planning business went so well – her clients would be too scared not to believe her if she said 'buy now'.

'I heard a boy went missing,' she said.

Nicholas nodded.

'They found him in the river . . .' He nodded to the north-east. 'Couple of clicks.'

Suzette kept her eyes on him. 'Mum said he was murdered, too.'

Murdered, too. He knew what she was thinking. *Murdered, like Tristram.*

He nodded again.

A stainless-steel train whummed past, sighing as it slowed to stop at the platform. Men in shirts and ties and women in sensible black skirts alighted and started up the wooden stairs of the crossover, heading home.

He saw Suzette was frowning. It was the same concentrated scowl she used to wear solving fractions at the dinner table and correlating statistical charts on her bedroom desk. *We don't change, do we? The patterns we slide into in childhood fit us for life.*

'What?' he asked.

She shook her head – nothing.

He looked back at the train station. There was just one person left on the crossover now: a girl in a yellow anorak. From this distance her face was a blur, her hair a dark pistil atop a fluffed golden bloom.

'I'm waiting for you to tell me that I couldn't have done anything to stop Cate dying.'

Suzette crumpled the empty popcorn bag and shoved it in her pocket. 'That it was an accident?' she asked.

'Or some similar shit, yes.'

Suzette nodded. 'Well. I don't really believe in accidents.'

Nicholas looked at her again.

'What are you saying?'

'I'm not saying it was your fault.' She met his gaze. 'But . . . nothing happens without a reason.'

He felt a warm knot form in his gut.

'Don't give me any God Wanted Her Home in Heaven bullshit, Suze. I saw her —'

He bit his tongue. He'd been about to say how he'd seen Cate falling from that invisible ladder time and again, over and over, her dead eyes staring at nothing, then rolling to him, blank as slate, without a trace of the person he'd loved and married. That wasn't heaven. That was hell. He felt Suzette watching him.

'If God is eternal, if time means nothing to him, I reckon he could have waited a few more years for her,' he finished.

On the pedestrian overpass, the girl in the yellow anorak pulled up her sleeve. To check her watch, Nicholas guessed. Someone was late meeting her. But then she climbed onto the crossover's rails, balanced for just a second, then stepped into space.

'Jesus Christ!' Nicholas leapt to his feet and his breath jagged in his throat like a hook.

The girl lay motionless on the track a moment. Her arm lifted a little as she tried to sit . . . then her anorak seemed to fly apart. She became a small, violent storm of feathers and red as an invisible train tore over her body, dragging pink flesh and one leg and shards of yellow thirty metres up the track. Then she was gone.

'You okay?' asked Suzette. 'Nicky?'

Nicholas saw his traitorous hand pointing at the track and willed it to fall by his side.

Suzette looked down at the train line, squinting. 'What is it?'

Nicholas looked around. And there, a flash of daffodil two hundred metres away. The girl in yellow was slowly making her way down the steep slope of Battenberg Terrace, her body whole, her face a smudged thumbprint.

Nicholas's heart was kicking in his chest.

'Nothing.'

Suzette frowned sceptically. 'Uh-huh . . .'

Nicholas put his hands in his pockets. He'd only been out of London a few days and he had already lost his poker face. The sun was now resting on roof ridges in the west, and here in the shadows the air had grown cold. The ground beneath the round lily leaves of the nasturtiums was black. He turned his back to the railway station. He didn't want to see that again.

'We should go home,' he suggested.

Suzette's careful eyes slid between him and the tracks. Then she cocked her head and fixed Nicholas with a hard look.

'I was in love with him, you know.'

'Who?'

'Tristram.'

Nicholas blinked, disoriented by the change of subject. 'I didn't know.' He thought a moment. 'That's ridiculous. How old were you? Nine?'

'Eight.' She took a breath. 'I saw him a couple of times.'

'You saw him more than that. He was over every time his bloody parents wanted a nap.'

Suzette's eyes were still fixed on him. 'No. I saw him *after* he died.'

Nicholas suddenly felt the air grow tight around him. His heart thudded slow, long beats as if his blood had suddenly taken on the consistency of arctic sea-water, just a degree away from becoming ice.

'Where?' he whispered.

Suzette looked him in the eye. 'Running into the woods.'

She got to her feet, dusted off the back of her jeans.

'Let's walk.'

•

They climbed back through the rusty fence and down onto the road. The sky in the west lost the last of its furnace glow and grew purple and dark. Birds hurried to find shelter before the last light was gone. A cold breeze stiffened.

A month or so after Tristram was found murdered, she'd defied their mother and walked down to Carmichael Road. There, on the gravel path through the grass verge, she'd seen Tristram kneeling, picking something up, then running away into the trees. The sight had scared her senseless.

'I reckon I felt how you just looked,' she said, smiling thinly. 'Like you just saw a ghost.'

She watched her brother. His dark eyes were fixed on the cracked footpath. He was motionless. Finally, he spoke.

'Do you still see them?' he asked. 'Ghosts?'

She shook her head. 'I saw him twice more. I snuck down one afternoon when you were sick, and another time when Mum went to work or something. He did the same thing. Picked something off the path, backed away, ran into the woods.' She shrugged. 'But after that, I never saw him again. Or any others.'

She watched him nod slowly. He let out a long breath. He was working up to telling her something.

'Why not?'

'I don't know,' she replied. 'Some books say that puberty either enhances or drowns clairvoyance and second sight, but it wasn't that with me. Maybe I just had a . . . a flash. Either that, or maybe Tristram had reached his proper time.'

'Proper time? To what?'

'Die.' She could see her brother's face tense as he digested this. 'That's what ghosts are, I think,' she continued. 'Spirits of people who are killed, or take their own lives, before their . . . you know, appointed time to die.'

Nicholas's eyes were shadowed shells beneath a grim frown.

'Ghosts,' he said so softly it was barely a whisper. 'Can I tell you about ghosts, Suze?'

The words made her heart start to trip.

She nodded.

He took a breath, and then he spoke for a long time.

He told her about the motorcycle crash, and borrowing the phone from the horse-faced couple he hit. About hurrying home to find Cate crooked like a broken exclamation mark, head bent too far backwards over the tub, her open eyes unable to blink out the dust that coated them. About the Yerwood boy with the corduroy jacket and screwdriver. About all the ghosts that silently conspired to send him home. He told her that there were ghosts here, too, including the suicide in the yellow anorak. The sun had sunk below the hills, and lights glowed orange in the houses they passed. The air was faintly spiced with scents of frying meat and onions. He finished by telling her how he'd chased the Thomas boy into the woods two days ago, and lost him at the same place he'd lost Tristram – the shotgun tunnels under the tall, rusted water pipe.

'Those tunnels full of spiders,' she said.

Nicholas looked at her, shocked.

'What?' she asked. 'Do you think I never went in there?'

He shook his head.

'More fool you then,' she said.

She stopped them outside a blue Besser-block fence, where fading graffiti demanded 'Free East Papua' and exclaimed that 'Fellatio Sucks'. She pushed the back of his head. 'Here. Let's have a look.'

She stood behind him and lifted his hair, finding the scar on his scalp. He'd never seen it of course, but he'd felt it. The edge of the concrete step of the Ealing flat had left a lumpy scar a thumb's length across.

'You think that's why I'm seeing ghosts?' he asked. 'A clout on the head?'

'Something started your seeing these things. Maybe it was the shock of losing Cate. Maybe that nasty bump just cleared the plumbing.' She rapped his head with her knuckle and grinned. 'When's my birthday?'

'My memory's fine, bloody hell —'

'When?'

Nicholas rolled his eyes. 'October thirty-first. Halloween girl.'

She sent him a dark smile. 'Yes and no. Yes, correct date – and by the way you owe me a present from last year. But, no, not a Halloween girl. Halloween's different down here. All Hallows Eve. The Celts called it Samhain.' She pronounced it *sah-wen*. 'For us in the south, the end of October is Beltane, the return of summer. Our Halloween is six months opposite.'

She watched Nicholas do a quick calculation in his head. 'April thirtieth.'

She nodded.

'My birthday,' he said quietly.

She nodded again, and bumped his shoulder with her own.

'You're the Halloween child. And a child born on Samhain is said to have second sight.'

•

As they walked, Nicholas felt a lightness in his chest. What did this mean? Was his sister just telling him what he wanted to hear? That they both had some gift – or some curse – to see the dead?

Or are visual delusions wired into our faulty genes?

He felt her eyes on his face, as if she could sense his doubt.

'You used to have inklings,' she said. 'I remember. Like the time you told me not to use the toaster. Mum ignored you and plugged it in, and it sparked and gave her a shock. You just knew, didn't you?'

'I'd forgotten about that.'

She quizzed him. That wasn't the only time he'd had a notion, a gut feeling, scraps of information of things, places, people that really he couldn't have known.

It was true, though Nicholas had never given it thought. Throughout his life, every few weeks or months, he had uninvited, inexplicable feelings that something wasn't quite right or that someone was ill or this thing was broken or that thing wasn't lost but in a mislabelled cardboard box under the house.

During a year nine school excursion to the state art gallery, he and four classmates had been about to cross the street to the footpath opposite when Nicholas had the strongest feeling that walking on the other side would be a bad idea. He convinced his classmates to remain where they were by saying there was, he was sure, a milk bar on this side not far along where they could chip in and buy cigarettes. Not a minute later, a speeding taxi mounted the opposite kerb and came to a shatterglass stop against a power pole. The cab driver had suffered a mild stroke and lost control of the cab. Had Nicholas and his fellow students crossed the road, they'd all be in hospital – in a ward or in a steel drawer.

At seventeen, taking his driving test, he'd disobeyed the transport officer and refused to take a right turn down a Rosalie side street. He failed the test, but saw on the news that night that an unapproved LPG cylinder on a caravan parked in suburban Rosalie had freakishly exploded, destroying the caravan and sending shrapnel shards of metal into the street that was, mercifully, empty of traffic – the very road Nicholas had refused to turn down.

And he recalled one night in London when he sat curled on his couch, miserable with a heavy head cold, only half-hearing his flatmate Martin's invitation to 'get off your lardy white arse' and come to a party off Portland Road. Nicholas felt lousy – it would have been a tight bet whether there was more mucus in his lungs or his stomach – but the moment Farty Marty mentioned the party he knew he had to go. Two hours later, sniffing like a coke addict but dressed in the best clothes he owned, he met Cate.

And, of course, there'd been his work around London. He'd

always seemed to know which village house would yield the fading valises and old carved bookends he was hunting.

Yes, he'd had inklings. Notions. Gut feelings. Until now, he'd thought everyone had them.

'What does it mean?' he asked.

Suzette smiled. He could barely see it in the dusk. 'It means I don't think you're crazy.'

•

The evening sky was gunmetal grey. Shadows were blue and amorphous. Headlights were diamonds. Her brother's profile was all dark angles. Finally, he looked at her.

'You're a financial advisor, Suze. How do you know all this stuff?'

'You see the dead. How do you not?'

'Well, I do go to phone Psychic Hotline but always end up dialling Lesbian Nurses Chat —'

'Do you have to make fun of everything? It's bitter.'

Overhead, a carpet of flying foxes flew west from their mangrove riverbank havens, an armada of black cuneiforms against the cloudless evening heavens, their leather wings eerily silent. The air was crisp, faintly spiced with car fumes and potato vine.

She took a breath. 'Well, of course it started with Dad's books.'

Nicholas looked at her. 'What books?'

She blinked, amazed. 'His books? In the garage?'

He was still staring at her. Finally, he guessed, 'In the suitcases?'

'Yes, in the suitcases! Jesus! Are you saying you never looked in them?'

She remembered the way her mother would tell her to go fetch Nicholas for dinner. She'd find him, a thin boy with a shock of straw hair, standing in the middle of the tiny, dark garage, staring. She knew he felt their father's death much more keenly than she did. Sometimes, he'd be staring overhead; stacked on planks strung through the trusses up there were three small cardboard suitcases. Their mother had never forbidden them touching the cases, nor had she ever encouraged it. They were just there, the only reminder at 68 Lambeth of a man that Suzette couldn't remember.

But, clearly, Nicholas could.

'I didn't want to touch them.' He spoke slowly, carefully. 'I figured he left them because he was coming back. Then when he was dead, I didn't want to touch them 'cause . . .' He shrugged. 'That would have meant he definitely wasn't coming back. But you . . . you had a look?'

More than a look. On weekends, when Mum was busy cursing her new potter's wheel and Nicholas was away at the library, she'd unfold the creaking wooden stepladder and pull down the suitcases. One was a pale olive green, the other two a beige and black herringbone. They weren't heavy – there wasn't much in them. One held a grey cardigan, patched trousers and half a dozen Dr Pat tobacco tins containing sinkers, spinners, hooks and fishing line. The other two cases contained what Suzette kept coming back for.

Books.

Some were cheap, flimsy things with titles like *Master Book of Candle Burning* and *Coptic Grimoires*. One book was thick with black and white plates showing turn-of-the-twentieth-century spiritualists pulling ectoplasm from their noses and ears. There was *Beowulf, The Sixth Book of Moses, A Pocket Guide to the Supernatural*. And the two books that Suzette had spirited into her own room to hide among her Susan Cooper novels: *Roots, Herbs and Oils* and *Signs and Protections*.

She explained all this to Nicholas. His face was shadowed, but she could see his eyes were bright; she wasn't sure if he was smiling or furious.

'I don't get it,' he said. 'Mum hates that shit. Any time there was a show with Doris Stokes or some spoon-bending freak, she'd turn it off.'

Suzette looked at him patiently. 'You might have noticed that our parents didn't have the jolliest marriage.'

'What do you mean, though? Dad was . . . what? A druid?'

'I didn't know him, Nicholas. All I know is what I found in his suitcases.'

Nicholas turned his sparkling gaze to her, as if finally realising a hidden truth. 'And you . . . Jesus! All those herbs and rubbish you grew in the garden when you were a kid. I thought you just liked gardening! That was . . . what? Hemlock and mandrake and double-double-toil-and-trouble shit?'

Suzette pursed her lips. 'You never asked.'

'So, what do you do? Sacrifice piglets while baring your buttocks to the harvest moon? Christ, you're a fucking economist. I thought you'd come up here to talk sense into me and tell me I need to see someone who can dope me up with Thorazine, and here you are telling me . . . Fuck, what are you telling me?'

Suzette fought the urge to snap at him. 'I'm just saying there's more to the world than the periodic table.'

'And what does Bryan think about you being into . . .' He fumbled for the word.

'Witchcraft?' she offered.

Nicholas laughed, but the sound blew away in the night wind.

'Bryan's fine with it. Weekends he helps me weed my herbs. He buys books that he thinks will interest me. And speaking of the moon, he loves it when my animal side comes out —'

'Fine, whatever.' Nicholas cut her short. 'And the kids?'

'Quincy, nothing. All she wants to do is look for Saturn's rings and bring home every creature from the pound. Nelson, though, he's . . .' She looked at Nicholas. 'He's like you. Gifted. But ignorant.'

Nicholas bristled. 'I'm not ignorant.'

'You are about magic.'

'That's because I don't believe in magic.'

'Christ, Nicholas.' She stopped, hands on hips, waiting till he turned around. 'You're haunted. You see the dead. How can you not believe in magic?'

'Magic is just stuff that scientists can't make any money out of explaining.' He turned and kept walking. 'Though I'm happy you have a hobby. Are you a good witch?'

She caught up with him. 'I own three Sydney houses outright and have five negatively geared investment properties. I'm good at everything I do.'

'I meant "good versus evil" good.'

'*People* are good or evil. Magic is magic. Some is performed with *good* intentions. Some isn't. Some is easy. Some is hard. It's like physics. For every action, there's an equal and opposite reaction. Nothing comes free. You need to put in effort. You need to make sacrifices.'

She saw Nicholas stiffen at the last word.

Then she glanced up. They were at an intersection. To the right, beyond hopscotch puddles of streetlight and shadowed picket fences, was the squat, heavy-browed building. The shops. Suzette felt a familiar old worm of fear turn in her belly.

They'd reached Myrtle Street.

•

They stepped under the awning and their footsteps echoed on the tiles. This had turned out to be a very weird evening. Suzette – sensible, nose-buried-in-financial-theory-textbooks Suzette – into magic? And his dead father, too? Nicholas brushed hair from his face. It felt unpleasantly like spider web and he shivered.

The shops were all shuttered and dark.

He'd expected a wave of pleasant nostalgia to suddenly overtake them, and they'd laugh about the lollies they'd gourmandised and the ice creams they'd loved that were no longer made. Instead, the dumb fronts of the shops were oddly hostile. This was their home suburb; it shouldn't feel so grim, so unsettling.

It's because we're being watched.

The thought shuddered through him like a shot of vodka. The streets were quiet. Nothing moved. They were alone.

'Mrs Ferguson's fruit shop,' said Suzette.

He turned. Suzette was peering in the window of the failed Tibetan restaurant, angled light from a distant streetlamp weakly picking out the empty bains-marie and bare shelves. 'She had an old set of imperial scales. Remember? She converted weights to metric and did all the maths in her head.'

Mrs Ferguson. A pleasantly plump lady with a gold tooth who wore a pencil perpetually tucked behind one ear. He remembered.

'Yep. And that old Texas Instruments calculator the size of a brick next to them? Only to prove to customers that her totals were right. They always were. Hey, we should go.'

But Suzette was staring, deep in memory. 'Did you know she tutored me?'

Nicholas was surprised. 'Mrs Ferguson? When? Where?'

'Nights you had soccer. At the back of her shop. I used to hate it.'

'Hated maths? But you're such a fucking nerd —'

'Not the maths, not Mrs Ferguson. But being back there . . . I hated that.' She shuddered.

Here, now, with the world more shadow than substance and the wind making the power lines moan, he could understand. And again the feeling struck him: *something's watching us.*

'We should go,' he repeated.

'Okay,' said Suzette. But instead, she nodded at the new shop: Plough & Vine Health Foods. All they could see in the glass was their own ghostly reflections; the shop within was as black as the waters of a deep well.

'This was Jay Jay's.' Suzette leaned closer, trying to see in. Nicholas fought an insane urge to yell 'Get back!' Her eyes were fixed on the dark shop window. 'Do you remember the old seamstress? Mrs Quill. She freaked me out. She was why I hated coming here at night.'

Nicholas had vague memories of a bent-backed old woman tucked behind a counter much too large for her, perched like some benevolent old parrot, nodding and sending a smile as he passed. Behind her hung ranks of shirts, pants, skirts and dresses that used to bring to mind a picture that, for a while during primary school, had haunted his dreams: from a book about the Second World War, a photograph of a dozen or so Russians – men, women, children – hanging dead and limp from a huge and leafless tree. A chill went through him and, as it did, another memory returned.

'You used to hate walking past these shops,' he said. 'When you were small. You used to cry.'

Suzette frowned. The line between her brows was just like their mother's. She nodded to herself. 'I think if I knew then what I know now . . . I'd say Mrs Quill was a witch, too.'

She shrugged her shoulders, as if to shuck off an ill thought, and reached into her pocket. She pulled out a tiny parcel wrapped in tissue paper. 'Hey. I brought you something.'

Not here. Not while we're being watched.

'Lovely. Can it wait till we get home?'

'Fucking hell, Nicholas,' said Suzette, cranky. 'I don't want Mum to see, okay?'

'Why not?'

'Christ! Because she doesn't understand that kind of stuff! We talked about this.'

Nicholas turned his back to the dark-eyed shop and removed the ribbon, unstuck the tape. Inside was a necklace. It was made of wooden beads and sported a polished brownish-white stone set in silver.

'The stone is sardonyx,' explained Suzette. 'You said you had some headaches, so . . .'

'They stopped.'

'Yeah. "Thank you" works, too. The wood is elder.'

Nicholas turned to face the streetlight. The stone was an inch across and cut in a square crystal, milky clear with tigerish bands of blood red. The beads were a dark timber, roughly spherical but each showing dozens of facets where they'd been cut by hand with a sharp knife. A woven silver cord held them together. It was, he had to admit, a piece both pretty and oddly masculine.

The feeling of being watched had gone.

'Thank you,' he said.

Suzette didn't answer. She was staring at the front door to Plough & Vine Health Foods. She leaned closer and frowned.

'Look.'

He followed her gaze and felt his stomach take a slow roll.

In the dim light it was just possible to make out an indentation in the wood doorframe. The mark had been painted over perhaps three or four times, and would be invisible in daylight. But in the angled light from the streetlamp, it was fairly clear. A vertical line, and halfway down it, attached to its right, a half-diamond. The mark that had been drawn in blood on the woven head of the dead bird.

Nicholas felt a cold wave of dread rise through him.

'Let's go home, Suzie,' he said.

She was entranced, leaning closer. 'This is a rune.'

'Wonderful. Come on. It's cold.'

'Wait,' she said, and reached into her purse. She pulled out a pencil and notepad and copied the figure.

Tell her! Tell her all about the bird and its twig head and the mark . . . the mark, what does it mean? But another voice was stronger, calmer. *No. Keep her out of it. She has children of her own to watch.*

'Mrs Quill,' she whispered to herself.

Nicholas put the necklace in his pocket, took his sister's arm and gently led her out to the street. 'We're going. I'm starved.'

The lie hurried him along.

•

Katharine turned the oven on low and started doling mashed potato onto three plates. How strange. She was out of practice being a mother. Nicholas had left home nearly twenty years ago. Suzette had lived in Sydney for ten. Katharine had grown used to the silence around her.

It wasn't fair. They left you and you coped. Then they came home and you had to worry all over again. Not fair. Not fair.

And yet now they were under one roof again, the instant they stepped on the street, she was anxious.

Because of the street. Because of Tallong.

'Nonsense,' she whispered and reached for the saucepan of meatballs.

Because you opened the door to something evil.

The front door rattled open.

Katharine jumped at the noise, dropping the ladle with a clatter on the tiles. Tomato sauce spattered blood red across the floor.

'We're home!' called Suzette.

'Miss us?' asked Nicholas.

Footsteps tromped down the hall.

Katharine quickly wiped up the sauce as her children stepped into the kitchen. Both of them blinked at the red flecks, and both seemed to sag a little with relief when they figured out what it was.

'You okay?' asked Suzette.

Katharine smiled thinly and nodded. 'You forgot the milk, I see.'

•

After dinner, the three members of the Close family sat on the lounge and watched the news.

No one said anything as the newsreader reported that Elliot Neville Guyatt, a thirty-seven-year-old cleaner recently moved up from Coffs Harbour, had presented himself at the Torwood Police Station and confessed to the abduction and murder of eight-year-old Dylan Oscar Thomas. The overlay pictures showed a slim paperclip of a man looking thoroughly confused as police escorted him from the paddy wagon into the watch house. Guyatt made no effort to hide his face. He walked as if he were caught in a dream.

•

Nicholas lay on the creaking single bed in his old room. He was awake, listening to the feminine lilt of his sister and mother talking. The wood walls filtered out the detail of words but left a melody that spoke of shared blood.

His old bed. The family together. Childhood again.

The shops remained the same. The woods remained the same.

Children were still dying.

He was suddenly wide awake.

Elliot Guyatt had confessed to killing the Thomas child, and the body was found in the river, miles from Tallong. Winston Teale had confessed to killing Tristram two suburbs distant, hiding his body at the construction site. Nicholas had always thought his memory of seeing Tristram's drained, dead body floating past a bad dream, a hallucination brought on by sheer terror.

But Suzette said she saw Tristram after he died, running from Carmichael Road into the woods. And Nicholas himself had seen the Thomas boy's ghost dragged into the trees. The boys didn't die miles away. The boys died in the woods.

Nicholas rolled to look out the window.

Suzette had probably reached the same conclusion and dismissed it as irrelevant. So the men killed the children in the woods, rather than out in the streets. What did that mean? Probably nothing. Would it bring them back? No.

Yet, it was disturbing. Disturbing and unsurprising that the woods were a killing place. A small piece in a newly begun puzzle that just seemed to fit with a satisfying click.

He would pull Suzette aside in the morning.

For a long while, he stared at the stars. Without knowing when, he slipped into sleep, and dreamed that gnarled, shadowy hands were carrying him away through dark curtains of silk.

7

Knocking woke him. His eyes flew open, and for the first time since leaving London he woke knowing exactly where he was. Home. KNOCK KNOCK.

The rapping of heavy knuckles on wood. Someone was at the front door.

The sea grey of pre-dawn stole between the venetian blinds. Nicholas rolled over and checked his watch. Quarter to six. He licked his dry lips and got out of bed. As he pulled on tracksuit pants, he caught sight of himself in the duchess mirror. A pale man with straw-blond hair, bleary eyes and a distracted expression. The look you saw on shoeless men in tube stations and on sparrow-fingered street-corner preachers – a face you'd give wide berth to because it seemed one ill-aimed word away from crazy. *So it's come to that*, he thought: *avoiding my own eyes.*

He pulled on his T-shirt as he lurched like a newly docked sailor down the narrow hallway toward the insistent knocking.

His mother's door was shut. Once again, hefty snores came from behind it. Suzette's door was shut too; from behind it rumbled snores a half-octave higher but equally lusty.

'How about I get it?' asked Nicholas.

Twin snores answered.

More knocking. The patient raps of a visitor who knows that someone is home.

Nicholas passed the kitchen. The sky outside was low and pregnant with rain. Who knocks at quarter to six in the morning? Only bad news.

He unlatched the front door.

A man stood there. He was perhaps forty, but his face wore fifty years worth of miles. His suit was expensive but rumpled. His tie was neatly knotted and his hair carefully combed. He'd shaved, but small tussocks of whiskers sat out like reeds in a grey swamp. The skin under his eyes looked as thin as old chicken meat; the eyes themselves were blue and overly bright.

Drugs, thought Nicholas. *Good drugs that are more than adequately compensating for sleeping pills. This guy is wired.*

'Can I help you?' he asked carefully.

He's lost. He's trying to get home from a huge night and needs a phone, a cab, a twenty.

But the man said nothing. He simply stared at Nicholas, fighting a smile and winning. The look on his face was . . . what? Desperate? Starved? Haunted?

Yes. Haunted.

The man finally spoke. 'Nicholas.'

Nicholas blinked. The voice was distantly familiar. Then the little smile bobbed again on the man's lips, a brave boat in drowning seas, and years fell away. Nicholas recognised a face he'd never seen as a man. It was a face he literally used to look up to. A Boye boy.

'Gavin?'

Gavin grinned. It was a skull's rictus.

'Wow. Gavin. You look . . .' Nicholas put out his hand. Gavin looked at it as if he'd never seen an outstretched hand before. After an uncomfortable pause, Nicholas let it fall. 'Right. Um. Listen, do . . . will you come in?'

The smile sank away and the years slipped back onto Gavin's face like the tide returning. He shook his head, and his gaze on Nicholas was unblinking. He was big, easily six-two, and Nicholas suspected he could move fast. *So take it easy . . .*

'How are you? How are your parents?'

Gavin didn't answer. Instead, he looked slowly over his left shoulder and then over his right. Above pine trees in a distant park, a dozen or so crows wheeled and dipped in the grey sky like windblown black ash. Gavin's movements sent a sudden chill flood through Nicholas's testicles. *That's exactly what Winston Teale did before he chased Tristram and me into the —*

'Woods,' said Gavin.

Nicholas stopped breathing. Pins and needles pricked the soles of his bare feet and his neck pimpled cold. He could see past Gavin's shoulders that the street was empty, not another soul in sight.

'You're up pretty early.' Nicholas wanted it to sound casual, but the words came out cracked, his mouth suddenly dry as sand. 'Do you want to do this another time? Come over for dinner? Suzette's up visiting.'

Gavin shook his head slowly, once. Nicholas noticed that he carried in one hand something wrapped in a black garbage bag.

'I was told you were back,' said Gavin. His voice was soft. Dreamy. He nodded, as if a subtle milestone had been met.

Nicholas found it hard to drag his gaze back up to Gavin's face; it was like looking at the sun, painful and dangerous. Gavin was unhooked, a boat adrift in rapids and rushing for the falls – but still afloat.

'Yeah. I'm back. What's in the bag, Gavin?' But Nicholas thought he already knew.

Gavin twisted his head, as if he hadn't heard the question. He was casting back in time. Remembering. He smiled – another death's-head grin. 'You know, Mum had tutors for us both. Tris really didn't need one. Mum only got him one so that I wouldn't feel stupid.'

'You're a smart guy, Gavin. You were never stupid.'

'Tris . . .' said Gavin fondly, his voice drifting far away. 'Trissy was the smart one.'

Nicholas watched the big man stand there, his eyes decades away. *Quick!* whispered the voice in his head. *Shut the door, now!*

That instant, Gavin's eyes flicked and locked on Nicholas's. A task remembered. 'I have a message,' he said.

In a motion so fast and fluid that Nicholas could hardly register it, Gavin pulled a gun from the bag. It was a hunting rifle, sawn off so short that the ragged cut sectioned through the front of its walnut stock. The severed barrel was ugly and raw as an eye socket.

What a waste of a good Sako, thought Nicholas, and was instantly dismayed by his reaction. Had it been a snake or a spider, his body's electric impulse would have been to leap back. But he didn't live in Baghdad or Los Angeles; fear of guns wasn't wired into his DNA. Instead, he was offended that a fine gun had been butchered. *You fucking tosser*, he thought. *You deserve to die.* A feeling like cold jelly filled his stomach.

Gavin cradled the gun easily in his hands so its rough snout pointed at Nicholas's midriff.

'A message,' said Nicholas, his mouth suddenly full of saliva, his empty cold-jelly stomach threatening to erupt. 'From who?'

Gavin watched him a long moment. Nicholas thought it was like staring into an insect's eyes – there was nothing human there. Gavin shrugged again and shook his head as if to say, *I just can't remember*. With an easy, firm movement he shifted the gun so that its barrel eye stared at Nicholas's face.

And suddenly the cold jelly was gone from Nicholas's gut. In its place was a warm, new idea. *Here it is. A way out. And I don't have to do anything. Just stand here a moment longer and it's over.* And from that warmth bloomed another thought: *No more ghosts.*

He looked up to Gavin's eyes. They were brimming full, and his patchy cheeks were wet.

'Tris loved you coming over. Saturdays. Cheese sandwiches. Watching *Combat*. Remember?'

Nicholas nodded. The two men looked at each other a long moment. A calm statement formed in Nicholas's mind. *He's going to shoot me now.*

'It's okay, Gavin.'

Gavin nodded. With a practised hand, he drew back the gun's bolt and chambered a round. The street was still. No one had an inkling that in a few heartbeats, a man was going to die.

Nicholas suddenly realised his fingers in his pocket had curled around something – wood beads and stone. The necklace Suzette had given him.

Gavin cocked his head. His eyes lost their sharp focus. His lips trembled. When he spoke, his voice was so soft that Nicholas wasn't sure he heard right.

'The message is: He touched the bird. But it should have been you.'

Gavin put the sawn barrel under his own jaw and pulled the trigger. The CRACK was sudden and as visceral as a lightning strike. Nicholas jumped.

The crows wheeling in the sky galvanised and took flight. Gavin was still standing. His lower jaw was mostly gone. He shook his head stupidly and the flaps of skin and white bone shook like a chicken's wattle. He shrugged, and his cheeks lifted the broken flesh – a macabre, embarrassed smile at his error. He swiftly reloaded, put the gun deep under his chin.

'Gavin —'

CRACK. This time, the top of his head seemed to levitate slightly. He crumpled to the ground like a dressing gown that had missed its hook. The gun clattered on the stoop.

In the next street over, a dog began barking. To the south, the grey sky became a curtain of slate where rain was falling.

Nicholas watched Gavin's body for a moment, then let himself fold to sit on the front step. A packet of John Player Specials poked out of the dead man's jacket pocket. Nicholas leaned forward and pulled it out. Then he fished in the pocket again, found a lighter.

'Nicholas?!'

Two pairs of bare feet rushed down the hall towards him. Nicholas lit a cigarette. 'It's okay,' he said. 'I got the door.'

'Oh my goodness . . .' whispered Katharine.

'Who is it?' asked Suzette. Her face was as white as paper.

'Gavin Boye.' He sucked in lungfuls of smoke. His hands shook. 'He was a smoker.'

'Oh my goodness.'

Nicholas fought the urge to cough. He could feel his sister and mother standing, staring. 'Maybe phone someone?' he suggested.

'I'll go,' whispered Suzette.

Heads were poking out of the doors and windows of neighbouring houses. Nicholas waved cheerlessly to them. Then he felt something on his lip and wiped it off. The gobbet was hard white and soft pink. He retched dryly between his knees.

'I'll get a cloth,' Katharine said thinly, and walked away on unsteady legs.

As Nicholas wiped the ropy spittle away, his eyes were drawn to the truncated rifle that lay neatly beside Gavin's body. Something was carved into the stock. The gouges in the walnut were fresh, pale against its darker burnished surface. The figure was a rough oval. From it sprouted two jagged lines like antlers. Within the oval was a symbol: a vertical slash with a half-diamond arrowhead on one side.

Nicholas flipped the rifle over so Suzette wouldn't see it.

•

By ten o'clock, Nicholas had counted eleven police officers step through the front gate, and Katharine Close had made tea for all of them. Four had arrived – lights and sirens – in answer to Suzette's telephone call, then another two who left soon after discovering the claim had already been staked, then the police photographer accompanied by the scientific officer who phoned an armoury specialist. Finally, two plain-clothes officers introduced themselves, a man and a woman. Nicholas instantly forgot the man's name, but the woman's was Waller, and he thought she would look quite pretty had her face not been saddled with a heavy scowl. By the time these last two arrived, Nicholas had told the story of Gavin's unexpected arrival and even more unexpected departure five times. He told it yet again to the detectives.

All through the recounting, the large male detective took notes and Detective Waller watched Nicholas and scowled. As usual, and without questioning himself, he omitted the bulk of the conversation he'd had with Gavin, restricting it to Gavin saying that he'd heard Nicholas was back, and that he felt it should have been Nicholas, not Tristram, who died in 1982.

'Died?' asked the male detective.

'Murdered,' answered Nicholas. 'Like the Thomas boy. You guys should keep records. They're quite handy —'

'You were involved in a homicide when you were a child?'

'I nearly *was* the homicide when I was a child,' said Nicholas.

He touched the bird, but it should have been you.

He was awfully tired. Shock, he knew, could weary a person, but this was just fucking tedious.

'I hadn't seen Gavin in more than twenty years. I don't know how he knew I was back, but it's not commercial in confidence. I'm sure he was resentful that Teale murdered his brother instead of me. And yes, these are his smokes.'

Nicholas lit another one, and offered the open pack to the detectives. They refused, and he saw them exchange a glance.

Katharine arrived quietly at the lounge room doorway with a refreshed tray of tea and cups, placed it, and just as silently retreated. Nicholas just wanted to sleep.

'Jesus Christ,' he said. 'You guys . . .'

'Is that it?' asked the male detective.

'I really fucking wouldn't mind if it was.'

He rubbed at his stubbled chin and felt a lump come away. It was a piece of pinkish bone the size of a match head. He felt his tongue sink back in his throat. He just wanted to shower and get to bed.

'Okay.' The male detective folded his notebook, then looked again into Nicholas's face. 'Why do you think he didn't shoot you?'

'Well,' said Nicholas, 'it took him two shots to hit his own brain. Maybe he was afraid he'd miss.'

'What sort of a relationship did you have with him?'

Nicholas sank his head in his hands. 'What relationship?! Christ, I thought we were done!'

'What sort of a relationship did you have with Gavin Boye as children?'

Nicholas smoked, and shook his head. 'He was my best friend's older brother.'

'Were you lovers?' asked the female detective.

Nicholas felt his eyebrows rise. He was almost delighted to be surprised. 'No. I lost my virginity at nineteen to a girl named Pauline McCleary who could probably have spent those three minutes much more productively. I've never had nor wanted to have sex with a male of any age, although if I was going to turn I think that Sean Connery has a nice voice but Robbie Williams looks like a harder fuck.'

Her scowl remained fixed on Nicholas, unshiftable as desert sandstone.

'We're done.' The male detective stood. 'Thank you, Mr Close. You've had a very disturbing morning and I strongly suggest you consider making an appointment with a qualified counsellor. We can recommend one if you like. Thank you for the tea, Mrs Close,' he called into the kitchen. Nicholas watched him reach into his pocket and switch off the tiny digital recorder there.

He followed them to the front door, where the female detective hesitated. 'Do you recognise the mark on the gun stock?' she asked.

Nicholas met her eyes. 'What mark?' Lying, he realised, was easy when you just didn't care.

The male detective nodded, and the pair left.

Nicholas helped mop the blood off the front steps before he finally took his shower, then he went to bed and fell into a sleep as deep and empty as the night sky.

•

Suzette popped another two ibuprofen from their foil card, put them in her mouth and concentrated on swallowing them. She had the unpleasant sensation of the hard pills ticking at her molars like loose teeth, and into her mind jumped the horrible flash of Gavin Boye folded on the front stoop, his eyes partly open and seeming to stare at the potted philadelphus, his own shattered teeth grinning from his red and ruined slash of a mouth. Her head throbbed. For the hundredth time she wished she were at home and could grab some mugwort from her herb garden. Finally, the pills went down.

•

When he woke, his room was dark. Thunder rolled grimly outside, stabbed by flashes of lightning. He was shaking and so cold that his muscles had spasmed tight, making it difficult to sit up. As soon as he did, a swell of nausea rode up to the back of his throat. He put his feet over the side of the bed and reached with jittering fingers for his watch. It was nearly two in the morning.

He touched the bird. But it should have been you.

Something had wanted him dead a long time ago. And now that something knew he was back. It had sent Gavin. *And it wants me to* know *that it knows.*

Why didn't Gavin shoot him?

Because he wasn't supposed to.

Nicholas kept his eyes open, because whenever he closed them he saw the top of Gavin's scalp rising on its little font of red and grey. *You're one small step from the loony bin, my friend. Not content with seeing reruns of suicides – you need premieres now?*

He felt hungover, foggy.

What possessed Gavin to do that?

The words hovered in his mind like smoke in a closed room. *What possessed him?*

Someone had left a glass of water on the bedside table. Nicholas reached for it. His hand quaked with every beat of his heart, making tiny, circular ripples.

What possessed Gavin? Was it the same thing that had possessed Elliot Guyatt to march into Torwood cop shop and admit he killed the Thomas boy? The same thing that had possessed Winston Teale to confess to Tristram's murder?

Teale did *murder Tristram!*

Did he? Teale certainly chased us into the woods . . .

Exactly!

Only . . . Teale was built like a bull. He couldn't have fitted through the tunnels under the water pipe.

Nicholas sat upright, suddenly wide awake.

That's right. Not too sharp, are you? Twenty-five years you've had to figure that out. Maybe Teale was just the sheepdog. Maybe Teale didn't kill Tristram.

'Then who did?' he whispered.

The same person that told Gavin to kill himself. The same person that made a talisman from a dead bird.

Nicholas put his feet over the bed edge. He had to talk about this, lance it before it swelled in his head like a sac of spoiled blood and poisoned him. He had to tell Suzette. He stood and struggled into his hoodie with shaking arms.

The hall was dark. Suzette's door was open. Her bed was unmade.

Nicholas frowned and padded to his mother's door. No snores came from inside.

'Mum?'

Nothing. He put his hand on the doorknob, but let it rest there. He could feel her wakefulness on the other side of the door. A dull slosh of anger rolled inside him, which he swallowed down.

Can you blame her, weirdo? You're an albatross.

Nicholas realised he was still shaking. His legs were weak and vibrated like cello strings. He shuffled to the kitchen and made tea, then stumped to the lounge room.

Suzette was curled asleep on the sofa, her face a deathly grey in the television's glow. The set's volume was so low it was no wonder he hadn't heard it.

He sat beside her and watched as he sipped his tea. After two infomercials (one for a company that implied it would loan you cash even if you'd just broken out of prison and held schoolchildren hostage, and another showing pretty women with loose morals who could not possibly make it through the night without *his* phone call), a news update. Elliot Guyatt, remanded in custody and due to face court next week charged with the murder of local seven year old Dylan Thomas, had been found dead in his remand cell, having apparently suffered a brain aneurysm. A coroner's report was pending. Today, the funeral service for Dylan Thomas had been held at St John's Anglican Cathedral, with his schoolmates forming a guard of honour . . .

Nicholas dropped the remote three times before he could switch off the set.

It took over an hour to fall asleep.

But once asleep, he dreamed.

He was Tristram. Sweat poured down his temples, his armpits, his crotch. He was on his good hand and knees, pushing through a dark, cobwebbed tunnel. With every inch forward, spider webs cloaked his face, clogged his nostrils, coated his lips. Tiny legs spindled on his arms, his neck, his lips and eyelids. He wanted to scream but couldn't, because spiders would get in his mouth. The tunnel seemed never to end, and the webs got thicker, and the numbers of spiders on his legs, his arms, crawling down his shirt, burrowing into his ears, became so great they weighed him down. Soon, the webs over his eyes as were thick as a shroud; they shut out the light and cloyed his limbs so he could not move. He screamed now, but the spider silk was wrapped tight about his jaw and he couldn't open his mouth. He struggled, but the sticky silk held him tight. And the spiders – thousands of spiders – stopped crawling and started to feed.

8

He woke to the distant clinking of metal spoons in ceramic bowls. He rose and wiped the corners of his eyes. It was just after seven.

Shuffling down the hall, he heard an elephantine rumble coming from behind Suzette's bedroom door. As he approached the kitchen, the sound of thick bubbling made him wonder whether he'd round the corner and see his mother in a hooded cloak, sprinkling dried dead things into a soot-stained cauldron. The imagining didn't amuse him; it made him slightly ill. He shook off the thought and entered the kitchen.

Katharine was in her pink nightgown, stirring a pot of porridge. 'Good morning,' she said. She didn't turn around.

He'd intended to tell her what he'd seen on last night's news: that Elliot Guyatt had died in his cell. But Katharine was stirring the bubbling oatmeal with such stiff briskness, her shoulders set so hard, that he remained silent. She was tense. Or angry. Or . . . *afraid*.

No. There'd be no talk about killers of children this morning.

She finally turned, wearing a bright, forced smile. 'Tea's made, and the porridge is nearly done. You look pale.'

'I call it PTSD-chic.' He sat.

'You could have a flu.'

Christ, he thought. *If only all I had was a flu.* 'Paper?'

She shook her head and nodded to the front door.

He stood again, shuffled back up the hall and opened the door. He yelped in surprise. Gavin stood there, the gun under his chin.

A moment later, the gun silently kicked and Gavin's jaw split open. The ghost smiled at Nicholas, repositioned the gun under his ruined chin, and it jerked again. Gavin's scalp jumped and he fell to the steps without a sound.

Nicholas stood frozen.

A moment later, Gavin was gone.

'For fuck's sake,' whispered Nicholas. His voice shook.

'What's that?' called Katharine.

Gavin was now fifty metres up Lambeth Street, walking towards the front gate. The day was harshly bright.

'Nicholas?'

'Nothing.'

He clenched his teeth and hurried down to the footpath where the rolled newspaper lay in dew. He sidestepped Gavin on the way back in.

Katharine had the porridge dished out. Nicholas stared wearily at his bowl.

'I think you're sick,' she said.

He shook his head. His stomach felt ready to disgorge, as if he'd swallowed a mugful of old blood. He was cold.

Katharine touched the back of her hand to his forehead. He could feel her thin skin vibrating. She was shaking.

'Bit hot,' she said.

He took a mouthful of tea and left his porridge untouched.

'I'll be in the garage.'

He felt her eyes on the back of his head as he walked to the back door.

•

Katharine sat watching a skin harden over the porridge in her bowl. It was, she decided, the exact colour of the poo that had come out of her children when they were breastfeeding – a wheaty shit with the sweet smell of just-turning milk. She dropped her spoon with a deliberate clatter.

'Fine,' she said to herself.

You bring these creatures into the world. You guide their little, darting dumb heads onto your swollen-then-aching-then-numb nipples, you change ten thousand nappies . . . but what does that guarantee? That they will love you? That they will talk with you? That they will be good?

No. No. No.

She was angry. And her anger stayed on a slow simmer because it fed itself; she didn't quite know why. Everything had been so normal a few weeks ago. Deliciously boring. A warm, smooth-sided routine. She could step from the shower and loll into every day: breakfast, tidying, check the last firing, discard the breakages, peel the thick plastic off the clay, boil the kettle, wet the wheel . . . and then it was dinner time and the possibility of a phone call from Sydney or London. But now . . . now things had changed very fast. Old things had reappeared; feelings and fears that she'd thought were long disposed of. It was like coming suddenly across the image of the man who'd dumped you in a stack of fading, happy photographs.

Oh, but it's so much more than that, she thought. *He's brought death to your doorstep.*

She set her jaw and stared at her tea. Whose fault was that? She didn't want to think about it, and busied herself sprinkling sugar over the gelatinous surface of her cooling porridge.

That's what happens, isn't it? Things are hot and dangerous for a while, then they cool, and you form a skin, a hide that keeps things nice and separate. Like keeping the practicalities of gas bills and leaking toilet cisterns – real-life stuff – from the dreaminess, the otherworldliness, that used to hover around Don like the scents of Arabia around a plodding climbing jasmine. That dreaminess was what had charmed her so many years ago, then alarmed her, then infuriated her. And now she saw it in her children and it infuriated her still. It was alien.

The answer was to ignore it and get on with the day, and so she started eating the lukewarm gruel, relishing that despite the fact it should be dumped, she refused to let it go to waste.

She was finishing the sweet, milky dregs when Suzette shuffled into the kitchen. Katharine nodded at the saucepan on the stove. Suzette nodded and pulled back her hair. Katharine felt the twin forks of pride and jealousy: pride that she had brought such a confident, good-looking person into the world; and an instinctive, primordial antagonism to another female in her space. A younger one at that.

'Your brother's sick.'

Suzette yawned and poured tea. 'I'm not surprised.'

Not surprised – was that a bait? Did Suzette expect her to ask: What do you mean? Why aren't you surprised? What do you know?

But to ask was to acknowledge foolishness, and she would not be party to that.

She pushed her cup towards Suzette's, and her daughter refreshed it. 'Ta,' said Katharine.

For a while, they sat in silence. It was Suzette who broke it.

'Do you remember the seamstress down the road, Mum?'

'Beg pardon?'

'The seamstress at Jay Jay's? Mrs Quill?'

Katharine felt her bladder go as loose as a hung bedsheet in the wind. It took all her concentration to clench and hold. Her expression didn't change.

'Quill? Not really. Quill . . . the old woman? She's been dead for years. Do you need something mended?'

She saw Suzette's eyes rise and lock onto hers.

She knows I'm lying.

But still the iron spike inside her refused to bend, and she met her daughter's stare.

'No,' replied Suzette. 'Never mind.'

•

The chamferboard sides of the garage were once white but decades of grinding sun and mindless rain had grubbied them to a weary grey that was flaking off dispiritedly, revealing tiny continents of bilious green undercoat. Its single window of four dusty panes stared darkly out at the lush garden that flanked the building. Lush monstera bushes with their broad, perforated leaves squatted around the outside, and Rangoon creeper snaked up the jagged timbers. The unused driveway, twin rails of concrete veined with cracks from which emerged tiny lava flows of moss, ran up to two wooden bifold doors that sagged, their tops meeting in the middle like the leaning foreheads of exhausted, clinching boxers. Nicholas slipped an old nickel-plated key into the lock of the right-hand bifold. It gave a desiccated groan as he drew it open.

He stepped inside and closed the door behind him.

Inside was dark and familiar as a lover's bedroom. There was no electric bulb; milky light trickled through the grime-fogged window.

Something was rattling. No wind shook the window; the dust motes hardly stirred. He realised the sound was his teeth. He bit down hard to stop them.

He inhaled. The taste of the still air was tinted with engine oil, with the scent of earth as fine and barren as desert sand, with dry rot . . . and underneath it all, as faint as a whisper, the sickly aroma of rum. *Because here was where he drank*, thought Nicholas. His mother had cleaned out the bottles after she kicked her husband out, but the smell of the booze lingered like a slow cancer. He walked across to the bench and pulled open the drawer. It wouldn't have surprised him to find half a dozen of the two hundred millilitre bottles his father preferred – but the drawer was empty except for dust and cockroach shells. He closed it.

It had been decades since he'd stood in here; yet the sight and smell of it had not changed. Time meant nothing. The thought sank like a slow blade into his gut. Those intervening years had been worthless. Twenty years of heartbeats, of travel, of conversations and work and sleep and wishes and laughter were dust. Cate had lived and died, and now existed only in his mind and in some cruel lantern show in the bathroom of a small flat in Ealing. This building was as much a crypt as any stone chamber in Newham Cemetery. Time was interred here.

He was tempted to step back out, return to bed and pray that his chill was something grave like pneumonia or dengue fever. Yet he knew he had to stay. He had an inkling. Something in here was waiting to be found.

His eyes were adjusting to the gloom. He craned his head back. Between the trusses overhead were strung side by side two old wood painter's planks, each thick as his wrist and grey with age, spattered with a muted rainbow of paints that had dried before Nixon resigned. Stacked on the planks were his father's suitcases.

Leaning against the rear wall was a timber stepladder, also speckled with paint. Loops of gritty cobweb hung between the treads like hammocks in a sunken ship. Nicholas drew in a deep breath – the effort set him shaking harder – and blew what dust he could off the ladder and pulled it from the wall. He set it below the planks, and climbed.

His head drew level with the first suitcase; inches from his face, a spider the size of a coaster hung from the plastic handle. He instinctively jumped back, and only stopped himself falling by grabbing the red hardwood truss. A splinter drove deep into the soft web of flesh between his finger and thumb. He steadied himself. The spider bobbed in the disturbed air, light as tissue. It was a carapace, hanging empty by a silk thread. Nicholas felt his heart fluttering like a trapped sparrow; he flicked the spider shell away and started carrying the suitcases down to the earth floor.

On the ground, they seemed smaller. Coated in dust and warped by seasons of damp and dry, they looked lost and vulnerable. Two were a matching herringbone, in beige and black; the third was once a cadaverous green.

He pulled that one towards him. Its plastic corners had cracked with age; its catches were brown and rusted. He pressed hard and something inside the lock snapped and the freed lid rose a fraction. He swung it open; the rusted hinges let out the sigh of a poorly sleeping man.

The clothes inside were so badly eaten by moth larvae that when he lifted what he guessed was a cardigan, it fell apart in his fingers. But his eyes lit on something untouched by the vermin: the synthetic label inside the collar. He read the cream rectangle: Size 38. A size smaller than mine, he thought. Before he knew what he was doing, he lifted the rotting fabric to his nostrils and inhaled. An unhappy blend of lanolin and wet soil. Nothing of the man. He dropped the rags.

Inside the upper lid was a sleeve for shoes; its elastic had long lost its pull and it sagged like a slack, dead mouth. Inside were some cardboard train tickets, each punched with a tiny hole, and a few bronze coins. Beneath the rotten chaff of eaten wool and grub pellets were some rusted tobacco tins. Nicholas pushed the case aside, and pulled another towards him.

It, too, resisted opening. He went to the workbench and found a screwdriver – its shaft grainy with rust – and popped open the stubborn latch. Within were books. These, too, had been exposed to insects, but clearly were less palatable fare and were only mildly damaged. They smelled potent: mealy and ripe. Nicholas lifted them out one by one. Some were cheap things, the spines of which lifted away the moment he touched them; others were weighty with dark, glossy covers. Books on spiritualism, clairvoyance, gods of the pagan world, Irish mythology – an even dozen. He pushed them aside and pulled the last suitcase towards him.

This was the smallest and heaviest. It opened without protest and Nicholas felt his stomach tighten. More books: herbs and magic. Druidism. Voodoo. The Apocrypha. Despite Suzette telling him the books were here, he was amazed to hold them in his hands. How could his mother, his pragmatic, no-nonsense mother, ever have cohabited with a man who read books like this? But of course, she didn't. Not for long. Their marriage had lasted just four years.

Nicholas stacked the books to one side as he pulled them out. What was he looking for? Would he have to go through all these dreary volumes one at a time?

No. It's here.

There were three books left. He lifted aside *The Curse of Machu Picchu*, and stopped. Beneath was a book unlike all the others. It was a slight staple-bound thing with a thick paper cover in jaundice yellow; in the centre of the cover was an etching of the Tallong

State School main building. The title read: *Tallong S.H.S – 75 Years – 1889–1964.*

Nicholas felt the pulse in his neck beat stronger. He flipped open the book.

The contents were broken into three chapters: the first twenty-five years, then 1914 to 1939, 1940 to 1964. Within the chapters were sprinkled black and white photographs of principals, of buildings being erected, of a governor's visit, and, of course, year photos of students, seated in four rows of eight or so, their teachers smiling cheerfully or wearily or dutifully from their midst.

Was his father's photo in here? Nicholas flipped through to the end of the book. As he did, a page slipped out and slid like a feather to the dark earth. He picked it up. No, not a page. It was a newspaper clipping, yellow and crisp: a truncated advertisement for Hotpoint clothes dryers. He turned the clipping over. As he read the headline of the small article, he felt his face go cold.

'Boy Missing – Police Seek Information'.

It took half a minute to read the article. A twelve-year-old boy named Owen Liddy had left his Pelion Street home on a Saturday morning; he was to catch a train into Central Station and visit a model aeroplane exhibition at the City Hall. His mother became worried when he hadn't returned by four. People attending the exhibition were interviewed; none recalled seeing a boy fitting Liddy's description. Police were inviting any information from the public.

Nicholas re-read the article. Then he noticed the last page of the Tallong schoolbook was dog-eared. He picked it up and opened to the marked page.

It showed a photograph of the 1964 year seven students. A grinning girl in pigtails held a pinboard with the class name: 7C. But it was the face of a short, smiling boy third along in the second to back row that Nicholas stared at. The face was circled in dark lead pencil. He slid his eyes down to read the caption below the photograph: 'Left to right: Peter Krause, Rebecca Lowell, Owen Liddy . . .'

Nicholas stared at the clipping for a long moment. What did it mean? Had his father known the boy? Unlikely – Donald Close would have been in his late teens in 1964. A friend's brother? Possibly. Had the boy turned up safe and well? Nicholas thought it unlikely; besides, why would his father have kept the clipping? There was only one answer.

Dad knew.

A boy went missing, and Donald Close thought it was odd enough a disappearance that he kept the article. Kept it for nearly ten years, until he himself had disappeared from his family's life and broken himself in two when his sliding car was sliced open by a poorly marked concrete road divider. *But he left it*, thought Nicholas. *He left it with his books.*

He left it for us.

He folded the clipping and slipped it into his pocket. Outside, the morning had gone grey and the air in the garage was cold.

He hurriedly put the suitcases back on the overhead planks, eager to be out of this room that was as uncomfortably quiet as a grave.

•

Nicholas let himself back in the house. The hall was quiet, and the air was freezing.

'Suzette?'

He rapped on her bedroom door, opened it. Her bed was made, her suitcase open on a chair under the window. From underneath the house came a low thrumming. His mother's pottery wheel: the electric hum of industry.

Halfway back down the hall, the walls took on a heavy tilt and Nicholas lurched. As he steadied himself, two large drops of sweat fell on the timber floor. He was feverish.

He fetched a change of clothes and went to the bathroom. In the bottom drawer of the vanity he found a half-empty box of Disprin and popped four in his mouth and felt them fizz on his tongue. Then he stripped off and turned on the shower.

As he showered, he chewed and took a half-mouthful of water, swallowing the bitter soup. His eyes slid down to his right foot and the scar: a faint line of pale skin where his sixth toe had been removed.

From his first job out of college – dish pig at the Kookaburra Grill – he'd saved every spare cent towards the elective surgery, and a lucky commission to design a logo for a new chain of wheel alignment garages topped his war chest to the required three thousand dollars. He booked himself in for the day op, had the offending appendage removed, spent a week recovering, then went out to the Lord Regent Hotel to find a girl to lose his virginity to, choosing the soon-to-be-unsatisfied Pauline McCleary. But every time he'd showered or bathed in the seventeen years since, his eyes had been drawn to his right foot, just to confirm that the horrid deformity hadn't grown slyly back.

As he looked at the jagged white line, into his mind sprang the image of pale scars in dark wood: the marking scratched with a blade into the stock of Gavin's rifle. Why had he hidden it from Suzette? And why hadn't he told her that same mark on the health food store door had been the very one on the dumb, round woven head of the dead bird? Something had stopped him. Now, under the steaming water with the aspirin starting to work, he realised why. *She has children.* Telling Suzette might somehow bring the danger latent in the mark closer to Nelson and Quincy.

Nicholas turned off the taps.

Now he had a piece of new information that he'd exhumed from his father's musty suitcases in the garage. He'd come into the house ready to tell Suzette about the child who went missing in 1964, but now he was glad she was out.

Don't tell her. Keep her ignorant. Keep her safe and send her home.

As he dried himself, his head began to throb again. Missing children. Dead children. Confessing murderers. Dead murderers. A strange mark. A strange message. *He touched the bird, but it should have been you.*

By the time he'd dressed, Nicholas had a plan.

He would find out when Gavin Boye was to be buried.

•

Suzette waved down a young waiter with a very nice bum and ordered a third long black with hot skim milk on the side.

A notepad with a page full of newly written notes was open in front of her, and a small pile of stapled cost projection reports, their margins crammed with her comments, all of which were now lined through. With one hand she flipped icons on the laptop screen, shrinking her address book, restoring her mailbox, opening an accounts summary spreadsheet, highlighting days in her diary. In her other hand was her mobile phone; on the other end was Ola, her PA, a blocky and unattractive girl with a voice that was as lovely as her face was not. It was Ola's good phone manner and skill at mail merging that got her the job.

Suzette was pleased. In the last hour and a half she'd concluded most of a day's business, and with the strong coffees removed most traces of her mother's awful porridge from her tongue. She asked Ola to send out a tender to a few architect firms, and confirmed she'd be back in Sydney in a day or two. Then she rang home. Bryan answered.

'Hello?'

'Hello yourself. What happened to "Hello beautiful wife, I miss you and can't bear another hour without you"?'

'Oh, hey gorgeous! Uh, yeah . . . the caller ID is . . . down.'

Suzette frowned. 'Down?'

'Nelson found my screwdriver set and did a bit of exploratory surgery on the handset. This is an old phone I found downstairs. I think it may have been used to convey the terms for the Treaty of Versailles. It's got a spinny thingy.'

'Rotary dial?'

'I think you'll find in telecommunications circles it's called a "spinny thingy".'

'Okay, Captain Hilarious. Why isn't Nelson at school?'

Her husband chuckled. He sounded much more than a thousand kilometres away. 'You won't like this.'

'Try me.'

'He didn't want to go.'

Suzette took a breath and told herself not to get snarky.

'Didn't want to go. Did he have a good reason?'

'He said he doesn't like his teacher because she isn't nice to her husband.'

'Not nice . . . to her . . . what? I don't get it.'

'Nels said she was married to her husband but kisses another man.'

Suzette's new coffee arrived, and she tried not to watch the taut young waiter saunter away. 'I still don't understand. Did he see her kissing another teacher?'

'No.'

'Then how —'

She suddenly understood. Nelson just *knew*.

'Aaah.'

'Yep,' agreed Bryan.

Inklings. Feelings. Nelson had them. Quincy didn't. Was Nelson's prescience as strong as Nicholas's? She didn't know. It was only in the last two days that she'd begun to realise how sensitive Nicholas was to things unseen. What was it in her family's blood that gave its men this odd sensitivity? Would Nelson turn out like Nicholas? She shivered at the prospect, then frowned at herself for being so uncharitable.

'He's napping now,' explained Bryan. 'I guess gutting a two-hundred-dollar phone takes it out of a bloke. Maybe call later, explain to him some stuff about women and kissing and misplaced love and all that stuff I don't understand because I'm married to the woman of my dreams?'

'You'll go far, charmer. I'll ring and tell him he's going to school or going to sea.'

Brian laughed. 'How's Nicholas?'

'He's . . . I honestly don't know. Sick, Mum said.'

'Hm. And you?'

She could hear the caring gravity in his voice. She knew what he meant. She'd seen a man dead on the front porch of her childhood home. God, was that only yesterday? The image of Gavin's broken teeth in his shattered jaw leapt again into the front of her mind and her stomach tightened.

'I'm okay.'

'Okay. Call later. Come home soon.'

They said their goodbyes, and then Suzette was staring at the cooling coffee with the disconnected phone on her lap. The thought of Gavin Boye crumpled on the porch stole all the joy out of her conversation with Bryan. Why had he killed himself? There were a thousand possible reasons, from tax fraud to child porn and everything in between. But why had he shot himself in front of Nicholas?

Tristram. Tristram was the link. She was sure of it.

She sipped her coffee and started to put away her paperwork. At the bottom of the pile was the small notepad she always carried with her. This was the last job she'd left for herself. Two nights ago, she'd been excited about this, but now, for some reason, it was a task she felt like avoiding. She flipped open the pad. Drawn there was the strange mark she'd copied from the doorway of Plough & Vine Health Foods. *Quill's shop*, she thought.

She clicked open her internet browser and typed: 'runes'. She started to hunt.

9

Nicholas couldn't help but admire the clerk at the convenience store. The young Filipino man managed to scan, bag and total Nicholas's purchase of milk, bread, peanut paste, toiletries and a newspaper without once looking up from the swimsuit pictorial in the men's magazine he held between his face and Nicholas's.

Nicholas carried the bags out into the angled afternoon light. The pearly clouds had cleared and faintly warm sunlight fell softly between the leaves of jacaranda and satinwood trees. In sober daylight, the Myrtle Street shops held no menace and the nostalgia he'd expected here with Suzette two evenings ago finally arrived – the excitement of what sweet treasures would be in forty cents' worth of mixed lollies (Cobbers? Freckles? Milk bottles? Mint leaves?) or how many pecans Mrs Ferguson would sell him for a dodecagon fifty-cent piece, or the tactile pleasure of stroking a burnished silver chrysalis found in the oleander bushes out front, now gone and replaced with topiary trees.

Nicholas strayed to the door of Plough & Vine Health Foods. The shop within was dark. A 'Closed' sign hung inside the door, with the shop's hours handwritten on it: '10 a.m. – 5.30 p.m.'. He checked his watch. It was five to ten. His eyes slid up to the doorframe. In the friendly light of day, the mark he knew was there under layers of gloss white paint was invisible.

He walked over to the curved galvanised steel handrail that separated the tiles outside the shops from the footpath, and then – with an easy swoop that defied the quarter-century since he'd done it last – he grabbed the rail in an underhand grip and swung to sit underneath it, legs dangling over the concrete buttress. Quietly pleased, he opened the newspaper on his lap.

A lowered sports car buzzed lazily past, chased by its longboat bass drumming. High in shadowed branches, a family of noisy miners quarrelled with a magpie, forcing it to fly beyond the distant rooftops.

Nicholas felt slightly cold and a little light-headed, but his flu symptoms seemed to have eased. He opened the paper and flicked through to the personal advertisements section and scanned for funeral notices. The page was full. Dying, he thought, remained as popular a pastime as ever. He followed his finger to the middle of the first column and found what he was looking for: 'Gavin Boye. Suddenly passed. Son of Jeanette. Husband of Laine.'

Nicholas blinked. Christ, Gavin had a wife. He read on.

'Loved and missed. Relatives and friends are respectfully invited . . .' He skipped to the end. The service would be at the local Anglican church the following morning.

A wife, Laine. Could she shed more light on why her grey-faced husband had risen early two mornings ago, grabbed his favourite sawn-off, and gone to the home of his long-dead brother's best friend to deliver a message . . . from whom?

It should have been you.

Was that Gavin's own wish, that Tristram had lived and Nicholas had been found with his throat opened up like a ziplock bag, almost empty of blood?

No. Those weren't Gavin's words. Gavin couldn't have known about the bird. The day Nicholas told Tristram about the talismanic bird, Tristram never returned home. And after his death, Nicholas never found a way to tell the Boyes about the tiny, mutilated corpse that Tristram had touched just before Winston Teale stepped from his olive sedan and strode like a golem towards them. The only person who could have told Gavin about the bird was the one who'd set the dead thing as a trap.

Nicholas checked his watch. It was after ten. He turned and saw that the sign on the health food shop door had been flipped and now read 'Open'. He went to door and pushed it inward. As it angled away from the light, the mark fell into relief – a vertical slash with a half-diamond. He felt the soles of his feet tighten vertiginously. He bit down the feeling and stepped inside.

As he looked around, his apprehension dissipated. The shelves were stocked with handmade soaps, cloth trivets stuffed with aromatic herbs, small wooden barrels of seeds with brass scoops stuck in their surfaces like the bows of cheerily sinking ships. The store smelled of mint and cloves and honey.

The pleasantly fragrant air was broken by a silvery crash of tin hitting tiles in the storeroom behind the counter, followed by the ticking skitter of tiny spheres skimming across the floor.

'Shit!' A woman's voice, followed by a stream of breathy words that could only be swearing.

'Hello?' called Nicholas.

Silence. Then a head poked out through the storeroom door. Her hair was light brown and her eyes were dark brown. Her eyes and mouth were rounded in three embarrassed Os.

'Oh, bum,' she whispered, and disappeared again from sight.

Nicholas set down his bags and picked up a few of the tiny objects that had rolled under the counter. They were wooden beads, not unlike those on the necklace Suzette had given him.

The woman stepped from behind the counter, tucking her hair behind one ear. 'Such a klutz,' she said.

Nicholas tried to guess her age. Twenty-five? Thirty? Her skin was milk pale and clear, lips red and pursed as she stooped to collect the errant beads.

'I fall down stairs,' he said.

She scooted about energetically, in and out of Nicholas's sight, picking up beads. 'Ah, but then you're only hurting yourself. These, now . . .' She stood and poured them from her hands into the tin. 'These can trip people very well.'

'What are they?'

She affected a wise expression as she slyly turned the tin's label towards herself to read furtively: '"Willow-wood beads – for Dreameing, Inspiration and Fertility". "Dreaming" spelt with an extra "e" for Olde English Effecte.'

Nicholas nodded.

The young woman smiled. It was a pretty smile. She shrugged. 'People buy them.'

'I have some myself.'

'Willow beads?'

'I think they're elder wood.'

She cocked her head and narrowed her eyes, then shook her head and shrugged again. Nicholas found it an attractive gesture. He was sure men shopped here just to look at her.

'Anyway,' she said. 'Since I can't trip you, can I help you?'

He thought about it. 'I don't think so. No.'

'Okay,' she said, frowning. A small, sweet line appeared between her eyes.

'There's a mark on your door,' he said.

'Oh?'

He nodded at it.

She stepped out from behind the counter. She was slim and nearly his height. Her dress was of an old cut, but snugly fitted. Simple, but flattering to her figure. She kept herself a few steps distant from him as she went to the door. He told her to open it, and pointed to the rune.

She frowned again as she peered at it. 'You know, I've never noticed that. Did you put it there?' She levelled both eyes at him with startling frankness.

He blinked, off guard. 'No. There used to be a seamstress here, when I was a kid. She was a bit creepy.'

'I've been here a year,' the young woman said. 'Before me was a pool supply guy. The place reeked of chlorine.' She shrugged again, and cocked her head as if to ask where this was going.

Nicholas realised it was going nowhere. 'I have a cold,' he said suddenly, and instantly wondered where the words had come from.

She looked at him for a moment. The frank gaze was strangely erotic – as if she were imagining him undressing, and finding the thought pleasing. Then she nodded to herself and ducked from sight. He could hear the sounds of tins opening and the crunching of slender fingers in dried leaves. She returned with a paper bag, which she sealed with a sticker from beside the till. 'Sage, ginger, echinacea, garlic. Make a tea with it.'

Nicholas took the bag doubtfully. 'How will it taste?'

She smiled. 'Dreadful. Eight dollars fifty.'

As she handed him change for his ten, she asked, 'Are you a local?'

Nicholas looked at her. This close, he could smell her hair. It smelled like vanilla, clean and good. He thought for a moment. 'Yes. Home again.'

She nodded approvingly. 'Next time, I'll try something much more treacherous than beads.'

'I look forward to it,' he said. 'Sorry about the mark thing. I just thought . . . You know.'

'Strange marks,' she said.

It was Nicholas's turn to shrug.

'Do you think it could be Chinese?' she asked. 'They used to have market gardens somewhere around here, I heard. It could be for luck.'

'Could be. I'm Nicholas.' He extended his hand.

She looked at it, and took it, and shook it firmly.

'Rowena.' She smiled. 'We're well met.'

'We are,' he agreed.

He found himself thinking about Rowena's smile on his way home, and so guiltily buried the memory of it.

•

He was emptying the letterbox when a man stepped through him. Nicholas jumped, his heart suddenly kicked into a sprint.

Gavin Boye kept walking up to the front porch of the house, silently carrying his gun in a black, glossy garbage bag. He stopped, then knocked silently on the door. No one answered.

Nicholas felt a greasy knot in the pit of his stomach. This was too much like the dead boy with his screwdriver outside his flat in Ealing. And that memory led back to Cate's death.

I can't face this every day.

He dropped the mail back in the letterbox and stepped out onto the footpath, closing the gate behind him.

•

It was just after lunch when a balding, constantly smiling real estate agent handed Nicholas keys to a furnished flat on Bymar Street. Nicholas had signed the lease, payed two months rent in advance, and been allowed to use the agency's telephone to connect power and gas.

He carried the keys and his bag of herbal tea up the concrete stairs to the first-floor flat, unlocked the door and stepped inside. The furniture was cheap and badly worn. The fridge had an asthmatic rattle. The carpet smelled faintly of cannabis and wet dog. The white curtains of the front room hung as listless as dressed game fowl. He pulled one aside, repulsed by the greasy feel of the fabric, and looked down the street.

At the end of Bymar Street was Carmichael Road, and beyond it, the heavy darkness of the woods.

In the sagging kitchen, Nicholas found a ceramic kettle with a wire element, and boiled water. How could the woods still be there? How did they survive the housing boom of the fifties, the licentious building rackets of the seventies, the fiscal orgy of the '03 spike?

It wasn't a loved park. No one went in there. In fact, people hurried past them. People *knew*, without even entering, that they weren't friendly woods.

Leave here, he thought. *Buy a ticket south. Get a job in a design firm in a nice new building and live in a new apartment where there are no ghosts. You can live with that. This place hasn't changed.*

No. Not yet. First, he would go to Gavin Boye's funeral. He would see Gavin's widow, and Mrs Boye.

Why?

Because it's the right thing to do.

Bullshit.

Well, then: to see.

To see what?

He chewed listlessly, staring, but the woods were a sea of shadow.

He didn't know. Perhaps . . . to look for more signs.

You're getting plenty of signs. Signs telling you that you shouldn't have come home. Just leave.

He could feel the weight of the woods, huge and drawing as the moon to the tides. Down there, in the green, secret velvet, the Thomas boy was being dragged between dark trees, his face a mask of terror, his last hours or minutes playing over and over, again and again.

You can bring no solace to the dead, he told himself. *Why not let the departed stay departed?*

Because I'm the only one who knows . . .

I'll leave after the funeral, he bargained.

He made the herbal tea. It was surprisingly pleasant. He drank it all, folded himself onto the thin fabric of the sofa, and fell into a dark and empty sleep.

10

To Nicholas, the sky seemed the same sea grey as the wet slate of the steeply set shingles on the church roof, so it was hard to see where the holy building ended and the heavens began. The rain darkened the rough stone of the church's buttresses, and the gloom made the green moss on the lowest course of its walls almost black. A fine day for a suicide's funeral.

He stood under a dark umbrella, listening to the rain strike a slack tattoo above his head as he watched mourners hurry inside like scolded black swans. The hearse – a long, modified Ford – was parked out front, its driver sitting upright and trying not to let passers-by see that he was reading a paperback.

He was among a small grove of she-oaks, waiting for the last of the crowd to enter the church. He smoothed back his hair with one hand, and surreptitiously sniffed at his armpit. Not too bad, considering. His sleep on the sofa had been as long as it was deep. His eyelids had drifted open just an hour ago; he'd been out nearly twenty hours. All traces of his feverish flu had gone. He'd jumped in the shower, but there was no soap. He patted himself dry with the few paper towels the previous tenant had left, pulled on yesterday's clothes, ran his fingers over his teeth and left for the church. Standing under his umbrella, he suspected that he looked exactly like the kind of rumpled weirdo one expects to see at the fringes of a funeral. The thought was depressing.

A final car pulled up and some elderly mourners slowly alighted. Nicholas turned his gaze to the church's damp granite flanks. From here, he could just read the lead lettering of the church's cornerstone.

It stated that the Bishop of the Western Diocese had laid this stone to the Glory of God in 1888, the funds donated by an E. Bretherton. Stained-glass windows, narrow and high and lit from within, were the blues and greens of deep-sea gems. Nicholas realised he'd never once set foot inside; his childhood church, two miles away, had been built in the 1960s of sharp, pale bricks and desperate angles determined to pierce heaven whether God wanted them or not. In contrast, this church looked as old as time.

He didn't want to go inside. The last time he had stepped into a church was for Cate's funeral, and every moment of that turgid service had felt an affront. The praise of God. The mercy of God. The enduring love of God. Even before the first reading, Nicholas had wanted to stand up and shout: 'God doesn't care! Go home! Go home and love each other while you have each other, before God snatches your loved ones away and snaps them on a bath like an unwanted pencil!' But for the sake of propriety he'd kept his silence and listened to the droning platitudes and tried not to think that his wife's cold body was in that garlanded, polished wood box at the front.

The rain grew heavier, tapping hard on his umbrella. The wet footpaths were empty. There were no more mourners arriving. He had no more reason to linger out here like a cowardly thief outside a petrol station.

He went inside.

•

Through the inner swing doors, he could see the casket wreathed in flowers on the front dais. Sprays of white lilies either side of the pulpit were as shocking as ice fountains.

The elderly minister, Reverend Hird, a small bulldog of a man in his late seventies, stood hunched at the side of the nave in discussion with a middle-aged mourner. A younger minister, a man of perhaps thirty with coffee-coloured skin, stood patiently behind his superior.

Nicholas shook off his umbrella, signed the book, and slipped quietly into the church proper.

He had hoped to sit unnoticed in the back pews, but there were only two dozen mourners so to isolate himself in the back would draw even more attention. He joined the fourth row. As he sat, several heads turned to see who was arriving this late and whether they recognised him. Most didn't, and returned their gazes to their orders of service, their neighbours or the festooned casket. But three women kept their eyes on him. Katharine and Suzette were frowning. Katharine shook her head and returned to chatting to the elderly lady next to her; Suzette's lips were as tight as a razor slash, and she mouthed, 'Where the fuck have you been?' Nicholas waved cheerfully and mouthed back, 'Later.' Suzette sent him one last furious glare, then turned back to the pulpit. The third woman held her stare at Nicholas longer, puzzled, trying to place him. At other times or in other lights, she would be striking, but the gloom of the church, the ubiquitous black, her shadowing half-veil made her seem carved severely from some cold and unyielding stone. He guessed this was Gavin's widow. Her eyes narrowed, unhappy that she hadn't identified this latecomer, and she turned her long neck again to the front. Beside her was a hooked old woman with a shock of white hair, visible under her small black hat.

Jesus, thought Nicholas. *That must be Mrs Boye.*

From where he sat, he could just see the corner of her face. Her eyes were fixed on the figure of Christ crucified. Nicholas followed her gaze. The image was carved wood, a century or more old. The raw chisel marks made his limbs seem more wounded, his suffering more pronounced. Something beyond the raw agony of the figure disturbed Nicholas. The setting carved behind him was not Golgotha, but an incongruous forest of Arcadian trees and lush vines. Old Mrs Boye's expression vacillated between a frown of confusion and a bluff of undisguised boredom; her head bobbed to its own unheard tune, and from time to time she'd look to her daughter-in-law to ask a question that Nicholas could guess: *Where are we?* Senile dementia. Her mildly confused eyes kept returning to the dying son of God.

Reverend Hird limped to the pulpit. He may have looked frail, but his voice was as strong as a Welsh tenor's. 'Please rise for hymn seventy-nine: "Saviour Again to Thy Dear Name We Raise".'

The congregation rumbled as it stood. And so the funeral commenced.

·

Speakers rose, praised Gavin, lamented the loss to his wife and his mother, opened spectacles, read poems, folded papers, dabbed tears, returned to their seats. The air was warm and still, the voices monotonous. Nicholas fought to stay awake. He did calf raises. Cleaned his nails. Took deep breaths. His eyelids sank, heavy as stones. He sat back in the hard pew and let his gaze trace up the stained-glass windows, across the curved timbers, to linger on the carved timber ceiling boss some ten metres overhead.

Suddenly, his weariness vanished like gunpowder in a flash pan. His heartbeat broke into a brisk trot and the hairs on his arms and neck rose into goose bumps.

The ceiling boss was carved as a face. A face with oak leaves sprouting from its sides and mouth. A face that was chillingly familiar. Nicholas dragged his eyes away, but they kept returning to the inhuman visage: a mouth drawn wide and thick, with vital leaves springing from its corners like fleshy tusks. It was a face he'd seen before, though he couldn't place where. It scared him.

'And now,' Reverend Hird rumbled, 'I'd like to call on Gavin's wife, Mrs Laine Boye.'

Nicholas dragged his startled eyes down from the ceiling.

Laine Boye held herself straight and took neat steps. Her black suit and skirt were well-fitted and expensive. She reached the pulpit, glanced at the casket, and then looked over the small congregation.

'Thank you for coming today.' Her voice was high-pitched but clear, a neutral accent that spoke of private schooling and careful grooming. 'Gavin left no children,' she continued. 'And he left too soon.'

Her gaze sought and found Nicholas, and rested on him. There was no puzzlement there any more; she'd figured out who he was.

He was close enough to see that her eyes, like the dark day outside, were grey and unyielding as stone.

Laine Boye was on her way back to her seat when a scream broke the silence.

Mrs Boye was on her feet; she ripped off her hat and hurled it at the carving of Christ. Her white hair flung out like lightning. She screamed again, a furious shriek, and the congregation was jolted into whispering motion.

'Blood is the only sacrifice that pleases the Lord!' she cried. Her voice echoed loudly in the transepts and hung unpleasantly on the air.

Laine hurried to Mrs Boye's side. The man beside the struggling old woman took firm hold of her arm. Hushed-voiced, they tried to comfort her, Laine's fluttering hands grabbing for hers. But Mrs Boye shook them off, her hair wild. 'Blood alone pleases the *Lord*!' She spat the last word like a curse.

Reverend Hird shot a nod to his young understudy, who hurried down to Mrs Boye. Fast as a snake, the old woman slapped the young reverend hard on the face.

'Fisher of men!' she cried. 'What do fishermen do with fish? Haul them from their water, drown them in air, and then gut them! Eat them! Or toss them back dead and empty! Fisher of men!' This time she did spit, a huge mouthful of foamy saliva that arced through the air to land on Christ's shin.

Nicholas stared, stunned. The old woman had said and done just what he'd wanted to at Cate's funeral.

Firm hands took hold of Mrs Boye. She fought for a while, then settled in a grump. Hird nodded to the organist, who started a lively rendition of 'To Jesus' Heart All Burning'.

And so the funeral finished early.

•

Nicholas huddled under his umbrella as the pallbearers loaded the casket into the hearse. Suzette and Katharine came to stand beside him. The rain fell steadily and cold.

'Nice service, I thought,' said Nicholas. 'Colourful.' His head throbbed. He couldn't remember the last time he ate.

'You might have called,' said Katharine. 'Your sister and I were worried sick.'

Suzette simply punched him hard on the arm. 'Fuckwit.' She leaned close and whispered harshly, 'I need to talk to you.'

'Okay. What, now?'

Suzette smiled primly. 'No.' Of course not; not with their mother right there.

'Later, then?' Nicholas suggested helpfully.

The church sat on a corner block, and graceful movement there caught his eye. Laine and the man that Nicholas now guessed was Gavin's cousin were shepherding Mrs Boye into a dark sedan. The old woman was hunched and docile, as if the outburst in the church had never happened. Before following her mother-in-law into the car, Laine hesitated, straightened and looked around. Her eyes lit on Nicholas. She said something to the driver, then strode over to stand squarely in front of Nicholas. They watched each other a moment. Then, deliberate as a chess tutor, she turned to Katharine and extended her gloved hand.

'Laine Boye, thank you for coming.'

Katharine took it. 'Katharine Close. I'm so sorry for your loss. This is my daughter, Suzette, and my son, Nicholas.'

Laine returned her steady, grey gaze to Nicholas. 'Would you be so kind as to excuse us, please, Mrs Close? Suzette?'

Nicholas smiled pleasantly at Suzette. 'Chat soon?'

'We'll see you at home *this afternoon*.' Suzette took Katharine by the arm and they walked away.

With them gone, the air between Nicholas and Laine seemed to chill. Nicholas found himself looking again into her cool grey eyes. Dark shadows at their corners betrayed the stress she'd been suffering since Gavin's death. But her face was without expression as she stared hard at Nicholas. When she spoke, her voice was barely a whisper.

'What happened?'

Something lurked beneath her fine features. Not fury. Not disgust. What? Nicholas watched her.

This is why you came, he told himself. *To find out what happened.*

'I was hoping you could tell me,' he said.

Laine's face was inscrutable, her features motionless as a portrait's, something from another time.

'What did you do to him?' she asked. This time, there was accusation in her tone, and Nicholas felt a burr of anger.

'I know the modern woman lives a full and vigorous life, but did you pick up any little hints that Gavin wasn't perfectly happy? The crazy stare? Lack of sleep? Love of firearms?'

She watched him, testing his eyes. After a long moment, she nodded curtly and turned away.

'I thought he was going to kill me!' said Nicholas, loudly. She kept walking. 'Mrs Boye!'

She stopped. Droplets of rain collected like glass beads on her shoulders. She turned. Her mouth was held tight. She lifted her chin and met Nicholas's gaze.

'How did he know I was back?' he asked.

He could see now what the emotion was, brewing behind her eyes. The knowledge surprised him. She was embarrassed.

'Thank you for coming, Mr Close.'

She turned, again with a grace belying her weariness, and hurried to her car to follow her husband's casket.

Nicholas looked around for his mother and sister, but they were gone.

He watched the remaining mourners drift away in twos and threes. In just a few moments, he felt awkwardly exposed, like a desperate adolescent still standing on the dance floor that all others have vacated at the first beats of an unpopular tune.

'I saw you looking.'

The unexpected voice behind him made Nicholas jump.

It was the young reverend. Nicholas saw he had misjudged his age. He was probably closer to forty than thirty.

'Looking at what?'

'At our Green Man.'

Nicholas steadied himself. 'At your what?'

'Our Green Man. Jack the Green. Green George.' The minister extended his hand. 'Pleased to meet you. I'm Pritam Anand.'

'Nicholas Close.'

The reverend inclined his head; he knew who Nicholas was. 'News travels fast. Bad news travels fastest.'

'I'm bad news?' asked Nicholas.

Reverend Anand laughed, then looked around to check there were no mourners he might have offended. 'News of what happened to Gavin Boye, I meant. A tragedy.'

Nicholas nodded, and looked at Anand's red cheek. 'Not a bad right hook for an old bird.'

Anand touched the spot where Mrs Boye had slapped him. 'Some people get upset when a loved one passes.' He inclined his head again, a very Indian gesture that Nicholas was sure induced parishioners to share secrets they'd rather keep.

The rain, which had been politely holding off, started falling again.

'You're getting wet,' said Nicholas.

'Then join me inside.'

•

'There,' said Reverand Anand, pointing. Nicholas followed his finger. Below the angular capital of the column was carved stonework: ivy leaves, fernery and a long face with oak-leaf tusks sprouting from the corners of its mouth. 'And there,' he pointed out another on the pillar's twin. 'And there.' In the carved forest curling ripe behind Christ crucified, another.

He sat on the front pew, drinking white tea. Nicholas sat beside him, drinking his black. The church, empty of everyone except the two men, felt to Nicholas suddenly huge and much colder. Hardly any light came through the tall, narrow stained-glass windows. The sheaves of stone of the roof killed the sound of the rain. *This is what it must feel like to enter an Egyptian tomb*, he thought. *Familiar, yet foreign. Cold and stony. And a sense of being watched by eyes ancient and not quite human.*

'What are they? These Green Men?' he asked.

Anand smiled. 'He is one entity, Jack the Green. Have you been to Europe? You'll find him in lots of churches there. Many, many in England; but also Germany, Poland.' He sipped his tea and looked over the cup's rim in a way that reminded Nicholas of his mother. 'But go further and you'll find similar images of this face – part man, part tree – in Nepal, India, Borneo.'

'It's not Christian?'

Anand laughed. 'Oh, no. His origins long predate Christ. His is a pagan image.' He smiled with barely disguised delight.

'I've seen it before,' said Nicholas.

Anand nodded, but said nothing for a long while.

'It is a disturbingly familiar face.' He cast his own gaze upward to the Green Man on the carved ceiling boss, then down to Christ crucified. 'The timeless man who dies each year and is reborn. Who symbolises triumph over winter and death.'

'Which? Jesus? Or the Green Man?'

'Exactly,' replied Anand. He turned to Nicholas, a small frown on his smooth forehead. 'A man killed himself right in front of you, Mr Close. Maybe he tried to kill you, too.' He shrugged, as if to say, not my business. 'But how are you feeling?'

The sudden change of tack caught Nicholas off guard.

'I have a shitty headache,' he said before he had a chance to think. 'Not as bad as Gavin's, perhaps. But still . . .'

The young reverend nodded, but said nothing. The men drank their tea in silence a moment.

'Where's that slack black bastard?' called an older voice. Reverend Hird bustled into the room. 'There!' he roared accusingly. 'Slacking!' He looked to Nicholas as if to a fellow witness of gross injustice.

'When are you going to die?' asked Anand pleasantly.

'Never! And when I do, I'll haunt you anyway,' replied Reverend Hird. He looked at Nicholas. 'You the chap that Boye shot himself in front of?'

'Yes.'

'Bad business,' said Hird, then gestured for his colleague to come along. 'We have an evening service to prepare for, you slack, slacking savage.' The old man entered the rectory.

Anand smiled at Nicholas. 'Reverend John Hird. He was in Korea. His approach to death is somewhat matter-of-fact.' He stood and extended his hand to Nicholas. They shook.

'It's a funny thing, Christianity.'

'An Indian Christian pastor certainly is unusual,' said Nicholas.

'Reverend,' he corrected. 'Next time we meet, call me Pritam.' He smiled and followed his superior, calling over his shoulder, 'And India has well over twenty million Christians. More than the entire population of this country.' He smiled again and closed the rectory door behind him.

Nicholas sat alone under the carved eyes of Christ and the Green Man.

Blood is the only sacrifice that pleases the Lord.

Their stony stares unnerved him.

He stood and quickly left.

11

Nicholas entered the house through the back door, carrying a posy of store-bought flowers. Suzette watched as he gave them to Katharine and told her he had moved out into a flat. Katharine nodded, put the flowers on the kitchen sink, went to her bedroom and shut the door behind her.

Nicholas looked at Suzette. 'I know they were cheap flowers, but honestly . . .'

Suzette narrowed her eyes at her brother. Katharine was angry with Nicholas, and Suzette couldn't blame her. The two women had spent hours after dinner last night arguing over whether or not to telephone the police and report Nicholas missing. Suzette had had the final word, saying that enough police had been to 68 Lambeth Street in the last week, and Nicholas was probably out on a bender and that might be a good thing. But she'd never guessed he'd gone and found a flat without telling anyone.

Nicholas explained about seeing Gavin's suiciding ghost every time he opened the door, and Suzette's anger ebbed a little.

'I know you couldn't tell Mum that. But you could have told me.'

'I'm telling you now. Besides, Mum never seemed too keen about having me back.'

'Uh-huh. Did you consider it might not be you that's worried her? The night you get back, a child goes missing and is murdered. A couple of days later, a face from the past knocks on her front door and blows his head off. Can you blame her for being a little fragile? Anyway. Here . . .'

Suzette reached into her bag and pulled out her notebook. She flipped it open to the page on which she'd copied the rune that they'd found faintly carved into the health food store's doorframe. She looked up. Nicholas was staring at the sketch with an odd expression on his face. 'It's the mark from Mrs Quill's old shop door.'

'Oh,' he said quietly.

'It is a rune. I looked it up.' She flipped to the next page and read from her scribbled notes. 'The third rune, Thurisaz, takes its name from the god Thor, from which is derived the old English word Thorn. But the rune has other meanings, including Protection and Devil. It's not a rune to be trifled with. Thurisaz is the most difficult and potentially dangerous of the runes of Elder Futhark. Only a strong will can control it; it will control the weak. It is a war rune. It is associated with the colour red for blood.' She looked up at her brother. He was staring out the window. 'Did you hear that? Was it a bit boring for you?'

He nodded.

'Well? It's a dangerous rune, Nicky. What do you think we should do?'

Nicholas looked at her, then he smiled. There wasn't a hint of happiness in it. He reached across for her notepad, flipped to a new page and started writing. 'I don't think we should do anything.' He stood, his chair scraping on the floor. 'That's the address of my flat. I'm going to get my stuff and go home. You should go home, too. Get home to Bryan and the kids.' He kissed her on the forehead.

Suzette was so surprised that she said nothing, simply watched Nicholas as he walked to the hall doorway, where he shrugged. 'So, it's a rune. It's old. Anyone could have put it there. But thank you for looking.'

He smiled again at her, and in a moment was just the sound of footsteps echoing in the hall.

•

Katharine could feel the stillness in the air of her house as Nicholas let himself out the squeaking front gate. She went to her bedroom window and watched him walking down the street carrying his suitcase. Afternoon sunlight cast a long, thin shadow behind him, and she watched it till he was around the corner and gone.

She cursed herself for her foolishness, locking herself in her room like some jilted debutante. But when Nicholas had handed her flowers and said he'd moved out, thirty-odd years cracked like some fragile ice bridge and fell away, and she found herself stranded back in time, staring at a man who looked so much like Don, hearing him say almost exactly what Don had said the night he finally listened to his wife and moved himself out. Katharine felt her eyes clouding with tears again, and angrily wiped them away. Christ, she'd told Don to move out. Screamed at him to go. He'd begun drinking and she had every reason to see him out of her and the kids' lives. But when he actually *did* it . . . And did she run out into the street and call him back? No. And now her son had gone, again, what did she do? Nothing. She dried her eyes and shoved the damp tissue in her pocket.

She went to the door and carefully opened it a crack. The kettle was starting to sing. Suzette was still in the kitchen. Katharine had heard Suzette's voice as she spoke with Nicholas; although she couldn't make out the words, she'd heard the urgent tone. What were they talking about? Why did the thought of having her children back here in Tallong knit her stomach into a tight ball of worry?

Because of her. Because of Quill.

Quill. A woman she hadn't thought of in twenty years. But was that true? Weren't there nights when she dreamed of that dark little shop where dresses and suits hung like the capes of villainous creatures in some bad old Christopher Lee film? Quill was long dead, long gone. Why had Suzette brought her name up the other night? Was it coincidence?

Katharine wiped under her nose, ran fingertips through her hair, straightened her dress. Yes. Of course it was coincidence. But to be sure, to be *certain*, a few questions might be asked about Quill.

She knew who to go to. She would go tomorrow.

She opened her bedroom door wide and went to sit with her daughter.

Ackland Street pastries. The sun-warmed timber of the wharf at St Kilda, daintily lifting its skirts as it stepped into summer waters. Good music. Great coffee. Life.

Nicholas lay on the couch in his flat, thinking of places to pack and leave for. Melbourne sounded inviting. So did Perth. And the Hunter Valley. And Launceston. In fact, anywhere sounded good. Anywhere but here.

He had no idea of the time, but it was long, long past midnight. He couldn't sleep. Every time he shut his eyes, images appeared, haunting his skull as surely as ghosts haunted his life: Gavin's scalp lifting, popping up like a magician's trick bouquet; Mrs Boye spitting at an impassive Christ; Teale, arms like Frankenstein's undead creation, chasing him through dense forest; a dead bird with a head of woven twigs; a strange arrowhead mark carved into the walnut stock of Gavin's gun.

A dangerous rune, Suzette had called it. Too fucking right. So dangerous that he hoped he'd confused her enough, or pissed her off enough, that she'd book a flight home to Sydney tomorrow.

His tired eyes slid shut, and straightaway more dark images played like a silent newsreel: Tristram dropping to his knees and crawling into the spidery tunnel; Laine Boye's eyes, inscrutable; Rowena's eyes, shining with youth; Cate's eyes, open and dusted with white powder; carved stone; the Green Man; dark woods dense with sentient trees; the oak grove at Walpole Park . . .

Nicholas's eyes flew open. He felt suddenly ill.

The face that he'd seen as he sped past overgrown Walpole Park at Ealing on his motorbike, the face that made him crash – a face glimpsed just for an instant, a half-memory, a ghostly dream from the other side of his life – had been shrouded in leaves, just as the ceiling boss at the church was.

The Green Man.

He shook his head. *You see things that would send a person insane; ergo, you are probably insane.*

But he wasn't insane; close, perhaps, but not yet. And he was sure of one other thing: he couldn't leave town. The Thomas child's body had been found three suburbs away, but Nicholas had seen his ghost dragged by invisible hands into the woods. Tristram's body had been found kilometres away, but Suzette had seen his ghost on the gravel path on Carmichael Road. The boys' bodies may have been found elsewhere, and their supposed killers had confessed to murdering them a long way from Tallong, but their ghosts didn't lie. The boys had died in the woods.

Something in there killed them, thought Nicholas. *And you and Suzette are the only ones who know that.*

As much as he wanted to, he couldn't leave.

There would be no sleep tonight. He stood, yanked on a jumper, snatched his keys and strode out into the pre-dawn chill.

•

Fog had closed the early morning down to a smoky dream. Nicholas had walked for what felt like hours, hoping that his long strides and the cold air would empty his mind long enough for him to rush home, pack his suitcase and speed to the airport. Instead, his traitorous feet took him through the thick mist to the 7-Eleven near the railway station. He agonised outside long enough for his light sweat to turn icy, then stepped inside and purchased two items, cursing himself for a fool every moment of the transaction.

Then he walked to Carmichael Road.

The fog swallowed all sound. No dogs barked. No cars passed. He could only see a few feet in front of him. As he crossed Carmichael Road, his footsteps on the tarmac were jealously hushed by the moist air. He stepped into the knee-high grass and felt the chill of it eat through his jeans to his calves. He ploughed a wet path to what he guessed was roughly the middle of the gravel track, and stood silent, waiting.

For twenty minutes, nothing happened. The wet, frigid air seeped into his collar, up his sleeves, into his shoes. He had to bite his lip to convince himself he wasn't still asleep on the couch, dreaming that he was here in this pearly grey world of cold. An elderly woman in a pink cardigan walked past on the other side of Carmichael Road with a tiny white dog – two faint spectres in the mist. She didn't see Nicholas, and was dissolved again by the cloudy grey. He waited another five minutes. The cold burrowed into his skin, his eyes, his bones.

Then a flicker of movement ahead on the path.

Nicholas hurried. As he grew closer, the figure grew sharper through the fog like a diver rising from obscure depths. A young girl crouched on the path. She was shoeless and wore a plain sundress. His first thought was that she must be freezing. Then he saw that tall blades of damp grass speared painlessly through her legs and arms. She was as insubstantial as the mist.

My God. Tristram. The Thomas Boy. This young girl. Maybe Owen Liddy. How many children have died in those woods?

Nearer, he could see the shift the girl wore was a pattern from the 1940s. Her face beamed in delight: she'd found something wonderful on the path. She looked around cautiously, hopefully, checking that its rightful owner wasn't around and she could claim the treasure for herself.

The girl bent again to pick up the invisible object she'd found. The moment she did, her translucent eyes widened in sudden disgust and she jerked away from the vile thing. Nicholas felt his stomach tighten; he knew what would come next. The ghost girl's head whipped up toward the woods and white terror slammed across her face. She jittered back to run, but got not a step before her arm shot out like a signal post's and she jetted away through the mist towards the invisible woods, mouth wide in terror, dragged by something unseen, powerful and fast.

A cold worm of fear shifted in Nicholas's stomach. But he didn't follow.

Instead, he started searching the path. It took less than a minute for him to find what he was looking for. He bent and parted the wet sword grass. There. A butcher bird. Grey wings, white belly, loose feathers over a swollen body. Legs snipped neatly off. Head gone, replaced with a sphere of woven twigs that was greening with mould encouraged by the recent rains. Hints of rust red peeked from under the ill green. The small bird's death-curled claws were stuck in like horns.

He knew without doubt that just a few days ago, Dylan Thomas had seen this same bird on the path.

Nicholas picked up the talisman. He plucked out the feet, pulled off the woven head, and angrily tossed the legs, false head and body in three directions.

There. Now I've touched the bird.

He turned and strode through the sword grass towards the woods he knew were waiting.

•

As he pushed through the tightly packed scrub, tendrils of fog curled in his wake. With mist obscuring everything but the few steps in front of him, there was less of an overwhelming palette of green to assault his eyes and he was drawn to details he would otherwise have overlooked: how close the trunks were to one another; how one tree was armoured in bark as dark and thick as a crocodile's hide, while its neighbour was pale grey and smooth as a girl's calf; how the carpet of leaves underfoot bled tea-coloured water as he squashed it, and how it sucked lightly when he stepped off; how the exposed rocks in gully walls bore spots of pale green moss rounded like spray can spatters on their tops and black shadows like beards below; how vines curled up trunks like possessive serpents, rose straight like jade zippers, or clung with their own green claws like headless jade dragons. Some trunks were metres wide – striated tendons in the wrists of straining giants. Some massive beeches had tumbled with time and lay prone like beached whales, barnacled with funguses that reminded him of human ears. Some had fallen and exposed clumps of roots twice a man's height – colossal, arthritic fingers probing the mist.

As he moved deeper, the fog drew even closer about him and moisture beaded on the fabric of his jumper and jeans. The half-light of misty dawn dimmed further as the dark canopy overhead closed tighter. He walked cocooned in a silent dusk, and had to stretch out his arms so he wouldn't collide with tree trunks that loomed suddenly, their limbs so madly twisted that they reminded him of Mexican catacombs where the dried dead were stacked standing, their leather-and-bone limbs crooked at angry angles.

He lost track of time. When he reached the low cliff that led down to the gully and the water pipe, he was unsure if he'd been walking ten minutes or fifty. The gully was thick with fog, and the dark green tops of shrubs poked through it like the mouldering heads of drowned people. He checked his watch and a shudder ran through him. It was nearly eight. He'd been in these cheerless woods an hour and a half.

He slung the plastic 7-Eleven bag over one shoulder and carefully descended the gully face. At the bottom, he walked cautious steps away from the steep bank until his feet clacked on the stones of the wash bed. Then he turned and followed the dry creek until a dark shape coalesced from the thick fog. The pipe. Its flanks loomed like the hull of some ghost ship. Below the red metal, the twin skull eyes of the tunnels watched him.

Okay, he thought. *Let's go.*

He felt his body vibrate with the hard thudding of his heart. He took a breath, feeling the biting harshness of cold air lick his throat, and knelt. From the plastic bag he pulled out a new torch and a squat spray can with a plastic lid.

You could just go back, he thought. *Just go back, never come down here again, never see another terrified ghost, just go back and leave town and get a job in a new office and buy a new flat and ignore the dead and —*

'Shh,' he told himself. He couldn't go back. Something was in there, beyond the pipe. Something that took children. Something that had taken Tristram.

He touched the bird. It should have been you.

Something that wanted him to come in.

Fine, he thought grimly. *I touched the bird. Here I come.*

He flicked on the torch. In the crepuscular gloom of the fog-bound woods, the white-yellow beam was cheery and bright. He clenched his jaws and shone the light into the nearest of the twin pipes. What he saw made him reel.

The tunnel's length, all four or so metres of it, was thick with spider webs: some were fresh and shining like silver wire; some were loose and dusky as old shrouds. Among the webs, dotted like black stars in a diseased firmament, were spiders. Thousands of spiders. The shaking torchlight scanned them: some had round, shining bodies with black osseous legs that stroked the air; others had abdomens orange as spoiled juice, swollen thick and looking full enough to pop; some were small and busy, tending webs with legs that moved as delicately as human fingers; others were as big as tea saucers, hairy and fleshy. Some fussed with spindle limbs over the silk-wrapped corpses of their prey or silk-wrapped bundles of their eggs. The torchlight winked off thousands of black, unblinking eyes.

Nicholas felt gorge rise from his stomach. *How did Tristram force himself through there? How did he not go instantly mad being dragged through that?*

Then another thought struck him: *Maybe he did go mad. Maybe he was lucky to, considering his bloody, lamb-like fate.*

Nicholas swallowed back the peppery bile and took the plastic lid off the can. It was a bug bomb. The illustration on its side showed a variety of cartoon insects clasping their hearts in theatrical death. The can rattled as he shook it. Satisfied, he aimed its nozzle at the pipe mouth, put his thumb on the tab and pressed it down with a plasticky click. Insecticide hissed out as the tab locked on, and he threw the erupting spray can hard into the curtains of web in the pipe. He guessed it travelled nearly halfway into the pipe until the webs snagged it.

He backed away till he could barely see the pipe's black mouth through the fog. The echoing hiss of the spray in the tunnel sounded low and mean, like the sighing exhalation of some entombed dark god, unhappily woken. The hissing slowed and thinned and died down to a stop.

For a few moments, nothing happened. Then spiders came crawling from the pipe – first in ones and twos, then by the dozen. They rushed out on panicked legs, or staggered out to perform mad pirouettes, or crawled out weakly, stunned. Some curled and perished on the spot. Some scuttered left and right into the woods. Some scrabbled weakly towards Nicholas; he crushed them with his shoe, nauseated by the dark liquids and small, glossy organs that shot from them.

It took fifteen minutes for the exodus of dying spiders to cease. Nicholas checked his watch. It was just after nine thirty. He waited a few more minutes for the poison to finish its killing work, then looked around for a stick with which to clear the cobwebs. He found one as thick as a pool cue, and returned to the pipe's mouth. *They'll all be lying on the bottom of the pipe. Oh, Jesus.* He hadn't thought of that. If he'd planned this at all, he'd have bought a disposable pair of plastic overalls, thick gloves, goggles and a mask. Moreover, he realised he couldn't hold the torch, crawl and clear cobwebs at the same time. He'd have to go in the dark.

He tucked the torch in the back of his jeans, slipped the one plastic bag he had over his left hand, gripped the stick with his right, sucked in a mighty breath and crept in.

As his body blocked the already thin light, the tunnel ahead fell into instant, sepulchral dark. He whisked the stick in front of him, left and right like a blind man's cane. It tick-ticked off the sides, echoing like chattering teeth. *Move fast. Don't breathe.* The first few feet weren't so bad, but he felt the give of spiny things crushing under his hand and under his knees. But as he went deeper, so became the bed of fallen spiders. His flicking stick grew heavy with web, coated thickly as if with hellish spun sugar from some demented circus sideshow. His knees grew sodden with the juices of squashed arachnids. But what was underhand was worst. The thin bag felt woefully insubstantial as he placed it again and again on the ragged, sometimes shifting bed of spider bodies. He felt the twiggy legs and rounded bulges of the large ones. As his weight shifted onto his arm, it pushed his hand down through a centimetre, then two, then three of inhuman flesh. He vomited. Tears welled and flowed. He sucked in lungfuls of acrid air and filaments of web invaded his mouth. The fumes made him retch again. He scurried forward. The stick, heavier and heavier, failed to clear the curtains of web and they shrouded his face and hair. Dead spiders knocked against his cheeks and eyelids. Those not quite dead clambered up his arms and in his ears. His bagged hand slipped forward and he fell like a horse on ice, his face burying in the hard-soft, dead-alive carpet of spider flesh. He screamed and let go of the stick, propelling himself forward as fast as he could. The circle of light at the other end grew larger and larger. His wet shoes slipped as he scrabbled for purchase, his hands squelched and his sleeves grew soaked. He hurled himself out of the tunnel.

He leapt to his feet and jumped in circles like a mad dog, wiping his hands furiously on his jean legs and clawing at the grey caul over his face and head. His lungs roared and his head swam. His stomach heaved again, vomiting nothing but salty spit. His heart raced and tears poured from his eyes.

'Jesus, Jesus, Jesus!'

He pulled spiders from his hair and wiped them from his jacket. Some had gone down the front of his jumper and T-shirt, so he jerked his shirt out violently, shaking the spiny cadavers onto the ground. He stopped his rabid dance. His panicked panting slowed to shuddering breaths.

He was through.

•

Clear of the pipe, Nicholas realised he had no plan beyond getting through the spidery tunnels. Without any other clear choice, he began following the rock wash bed of the gully floor.

The woods here were even denser than on the other side of the pipe. Ancient trees conspired together, dark limbs intertwining so closely that it was almost impossible to tell where one ended and another began. Vines with ribbed stalks thick as shins curled up trunks and over one another. The forest floor was an unsteady sea with tall waves of damp roots and deep troughs filled with decaying leaves that smelled as cloying and vital as human sweat. The fog was lifting, yet here it remained as dark as evening, and Nicholas couldn't see more than five metres ahead before the trunks and curling vines merged to become a thick curtain. No breeze stirred the dark ceiling of leaves overhead.

How could he possibly explore the entire area? What would he find? And if he did find something, what could he do once he had? *Did you bring a camera? A compass? A weapon?* No, no and no. What an idiot. And then a thought bloomed brightly, trampling his foolish feeling and chilling him: *Nobody knows you're here.*

He noticed the stream bed underfoot was narrowing. He sensed that he was heading slightly uphill, but the hunched trunks, the fallen trees leaning against each other like drunken titans, and the clutching undergrowth made it impossible to judge. Roots arched over the rolling ground like stealthy fingers. He knew from the street map that if he could travel straight, he would eventually meet the river. He couldn't be sure whether the dry watercourse was running straight, twisting left or right or meandering wildly – it hunted under dark schist and round knobbed elbows of roots. So was the river half a kilometre distant, or would he cross the next ridge and slide down into brown, frigid water?

He was lost.

Worse, he was thirsty and, now his empty stomach had recovered from the crawl through the tunnel, hungry as hell. As he climbed, the rocks grew sparser and the undergrowth wilder. Leaning trees had been covered in thick curtains of vines so they took the form of elephantine beasts, hulking antediluvian monsters with shimmering hides of shadowy jade. Soon, Nicholas was scrambling, climbing hand and foot over saplings and fallen, rotting trunks hoary with moss. He seemed to reach a low crest, and stopped.

Below, visible through a narrow gap between the tight-packed trees, was a path.

He carefully edged his way down to it, pushing aside thorny shrubs and crawling between close trunks. After much panting and straining, he slid out onto a narrow stony track that wended between the trees. To his left, the path seemed to go slightly uphill; to his right, it seemed to fall slightly. Which way? Any sense of direction was long gone, and without glimpse of the sun, he couldn't pick north from south. He was trying to decide when a flicker of red caught his eye.

Tucked nearly out of sight behind a tree root off the path was a small patch of strawberries. The plants' serrated leaves were peppered with tiny fruit each as small as Nicholas's thumbnail. Seeming to sense that food was near, his stomach growled. He pinched one of the berries off – it was firm but yielding and ripe. *Well, thank God for small mercies*, he thought, and popped the fruit in his mouth. It was deliciously sweet. He knelt and plucked and ate, only stopping when he recalled standing on St James's Street eating a large punnet of strawberries while Cate had a job interview; the runs they gave him an hour later were a loud and painful reminder of the paucity of public toilets in central London.

Cheered by the pleasant fullness in his belly, Nicholas regarded the path again. The trees lining the downward slope seemed less tightly packed and sinister, so he headed that way.

A small thought nagged him: *Why is there a path here at all?*

Never mind, he told himself, *I'll find out soon enough.*

And why haven't you seen any dead children? Clearly, he was in the wrong part of the woods. *Let's see where this path goes, and if it goes nowhere, I can eliminate it from my next search.* This seemed completely reasonable. He'd follow this path to its terminus and then follow it back. *Yes, but why is there a* path?

Nicholas grew annoyed with his own arguing voice. *Animals? Maybe a feral goat or something – who cares?* This was the easiest going he'd had all morning. He could walk without being scratched, there was a mild breeze, glimpses of sunlit sky winked between the leaves overhead. The woods either side were actually quite pretty. Elkhorn ferns grew from the trunks of some, their green fronds hanging pleasantly like peacetime pennants. The air was crisp and smelled clean and lively. He was, he discovered, in a good mood. Regardless of this hunt for . . . whatever, he must make a point of returning to this delightful little track.

The path curved as it circumvented first one wide, friendly trunk of a fig tree, and then another, and then straightened again.

As Nicholas stepped around the last trunk, he stopped and stared.

The path kept straight ahead, widening slightly. The woods each side retreated to allow a clearing. Its gently sloping ground was a carpet of low ferns and guinea flowers; at the bottom of the grade was a fast-running creek that burbled over glistening rocks before its clear waters broke into a wide pool a stone's throw across. An almost perfect circle of blue sky rode overhead.

But what made Nicholas blink in wonder was the boat.

Moored at one edge of the pond was a wooden sloop. It was, he thought, the loveliest ship he'd ever seen. She wore white lapped timbers, a fresh blue canopy and waxed hardwood rails. Her style was old, from the century before last, but her proportions were neat and spry, and she sat very prettily parallel to the shoreline. Sunlight winking off the glass portholes of her wheelhouse made her seem to smile and sparkle.

Nicholas beamed back, delighted.

Why is there a boat here?

'Shh,' he hushed himself again. He stepped off the path over the soft, fragrant blanket of green down to the water's edge, and ran his hands along the boat's timber flanks. Her white paint was almost blinding after the gloom of the forest. What a beautiful surprise!

Footsteps. Nicholas turned.

Coming down the path was the old woman in the pink cardigan, walking her tiny white terrier – the pair he had seen outside the woods on Carmichael Road so many hours ago. The old woman was speaking quietly to her dog, whose tail wagged contentedly at the praise. She held herself tall, reminding Nicholas of the proud elderly women of Paris, always dressed beautifully, walking with grace. Suddenly, the woman noticed him and stopped in her tracks; she was so startled that she dropped the dog's lead.

'Garnock,' she called to the terrier.

Garnock took a few brave steps towards Nicholas.

This isn't right . . .

'Shh,' he reprimanded himself again – he didn't want this good mood to pass, and here was someone to share it with.

'Hello!' he called.

The woman looked anxiously behind her to see if there was anyone coming up the path who she might summon help from.

'It's all right,' called Nicholas.

It's not all right.

'I don't usually see others here,' said the woman. Her voice was clear and strong. Nicholas could see that she would have been a pretty thing in her youth. Garnock took a few more steps towards him, and his tail wagged cautiously.

Now you have to go, said the voice in Nicholas's head. *It's not too late if you go now.*

He patted the hull of the boat. 'I just found it myself. She's a beaut, isn't she?'

The old lady smiled and nodded agreement, some small relief in her eyes. Still, she watched Nicholas cautiously. 'She is indeed.'

Garnock was just a couple of feet away now. His eyes were brown and shining, his tail started wagging faster.

Go! For God's sake, go NOW!

'What's her name?' he asked.

The old lady nodded at the bow. Nicholas followed her eyes. The boat's name was printed in black on the white timbers: *Cate's Surprise.*

Nicholas blinked, and looked back at the woman, a question on his lips.

Garnock jumped, and his teeth sank deeply into Nicholas's hand.

It was as if a black shroud fell over the world. The trees rushed in, gnarled branches and green-black leaves closing over the sky. The pond drained into itself, drying in an instant to become a choked bowl of wild and vital thorn bushes. The largest and oldest of the trees all leaned in the same direction, as if away from a mighty gale, and the lush elkhorns that nodded from the tree trunks became hanging shards of rotting cloth or harshly bent rusted iron. The boat heaved over on its side, sucking into itself like a collapsing lung, its white paint stripping away to reveal a skeletal wreck of grey, warped boards. The painted name flaked away to different letters: *Wynard.*

Nicholas tried to turn his head, but it whirled vertiginously and his eyes struggled to focus. He looked down at Garnock the terrier.

The dog's white coat dissolved away as if by invisible acid, revealing a dark brown shagginess beneath. Its legs cracked and grew, and from its flanks sprouted another four long, cadaverous shanks. Its snout and face split and peeled away, revealing another one, two, four, six unblinking eyes, and its white teeth cohered to become two curved fangs as big as bear claws; wet and sharp as needles.

Nicholas looked at his hand – two ugly, red-circle punctures were bleeding slowly. The world of the dark woods spun. With huge effort, he lifted his gaze to the old woman.

Of all the things, she alone had remained unchanged.

'How did you enjoy my strawberries?' she asked pleasantly.

Nicholas's eyes rolled back in his head and the world went black.

•

Suzette knocked on the cheap front door of the flat. 'Nicholas?' she called loudly, and knocked again.

No sounds behind the door. Crickets chirped in the hibiscus bushes below. From the flat two doors up came the perky jabber of a daytime chat show. Nicholas wasn't home.

Suzette let out a long breath and sat on the concrete steps. It afforded a view of the monolithic slab side of the building: pale bricks and pale mortar, its only feature being the flat's street number in pressed metal, the numerals attached to a motif of a Mexican in a sombrero sleeping under a lolling palm tree.

The anger that had been leaking out of her like lava all morning was finally spent, and she was weary. Nicholas had stunned her yesterday afternoon; his dismissal of the rune in Quill's old door as happenstance left her momentarily unsure what to do. He was out of the house and gone by the time she'd rallied her thoughts, and her confusion had begun to heat into a boiling fury. It was so typical of Nicholas to turn his back on a gift of knowledge and walk away. He'd been like that as long as she could remember, and it made her sick with fury. Everything came so effortlessly to him: he'd never studied and had sailed through school, while she'd had to study with monkish devotion; he'd pick up a pencil and draw with easy flair, while the few times she'd secretly tried to sketch a face or vase, the monstrous results had needed swift abortion; he was born with this blessing of second sight, something she had spent thousands of her free hours reading up on, working on her craft with herbs and charms and signs of earth and water . . . and now he was simply walking away from an opening truth, and expected her to do the same, to just pack her bags and go home. She was so furious, so red-eye-blind with anger at him, that she did pack her bags, stumping past Katharine as she huffed from bedroom to bathroom to the telephone where she checked for the next flight to Sydney . . .

But she didn't go.

Her conscience wouldn't let her. The rune on the health food store door was just what she'd told Nicholas: a blood rune; a dangerous rune. Yes, maybe it was coincidence that they'd found it on the door of an old woman who used to give her the willies, but as her life went on, Suzette believed less and less in coincidence. Was it coincidence that two boys, almost the same age and from the same suburb, were murdered in the same way by different men a quarter of a century apart? She didn't think so. Quill was certainly long in the ground, but a rune did not die, and Suzette was sure it had something to do with the deaths of Tristram and the Thomas boy. The fact that Nicholas wasn't in his flat, lolling on the sofa, made her feel that he believed that, too. What was he hiding from her?

She picked herself up and wrote a tersely worded note, which she stuffed under his door.

It took around ten minutes to get to Myrtle Street and its heavy-lidded shops. Even in daylight, the sight of them sent her heart tripping and her feet tingling, ready to run. But she wasn't a child any longer; she had knowledge of many things. She climbed the low steps to the tiled veranda outside the shopfronts and walked briskly to the door of Plough & Vine Health Foods.

A handwritten sign inside the glass of the door read 'Closed for stock take'. The 'o' in 'stock' was a smiley face with petals around it. The shop within was dark.

Suzette let her eyes probe the gloom, expecting any moment to see something shift, to see a small, bent lady peer from between the gibbets of hanging things . . . but the shop was still.

She flicked her eyes to the doorframe. The glossy white paint was a bright ice storm of reflections of the day outside the awnings and of her own face. She ran her fingers over the silky surface . . . and felt the small, invisible grooves. It was there. Her fingertips tingled at the touch of it. Blood rune. War rune.

She pulled her hand away.

If she felt it, Nicholas must, too. What else did he know?

•

Kelmscott Heights had a small driveway entrance flanked by two dark brick piers crawling with ivy. The drive itself was gravel and crunched under the tyres of Katharine's car. Old camphor laurel trees lined the drive; their crocodile-bark trunks cast cool shadows and their branches met overhead, creating a cosy leafed tunnel. At the end of it was the main building of the retirement home: a two-storey brick house with steep eaves and, like the front fence, frocked in dark green ivy. A newer wing ran off at an angle, and separate cottages were divided by neat hedges, politely pruned citrus trees and red-flowered bottlebrush. Kelmscott Heights, Katharine realised, was no ordinary retirement home. Pamela's family must have money.

The young man at the counter seemed delighted that Pamela had a visitor. His name badge read 'Nathan', and he gave Katharine very clear, if slightly patronising, instructions to Pamela's room in Roseleigh. 'That's the AR wing,' he explained in a stage whisper.

Katharine just bet his boyfriend liked Nathan to whisper 'Come on my face' in that exact tone of voice.

'And "AR" is . . . ?'

Nathan rolled his eyes, as if Katharine were joshing; surely a *good* friend who visited *often* would know that? 'Assisted Residents. Pamela requires quite a bit of care now.' He let the last word linger like an accusation.

Katharine smiled thinly and leaned closer. 'Couldn't give a fuck. I'm just here to see what I can steal,' she stage-whispered back. She enjoyed the shocked expression on Nathan's young face. 'Kidding, of course.' She waved and headed to the lifts.

The walls of the AR wing were adorned with bright pictures painted by residents' grandchildren and dozens of photographs that invariably showed smiling faces anchored by the blank stare, scowl or confused off-centre look of an elderly wrinkled man or woman. *They're mostly senile*, realised Katharine. She started reading door numbers, and found her way to room sixteen.

Pamela Ferguson was sitting under the window reading a Tami Hoag novel. The room was surprisingly large, and furnished with some pieces that must have come from Mrs Ferguson's own home: a blackwood bookcase, a small china cabinet full of Lladró figurines, a small silky oak coffee table on which sat a Chinese abacus that looked – and may well have been – five hundred years old. On the bedside table was a fading framed photograph of a jolly-cheeked man with wrinkly eyes and a bad combover; the deceased Mr Ferguson, guessed Katharine. She realised suddenly that even though she'd shopped at Mrs Ferguson's greengrocery for nearly two decades, she had never asked Mr Ferguson's first name.

Katharine coughed into her fist.

Pamela Ferguson looked up and pulled her bifocals down on her nose to peer over them. Her eyes brightened in recognition. 'Katharine!'

They hugged and exchanged pleasantries. Pamela Ferguson had shrunk with age – nature's way of finally letting us buy smaller dress sizes, she explained – and Katharine watched with sadness as the once sprightly woman strained to reach into the bar fridge for milk as she made tea for herself and her guest.

They sat and chatted for a while. Katharine complimented Pamela on the lovely grounds and the gorgeous view; Pamela explained her brother had developed and sold a software company and had left her quite a bit when he died, which allowed her to stay here.

'Pam, this is going to sound . . . honestly, a bit stupid. You seem just fine. Why are you in here?'

'In the Alzheimer's Revenge wing?' suggested Pamela. 'It's temporary, until a cottage becomes vacant. And the only way to speed that up is to sprinkle a bit of rat poison in someone's cacciatore.'

The women laughed. The easy silence that followed encouraged Katharine to state her business.

'Have you been watching the news, Pam?'

Mrs Ferguson shook her head. 'I've given it up for Lent. Sudoku, that's my thing now.'

Katharine nodded, then recounted how Nicholas had returned from London, how the Thomas boy went missing, and later was found with his throat cut. The man who confessed to his murder died in prison within days of the crime. Katharine looked carefully at Mrs Ferguson. The older woman drew a deep breath through her nostrils.

'Anyway, all this got me thinking of when Nicky's friend Tristram died,' said Katharine.

'Of course,' said Mrs Ferguson. 'All a bit similar, isn't it?'

Katharine nodded. 'Suzette asked me if I remembered Mrs Quill.'

She watched the older woman. Mrs Ferguson said nothing. She nodded to Katharine, go on.

'Mrs Quill,' repeated Katharine. 'She used to scare Suzie, remember? Do you know . . .' She hunted for the right words. 'Why do you think she worried her?'

Mrs Ferguson drew in another of those long breaths. It was a sad, finite sound. 'I worked next to Mrs Quill from the day I took the lease on my fruit shop to the day I dropped the shutter for good. And not one second in between did I like that woman.'

'Why not?'

Mrs Ferguson fixed Katharine with a firm stare. '*Baobhan sith.*' Then she laughed and shook her head. 'Fiddlesticks. That's my

nanna talking, superstitious Scot she was. I just never took to Quill.
She was always polite. Always said hello. She always paid her rent,
never a day in arrears, though who knows how she turned a quid
in that haberdashery. There were days went by when I never saw a
soul enter her shop.' Mrs Ferguson shrugged and looked again at
Katharine. 'But nights when I worked back, making fruit salad from
the bruised stock or cleaning up the grapes where such-and-suches
went picking at them, and I knew Quill was still in her store two
doors up . . .' She shivered. 'I didn't want to go up there. I thought
if I did, I wouldn't come back. I have to say it was a happy day
when I heard her sister won the lottery and bought her a house
in Hobart.'

Katharine frowned. 'I heard she moved to Ballina and died.'

Mrs Ferguson's eyebrows rose. 'Oh? Well. That's funny, because
I also heard . . .'

She looked out the window at the gently swaying callistemon.
Bees hummed on the red fluffy flowers. Clouds had crept over the
sun and the day had gone dull and cool. She fell silent.

'Pam?' said Katharine. 'Pamela?'

Mrs Ferguson jerked at Katharine's voice and turned. Her eyes
widened in surprise.

'Katharine! What are you doing here? How lovely. Here . . .' The
older woman stood and shuffled to the kettle, switched it on. 'I
should be at the shop, but I'm not a hundred per cent today. How's
your Donald? Where's little Suzette?'

Mrs Ferguson peered around the room. Katharine realised Pamela's
placement in AR was no temporary measure.

'She's at home, Pam. So's Nicky.'

'Oh.' Mrs Ferguson was disappointed. 'You don't look well,
Katharine.'

'I'm fine. Pam, can I ask you something?'

'Don't ask me for limes. The markets want eighty cents a pound
for them and that's robbery, I won't pay it.'

'No. What's a . . .' She hoped she had the pronunciation right.
'What's a *baobhan sith*?'

Mrs Ferguson's eyes brightened. '*Baobhan sith*? I haven't heard that since my nan passed on. Funny old cow. She was sure there was a woman in her street when she was a lass who was one.' Mrs Ferguson looked at Katharine slyly. 'The white women of the Highlands. They sometimes appear in a green dress. They prefer the night. They seduce young men, charm them with their dancing . . . then drink their blood.' She chuckled at the foolishness of it.

Katharine stayed just a little longer, waiting until Mrs Ferguson was again staring out the window before she quietly stood and crept from the room.

She was glad to get to her car.

•

Singing.

A woman's voice from across dark air, a siren song; faint, tugged at jealously by the wind.

Awareness swam up out of nothingness, like a slow bubble rising through the night sea. Nicholas realised he was moving. His feet and hands felt a million miles distant, ice cold and unreachable. He could not command his legs, arms, lips, eyelids. But he could sense the subtle rise and fall of his chest, although there was a heaviness there. He could hear the rustle of leaves, a surf-like whisper. He was supine and yet he was moving. Under his back, his buttocks, the underside of his thighs and calves, under his forearms and head, were thousands of tiny shifting knuckles. He willed himself to breathe deeper, but his lungs kept at their shallow work, tight and pained as if labouring under a weight.

The singing grew clearer: '. . . his face so soft and wondrous fair . . .'

The woman's voice was lovely and high. Where was he?

Open your eyes.

He couldn't. He tried another deep breath, but his lungs ignored him and kept their own shallow rhythm. A memory surfaced: *I was poisoned.*

'. . . the purest eyes and the strongest hands . . .'

He was being carried up a grade. Slowly, recollections of his last few lucid moments came back in pieces: the boat, the sky, the old woman, the wild strawberries, the juice, the bleeding holes in his hand . . .

Open your eyes.

He tried again. Nothing. He was deep inside himself; only his ears were unfettered, letting in the chittering of tiny legs underfoot and the lilting song.

'. . . I love the ground on where he stands . . .'

Open your eyes. You can't fight what you can't see.

But another voice in Nicholas's head spoke just as loudly: *Are you sure you* want *to see?* He remembered the dog's flesh falling away, and the huge spider crouched there, dull spiny hairs on its long, multi-jointed legs, its black eyes sparkling. Then another flash returned. The name on the boat: *Cate's Surprise.*

Was that a memory? Or a vision infected by . . .

How did you like my strawberries?

A dark thing bloomed inside him. Anger.

Whatever, it was mean, he thought.

He focused on his ire, blowing on its embers, brightening it. *How dare she? How dare she use Cate's name?* His heart thudded. He told his lungs to breathe deeper. The air sucked in.

'. . . I love the ground on where he stands . . .'

Okay. Open your eyes.

With a mental fist, Nicholas gripped the bright coal of outrage in his belly, letting it burn and hurt. *Good. Now, move it up.* He lifted the bright pain to the spot behind his eyes. *Forget what you saw before. You don't know what was real and what was not. What matters is what you see now.* He grimly tightened his imagined hand around the coal, letting the pain and the anger grow brighter and sharper, focusing it like the pinpoint of light from a magnifying glass behind his eyes. *Ready? Open!*

One eyelid cracked open a sliver.

In the gloom, he could see the weight on his chest was no poisoned hallucination. Perched there like a spiny, deformed cat was the spider

Garnock. All eight orbs of its stygian, unblinking eyes seemed to be trained on Nicholas's face – and they noted the movement of his eyelid. The spider's forelegs shifted, readying to pounce.

Oh, Christ, thought Nicholas. *This is going to send me insane.*

The spider's two curved fangs were as dark as ebony, rooted in hairs in its head and underslung with two swollen, grey-pink sacs. The points of the fangs were wickedly sharp and glistening. They tack-tack-tacked together, a bony clicking like knitting needles that was surprisingly loud.

'Really?' came the old woman's voice. 'Well. We're here, anyway. Put him down.'

Nicholas felt the wave beneath retreat as the knuckle lumps supporting him slipped away first from his head – depositing it on moist-smelling earth – then his shoulders, arms, back, buttocks, legs. From the corner of his eye, he glimpsed hundreds of spiders, dark grey and hunched and large as sparrows, streaming away. A jolt of new terror went through him like a spasm and his stomach heaved.

Maybe I'm insane already.

Above him were small gaps in the dark treetops; smoke-coloured cloud drifted overhead. Then the view was obscured by the old woman's face.

She wasn't that old, Nicholas could see now, maybe in her mid-sixties. Her eyes crinkled as she smiled, but there wasn't a speck of warmth there.

'Hello, Nicholas.'

He opened his mouth to speak, but only a shuddering breath escaped his throat.

She took her eyes off his and ran her gaze over his forehead, his hair, his cheeks, his neck. She clucked to herself, then resumed singing in the softest voice: '. . . and where he goes, yes . . .'

Nicholas closed his eyes and concentrated. His limbs felt carved from frozen meat. But he willed his head to turn. It did, just a few degrees. The new angle afforded him a little more view of his surrounds. He could just glimpse the tip of a stone chimney, topped with rusty iron baffles to dissipate the smoke and send it out widely.

The top of a wooden trellis, lush with leaves – maybe beans or pea stalks. And the tops of a circular grove of trees.

'. . . I love the ground on where he goes, and still I hope . . .'

He flicked his eyes down. The old woman knelt over him, her eyes taking in his arms, his chest. He was wrong: her hair wasn't white, it was grey, and she would have been sixty at the most, closer to fifty. A smile teased her lips. '. . . that the time will come . . .' The tip of her tongue darted out, slick with saliva. Her hands were trembling.

'Who . . . ?' whispered Nicholas.

Her eyes rolled back to his and her smile broadened.

'Who, indeed. Who, indeed . . .'

She stroked his face, and her eyes returned to his belly. But her hands stayed on him, drifting down his cheeks to his neck, across his chest.

'And how is your little toe? Still there, eleven of ten? Or have you tried to hide your little deformity?'

Nicholas felt his blood thud in his ears. How did she know?

'Garnock,' she whispered.

Nicholas's heart tripped as the huge spider appeared in his periphery, then stepped, one delicate leg at a time, onto his chest to stare down at his face. He groaned and shut his eyes. Her hands were down at his groin. He felt her unzip his fly. *Oh, God, no.*

'. . . When he and I will be as one . . .' sang the old woman. Her hand slipped inside and softly curled around and cupped his penis. *No, no, no, no . . .* He screwed his eyes shut. '. . . when he and I will be as one . . .'

As she stroked him, he grew harder. *No!* he screamed, but again only a whisper came out, and his body – untouched since Cate died – didn't listen and stiffened more. Her stroking grew faster.

'. . . When he and I will be as one . . .'

The weight of the spider on his chest was horrible, stifling. He couldn't move. The old woman's hand was eating him as hungrily as her eyes had.

'Yes, yes, yes,' she whispered.

Nicholas wanted to leap out of his skin and run. His brain screamed. *This*, said the cheerful voice in his head, *is what it's like to lose your mind.*

'Yes!' said the old woman, and he came. The warm spasms rolled up through his guts and his body jerked involuntarily.

'Yessss,' she whispered. Nicholas heard the scraping sound of tin on glass – a lid going on a jar. 'Garnock. Off.'

The weight stepped from Nicholas's chest. Then he felt a damp, cold hand pat his cheek. He opened his eyes. The old woman was regarding him. She would have been ninety or more; her face was grey and wrinkled as a kicked blanket. Yet her dark eyes shone with the same delight.

'We'll see you again soon, pretty man.' Her ancient voice was now as dry as ash. 'Garnock-lob?'

Two hot skewers drove into the flesh of Nicholas's exposed thigh, and fire swept up to his skull. The world shrank and fell away into oblivion.

•

He dreamed he was a bird.

His legs were numb, because they were gone. His head was gone, too, painless and vanished. But his body – dead though it was and swelling with rot – still had feeling. It was sodden wet and cold. Ants were crawling over it, exploring for places to nest and feed. He was quite content to lie there and decay, until his body felt something poking into its side. Without eyes, he couldn't see, but he knew it was a boy holding a stick, poking him, disturbing his death, seeking to drag him out onto a path. He was the bird, but he was also the boy. All was well, though.

Because this is the plan. This is what we need to bring him. It is the cycle.

But the prodding stick?

Flesh, not stick! Flesh and blood! Because blood is the only sacrifice that pleases the Lord . . .

Nicholas's eyes blearily opened.

A large woman stood above him, poking him with the tip of a brightly coloured umbrella. Nicholas screamed. The woman screamed, too, and skittered backwards. Despite her size, she moved surprisingly fast.

'He's alive!' she called to her husband in the car on the road. She hurried into the passenger seat and the car roared past.

'Dirty druggie! Disgrace!' shouted the man before he swiftly wound up his window and sped away.

Nicholas was lying in the dry sword grass outside the woods. Everything hurt. His hands and feet felt like they weren't flesh but wet dust, heavy and lifeless. His clothes were damp. His heart thudded dully, and his head felt full of acid sand. But he could move. He rolled onto his side, dragged his knees to his chest and slowly pushed himself up onto all fours. Ropy spittle fell from his slack lips. The minute it took him to sit on his haunches seemed an eternity.

He sat on the path, breathing heavily from the effort, and squinted at his watch. It was four thirty; the sun was kissing the rooftops in the west. An arm's length away on the path lay the body of the butcher bird, its woven head re-attached to its perishing, lifeless body, its pathetic severed legs again poking out like antlers. Beside him was a clean plastic 7-Eleven bag. He reached painfully and picked it up. Within were a new torch and a bug bomb can, the latter also unused, its lid still attached.

Nicholas looked at his knees. No sign of the virulent sludge of squashed spiders – but his clothes were all wet; soaked through.

Was it all a dream?

He looked at his hand. In the flesh between his forefinger and thumb were two red-rimmed and throbbing punctures. The pain in his upper thigh told him he would find two more wounds there.

She did this, he thought. *She washed my clothes. Bought new goods. She did it so no one would believe me if I blabbed. She did it so I wouldn't believe* myself.

But he could prove it! He could run now, into the woods, to the tunnels under the pipe, and the left one would be full of torn cobwebs and squashed, dead spiders. But he knew, with cold clarity, that the pipe would have been emptied of dead spiders and filled with live ones busily spinning fresh webs. The empty bug bomb container would have been spirited away.

He looked around at the woods. In the late afternoon light, they brooded, patient and dark. There was no way he wanted to go back in there, not today.

She got what she wanted.

He remembered, then, the wrinkled hand stroking him, his jerked expulsions, the horror of the catlike weight on his chest as he heaved in orgasm. He felt utterly exhausted. Raped. Emptied.

He climbed to his feet and began a slow stagger towards Bymar Street.

12

Nicholas sat on his sofa. His throat was raw and his stomach was sore from retching. The bites (*spider* bites, he reminded himself) throbbed, and for the hundredth time he dully considered a trip to the twenty-four-hour medical centre. And, for the hundredth time, reasoned that the resultant questions would not go well. *Giant spider, you say? Oh, yes, we get those all the time. Excuse me just a moment while I phone security.* Suggesting the wounds were a snake bite would only demand more tests, more questions. The punctures weren't infected, and he was feeling incrementally better. He'd stay here.

So tired. As soon as he began drifting towards sleep, the nightmare image of the old woman stroking him while her pet sat on his chest returned with awful vividness. Shutting his mind's door on the vision and leaning against it to keep it closed was draining. To let it open and relive those moments as a supine captive in the woods would send him crazy.

How do you know you're not crazy?

He skipped to the next groove in the scratched record of his mind: *Go to the police.*

And say . . . what? That the men who'd confessed to the murders of Tristram Boye and Dylan Thomas were lying? 'Forget their confessions, their fingerprints, their car tyre tracks, Sergeant! The real killer is an old woman who lives in a strange little cottage in the woods. That's right, just down the road from me. Her hobbies include spider farming and jerking off hostages.'

'That's amazing news, Mr Close! The very break we needed to re-open these already neatly closed cases. By the way, how did you find out?'

'Oh, here's the clever bit: a *ghost* led me there.'

The bitch knew.

The old woman knew there was no room in a sane world for stories about huge spiders and Brothers Grimm strawberries. Relating what happened would be the babblings of a madman. No, she knew there would be no police.

Go away. Move to Melbourne.

And when you read of another Tallong child going missing? How will you feel then?

Fuck off. I'm not the murderer.

Ah. But she has your sperm in a jar.

Nicholas was suddenly fully awake. An image appeared in his mind complete: an autopsy table, a small boy face down on the stainless steel, a lab-coated man with a syringe withdrawing milky white liquid from the dead boy's anus and squirting it into a jar theatrically labelled 'Evidence'.

Oh, Jesus. He definitely had to move! Create an alibi! Live a visible life and surround himself with people who could testify that he never came to this city again!

But Mum lives here.

Katharine was just a chassé away from thinking her son a killer already. *Wipe her!*

He paced.

No. He and his mother might not get along, but leaving her in this suburb – this haunted, killing place – would be wrong.

Move her down south, too!

You know she wouldn't go.

He was running out of options.

You could kill yourself.

Suicide. He rolled the thought in his mind like an ice-cube on his tongue, tasting it, feeling its smooth chill. Death. He'd thought about it a lot immediately after Cate died. He'd been thinking about how he might do it (Pills? Stanley knife to the carotid artery?

Sneaking up to the roof of the Leadenhall Building and taking a dive?) as he moved the last of his and Cate's belongings the afternoon that he slipped on the front steps of their Ealing flat and rose to be stabbed by the ghost of wild-eyed Keith Yerwood. After that, his visions of the dead – in particular, his vision of Cate's last few moments, slipping, falling, breaking, over and over – convinced him that nothing good waited after his own heart stopped. Certainly, suicide would bring a blissful end to the sightings of dead children, but would it stop live ones dying? No.

So, what then?

Kill the old lady. Kill the witch.

Nicholas stopped, stock-still.

Witch.

Suzette's words came back to him: *If I knew then what I know now, I'd say she was a witch.*

Very good. He had something to label the old woman now. The witch.

The witch killed Tristram. But she wanted you. *She found out you were back, and she taunted you with Gavin and drew you down there like the idiot you are.*

But then the realisation clarified slowly, like steadily clearing liquids of a science experiment.

She can't know I see the ghosts.

Nicholas set his jaw.

What does that mean? How does that help?

'Why me?' he asked aloud.

The room was silent.

Then, a small noise. The front door's knob was turning.

With a start, Nicholas realised he hadn't locked it.

•

Pritam reached with one shoe and switched off the vacuum cleaner. For a long moment, the baby-cry whine of the electric motor echoed down the nave and in the transepts, and seemed to keep the tall brass pipes of the organ humming disconsolately. The stained-glass windows were dark; it was night outside, and the occasional car headlights set the tiny panes sparkling like a handful of scattered diamonds. The candelabra overhead held electric bulbs, but their light wasn't strong and the church seemed to Pritam yawningly huge, more dark than light. He would talk with John Hird about gradually increasing the wattage of the bulbs.

As he followed the electric lead to the wall socket, he stepped off the burgundy carpet onto marble and his footfalls rang emptily in the choir stalls and up to the high, dark rafters. He preferred to dress well when he was working in the church, even when doing everyday chores. He regarded dressing well as a sign of respect, for the institution and the office, and he wore his leather dress shoes and ironed trousers despite the countless occasions when Hird, sidling past in thongs and shorts, snorted amusement at his understudy's formality. But now, alone in the church at night, the clack-clack of his heels on the cool stone floor sounded stiff and distant even to Pritam. He unplugged the cord, walked back to the vacuum and pressed the retractor – the cord reeled in so fast that the plug overshot the machine and whipped past, the tiny fist of a thing striking Pritam sharply on the shin and sending a flurry of pain scampering up his leg.

He let out a short hiss and bent to lift his trouser leg. One of the metal prongs had taken a scrape out of the tight skin on the front of his shinbone, and a ball of claret-coloured blood had already seeped to the surface and was running down to his dark sock.

The sight of the thick, descending droplet suddenly reminded him of that shocking moment during the funeral earlier this week, when the deceased's elderly mother had risen to her feet and spat at the image of Our Lord. Pritam had been unable to stop himself watching her creamy-coloured spittle run down His wooden shin, down His pinned foot, to collect in an offensive egg-like sac before gravity drew it down to the carpet he'd only now just vacuumed. After the service, Hird had laughed, saying the 'old bird was a bloody good shot', but Pritam had been stunned by the action. Or was it the words that had preceded it? Something about the Lord only being pleased by the letting of blood.

He knelt and gingerly touched the flap of raw skin on his shin – it hurt like a bugger. He reached into his trouser pocket and removed a neatly ironed handkerchief, which he tied around his shin. Blood pleases the Lord. While he no longer laboured over it, the two faces of God had troubled him greatly in seminary. How could the God of the Old Testament be such a jealous, needy being, so demanding of fealty and, yes, blood, while the God of the New Testament was so much less proscriptive, so much more forgiving. An answer was carved not a metre from Pritam: He had a Son. But how could the Creator of the universe change so fundamentally simply by coming to earth in human form? Pritam had once described God's behaviour in hypothetical terms to a psychologist friend, whose straightforward diagnosis was 'bipolar disorder'. Pritam couldn't accept that; there had to be more to this Holy mystery, The need to better understand his God became the reason he stayed in the clergy.

Pritam tied the handkerchief tight, rolled his trouser cuff down. Someone was behind him.

'Is that you, John?'

He got to his feet and turned.

The church was empty. The windows were unrelieved black. The shadows in the apse behind the figure of Christ seemed as solid as the dark timber. Yet still Pritam had the feeling someone was watching him.

'Hello?' he called. His voice, carrying only the slightest hint of his Indian childhood, echoed among the polished pews and fell away to still silence.

He found his gaze settling on the spot where the strange man had sat during that same funeral service. Close, that was his name. Nicholas Close. That was the second unsettling thing about that day: the expression Pritam had seen on Close's face as he looked up at the ceiling. Close looked as if he'd seen the hooded skull of the reaper staring back at him.

Pritam looked up through the chill air to the carved boss six metres overhead. Even in the dim, ineffective light cast by the fake candle globes, he could make out the carved timber face wreathed in oak leaves. Suddenly, a chill went through him.

He's looking at me.

He blinked. The Green Man's face was mostly shadow, its eyes dark sockets. What nonsense. It wasn't alive. It couldn't see. It was inanimate; a decoration made from a tree felled by human hands not much more than a century ago; nothing more than wood shaped by iron.

Like your image of Christ? Let's not forget how offended you were when that old nari *spat on Him.*

Pritam reprimanded himself. *That is different.* He *is my Lord and saviour, but him up there, he is . . . what?*

He remembered a similar cold thrill of recognition when he was taking his elderly mother on her last trip back to India before she died, and visiting one of the huge, amber-stoned Jain temples in Ranakpur. He'd felt the same sensation of being watched – which one always is in a country of a billion people – and turned to see carved into a column a face with long, slender leaves sprouting from the corners of its mouth, blank eyes regarding him dispassionately. Then, as now, he'd felt a frisson of apprehension and the sudden desire to be well away.

He'd assumed his discomfort with the alien visage was due to his own firm commitment to a Christian faith. However, when he'd received his appointment to this diocese and first walked into this church, he'd seen a strikingly similar carved face among foliage. He'd asked John Hird about why such an unchristian image was in such a holy place. 'Christ knows,' Hird had grumbled. 'What am I? An architect?' Then he'd lumbered into the presbytery to make tea.

And now, alone in the church, Pritam couldn't shake the feeling that the Green Man was watching him from his headdress of hewn leaves. Suddenly, the words of the old Boye woman came back with sharp clarity. *Blood is the only sacrifice that pleases the Lord.*

He can smell my blood, thought Pritam.

The thought was irrational, childish, stupid. His heart was racing. His feet in his leather dress shoes were tingling and ready for flight.

But he bent with deliberate slowness to pick up the vacuum cleaner. This was his church. He would not run from it.

'This is a house of God,' he said, loudly. The words rang against the cold, shadowed stone and among the dark old timbers.

He turned and walked to the apse door, all the while feeling the hairs on the back of his neck prickling like live wires.

•

When Suzette swung open the door of Nicholas's flat, the first thing she saw was her brother's pallid face, eyes wide in fright. The expression, quite frankly, scared the shit out of her. 'Who did you expect?' she'd asked. He'd simply shaken his head, and replied, 'I don't know if you'd believe me.'

And now she'd heard it, she wasn't sure she did.

Nicholas had made them both coffee, sat her down, and told her about his day in the Carmichael Road woods. Following the Thomas boy's ghost. Going under the water pipe through the cobweb-choked drain. Wandering lost. Finding a boat, of all things! Seeing an old lady and her dog; a dog whose bite marks he showed Suzette. They were two small red circles that looked days old. 'They were much bigger earlier,' he'd explained sheepishly. Falling unconscious. Waking to find himself unable to move, lying outside the old woman's cottage. Bitten again by the dog – and the way he said 'dog' made Suzette feel there was a lot her brother wasn't telling her. Waking wet, clean and nauseated in the tall grass on Carmichael Road, and staggering home.

'Didn't you get my note?' she asked.

Nicholas's blank stare was answer enough. Suzette turned and saw the folded paper still lying on the floor. Typical.

'What do you think?' he said. 'You think I've gone bonkers?'

'I think you're a fucking idiot eating berries without knowing what they were.'

'I told you. They were strawberries.'

'Oh, you're the Bush Tucker Man now?'

Her expression must have been cynical; she saw her brother's face harden.

'Look at it from my point of view, Nicky. You were starving. You ate some berries —'

'Strawberries.'

'Would you bet your life on that?' she snapped, suddenly angry. 'Would you bet your sanity on that? 'Cause that's what you're doing.'

'What do you mean?'

'Everything weird you saw, everything weird that happened to you, happened after you ate those berries.'

She watched him as this sank in. She could see the wheels in his mind turning behind his eyes, see him realise that everything could have been a hallucination brought on by the berries. A seed of doubt had germinated. She pressed the opportunity.

'Trust me, I know how potent some herbs and berries can be. Datura, peyote, morning glory seeds . . .'

She watched Nicholas frown, and his eyes turned to the wound on his hand.

'And that isn't a dog bite.'

'No,' he agreed, but he didn't say anything else.

Suzette changed tack. 'The old woman . . .' She waited until Nicholas was looking at her. 'Was she Mrs Quill?'

He seemed to take his time thinking about this. Then he shook his head slowly. 'She didn't look like Quill. Like I remember Quill.'

Suzette nodded. For some reason, that answer was a relief.

Brother and sister drank their coffees in silence for a long while. Nicholas shifted on his seat, as if uncomfortable and wanting to speak. But he kept his silence.

'I don't think you're crazy,' said Suzette quietly.

'I think you might,' whispered Nicholas. He looked up at her. His eyes were grave. 'You were the one who said the rune was dangerous. You were the one who wanted to know more. And now I tell you more, you think . . .' He shook his head. 'You think I was tripping on shrooms.'

Suzette met his gaze. She couldn't lie. Her next words she spoke carefully.

'I believe you ate something. Maybe they were strawberries. Maybe they just looked like them. Maybe it doesn't matter. 'Cause these things you say you saw, well . . . it's only a couple of days since a man shot himself to death in front of you.'

She watched these last sentences sink into Nicholas's mind. He sat rock still in his chair for a long moment, staring at the mud-coloured, threadbare carpet. Finally, he took a long breath.

'You're probably right,' he said. He nodded, stood and collected their coffee mugs, and repeated, 'You're probably right. Yep. How do you think I got these bites?'

Suzette felt a warm glow of relief in her stomach. Her brother was odd, sometimes lazy, a fucking *idiot* for eating any old shit he found on the forest floor . . . but she loved him. The idea of his gift sending him mad was scary.

'I dunno. Maybe a tree snake bit you in the woods? They're not venomous, you wouldn't even realise it till later.' She shrugged.

He nodded again as he dried the mugs – that sounded reasonable. He checked his watch, and Suzette looked at her own. It was nearly nine o'clock.

'I'd better get home. Mum will think we've both bailed on her.'

Nicholas smiled. 'Thanks for coming over. Sorry I . . . you know. Worried you. Et cetera, et cetera . . .'

Suzette gave him a quick hug. 'Fine. Glad you're feeling better.'

He saw her to the door.

'Just the same,' she said as she stepped into the cold night, 'I don't think you should go into the woods.'

He nodded again. 'Good advice.'

He closed the door on her.

•

Nicholas carefully pulled aside the limp, once-white curtains and watched his sister walking up Bymar Street, until the darkness between the tiny footprints of streetlight consumed her. Then he sagged.

She thinks I've lost it. Well, when ninety-nine people say the sky is blue and one guy with bad hair says it's green, who do you side with?

Suzette thought he had a wee touch of Gulf War syndrome after seeing Gavin off himself; that was fine. But she was still here – she hadn't flown home to Sydney. That wasn't so good. He wondered if he'd told her too much; she'd scared him coming through the front door, he couldn't help himself. When that knob had turned, he wouldn't have been surprised to see the old woman with her blue, unsmiling eyes opening the door wide to let some eight-legged thing step silently in. When he saw it was Suzette, his relief was so great he just . . . blabbed. Thank God he'd had the good sense not to tell her about what the small terrier Garnock really was. Or about the raping hand job.

He hadn't imagined it. Certainly, the old witch's strawberries had made him see things – the beautiful vale, the glistening pond, the pretty boat, *Cate's Surprise*, that was the most sadistic of them. But he'd also seen things as they truly were: that the boat was a collapsed hull, the witch's secretive cottage, the nightmarish, fox-sized spider Garnock . . .

Overhead, in the winter sky, the moon was high and small, just a slivered narrow eye.

Was that the last thing Dylan Thomas saw? The moon? An old woman? A knife? Eight unblinking eyes?

He'd told Suzette a lot, but not too much. If he could keep his new, horrible knowledge inside for a few more days, he was sure he could get her to leave and go back to her family. Then there was only Mum to worry about.

The old woman doesn't want your mother. She wants you.

Nicholas felt his eyes drawn to the end of Bymar Street, where it intersected with Carmichael Road. He could *feel* the wall of dark trees there, as solid and hostile as an army camped outside a city under siege.

He was about to let the greasy curtain fall when something closer to his flat caught his eye.

Across the road, under a moth-flickering cone of light cast by a streetlamp, a small white terrier sat on the footpath. As soon as

Nicholas's eyes fell on the creature, its tail wagged slowly. It was looking directly at his window. It was watching him.

Now that Nicholas had recognised it, Garnock lazily got to its haunches and trotted down Bymar Street in the direction of Carmichael Road.

Nicholas watched it go, and realised he was shaking.

I'm terrified.

13

He sat shivering on wide, cement steps. Behind him rose the blocky sides of the State Library, wide slabs of raw concrete and dark glass, looking for all the world like a colossal stack of unwanted telephone directories.

The morning sun seemed a tiny, fustian token in cloudless brittle blue. Nicholas was curled tight around himself in the cool shadows – the sun's rays were still creeping down the monolithic sides of the library building, their small warmth teasingly close yet out of reach. Around him waited other library patrons: bearded men in anoraks, precise women with tight hair and string bags, university students with deadline faces, old men straight as their canes. Nicholas reluctantly pulled his hand from a warm pocket and checked his watch.

It was nearly nine. The drive in had been slow and dejecting. Caught in peak-hour traffic, he had been forced to crawl past a man lying at the side of the road. The man's lips had been white, his eyes wide with confused terror, chest caved in and ribs protruding, head held off the ground by invisible hands. It took minutes for him to expire, and appear again a split second later, falling from a car that had crashed weeks, months, years ago. Nicholas tried not to watch, but found himself looking. *Why are you still here?* he had wanted to ask. *Why can't you move on? You weren't evil, were you? The Thomas boy wasn't evil. Cate wasn't evil. Why are you doomed to this horrible, endless re-run?* As if hearing Nicholas's thoughts, the dead man rolled his eyes towards him as his crushed body jerked. Fear and confusion. That was all Nicholas ever saw in their eyes. Terror, bafflement, a glum desire to be done with. Never enlightenment. Never hope. Never portents of heaven or signs of the divine. He had looked away and forced his way into the next lane.

There was a twitter of excitement among the people waiting outside the library. They all started moving, like cows at milking time, as the tall glass doors opened. From their hurried rush, they might have been racing to read the last books on a doomed earth. Nicholas rose wearily. *I fit in here*, he thought. An unkempt man with strange fires burning behind his eyes. He shuffled into the library.

He watched the last of the small crowd of patrons disperse like swallows to nests: some scurried to the information desk, some to the reference books, some to the microfiche catalogues, most to carrels where they placed proprietary bags beside the LCD terminals. Nicholas wandered to a far stall and staked his own claim with a pencil, notepad and a bottle of water. He furtively checked no one was watching, then reached into his satchel and produced a spray can of insecticide that he sat close by his chair. Then he settled to work.

Half an hour later, he'd mastered the online photograph library. On the screen was a box labelled 'Search terms'. Into it he typed 'Carmichael Road'. An icon bar gradually filled as the computer searched.

'Search results: 15 hits'.

The first photographs were of different Carmichael Roads in other towns and many suburbs. Then he found Carmichael Road, Tallong. He clicked the link. The black and white photograph was from 1925; the caption stating it showed 'R. Mullins's delivery truck'. Behind the oddly fragile-looking old vehicle was a nondescript house, strangely naked without connected power lines or a crowning television aerial. He clicked another link. This revealed a posed photographic portrait of 'Clement Burkin, meteorologist'. Another link: 'C. Burkin's home, Carmichael Road'. Yet another: a plan of the suburb of Tallong, Parish of Todd, 1880. The fold lines were as dark as the faded streets with their handwritten names: Madeglass Street, Ithaca Lane, Myrtle Street. The thirty-two perch house blocks hung like ribs from the spines of roads. To the east of them sat a large rhomboid flanked by Carmichael Road on one side and cradled by a loop of river: 'Arnold Estate'.

Nicholas realised what the Arnold Estate was. The woods. He leaned closer to the screen.

Dotted lines ran through the rhomboid: 'Proposed subdivision. Raff & Patterson, Surveyors'.

He wrote down the names.

Another link – a flyer for an auction from 1901: 'Fifty-eight magnificent new sites! High-set views!' Again, the area of the woods was divided into dotted lines of proposed streets. '£5 deposit. Thorneton & Shailer, Auctioneers'.

He wrote down their names, too.

'Flood damage to jetties and boat houses, 1893'. A jetty on leaning piers seemed to slide down into still, sepia waters. Nicholas blinked. *Of course, the '93 flood.* The river would have broken its banks in lots of suburbs, including Tallong. He flicked back to the auction flyer, its map showing the loop of river around the woods. *The river waters would have torn right through them.* A memory rushed back of leaning trees festooned with bent iron, and the heaved, rotting boat, her *nom de guerre, Cate's Surprise,* flaking away to show her real name.

But what was it?

For a silent room, the library was annoyingly noisy: rustling paper, the phlegmy clearing of throats, the *sotto voce* titter of chatting librarians.

Nicholas shut his eyes and tried to silence his thoughts, ignored his racing heart, emptying a space for the memory. *What was the boat's name?* It had been written in black, cracked and faded, barely visible on the grey, splitting timber. One word, it was one word. Started with 'W' . . .

Nicholas opened his eyes.

He typed 'Wynard', then 'Boat'. *Search.*

He held his breath.

'Search results: 1 hits'.

He clicked the link.

The caption of the photograph read: 'Former ferry boat *Wynard* docked at private jetty, Sherwood, 1891'.

There she was. The sepia photograph was of the same boat he'd seen resplendent in fresh paint on a mirage pond, then decrepit and collapsed in a choked gully.

Here's proof I'm not crazy.

Nicholas sipped his water as his heart thudded. What did this all mean? He closed his eyes and concentrated, trying to get all the images he'd seen into some order in his mind.

The woods. Many planned subdivisions. Many scheduled auctions. Yet none had transpired; the woods had remained undeveloped and untouched. Why? Had the auctioneers been unable to sell them?

He opened his eyes and typed 'Auctioneer, Thorneton'. *Search.*

Three thumbnails: that same flyer for the Arnold Estate subdivision; a photo of a rakish, smiling man in a boater hat accompanied by a heavyset woman in a bustle that was an explosion of tulle; an old photo of the stone Anglican church where Gavin's funeral service was held.

Nicholas felt a flutter of fear. But why should that be surprising? The church had been the centre of Tallong for more than a century. He clicked to enlarge the image.

The caption read: 'Funeral service for P. Thorneton, Auctioneer. 1901'. The photograph showed undertakers in top hats with black ribbons sitting atop a horse-drawn hearse. Mourners grim as crows were grouped around the dark stone church. Pritam's Anglican church. The church of the Green Man. The building, only decades old then, looked centuries old, as grim and severe as something that had forced its way bitterly up through hard earth.

Nicholas typed another search: 'Surveyor, Raff, Patterson'. He bit his lip, then typed 'Funeral'.

He sipped water while the search bar filled.

'Search results: 2 hits'.

The first photograph was unrelated – it showed the tombstone of a Glynnis Patterson from Toowoomba. But the second made Nicholas's breath hiss in through clenched teeth. 'Funeral Service for Elliot Raff, Surveyor, 1881, Henry Mohoupt, Undertaker'. The image was cracked, making the dull grey sky look fatally wounded. A crowd of mourners beside a horse-drawn hearse outside Pritam's church. The trees were shorter and the dresses were fuller, but otherwise the photograph was almost identical to the one taken twenty years later.

Nicholas wrote a note to himself: 'Church?'

He sat back and rubbed his eyes. It was midday. The surrounding carrels were full. He looked outside. The river ran alongside the library, swollen and brown. Its opposite bank was laced tight with an expressway that ducked and weaved in and out of itself, feeding into a business district studded thickly with skyscrapers and office buildings. Bruise-blue clouds loitered discontentedly at the horizon.

Nicholas stretched his neck, trying to get all the new facts straight in his head. Auctioneers plan to sell the woods. Each dies the same year they try to sell them. Surveyors plan to divide the woods. Each dies the very year he plans to slice up the woods.

He turned back to the monitor and typed 'Water pipe, construction'.

'Search results: 21 hits'.

It took him ten minutes to reach the last, telling image. The caption didn't surprise him: 'August 3, 1928. Workers boycott construction of water pipeline through western suburbs following multiple fatalities'. The photograph showed a bullock team and an empty dray beside dislocated sections of three-metre-high pipe. Behind the dour men and lumpish oxen, the woods glowered. He skipped to the end of the text accompanying the photograph and read the words: '. . . the unpopular pipeline was diverted through a neighbouring suburb'.

He reached into his satchel and pulled out Gavin's cigarettes, slipped one into his mouth. A woman opposite levelled a scornful stare at him. The middle-aged man sitting next to him sent him a thundery look, then got up and walked away. Nicholas jiggled the cigarette in his mouth; the dry whisper of the filter on his lips was comforting. The woods had been unassailable. Auctioneers, subdividers, council pipes . . . something wanted no one in those woods. But the church . . . why did the church keep cropping up?

He typed 'Anglican church', then hesitated. What had he seen written on the foundation stone? He closed his eyes and concentrated. Standing outside the cold, mossy church in the rain, peering over to the marble stone, reading the lead letters . . . 'Dedicated to the Glory of God, 1888'. He typed the year. *Search*.

'1 hits'. He clicked the link.

He stared. His good mood vanished as suddenly as if a door had opened and an arctic night world of cold had sucked away all warmth.

'The Right Reverend Nathaniel de Witt stands beside Mrs Eleanor Bretherton who lays foundation stone for Tallong Anglican Church, 1888'. While the Reverend de Witt smiled, Bretherton looked at the camera with undisguised contempt. In one gloved hand, she held a guide rope attached to the heavy stone that was suspended by an overhead crane outside the frame. But it wasn't her expression that held Nicholas's stare. It was that he recognised her.

Eleanor Bretherton looked exactly like the old seamstress from Jay Jay's haberdashery that he remembered from his childhood. The old woman who'd freaked out Suzette. Mrs Quill.

That's impossible, he thought. *How could Mrs Quill appear identical nearly a century later? Bretherton must be her grandmother, or great-aunt or something.* But those explanations rang hollow. Certainly, Nicholas was trusting memories twenty years old, but the similarity between Bretherton and Quill was an uncanny coincidence.

Only the voice in his head said it was no coincidence.

He typed 'Quill, Haberdasher'. *Search*.

'Search Results: 0 hits'.

He thought a moment, then typed 'Myrtle Street', hesitated, then, 'shop'. *Search*.

His jaw tightened as he watched the search bar fill. '1 hits'.

As he reached for the mouse, he saw his fingers were vibrating. He was shaking. He moved the cursor over the link. *Click*.

An old image appeared. 'Sedgely Confectionery shop, Myrtle Street, c. 1905'. A solitary, timber-clad shop with a deep awning sat alone on the corner of unpaved Myrtle Street. Words painted in its windows proclaimed 'Boiled sweets', 'Choicest Fruits of the

Season' and 'Teas, Light Refreshments and Ices'. Nicholas peered. It was in the same place where the group of shops stood today – the convenience store, Rowena's health food store, the computer repairer. In front of the confectionery store stood a woman in a white dress. She must have turned away from the camera as the photograph was taken because her head and face were smoky and blurred. The caption read: 'Possibly proprietress Victoria Sedgely'.

Nicholas's mouth went dry as a crypt.

The woman in the photograph held in her arms a small, white terrier.

•

Katharine swore as the spinning clay collapsed in on itself and what was to have been a tureen folded into a damp, malformed thing that brought suddenly to mind a birthing film a nurse had shown her when she was pregnant with Nicholas – the folded, exhausted clay lips looked horribly like that film's mother's bloody vulva. Katharine ground the spinning wheel to a halt with the heel of her hand, scooped the aborted pot off and pounded it into a ball that she slapped onto the block of clay at her feet.

Why am I angry? she asked herself. Normally, a few hours in her under-house studio was distracting enough to wick away any vexed thoughts. Not today. She switched off the wheel with her toe. In the new quiet she could hear the steady patter of rain on the bushes outside the window. The day was dark. She rose and went to the tubs to wash the already drying patina of pale clay from her hands.

Her anger confused her. She'd returned from seeing poor Pam Ferguson feeling detached from herself, like those patients one reads about who observe themselves from the high corners of operating rooms while undergoing surgery. *Quill.* Katharine hadn't thought about the woman in twenty years, and then, suddenly, she couldn't get the sight of the wizened old thing out of her mind.

Pamela's words had disturbed her, and she'd slept poorly last night. Stuff and nonsense, she'd told herself while she lay in bed, stiff as a corpse, fruitlessly willing sleep to come. Stuff and nonsense;

Pamela was a superstitious old Scot. So what if Katharine had heard that Quill moved to Ballina but Pamela Ferguson thought she moved to Hobart? Christ, the old seamstress must have been dead at least fifteen years, what did it matter? What had she called her? White woman of the hills? Osteoarthritic woman of the overlocker, more like it. Stuff and nonsense.

What would Don have said?

Katharine shut off the tap with an irritated twist. What would Don have said? *'Can you make that a double, love?'* she thought bitterly.

Ah. But the drinking came afterwards. What did he say about Quill before all that?

Katharine dried her hands. She didn't need to think about that. Don was long dead; dead, in a way, even before he died. Quill was long gone, too. Life was for the living.

'Stuff and nonsense,' she repeated to herself, and reached to switch off the light. The warm yellow of the tungsten bulb clicked off, leaving the room a dull aquarium slate; light swimming in through the window fell on the distorted lump of clay under clear plastic. It looked horribly like a broken head, and in Katharine's mind appeared a vivid memory of Gavin Boye's shattered face as a white plastic bag was zipped up around him. Yes, life was for the living, but the living were dying again. She closed the door and hurried upstairs.

The house was quiet. Even a week ago, returning to this silence would have been welcoming, a cocooning balm for her to luxuriate in, a private hush in which she could curl up, read a book, doodle designs on a sketchpad, stare idly out the window at the hibiscus . . . But today, the silence was eerie. The furtive whisper of the rain on the roof made it even more unnerving.

'Suzette?' she called. For a moment, she had the terrible thrill that her daughter was down at Myrtle Street with Pamela Ferguson and something bad was about to happen. Then she remembered Suzette was a grown woman now. She was in no danger.

'In here, Mum!' Suzette's voice came from her old bedroom up the hall.

Katharine walked up and looked through the doorway. Suzette was leaning over an open suitcase that was half-packed. It was a sign of how effectively the Close women had been avoiding one another; Katharine had no idea her daughter was returning to Sydney today.

'Almost done?' she asked lightly.

'Almost,' agreed Suzette. 'I'll have to ring a cab. Black and White or Yellow?'

'Stork or Flora?' replied Katharine. 'They're much of a muchness.'

Suzette nodded; she'd figured as much.

'Your brother all right?' asked Katharine.

'I think so. A bit . . .' Suzette stopped folding clothes and thought for a moment. 'I don't think it's good for him here. I'll go home, and maybe talk him into moving down.' She fixed Katharine with a look. 'Then I'll get you down.'

'I'd have to sell both kidneys to afford to live in Sydney, and then where would I be?'

Suzette shrugged. 'I could help.'

Katharine bristled, and fought back the stubborn urge to bite. 'Thank you, love, but I own this place and it's fine.'

Suzette smiled thinly, as if hearing a safe bet won.

'Listen,' began Katharine. 'The other morning, over breakfast . . .'

'It was fine, Mum, I just don't like porridge —'

'No, no. You asked me about . . . about Mrs Quill.'

Katharine saw her daughter's hands freeze for a moment in midair, before they continued their busy packing.

'Yep,' agreed Suzette.

'Why?' asked Katharine, still trying to keep her voice as airy as possible. 'What made you think about her?'

Suzette cocked her head. 'I thought you couldn't remember her?'

Katharine shrugged. 'Since you mentioned her . . . bits and bobs. Little old thing. Pleasant enough. Hardly saw her outside her shop. I don't know where she lived, but it couldn't have been far.'

Suzette was looking at her hard. 'What makes you think that?'

Katharine thought. What *did* make her think that?

'I never saw her drive. And on the odd evening I saw her walking with her silly little dog —'

Katharine fell silent as Suzette's face became a hard mask.

'Little dog?' she repeated.

'Yes, I think . . . a little – I don't know – Maltese or something . . .'

Suzette was staring at her. 'What colour was it?'

Katharine frowned. 'Honestly, it's so long —'

'Mum?'

'White. But why . . . ?'

Suzette didn't answer. She dropped the clothes she was folding and hurried out past Katharine.

A moment later, Katharine heard the fluff of an umbrella opening, the door slamming and her daughter's footsteps hurrying down the road.

14

Rain on the windows turned the world into a smear, making car headlights larger but stealing their form, fusing blues and greens, killing reds and yellows. It was sometime after four in the afternoon, but low-throated winter rain clouds conspired to induce evening early.

Steam rose as Nicholas poured tea.

'Sugar?' he asked, and placed a packet of cubes in front of his sister.

'Given up,' Suzette replied, taking the cup with a nod. She hesitated, then dropped three cubes into her tea. 'Fuck it.'

Her gaze slipped down to Nicholas's hand. He remembered her expression changing from mild cynicism to pale fear when she saw the puncture wounds in his hand. Right now, she looked ready to cry. And why not? He just piped her aboard the good ship *Flip-out* and set sail for Crazy Island.

They sipped their tea without speaking, listening to the ocean wash of distant tyres on wet road.

It had been about an hour since he'd heard the sharp rap on his front door. He'd hurried to hide away the papers he'd been laying out on the scarred and peeling coffee table, and opened the door on his drenched, dreadfully pale sister.

'I believe you,' she'd said.

He let her in, gave her a towel, boiled the kettle. He asked her what made her change her mind.

'Quill had a little white dog,' explained Suzette. That was when Nicholas felt the mug slip from his dumb fingers, and hot tea and shards of ceramic scattered everywhere. She was helping him clean up when she noticed the pile of papers he'd hurriedly hidden under the coffee table.

'What are those?' she'd asked.

He'd lied so badly that she simply walked over, picked them up and started flicking through them. Then it was her turn to be struck silent.

Now, on the coffee table, the A4 pages were spread out again: printouts of old black and white photographs from Nicholas's search at the State Library. Bullock team and the abandoned water pipe. The funerals of the surveyors and auctioneers. The old real estate flyers. The unnerving image of the Myrtle Street shop in 1905, with the ghostly blur of Victoria Sedgely holding her white dog.

He'd talked her through them all one by one. The last printout was now face down on Suzette's lap; on its hidden side was the photograph of Eleanor Bretherton laying the foundation stone of the Anglican church. When Suzette first saw it, her lips thinned and her eyes grew as wet and unfocused as the rain-smeared windows.

'Quill,' she'd whispered, then turned the image over so she didn't have to look at it.

He'd made another pot of tea while she collected herself. And then they sat, brother and sister, trying to believe the impossible.

'It's . . .' Suzette shook her head.

'It takes a while,' said Nicholas. He watched her carefully.

'Did you look up other records for Eleanor Bretherton?'

He nodded.

'And?'

'One paragraph in the *Ipswich Times* mentioning a donation for children with rickets from "philanthropist spinster E. Bretherton". That's all.'

Suzette fell silent. She turned her head and looked out the window in the direction of the woods.

'I don't know what to think.'

She put down her tea and delicately picked up the photograph of Eleanor Bretherton by its corner, stared at the old woman's hard face. She was in her sixties, her brow furrowed, staring at the lens, trying to penetrate it and memorise the photographer for retribution later. This was the face they'd passed almost daily on their way home from school, coolly looking out from her gloomy shop over her tall counter or her sewing machine. Suzette handed the offensive image back to Nicholas and he placed the sheet with the others.

'It is her, isn't it?' he asked.

'Mrs Quill? Yes.' She crooked her arm around a knee.

Nicholas nodded. 'There's more,' he said. 'You okay to see it?' She looked at him and shrugged.

Am I okay, though? he wondered. He took a breath and reached into his satchel and produced another handful of A4 pages held with a bulldog clip. 'I had to go into the microfiche catalogue for these.'

The printouts were of enlarged newspaper articles.

'Two thousand and seven,' he said, and laid down the first. The headline read 'Confessed Killer Charged with Murder'. It showed thin, harried cleaner Elliot Guyatt stepping awkwardly from a police paddy wagon behind the Magistrates' Court.

Nicholas laid down the next. 'Nineteen eighty-two.' The bold text read: 'Missing Boy Found Murdered'. The half-tone black and white photograph was a portrait of Tristram Boye smiling at the camera, forever ten years old. Suzette let out a sad sigh like a tiny 'Oh'.

'Late fifties,' Nicholas said. 'Local Twelve-Year-Old Found Dead – Tragedy'. The photograph captured two distraught parents being comforted by police detectives wearing fedoras.

'Early forties,' sandwiched between an item on jungle troops and ration changes: 'Young Girl Missing – Public Asked for Information'.

'Nineteen thirty, 1912, 1905.' He laid down three that were just paragraphs without pictures: 'Western Suburbs Boy Missing'; 'Oliver Girl Found Murdered, Killer Confesses'; 'Police Lose Hope for Missing Child – Presumed Dead'.

He watched Suzette. Her face was almost white.

'Third-last one,' he said. 'From the *Moreton Bay Courier*, 1888.' The small paragraph was headed 'Murdered Boy Had Throat Cut'.

Neither of them spoke for a long moment. The pile of papers sat between them, and Nicholas could almost feel their presence, as if something alive and poisonous was lying on the table. The rain drummed on the road, on the tiled roof of the flat, the window.

'Mostly boys. Some girls. Average fourteen point four years apart,' said Suzette.

Nicholas raised his eyebrows, impressed.

'Economist,' she explained. 'Statistics are my thing.' She lined up the papers, moving them around quickly like cups on the table of a sideshow swindler. She frowned. 'Three of the child murders occurred in the same years as other events.'

Nicholas nodded in grudging admiration. It had taken him over an hour to make that connection. One child was murdered in the same year the auctioneer Thorneton died; another child had been found dead the year the pipeline was abandoned; another was killed the year Eleanor Bretherton funded construction of the Anglican church.

'How far back does it go?' she asked.

'I checked back as far as I could, right back to the first year of the *Courier* in 1846. There were lots of gaps, sometimes weeks without entries, so any articles about child murders or missing children could have been in papers that weren't archived. But I did find this.' He placed down the last A4 printout. 'It's an excerpt from the captain's log of a ketch named the *Aurora*.' Nicholas read aloud: '"Monday, 24 April 1848. Posted notice to positively sail for Wide Bay from Kangaroo Point on 6 May. Discussed with First and agent an increase of charges to 30s per ton, agreed same. Commenced taking cargo this afternoon. Received news that William Tundall (cabin boy) missing. Raised volunteers from crew to search nearby bushland tomorrow."'

He looked at Suzette. She lifted her chin and gazed out the window. No light was left in the day outside, and the rain fell steadily. He felt a sudden pang of fear.

You're a fool for letting her in on this.

'You can see why I wanted you to just go home —'

She cut him off with a glare.

'I'd never have forgiven you,' she said. 'Where's the last one?'

'What?'

'Before, you said "third-last". There's one more clipping.'

Nicholas nodded. From his pocket he withdrew the folded sheet of paper that had slipped out of the Tallong High School yearbook he'd found in their father's suitcase. He opened it up and let her read about how young Owen Liddy never made it to his model railway exhibition in 1964. Suzette delicately picked up the old clipping, turned it in her fingers.

'Where did this one come from?'

'Dad's suitcase.'

She blinked at him. 'Dad . . . Dad knew?'

Nicholas shook his head as if to say, your guess is as good as mine.

Outside, the rain grew heavier. They were silent a long while. Suzette finally spoke.

'A lot of children,' she whispered.

Nicholas nodded. 'Have you ever heard of this . . . Have you ever, in your readings about witchy shit, ever come across this kind of thing?'

She sent him a quick glare, then took in a long breath, composing her thoughts.

'Blood is an ingredient for some of the most powerful magics,' she explained. 'Blood is the only element that satisfies some spells. Some quite . . . extreme spells.'

Blood is the only sacrifice that pleases the Lord.

The flesh on Nicholas's arm raised in goose bumps. Suzette's words were frighteningly similar to Mrs Boye's outburst in the church.

'Like staying alive for a hundred and fifty years?' he asked. He'd meant it to come out jokingly, but the words hung in the air.

Suzette wrapped her arms tighter around herself. 'Yes,' she said, and looked up at Nicholas. 'Quill put herself in a quiet shop at the centre of a quiet, working-class neighbourhood so she could sit and watch. See for herself which families had children. Learn who lived where, who was happy, who was alone. Tiny, patient questions. Hatching plans.'

'Like a spider in her web,' he said.

The analogy had slipped easily off his tongue, but struck both of them keenly. That's exactly what she had been. A hungry, perched thing, ever observant, watching and spinning thread while she waited, and . . .

'And . . .' Suzette seemed unwilling to take the next logical step.

'And killing children,' said Nicholas.

'Yes,' she agreed softly.

Night had fallen outside. Streetlamps turned droplets sliding down the windows into slowly descending diamonds.

'I don't understand the connections. The church? The woods?' Suzette shook her head. Neither did she.

'And the men,' she said. 'The men who confessed? Teale. Guyatt. Maybe others. She found ways to influence them.'

Nicholas remembered jetting into the old woman's hungry palm, and the memory sent his stomach into a nauseating roll.

'There's something else I haven't told you,' he said. He slowly, carefully, recounted coming across the old woman in the woods, her dog Garnock biting him, the pleasant veil of the world dissolving to reveal the woods darker than ever and Garnock the terrier as the largest spider Nicholas had ever seen. Then, waking in the grounds of her cottage, and the way the old woman had reached into his pants, milked him, and saved his spurtings in a jar. He'd never spoken about things sexual in front of his sister, and by the end of it felt a fool for blushing like an adolescent. He looked up at Suzette.

She was as pale as the stack of paper in front of her.

'Spider?' she whispered.

He nodded, watching her stare down at the floor, expecting any second for her to laugh aloud and call what he'd just said drivel. But instead she leaned forward and again shuffled the photographs and picked out the image of a blurred Victoria Sedgely outside her confectionery shop cradling a small, white dog. She stared at the picture for a long moment.

'What does she want?' she whispered to herself. She looked up at Nicholas. 'Have you been in the health food store?'

Nicholas recalled the pretty girl with the brown eyes and easy smile. Rowena. There was no similarity between her and the flint-faced Bretherton or the watchful crone Quill. So the lie came easily.

'No.'

Suzette watched him for a few seconds, then nodded again. 'We should go in sometime,' she said. 'Together.'

'Sure,' he agreed. He was already regretting the lie, but decided to deal with it later.

'The rune makes some sense,' Suzette went on. 'The mark on Quill's door – the blood rune, Thurisaz. I don't quite get it, but it makes sense she'd use it.'

Nicholas stared at the floor. He felt Suzette looking at him.

'What?' she said.

'Quill's door isn't the only place I've seen that mark.'

'Where else?' she asked. 'Nicky?'

He told her about the dead bird talismans with their macabre faux heads made of twigs. He told her about the same mark on Gavin's rifle.

'Fucking tosser,' she whispered, and looked up at him. 'But I'm glad you told me. Better late than never.'

Neither spoke for a long while. The rain grew more insistent on the roof. The refrigerator compressor suddenly chugged nearby, and Suzette jerked.

'Suze? Are you okay?'

She shook her head slowly. 'I think I'm pretty scared.'

Nicholas nodded. 'That's why I didn't want to tell you.'

He checked his watch. It was nearly seven.

Suzette pulled out her mobile phone. 'Where's your phone book? I'm cancelling my flight.' Her expression dared him to argue. He went to the linen press and produced a grubby phone book.

'Okay,' he said, placing it in front of her. 'Then there's someone I think we should see.'

•

The Anglican church squatted darkly on the street corner like some colossal, ancient hound: spiny and carved and solemn as dolman stones. Opposite was parked Nicholas's Hyundai. The windows were fogged; Nicholas and Suzette had been arguing inside for nearly ten minutes.

'How? Easy!' said Nicholas. 'We just tell him we want to see the records.'

'Genius, he's a *minister*!' snapped Suzette. 'He's going to think we're insane.'

'Reverend,' corrected Nicholas.

'He doesn't believe what we believe.'

'He will when he sees the pictures.'

'Nicholas,' she said, 'he may never have met Mrs Quill. It's only our say-so that she looks like this Bretherton woman, who, I must point out, *paid for his church*! For all we know she's a fucking saint!'

Nicholas shrugged – so?

'And while *I* know that I saw Tristram's ghost when I was a kid,' continued Suzette, 'ten out of ten people would suggest that I had a crush on Tristram and so I made myself *imagine* that I saw his ghost out of wishful thinking.'

Nicholas snorted. 'I see ghosts all the time. That's not wishful thinking.'

Suzette watched him impatiently.

'Your wife died, Nicholas. Think about it.'

He opened his mouth to retort, but her words had caught him. *My wife died.* People forgave a lot when they heard that. But they also expected a lot. They expected you to be a little irrational. A bit unhinged. And irrational, unhinged people didn't make credible witnesses.

When Suzette saw that he was getting her point, she spoke quietly. 'We have a string of coincidences that simply fall apart unless you believe in ghosts.'

He shifted. Across the street, the church was a silhouette, solid as rock. And inside were Quill's Green Men, the strange, half-human faces with shadowed, carved eyes. It was her church.

'She murders children,' he whispered.

'I think so, too.'

'So that she can live longer. And – Christ knows why – to stop people going into those woods.'

Suzette licked her lips. 'Yes. I believe that, too.'

'So, why would she build a church?'

Suzette rolled her eyes. Their argument had come full circle – again.

'I don't know!'

'And how else are we going to find out if we don't ask the people *who run the church*?'

They looked at each other. This seemed no different from the spars they'd had as children: him railing, incensed at her dispassion; her countering every point with quiet logic. Rain tapped insistently on the bonnet of the car.

'We'll tell him we *love* Tallong and we've decided to make a . . . I don't know, some sort of community historical newsletter,' said Nicholas.

Suzette looked at her brother for a long moment.

'This is a bad short skirt,' she said finally.

He looked at her blankly. 'I don't —'

'Some economists theorise that short skirts appear when general consumer confidence and excitement are high. So those positive economic periods are called "short skirts". But when that confidence and excitement is unfounded: bad short skirt.'

'Watch and learn,' said Nicholas, alighting.

She reluctantly followed him to the rectory.

15

Reverend Pritam Anand sipped the last of his dissolved codeine tablets and winced at the taste. *Still,* he thought, *if it takes the edge off this headache, I wouldn't care if it tasted a hundred times worse.* He'd woken that morning with his head throbbing and feeling as if his brain had been grabbed by invisible hands and wrung like a wet hand towel. Nothing had eased it all day, and he was looking forward to a quiet rest before resuming his chess game with John when he heard the knocking at the presbytery door.

Now, two guests were in the sitting room.

Pritam quietly shut the door at the far side of the room that led to the bedrooms, bathroom and kitchen.

'I don't want to wake the Right Reverend,' he explained. 'He's an odd sleeper. He'll rise about ten tonight till two or three in the morning.'

He returned to sit opposite Nicholas Close and his sister, Suzette Moynahan. The siblings each held a cup of steaming coffee.

The sitting room's walls were lined with bookshelves. Its chairs were old but comfortable leather club seats. A chessboard was set mid-game on a small occasional table. A mantel clock tocked and a bar heater ticked pleasantly; warm bricks, dark timber. On one wall hung a Turner print and a framed map of the world; on another, a solitary crucifix; the opposite wall held two-dozen framed photographs of the church's reverends, from the present Reverend Hird back to the nineteenth century and its first: de Witt.

Pritam noted that Nicholas was straining not to look at the last photograph. He liked Nicholas; he'd proved an interesting

186

conversationalist when he'd invited him into the church after Gavin Boye's funeral. But tonight he looked pale with dark shadows under his eyes. If he'd not met the man before, Pritam would have guessed he was a smack addict.

'So. You two guys live here?' asked Nicholas.

Pritam explained that Reverend Hird was the rector but was planning on retiring at the end of the year. His health had been poor, and when the synod had asked him for suggestions about what to do with an upstart reverend from Goa, the old man had a delightful solution: to make Pritam his successor.

'Above all, I think he enjoys having someone around to argue with,' said Pritam.

'I know the feeling,' said Nicholas, smiling pleasantly at Suzette. She narrowed her eyes.

'Pritam, are the church's records kept here?' he continued. 'Or at . . . I don't know, Anglican HQ?'

'Here.' Pritam pointed at a closed door marked 'Storeroom'. 'Everything. Weekly tithes. Repair bills. Who married here. Baptisms. Funerals. Tax records. Copies are sent to "Anglican HQ",' he said dryly, 'but we keep the originals here. There are . . . oh, perhaps nine or ten archive boxes in there. Why do you ask?'

'Dating back?'

'Dating all the way back.'

'Can we see them?'

Pritam stretched his neck, but kept his eyes fixed on his guests. He hadn't expected to open the door to such a strange line of questioning. *But then*, he thought, *it has been a strange couple of days.*

'That depends,' he replied. 'Once again: why do you ask? And please bear in mind that I have a rotten headache and am really in no mood for this ill-advised masquerade about your making some community history newsletter.'

He saw Suzette level a cool look at her brother.

'I'm sorry, Pritam. I don't think we can tell you why we're really here,' said Nicholas.

Pritam felt the veins in his temples throb.

'Why not?' he asked.

'You won't believe us.'

'Won't believe him,' clarified Suzette, pointing at Nicholas. 'I thought it was a bad idea to trouble you with our . . . suppositions.'

Pritam regarded them both.

'It is quite a dismal night out. And neither of you – forgive me for this assumption – look the sort to prefer the polite company of an Indian priest over a night on the couch in front of *Californication*. So this is somewhat important, yes?'

Nicholas met Pritam's gaze and nodded.

Pritam inclined his head.

'And does it have anything to do with Gavin Boye's suicide?'

Nicholas and Suzette exchanged a glance. Nicholas nodded again. 'And Eleanor Bretherton,' he said.

Pritam let out a breath and squeezed the bridge of his nose. The codeine was beginning to work, but was a long way from making him feel sociable. He shifted in his chair, unable to get comfortable.

'Did you know that I was offered a Rhodes scholarship?' he asked. 'So I'm not an idiot. Well, I went to seminary here instead of going to Oxford, so some would argue that does make me an idiot. Regardless, I cannot think of *any* connection between Gavin Boye and a long-dead patron of this church.'

'Yeah,' sighed Nicholas. 'I don't think you're gonna fancy the one I'm about to tell you.'

Pritam smiled. 'My father was fond of an old saying: when an elephant is in trouble, even a frog will kick him. You, my friend,' he pointed at Nicholas, 'look like you're in ten different kinds of trouble. So may I suggest trying me.'

Nicholas looked at Suzette. Pritam saw her shake her head as a final discouragement. Nicholas ignored her.

'Every twenty years or so,' he began, 'for the last hundred and twenty years at least, a local child – a child from around here in Tallong – has been murdered.'

Pritam nodded – go on.

'The second-last murder was a childhood friend of ours, Tristram Boye,' continued Nicholas. 'Gavin Boye's brother. He was killed in 1982. Tris was chased into the woods on Carmichael Road but found a few miles away with his . . .' Nicholas licked his dry lips, '. . . with his throat cut. The last child murdered was the Thomas boy. He also had his throat slit.'

Pritam said nothing, but watched his guests. Suzette broke the silence.

'We think the murders are connected,' she said.

Pritam's eyes narrowed. 'Which ones?'

'All of them,' replied Nicholas.

Pritam stopped moving in his chair.

'Connected? Over a hundred and twenty years?'

Nicholas nodded. 'Or more,' he said. 'Maybe a hundred and fifty years.'

'We should go,' said Suzette.

Nicholas shook his head at his sister.

Pritam frowned. The news about the murders was new to him, an unpleasant surprise. Since he'd arrived in Tallong, he'd found it a pretty, hospitable, slightly dull suburb. But now a suggestion that the murders were not a string of chance happenings, but linked . . . Maybe a few days ago, he'd have laughed this off. But his aching skull and the dark mood he'd felt since his evening alone in the church had punched down his sense of humour.

'Are you talking about . . . Are you suggesting ritual killings?' he asked.

Nicholas watched him carefully.

'Kind of,' he replied.

Pritam nodded, and stared at the floor, deep in thought. The ticking of the mantel clock seemed suddenly loud. 'I urge you to be very careful answering this next question,' he said. 'Are you also suggesting a connection between all these murders and this church?'

He realised he was gripping the arms of his chair tightly. He looked up at his guests; they'd both noticed the same thing.

'No,' said Nicholas slowly. 'To her.' He nodded at the leftmost photograph. It showed Reverend de Witt smiling beside dour Eleanor Bretherton as she laid the church's foundation stone.

Pritam felt his headache returning like a flash tide and he closed his eyes at the pain.

'Pritam?' asked Nicholas.

'I'm sorry,' he said, standing. 'This is all a bit fantastical for me this evening. Perhaps . . .' He indicated the door.

'Jesus, hear us out,' said Nicholas.

Pritam blanched at the blasphemy.

'Let's go,' said Suzette firmly, taking her brother's arm. 'Maybe another time, Reverend.'

Nicholas shook her grip off.

'Pritam, we know it's all pretty airy-fairy, but if you just let us look through your records —'

Pritam found his voice rising, riding the unwelcome wave of the headache, and was powerless to stop it. 'Nicholas, you are suggesting cult murders, you're suggesting some cover-up. It is insulting to my congregation, it's insulting to Reverend Hird, and it's insulting to me.'

'I don't give a fart about him or your congregation,' said Nicholas. He jabbed a finger at the photograph of Eleanor Bretherton. 'It's her!'

Suzette yanked Nicholas out of his chair and dragged him to the door.

'We're sorry,' she said.

'I'm not sorry,' snapped Nicholas, eyes locked on Pritam. 'Maybe there *is* some cover-up!'

Pritam saw the wildness in Nicholas's eyes. *Maybe I was wrong*, he thought. *Maybe he is on drugs.*

Suzette threw open the door and dragged Nicholas out into the drizzle, hissing unheard words at her brother.

'No, it's a fucking *joke*,' he snapped.

'Good night,' said Pritam, eyes hard.

'Sorry,' said Suzette, closing the door.

Nicholas seemed to think of something, and again slipped out of her grip and stuck his foot between the door and the jamb.

'Please, Nicholas . . .' began Pritam, walking wearily to the door.

'One last question and I'll go.'

Pritam hesitated a moment, then waved his hand – fine.

'How long has Hird been in Tallong?' asked Nicholas.

Pritam took a breath, shook his head. 'Thirty years or more.'

Nicholas nodded, eyes bright; Pritam could again see the pleasant young man who had looked so terrified at the sight of the Green Man.

'Then get Hird to look at the photograph of Mrs Bretherton. Ask him if he remembers a seamstress named Mrs Quill. Quill, like feather. Will you do that?'

Pritam watched Nicholas for a long moment. He was a nice guy, he was sure, but looked on the edge of some very dark cliff.

'You should consider getting some grief counselling, Nicholas.'

For some reason, Nicholas let out a bark of a laugh and withdrew his foot.

Pritam shut the door with a loud, solid click. Outside, retreating footsteps and the surf-like hush of rain. Already, his headache seemed to be withdrawing.

He went to the nearest window and eased aside the heavy tapestry curtains. Across the rain-shiny street, brother and sister hurried to their car. He heard their doors close, then the car start and take off. Soon, the only noise was his breathing, the tocking of the clock, the soft clicking of the bar heater element.

Pritam took a deep breath and walked over to the photograph of the Right Reverend de Witt and Eleanor Bretherton laying the foundation stone. The photograph had disturbed him since he first laid eyes on it. He'd always assumed it was because the church, now so solid and real, was in the photograph merely a slab; looking at the old photograph was like seeing an autopsy picture of a close acquaintance lying naked and too exposed. But now, fixing on the severe gaze that Eleanor Bretherton sent back through the glass and a hundred and thirty years, Pritam realised he might have been wrong. The reason the photograph was disturbing was *her*.

He berated himself. Nicholas Close had undergone trauma. *I should have been more sympathetic*, he thought. Tomorrow, clear of this awful headache, he'd call the man and apologise. But as for child murders . . . there was no way he would upset the Right Reverend with talk of cult killings.

He switched off the outside light.

16

Suzette sat in a silent simmer the entire drive back from the church to Lambeth Street. Nicholas pulled up the hire car. Rain pattered on the roof.

'You are your own worst enemy, you do know that,' she said.

He nodded. 'Cate used to say that.'

Suzette blinked. He hadn't said it for sympathy; it was true. Cate had often chastised him for acting before he thought things through. But the mention of Cate turned down Suzette's thermostat just a little.

'She was right. What did she ever see in a twit like you?'

He shrugged. It was a mystery he'd never be able to clarify.

Suzette opened her door. 'Coming in to see Mum?' she asked.

He begged off; his mother's forced pleasantness so soon after the defensive hostility of Pritam Anand would give him the bends. He agreed to meet Suzette the next morning for a decent breakfast at the café near the railway station, and make a plan for visiting Plough & Vine Health Foods. He waved, watched her hurry across the front yard and through the form of Gavin Boye. The sight made his stomach tighten. He looked quickly away and drove off.

By the time he'd parked outside his flat on Bymar Street, the rain had dropped to a steady drizzle. He was halfway up the concrete stairs when he stopped. What was inside? Frozen pizza and television channels overladen with half-baked reality or over-cooked comedy, all broadcast with mephitic monotony. A sane and solid bedrock where north was north and home was safe and marriages lasted . . .

the frippery of evening television made a mockery of the unpleasant things he'd learned today.

What was out here? Night. Shadows. Questions.

Garnock?

Nicholas shuddered. But he'd been bitten twice by the spider and he was still fine.

Fine? My dear boy, this is hardly fine.

He thought the best thing he could do was go inside, find as much alcohol as he could and get roaringly, disgustingly, forgetfully drunk.

Yet he didn't want to go inside. His feet were anxious to move. He shoved his hands deeper into his pockets and walked back down the stairs and onto the street.

The rain finally petered out and a wind had invited itself to shift the air, turning it cold and nudging the black tops of trees. Nicholas was angry with himself. It could have gone so much better with Pritam. Suzette was right. And now he'd alienated a person who felt like a man who could be trusted. Nicholas couldn't blame the reverend. Spoken aloud, his theory on the murders was a fabulist's: the stuff of nineteenth-century fairy tales where endings weren't happy and evil was as powerful as good. A woman a hundred and fifty years old killing little boys and girls to stave off her own death and, for some reason, to keep her dark woods whole.

Woods. Floods. Spiders. Church.

How had everything gone so wrong so fast? Four months ago, he and Cate had had a life to be envied. Was that the problem? That they'd had the gall to be truly happy? Had they offended the gods by flaunting their pleasure with their simple plans and simple love? One motorcycle trip. One ladder. One phone call. Halloween child. Samhain child.

Church. Green Man. Walpole Park. A face wreathed in leaves.

One fall down cement stairs and a day world becomes a night world. The dead walk unmollified, doomed to mark time while some cosmic starter gun fires, reloads, and fires again and again . . . Cruel. Cruel.

They saw him, the dead. And they knew he could see them; they watched him. As some respite from their own morbid television re-run performances, perhaps they looked to Nicholas for help. But he couldn't help them. Nor could they teach him. *This isn't like some TV show where the gold-hearted clairvoyant heals the departeds' suffering and sends them on their way. No; this is excruciating impotence. This is jumping all the way to the end of the book and finding the last chapter has been torn out and lost. Cruel.*

Why hadn't he died in the bike crash?

Why had Cate died instead?

Why hadn't Gavin shot him?

Nicholas stopped. He was at the corner of Lambeth Street. If he turned up it, in two minutes he'd be with his mother and Suzette. But he could feel no answers waiting there.

He walked on.

Another block and he reached the corner of Airlie Crescent.

Without thinking, he let his feet change direction – just as he used to let his hands turn the wheel of his van when he trundled through narrow-laned English villages hunting for knick-knacks. He strode up a shadowy footpath he hadn't walked in two decades, in and out of tiny pools of streetlight, to stop outside number seven.

The Boyes' house.

It lay watching from within a nest of tall laurel trees, which hissed disapproval at his arrival. Though the house was, to his adult eyes, smaller than he remembered, it was still huge – a looming colonial with deep verandas draped with filigreed ironwork that had greyed with neglect and hung between posts like cobwebs. The hedges had rambled and shrubs were creeping out to reclaim the yard. Dim lights shone within; a brooding Halloween pumpkin.

Nicholas entered the yard and mounted the wide wooden steps to stand outside the lattice doors. He rang the doorbell.

Here was the landing that he and Tristram had dared each other to jump off, commandoes from a C-47. And Nicholas, to his credit, had jumped, albeit pale and terrified. Tristram had jumped whooping. Tristram had been the brave one.

Across the shadowed veranda, the dark, glossy front door opened a crack and Mrs Boye squinted at him through the gap. Her white hair spilled like a judge's wig around her dressing-gowned shoulders – she could have stepped from a scene of Shakespearean mania. Her eyes narrowed.

'Yes?'

'It's Nicholas, Mrs Boye. Nicholas Close.'

Mrs Boye set her lips. 'Oh, Nicholas. I'll tell Tristram you're here. But I don't want you two yelling about the yard! Mr Boye has had a very full week.'

Nicholas thought the better of arguing with her.

'Thanks, Mrs Boye.'

'Tristram!' she called. 'Tristram Hamilton Boye? Gavin, where is that brother of yours?'

The old woman walked back into the house, shutting the door behind her. Again, Nicholas was alone on the steps. *Why am I here? Avoiding my own mother. Avoiding my sister. Avoiding sleep.* A minute passed, and no one returned to the door. Nicholas gave up, and was halfway down the stairs when he heard the front door open again.

'Hello?' A younger woman's voice. He turned.

Laine Boye's hair was dripping wet and she held a bathrobe closed with one hand.

'It's Nicholas Close, Mrs Boye.'

'I can see that,' said Laine. Her face was in shadow. 'Can I help you?'

He walked slowly back up the stairs. 'Yes. Well . . . I just was walking, and happened to be . . .'

He watched her watching him. She was barefoot, drenched, even thinner than when he saw her last. She held her chin up and out, her head cocked.

'I'm sorry to come unannounced, Mrs Boye, but . . .'

He felt his hand close around something in his pocket. He pulled it out. Something silver and small rested on his palm.

'I found Gavin's cigarette lighter. At home. I thought . . .'

He held out the Zippo.

Laine took a half-step back, as if the sight of the lighter offended her. Again, Nicholas noticed the colour of her eyes. A seashell grey; an equivocal colour that could be contented or angry, serene or melancholy.

'I thought maybe we could talk a little,' he said. 'About Gavin.'

She watched him a moment, frowning at some argument in her head. Then she nodded and unlatched the lattice door.

'Come inside.'

Nicholas followed her in.

The sensation of being drawn back through time made him wish he'd walked instead up Lambeth Street. Some rooms had been refurbished, and a few of the furnishings had changed. But the tall panelled walls, the polished cherrywood dining suite, the fireplace over which were mounted two painted portraits of Tristram and Gavin as boys, were all exactly as when he'd seen them last, twenty-five years ago.

Laine stopped in the dining room. She seemed shorter in bare feet. Square-shouldered. In the softer light, her features were finer, less angular. Her skin had an olive hue.

'Give me a minute. I have to dry my hair.'

She frowned at Nicholas, then stepped into the room that had been Gavin's and shut the door. On the floor outside it, Nicholas saw a small collection of packing boxes. Some were taped shut, and over the tape the boxes' contents had been neatly printed in permanent marker: 'Shoes', 'Shirts & Trousers', 'T-shirts'. Their ordinariness – as if Gavin were simply moving house, not dead and being filed away for good – was prosaic and mournful. One box remained open, only half-filled. He stepped closer to peer inside.

Some VHS tapes with documentary titles handwritten on the spines. A pair of worn hiking boots. A curled bunch of shooting magazines . . . and something else. Nicholas bent closer to see –

'Who are you?!'

He whirled at the shout, startled.

Mrs Boye stood behind him, brandishing a fireplace poker.

'Nicholas. Nicholas Close,' he replied, hiding the tremor in his voice. A woman who could spit on Christ from twenty paces would be a wildcat with a poker. 'How are you, Mrs Boye?'

'Ah, Nicholas,' said Mrs Boye, lowering the weapon. 'You want to see Trissy. Tristram!' She wagged a bony finger at Nicholas. 'I don't want you two making a racket.' She gestured for him to follow.

She led him through the house to Tristram's bedroom door. The sight of it made Nicholas feel suddenly cold. She rapped sharply.

'Tristram? Your friend is here.'

She looked at Nicholas with an expression that said: boys, how intolerable. 'Go in, but I need you going home by five. We're dining early.'

'Thanks, Mrs Boye.'

She walked away, stiffly whistling a tune that should have been tripping and joyful, but from her sounded broken and lost.

The large house became eerily quiet.

Nicholas twisted the low-set knob and opened the door.

He flicked on the light.

The room had not been touched since Tristram's death. A *Battle Beyond the Stars* poster was stuck to one wall with yellowing tape, one corner detached and weeping down. The alarm clock had burnt out, its panelled numbers frozen at 11.13. The air was husky and dry, and smelled like sick soil. A thick film of dust coated the wooden floorboards. In the middle of the floor sat a board game; at its centre was a hard plastic bubble in which was a die on spring steel that would have click-clacked loudly when it was last pressed by small hands. Now, the steel was rusted and dust had painted the dome a cadaverous brown. Cobwebs hunched in the ceiling corners and around the depending light shade. A large spider had spun a web above the bed; the creature seemed to creep a sly step towards him. Watching. The small single bed was still unmade, a gritty patina of insect husks on the *Empire Strikes Back* sheets. The room was unutterably sad.

'Nicholas?'

He turned.

Laine stood behind him, dressed in jeans and a woollen jumper. Her anxious fingers twined amongst themselves.

He stepped out of Tristram's bedroom and closed the door.

Laine looked at the floor a moment, then up at him again. 'I'm sorry,' she said. 'Getting changed, I thought about it. I don't think I really want to talk with you much about anything.'

Nicholas felt a guilty stab of relief. He nodded. 'I don't think I have anything to ask.'

She gestured towards the hall. He could see her fingers vibrating. She was holding herself together with sheer willpower. Husband suicided. Yoked instantly with the care for a senile mother-in-law. No one to help. She led him to the hall.

'I do have a question,' she said.

'Yes?'

'Did you shoot him?'

She lifted her chin and watched him with those inscrutable grey eyes.

'No,' he answered.

She pursed her lips and stepped away.

They walked past Gavin's bedroom. As they passed the boxes, Nicholas peeked down again into the half-filled one. And he saw what had caught his eye earlier: the rifle magazines were roughly rolled together and shoved in a plastic bag. On the side of the bag was printed Plough & Vine Health Foods. Rowena's store. Mrs Quill's old shop.

'Do you shop there?' he asked, nodding at the bag.

Laine stopped to see what Nicholas was looking at.

'No. Gavin took a liking to dried pumpkin seeds. For the zinc,' he said.

And rifles for the lead, thought Nicholas.

She opened the front door for him.

'Good night, Mr Close.'

Before he could reply, she shut the door, closing him out in the cold.

•

Nicholas placed the phone book on the coffee table. Its cover was torn and heavily graffiti'd by the previous tenants: a Rosetta stone of cartoon tits and spurting phalluses.

As he walked home from the Boyes' house, the sight of the plastic bag from Rowena's health food store kept popping into his mind. *Gavin took a liking to pumpkin seeds; for the zinc*, Laine had said.

He'd shopped in Quill's old store. The mark on her door, on the rifle, on the bird. *He touched the bird. It should have been you.*

It wasn't coincidence. He knew it wasn't. The links were growing too strong.

He flicked quickly through the directory's residential listings for 'G'. He had an inkling.

I'm right, he thought. *I know I'm right.*

His finger ran down the surnames. Gull. Gunston. Gurber. Guyatt. There were a dozen Guyatts.

Guyatt, A., Guyatt, A. & F., Guyatt, C., Guyatt, E., Linning St, Toorbul. Guyatt E., Paschendale Ct, Mt Pleasant.

Then he found it, just as he knew he would. Guyatt, E., 93 Myrtle St, Tallong.

Nicholas sat back.

Elliot Guyatt, the unprepossessing cleaner who had confessed to the murder of Dylan Thomas and died of a stroke just days later, had lived on the same street as Plough & Vine Health Foods.

Rowena's shop. Sedgely's shop. Quill's shop.

Gavin Boye – deliverer of a cryptic message with a self-destruct ending – had shopped at Plough & Vine Health Foods. Nicholas was certain that Winston Teale, the huge man with the small voice who had chased Tristram and him into the woods, would have had the frayed linings of his work suits repaired at Jay Jay's haberdashery.

He reached into his satchel and pulled out Gavin's rapidly emptying packet of John Player Specials, and realised he no longer had a lighter. He turned on the coil of the electric stove and waited for it to glow. Ridiculous. Rowena was young; Quill and Bretherton were old. Rowena was unthreatening and guileless; Quill had stared from her shop and Bretherton from her photograph through the same cunning eyes. Rowena was pretty and without any air of perfidiousness; Quill/Bretherton/Sedgely was malevolent.

And yet. And yet . . .

Someone lumbered into the front door with a crash and Nicholas jumped.

'Nicholas!!' came the voice on the other side.

'Suzette?'

'Open it!' she yelled.

Nicholas felt his stomach swirl – something bad had happened. He ran for the door, undid the latch and threw the door open. Suzette sagged inside. Her face was pale and her eyes were wet. She was on the edge of hysteria.

'Jesus, Suze . . . ?'

'I finished dinner with Mum and heard something scratching at the front door,' she whispered. 'I opened it . . . idiot . . . and a white dog bit me.'

•

Suzette staggered to the toilet, smacked up the lid and vomited. The air thickened with tangy brine.

Nicholas felt the world suddenly grind into slow motion. 'We have to take you to a doctor,' he said quietly.

She held on to the porcelain pedestal with both hands. Her right had twin puncture marks just above her thumb, as if two sharp pencils had been driven into the flesh.

Oh, God, he thought. *My fault. My fault . . .*

'I didn't even think,' Suzette mumbled, wiping her mouth. 'I opened the door and didn't even think about insect spray.' She rolled onto the floor, ripped off toilet paper and blew her nose. 'Jumped out of nowhere . . .' Her hand slipped out from under her and she slid to the tiles. Her eyes struggled to focus.

'Jesus, Suze! I'm taking you.'

She shook her head. 'Bed.'

He lifted her and carried her to the spare room.

'I don' thing I really believe joo . . .' Her words were slurred.

'That's okay.'

'Do now. 'S not a dog . . .'

'It's okay.' He placed her down.

She nodded at the bite marks on her hand. 'Necklace,' she whispered.

Nicholas shook his head – I don't understand.

'Necklace. I gave you . . .'

She was sliding from consciousness.

Nicholas ran to his room and pulled the elder-wood necklace from his bedside table. The beads felt good in his hands, the polished stone warm and substantial. He returned and put it around Suzette's neck.

'You should ha' be wear . . . this . . .' she said.

As Nicholas rested her head on the pillow, he saw a spot of blood appear on the white pillowslip.

'Suze?'

No answer. She had passed out. Her breaths came slow and deep. He gently parted the hair of her scalp and found a patch of blood. A clump of her hair had been torn out by the roots.

He sat back, jaw tight. Suzette was breathing evenly. He fetched antiseptic and cotton balls, cleaned her scalp and then the punctures in her hand. He'd been bitten twice by Garnock, so wasn't worried that the bites were fatal. But why Suzette?

She has kids, came the voice in his head. *You knew that, fool. And you let her stay.*

He felt anger heating inside him: anger at Suzette for not being careful; anger at himself for letting her come up here; angriest of all with the little white shitlicker that had bitten them both.

And Quill?

The thought of her didn't make him angry. He ran his mind over the feeling like hands over a hidden gift. This was something colder and more solid; a heavy stone to bind with rope and drop into the water, to drag her down and down into the still, brown deeps.

He would make a plan to kill her.

17

Pritam moved his knight to threaten the Right Reverend's bishop.

'You dirty black bastard,' muttered Reverend Hird, wiping his spectacles on a handkerchief. The old man was swaddled in a padded robe, his striped pyjama pants just poking from beneath it. Pritam could see that his flesh between the pant cuffs and brown slippers was swollen as tight as a sausage and marbled with veins. Hird moved his bishop.

'Is that why you never let me play white?' asked Pritam. 'So you can slag off at me?' He saw that the white bishop was now stalking his one rook; Hird was the superior player. 'You degenerate old chiseller.'

Hird shrugged. 'Now you're blackening my good name.'

Pritam advanced a pawn. He looked at the mantel clock; it was nearly midnight. They often played till one or later, discussing the foibles of the congregation, the vagaries of the synod: serious matters couched in trivialities as the old man groomed the younger to take his job.

'And I feel compelled to point out, yet again, that I'm not black. Of course, if I were black, I'd be proudly black. But I'm Indian. Sub-continental. Hindustani. Whereas you are the ill-favoured offspring of deported criminals.'

'Touché,' replied Hird. 'And, in response to your brassy defence of your low-slung heritage, let me just say this: check.'

Pritam sighed and took a sip of sherry. He could now save his king and lose his bishop, or resign. Just once he would love to see the old man's face in defeat. He scoured the board for alternatives that he knew would not be there.

'Who were your visitors earlier?' asked Hird.

After Nicholas Close and his sister left, Pritam had made himself some green tea, taken another two codeine tablets, and within a half-hour his headache was gone. Which was responsible for the respite? The pills, or the departure of Close and his ridiculous questions?

'Never mind,' he said.

'Well, I do mind. What if they were more Hindustanis? Unwashed half-breed cousins you're trying to slip in under the radar? You breed like frogs. Or worse: what if they were Liberal voters? Soliciting your venal, oily hide for your curry-fingered vote?'

Pritam looked up at the old man. His eyes were sparkling with delight.

'You met one of them at Gavin Boye's funeral,' he said.

Hird's white eyebrows knitted together. 'In the church?'

Pritam nodded. 'And his sister.'

Hird thought for a moment. 'Here to discuss the suicide?'

'I resign,' said Pritam.

'At last!' crowed Hird, then sobered slyly. 'Oh, you mean the chess game. No, I won't let you. Always to the death.' He looked at the younger man. 'Well?'

'They were talking about the murder of the young Thomas boy.'

The older reverend nodded. 'And?'

'And nothing.'

'My friend Bill Chalmers baptised Nicholas Close. The boy's agnostic, like his mother and, I presume, his sister. Their father was a dodgy bastard: turned to drink, left his wife in the lurch with the kids, wrapped himself round a power pole.' Hird carefully cleared one nostril with a thumbnail. 'I might be old and foolish in my choice of housemates, but I still have capacity to wonder why two agnostics would come to see an Anglican reverend on a rainy winter's night. Unless Nicholas wanted to show his sister how ridiculous you Indians look in a white man's clothes.'

Pritam waited. There was no getting around this. Hird would harass and hassle him into answering as inevitably as he would extract a victory on the chessboard. He sighed.

'They mentioned a Mrs Quill. A dressmaker, I think.'

The older reverend nodded, very slightly. 'And?'

'And, nothing. I didn't want to worry you with this sort of nonsense, John.'

Pritam fell silent, and Hird watched him over his spectacles.

'I know English isn't your first language, so take your time.'

Pritam threw up his hands. 'Fine! He wanted you to look at the photograph of Eleanor Bretherton and then for me to ask you about this Quill woman.'

Hird looked over his shoulder at the old photograph of the church's construction, and wearily got to his feet.

'And now you're going to do it?' asked Pritam, incredulous. 'Is this your way to draw out my misery?'

Hird waved cheerily and hobbled over to the picture. He adjusted his glasses.

'I remember Mrs Quill,' he mumbled.

Pritam returned to the board. If he couldn't find a graceful way out of this game, he could at least backtrack and see the mistakes that had led him to lose.

'Did you learn to play in Korea? John?'

Pritam looked up at the old man. Hird was staring at the photograph. His face was white and his hand shook with a palsy.

'John?'

Hird looked at Pritam and shook his head slowly.

'Oh, dear,' he said quietly.

Then he dropped to one knee, and slumped onto the floor like a shot beast.

'John!'

Pritam ran to the old man. His breaths were shallow and fast, and his mouth formed silent, unknowable words. Pritam scrambled for the telephone.

•

The rain had finished, and the clouds were leaving like concertgoers after the final curtain. A beautiful night: chill and clear, moonless; the sky was a dark glass scrubbed clean and waiting.

The suburb of Tallong eased itself to sleep. House lights switched off one by one, two by two, by the dozen, until it seemed only the bright pearls of streetlamps strung their beads around the dark folds of the slumbering suburb. The narrow roads were glossed with the rain, and tiny streams chuckled in the gutters and fell with dark gurgles into storm-water drains to rush underground towards the nearby river. No cars disturbed the stillness. Only the trees sang softly their night-breeze song, whispering.

The woods were all shadow and moist as private flesh.

At their heart, a fire flickered. In a cottage that had been long built even before the suburb's old Anglican church had been started, flames licked fallen twigs in a stone-lined fire pit. The fire cast tall, thin shadows that jerked and clawed up the timber walls as if desperate for escape.

Over the flames hunched an old woman. Her withered lips moved, but her words were soft; intended, perhaps, for the flames, or for something unseen already listening for her offer. Her hands, more like bone than flesh, moved quickly. In the uncomforting flicker of the hungry flames: a flash of silver, a splash of dark liquid, the ash of something crumbled through deft fingers. Then a final item, and the old woman's hands slowed and moved with care. Tweezered in her skeletal fingers, a few long hairs joined by a small patch of blood-crusted skin. In went the hair and skin.

Her lips moved again.

The fire rose.

Outside, a chill wind grew, as if to carry across the dark, sighing treetops, along the empty streets and into the slumbering suburb something urgent and baleful.

18

Instead of being welcomingly warm, the sunlight felt harsh and brittle. Nicholas squinted against it as he watched Suzette speak on her telephone. He was exhausted. Even thinking about the simple choice – whether to stand and close the greasy curtains, or sit here squinting – was debilitating; the distance across the room could have been a thousand kilometres. Just too far.

Suzette finished her call and looked at her brother. There were bags the colour of soot under her eyes. She'd aged ten years in a night.

'Nelson has a fever,' she said.

They had talked about this possibility for a half-hour over tea this morning. She'd risen from her deep, unnatural sleep and her hand went to her raw patch of scalp. Nicholas had argued that she must have lost the clump of hair scrambling away from Garnock. She disagreed, and stated plainly that the dog – and she said the word 'dog' the way most people said 'cancer' – had wrenched it out right after it surprised her with the bite.

'It wasn't sent to hurt me,' she explained with a smile. 'It was sent for my hair. She's going to hex me.'

And not a minute after she'd said those words, her mobile phone rang. Bryan was calling with news that their son was suddenly ill.

Nicholas and Suzette sat silent for a while.

'Bryan's taking him to the twenty-four-hour clinic in Glebe,' said Suzette, finally. She licked her lips. There was more she wanted to say, but wouldn't.

'You have to go home,' said Nicholas.

For a long while she stared at her hands, saying nothing.

'How sick is Nelson?' he asked.

'I don't know.'

'Is she . . .' Nicholas hesitated, but there was no easy way to phrase it. 'Is she trying to kill him?'

Suzette thought about this, then shook her head. 'I don't think that's her plan,' she said, and looked up at Nicholas. 'She's dividing us.'

He nodded.

'But you can look after him? Nelson?'

'If it came out of the blue, maybe not. But since I know this sickness is . . . an attack . . . yes. I think so.' She couldn't meet his eyes. 'But I have to be there.'

'I know.'

'She's afraid of us,' she said.

Nicholas snorted. 'She has no need to be.'

He produced the telephone book and hunted for the airline's listing.

'We know more about her than anyone else in a century and a half,' said Suzette, turning one hand over. The puncture marks were healing remarkably fast and already looked days old. She touched them uneasily.

Nicholas imagined little Nelson a thousand kilometres away, face slick with sweat and turning fitfully as he dreamed of Christ-knew-what. Nothing pleasant, he was sure of that.

'She's halved us in one easy move, Suze. If you think she's afraid, you're an idiot. She's just playing.' He slid the open phone book towards her.

Suzette stared at it a moment, then picked up her phone.

•

Nicholas shut the cab door. His sister wound down the window.

'Show me,' she said.

He unzipped the front of his hoodie, revealing the burnished brown of wood beads. Suzette nodded approvingly. She looked into his eyes.

'I don't know, Nicky.'

He drove his hands into his pockets. 'I'll keep you posted.'

'Okay.'

She spoke to the driver and the cab pulled away into the bright street and soon became a winking spot of yellow too bright to watch.

•

Katharine nodded while Suzette rushed around the house collecting her suitcase, her make-up bag, her toiletries bag, her spare shoes. Outside, the cab horn tooted again. Katharine had swallowed not a word of the tripe Suzette had dished up about her and Nicholas having a few too many Jägermeisters last night and forgetting to tell Katharine she was crashing there at the flat.

I may be getting long in the tooth, she thought, *but I can still tell the difference between panic and hangover.* The way Suzette was rushing around like a dervish, the only drug in her veins was adrenaline. All that rang true was that Nelson had come down with something.

'Okay. That's everything,' said Suzette, pulling her hair back behind her ear.

'Great,' said Katharine. It was ridiculous. Nicholas was like his father – strange and handsome and flighty – but Suzette was supposed to be like *her*. Grounded. Sensible. Why were those two still keeping secrets like children? Why had Suzette flown out of the house like a bolt from a crossbow yesterday as soon as talk turned again to Mrs Quill? She was tempted to march to the porch, throw the cabbie twenty bucks and dismiss him, sit her daughter down and demand an explanation.

And do you think she'd tell you? Would you tell her? Have you told her everything?

No. No. And no.

The cab horn beeped again, longer and more insistent. Suzette wheeled her suitcase out of the room and kissed Katharine on the cheek.

'Gotta go.'

Katharine nodded.

It seemed to take just a moment, and then an engine rumbled, an arm waved, and the house was quiet again.

Katharine went to the kitchen and filled the kettle.

You brought this on yourself.

She sat, determined not to think as she waited for the water to boil.

•

For the last three-quarters of an hour, the young man had shuttled between his dirty brick-veneer house and a lopsided back shed.

Nicholas was standing behind an unkempt stand of lasiandra a few doors up from and opposite the Myrtle Street shops. He stood with his hands in his pockets, shifting from foot to foot as the sun crept low to the horizon and the lengthening shadows grew cold. He was turning and stamping his feet for warmth when he noticed movement in the backyard of the house behind him. At first, he gave no mind to the portly young bloke, but within minutes could hardly take his eyes off him. The lad would stride purposefully from the house with a small cardboard box of who-knew-what, across the unmown and weedy back lawn to a small old shed. A few minutes later, he'd emerge again, cross to the house, then return carrying some plastic bottles and rags. Then he'd wait in the shed about ten minutes, before returning empty-handed to the house and emerging with . . . a small cardboard box.

Nicholas let himself in the front gate and walked around the small house to the backyard. The young man was again carrying his bottles of cleaning liquids across the yard.

'Hey,' said Nicholas.

The boy didn't break stride, but his eyes slid over to Nicholas.

'Stop,' said Nicholas. He could hear how quiet his voice was. 'You can stop.'

But the young man didn't stop. Nicholas could see the eyes in his round face were puffy and red.

He told himself to turn around and go back to his hiding spot on the footpath. Yet he found his feet carrying him to the open door of the garden shed.

Inside was a folding card table on which the boy had placed his bottles. Nicholas watched him pour bleach, ant poison and – he found himself with the insane urge to laugh – Listerine into a jug. Spread out on the table was a short letter on floral notepaper, the soft, swirling handwriting of a woman. There were no hearts, circles or crosses at the bottom.

'Please don't,' said Nicholas.

The boy lifted the jug, locked his eyes on Nicholas, and drank deeply.

Of course he can't stop. He'll never stop.

The boy gagged silently, but kept swallowing.

'Are you in there?' asked Nicholas.

The boy's face started turning bright scarlet. His eyes closed tight with pain.

Nicholas left and hurried back to the street.

What had happened to the joy in that boy's life? Or in Dylan Thomas's life? Or Cate's life? Were the happy moments of their lives evaporated, boiled instantly away until all that was left was the moment of their death? What happened to the laughter? What happened to the years of contented sighs, when Cate fell asleep curled in his arms, knowing she was wanted and loved? Did it last anywhere, in some other universe, in some distant heaven? Or only now in his own memory? How much of her was trapped in that tiny bathroom in Ealing, or underground in Newham Cemetery, or in his own miserable heart?

No answers.

He stepped back behind the lasiandra, which suddenly whispered as a cold breeze hurried up the darkening street. Afternoon was turning to dusk.

Across and down the road, the Myrtle Street shops were quiet. A car parked. A man entered the convenience store and emerged shortly after with two stuffed bags of groceries. The light in the computer repair shop went out. Two minutes later, a lanky man stepped out and locked the front door. He leaned and sidestepped to peer into Plough & Vine Health Foods, gave a short wave, then trotted around to the side street where his Nissan was parked. He drove away.

Nicholas checked his watch. It was 5.34.

The lights inside the health food store went out.

He took a small step back, lowering himself a little behind the tangled shrubs.

A moment later, the door of Plough & Vine Health Foods opened and a tall, slender young woman stepped out. Rowena. She reached into her handbag for keys, dropped them, knelt to pick them up and locked the door. Nicholas watched her test the door was secure, then she checked her watch and hurried out from under the awning of the shops, away from his hiding spot. He watched her draw her long, knitted coat about herself as she strode away. He waited until she was far enough away that he would be just a shadowed stranger in the distance before stepping out from behind the lasiandra to follow.

Sedgely had her shop here. Quill had her shop here. But did that automatically cast any tenant of the shop under suspicion? Of course not. Ahead, Rowena's coltish long legs took her across Myrtle Street and up to the corner of Madeglass, where she turned left. She was moving fast, so Nicholas picked up his pace.

Old Bretherton. Old Sedgely. Old Quill. The old woman walking in the woods with Garnock. Were they the same person? He'd come to think so. But was there any connection between them and the vital young woman hurrying ahead of him? Was there any similarity between the friendly, clumsy woman who sold wheat germ and organic liquorice with a lovely smile and the sinister, bent thing that had watched with glittering eyes from her nest between hanging dresses? He couldn't see it.

At the end of Madeglass Street was a busier road that led under the railway line. At the corner, a small huddle of people waited at a bus shelter. Relief seemed to soften Rowena's tall form, and she slowed her pace as she moved to the end of the queue.

Nicholas slowed and stopped behind a power pole fifty metres away. He leaned against the hard wood and the faint tang of creosote rose through the chill air. The sun was gone now, and the first sparkles of stars were appearing in the purple sky. He watched Rowena. She was chatting with the middle-aged woman in the queue ahead of her. Both women laughed. Rowena's teeth were white in the gloom. The headlights of a bus appeared in the railway underpass, its windows glowing warm yellow. A moment later it let out an elephantine sigh and stopped to take on passengers. Rowena got on board. Nicholas watched her pick her way down the aisle to a seat halfway back. The bus rumbled and soon was gone.

Nicholas drove his hands further into his pockets. There was no malefic air about Rowena. Her shop was Quill's and her door still bore Quill's mark, but was that her fault? Of course not. Was she in danger herself? He didn't think so. The old woman who had been Quill had found somewhere else to hide, a new centre for her web. She was in the woods.

He felt the cold wind of night grab at his hair. He turned and walked slowly home to Bymar Street.

•

'. . . and then the princess realised he was the kindest, gentlest and best of all the animals, and she loved him most of all . . .'

Bryan's voice flowed down the hall like warm water, soothing and calm. Suzette could picture Quincy's eyes rolling and straining to focus as she fought to stay awake and hear the rest of her favourite story. Bryan had been so good, keeping Quincy occupied all day and well away from her sick brother.

Suzette was in Nelson's room. It was dark. He lay on the bed, his chest barely rising and falling. The doctor had suggested it was some kind of chest infection and, after conducting all manner of tests for meningococcal, pneumonia and SARS, had let him go home. Bryan had argued that he needed to be in hospital, and Suzette loved him for it. 'Trust me,' she said. He did, and she loved him for that too.

She finished writing Nelson's full name on a candle that was so purple it was almost black. Already waiting on a tray was a small poppet, a roughly human-shaped thing of white cotton and smelling strongly of sage, garlic and lavender. She'd sewn the poppet closed with Nelson's hair.

How dare she? thought Suzette. *How dare she attack my child?* But a part of her begged her to be quiet, to be grateful. *Quill's done so much worse.*

She listened. Silence from the far end of the house. Story time was done; Quincy was asleep.

Time to start.

She lit the candle.

19

Pritam sat on the Right Reverend Hird's bare mattress, unsure where to begin.

The ambulance had taken John's body away in the early hours of yesterday morning. Yesterday itself had been a blur: phone calls, discussions with the archdiocese about funeral arrangements, hunting through John's telephone book and finding with relief that he had no siblings or hidden children that needed contacting. At the end of the long day, Pritam, utterly spent, had collapsed in his room ready for sleep, but instead had lain awake for hours, playing over and over the last few minutes of his friend's life.

When John collapsed, Pritam had phoned 000. He'd surprised himself – maybe disappointed himself – with how calm he'd sounded talking to the emergency operator. He'd performed CPR at the operator's instructions, wincing guiltily at the papery dryness of the old man's lips beneath his own. As he pressed the heel of his palm into John's chest, counting, breathing, counting, his eyes had drifted up to the photograph of Eleanor Bretherton. Was it coincidence that John had suffered such a severe attack while looking at the photograph? Surely. But Pritam had seen the look on John's face. It began as one of wonder, and became something he'd never seen in the old man before. Now, sitting in his room and waiting to pack his few belongings, Pritam had convinced himself that he knew what the expression was.

Fright.

A man who had been seemingly afraid of nothing saw something in that photograph that had literally scared him to death.

Pritam rose from the bed and walked into the rectory sitting room. The chess game was as it had stood fourteen hours ago, when he had wished to see John's face in defeat. Well, he'd seen that last night and it cheered him not at all. He opened the storeroom. Two sets of wooden shelves lined opposite walls. One held spare hymn books, sacramental wine and wafers, collection plates, vestments, Christmas decorations and the cast plastic nativity scene John steadfastly refused to replace. The opposite held archive boxes.

Pritam didn't know what he was looking for, so he took down the first box, removed its lid and sat on the floor. He pulled out the topmost piece of paper and began to read.

•

While Pritam was unpacking boxes, Laine was taping her last one shut. That was the last of Gavin's belongings put away; some for charity, some for the tip, some to be saved for a happier 'one day' that Laine felt, right now, was as distant as the stars.

She and Gavin had moved into the house fourteen months ago to look after his mother. Mrs Boye's husband, Gavin's father, had passed on two years earlier, and the widow's decline had accelerated in those twenty-four months. Three personal carers had quit, finding her manner too abrasive even for their seasoned experience.

Twelve months ago, the arrow on Laine's marriage fire-danger sign had pointed to 'moderate'. Over the subsequent six months it had escalated to 'high'. She and Gavin had been trying for a child for more than a year, and had finally started IVF treatment. The hormone injections gave her an immovable headache that soured every heartbeat. Waking up sick, commuting to her grinding job at a graphics company that seemed to tender only for redesigns of cereal boxes and fridge calendars, then returning home to Mrs Boye's increasingly nonsensical and voluble rants made it hard to unearth even minuscule moments of pleasure.

Gavin got a promotion: sales executive, Asia Pacific. He wasn't the brightest man, but he was good-looking and seemed to get along well with everyone. He had a natural charm. He'd certainly charmed her.

But he had also put her through the humiliation of two affairs. Both times Laine had caught him out, and both times he had collapsed at her feet in a ball of remorseful tears promising never, *ever* to be so stupid again. While most of her softened to his grief, one deep part of her remained ice, half-wishing that he had stood his ground and explained his infidelity without remorse. *If you're going to pretend your wife doesn't matter while you're fucking another woman, show that same face to me,* she'd thought. *Sure, I might slap it, I might leave it, or I might forgive all of you instead of most of you.* But he'd simply sworn never, never, never again . . . then landed another overseas job that would deliver him into temptation for weeks on end. The needle moved to 'extreme'.

Then, the unforeseeable. A month ago, Gavin had given his employer four weeks notice. 'I'll get a job around here,' he'd told her. 'Something low-stress, part-time, maybe. We're not paying rent, and Dad's left us plenty. You should quit too.' A year earlier, this news would have filled her with delicious, full fat, chocolate-coated joy. But now, after a gruelling routine of shitty work, shitty weird home life in a house where the shadow of a dead boy walked more solidly than the grown-ups, shitty headaches, shitty worry about a husband who couldn't keep his dick out of other women, the golden offer just weirded Laine out. She didn't trust it.

But Gavin seemed to mean it. He began eating properly – health food and raw vegetables. It should have been good. It *would* have been good. Had he not started talking in his sleep.

In the middle of the night, when the huge house ticked uneasily, Gavin's whispering would wake her. She had to lean close to hear his words. '*Bird. Tris. Back. Dead.*' By the watery light coming through the window, she could see he was deep asleep as he spoke, yet his expression was adulating, hungry. '*Bird. Please. Bird. Dead.*' The words kept her awake long after he'd rolled over, snoring. Two people muttering to themselves in the house made her feel guiltily glad she hadn't fallen pregnant; she didn't want a child infected with this family's madness. She stopped taking the fertility drugs, but didn't tell Gavin.

Then, just a few days ago, Gavin had risen early. Laine had been so exhausted, having finally fallen asleep at four, that she hadn't stirred. Mrs Boye had slept uncharacteristically late too. They'd both been roused at seven by police knocking to bring 'some very bad news'.

And now? Her lawyer was battling with Gavin's life insurer, but Mr Boye's inheritance was hers. She would find a carer for Mrs Boye and get the hell out of this quietly haunted house. Two nights ago she had been in the shower making plans for just that when Nicholas Close had visited.

Close was pale and odd-looking. Not unhandsome, but held together inside by wires stretched too tight. Laine had heard that his wife had died, and that he'd been with Tristram when he was taken way back when. Close had said he wanted to talk about Gavin, and she'd had to clamp her mouth shut. She had wanted to yell: *Tell me about the bird! What does it mean? What bird?!* But that would have signed her application into Bedlam, so she sent him on his way.

Now it was done. The last box was packed. She could go and put all this behind her.

Except she wanted to know.

Gavin's brother had been murdered. His killer had suicided. A boy had gone missing a week or so ago. His killer had suicided. Gavin had suicided. What linked all this death? Nicholas Close.

She was leaving this awful city. Who cared if he thought her mad?

She would go to see him.

20

Hannah Gerlic was so angry she could spew. Miriam, who was two years older and in year seven and *supposed* to be more adult about things, had chucked the most dangerous kind of spaz when she caught Hannah using her lip gloss. Jeez, come on! Miriam *knew* Mum wouldn't let Hannah buy her own lip gloss! But catching her, Miriam hadn't yelled and spacked out; she'd gone silent. This meant one of two things: either she'd march straight to Mum and reveal some secret she'd crossed her heart not to tell, or she'd Get Even Later.

As Hannah stumped along alone, she understood very clearly that Miriam had chosen the latter.

They'd walked off towards school together, Miriam all sweetness and light and *miss-you-Mum*. But out of sight of home, she had turned on Hannah, fast and harsh as those peregrine falcons you see on TV documentaries, diving like lightning on field mice and ripping their guts out. 'Just wait, you little bitch,' she'd hissed, and then had given Hannah eighteen-carat, diamond-studded, first-class silent treatment the whole two kilometres to school.

Once there, Hannah quickly forgot her older sister's fury and the day ambled along nicely to its final (and Hannah's favourite) lesson: Art and Craft. Hannah was good at art, and loved the luscious sense of creation that came from spooning thick acrylic paint onto a brush and sliding it over pristine white paper, of making something out of nothing. Mrs Tho (who Hannah thought was the prettiest woman in the world and who was always patient) said Hannah's paintings were magnificent and told her to keep in mind that the school fête was coming up, where she might be able to exhibit some of her work. The idea plucked pleasant shivers inside Hannah, and the thought of other people seeing – and maybe *buying* – her work was . . . well, just awesome.

Afire with this, she had attacked this afternoon's blank paper with excitement, and come up with something vibrant and pretty and deliciously weird. It was a horse in a man suit in a supermarket aisle shopping for seahorses. Where the image had come from, who knew? But it made her classmates laugh and Mrs Tho smile. Hannah couldn't wait to show Miriam, who was usually the biggest fan of her creative talents.

Not this afternoon, though.

A glacial freeze surrounded Miriam as they started to walk home. Hannah tried to engage her older sister by telling her about the fête. She started to unroll the new painting, but at the top of the hill past the school Miriam stopped in her tracks.

'I don't want to talk to you, you thieving little dog. I'm going along Silky Oak Street. *You* walk the other way.'

Hannah felt a small thump of fear in her tummy. The 'other way' was along Carmichael Road.

Since Dylan Thomas went missing, she and Miriam weren't allowed to walk along Carmichael Road. 'How come?' they'd both asked in a singsong complaint – although both of them preferred the Silky Oak Street route because it took them past the Myrtle Street shops, where they could buy a Cornetto if funds were plentiful or (if times were tight) share a Bounty bar. Mum had explained with gravity that the woods off Carmichael Road were too big and it was very easy for careless girls to get themselves lost. And now Miriam was forcing Hannah to go past them.

'Miriam . . . ?'

Miriam walked a few steps and whirled again, eyes brightly ferocious. 'I mean it, shithead!' she spat. 'You follow me and I'll kick you to death!'

Hannah stood frozen. She'd never seen her sister this angry. She remembered a half-heard warning from Mum: *Miriam's going through a phase right now. She's growing up fast and lots of changes are happening to her. She's liable to be a bit testy.*

Wow, you reckon? thought Hannah.

She watched Miriam stalk off on her long, thin legs. She fought the sudden urge to bawl, slowly rolled up her painting and walked to the terminus of the school's avenue, which turned down Carmichael Road.

I'll tell, Hannah thought hatefully. *I'll tell Mum that Miriam used the F-word. And I'll make it stick worse because I'll fess up to using her lip gloss first, and second I'll cry.*

Cheered a little by this plan, she walked easier. The afternoon was warm and she opened up her school cardigan. The woods grew closer on her right. They looked fine: thick and secret and old. When Dad used to read stories about enchanted princesses sleeping the years away in emerald groves, it wasn't forests thick with European pines that Hannah had imagined, but woods like these: lush and healthy and wild and filled with hefty-trunked paperbark, glossy ash, lumbering and shadow-branched figs and scrambling, dark-footed lantana. Trees as tall as churches, some so thick with vines they looked like green-furred dinosaurs. The woods were beautiful. As she passed them, she left the footpath and took the gravel track that cut through the dried grass strip that fringed the tree line.

Besides, it wasn't *woods* that hurt people. Sure, you could get lost and freeze to death, or you could break your leg or your neck, but if you were careful, the woods were safe as anything. It was *people* who hurt people.

With this thought in mind, it seemed to Hannah that she saw three things at once.

The first was unimportant: someone had driven black star pickets into the ground near the footpath and wired between them a sign made of white plastic.

Secondly, a man stood on the other side of Carmichael Road. He had been staring at the sign, but now was watching Hannah.

The third was so exciting her heart began to race. The sight of it made her forget the other two things instantly. It lay smack in the middle of the path, glinting like a huge gem in the sunlight.

It was a unicorn.

It looked like it was made of glass, but as Hannah stepped closer, she wasn't so sure. Glass was usually smooth and bulgy; this had fine, chiselled legs, rippling and strong. She could see the striations in the horn, the fine detail of the creature's course mane hairs, its beautiful wise eyes. Its flanks were scalloped and muscular. It looked alive and frozen at the same time, more made of ice than glass, or perhaps carved from some magical, transparent wood. It was the most beautiful thing she had ever seen.

'Excuse me!'

Hannah reluctantly looked up – she didn't want to take her eyes off the unicorn. The man had crossed the road and was coming towards her. *He wants the unicorn*, she thought wildly. *It's his unicorn, but I want it!*

'Young lady?' he called.

Hannah calculated. She had time. She could grab the exquisite figurine, put it in her bag, and run.

'Don't!'

She reached down and snatched the unicorn.

And as she did, it felt as if the earth jumped a step to the side. She lurched. The sky seemed to dim. The sun sank lower. The woods, so benign and inviting, suddenly loomed dark and dreadful. She looked at her hands.

Instead of the lustrous unicorn, she held a dead plover. The bird sagged limply. Its head was gone, cut off and replaced with a ball made of twigs and painted with a funny mark. It was hideous. So horrible. So *dead*.

She was staring at it, about to scream, when the man grabbed her arms.

•

Nicholas was staring at the ceiling of his flat and deciding that it was indeed stucco. This was the sole conclusion that he had reached in two hours. He had bumbled around the flat, circumnavigating the dining room table and the open notebook lying there. He had rung Suzette to find that Nelson's fever had diminished but not gone, so she had moved him onto a cot in her and Bryan's room.

Nicholas had forced himself to sit, intending to make a list of names and places – Quill, Bretherton, Sedgely; shop, woods, church – to see if their placement together might catalyse some epiphany he felt was ripe and ready. But the instant his buttocks hit the chair, he was up again. He couldn't stay inside any longer. He had to go out.

He willed his feet to take him to Lambeth Street. Suzette had said that their mother had sounded short on the phone, and some placating might not be a bad idea. But the instant Nicholas's feet touched the Bymar Street footpath, they started towards Carmichael Road.

The wind had risen through the night; it tugged urgently at treetops and made the power lines sway and moan. High overhead, clouds were hounded fast across the sky, and the sun, though impoverished of warmth, was so bright it hurt the eye.

Nicholas walked onto Carmichael Road. He stayed on the footpath opposite the woods and walked towards the point where Winston Teale had once stopped his olive green sedan. Movement flickered in the grass verge and Nicholas squinted.

Dylan Thomas took a few frightened steps back, then his arm spasmed out straight as a mast's boom and he jerked as he was rushed towards the woods and into the dark trees. Then, in an orchestration that was unsettling, high clouds passed over the sun just as Nicholas saw something else that made him flinch. A sign had been hammered into the hard strip of grass bordering the woods.

Stiff-legged, he walked along the footpath till he was opposite the new notice. 'Application for Subdivision' it said; 'Barisi Group, Developers'. A small logo of a black Romanesque stallion flanked the large print.

Nicholas's mind flew back through the old papers he'd found at the library – auction flyers, auctioneers' names, surveyors' names. Funerals of men. Murders of children.

He blinked as a terrible realisation dawned on him. Every time the woods were threatened, a child went missing and died. Here was another application to invade the woods. Quill was going to kill another child.

At that very moment, a small girl appeared on the path.

She was maybe nine or ten, with dark brown hair in a ponytail and thin legs ending in shoes that looked too big. She spotted Nicholas and looked quickly away back to the path. Then her scissoring steps slowed and stopped. Her eyes had found something on the ground.

Nicholas felt the world slow to a quiet halt. The wind seemed to cease. The very sunlight seemed to freeze in the air, becoming so fragile that a single gesture would shatter it and let darkness flood the sky. The woods, a wall of black shadow, ghostly trunks and dark green waves, seemed to swell, growing taller and closer to the girl.

Bring her.

The voice in his head was low, as old as stone and as strong as night tides, a powerful rumble almost too low to hear; it vibrated through him like a whale song or thunder.

Bring her.

He shook his head as if to clear it. 'Excuse me!' he called out to the girl. His voice sounded impotent and exhausted.

The girl looked up at him, frowning. She was so small. It would be easy to grab her, to fold her in his arms and . . .

Bring her in.

He took a step towards her, and stopped himself. *No.*

She was looking at the path again. Nicholas knew what lay there. A dead bird with a woven head, and if she touched it she would die.

She will *die.*

'Young lady?' he called. His feet moved again, and this time they wouldn't stop. They were carrying him to her, across the road. It was hard to breathe. His throat was tight. His hands went to his collar and pulled it away; as he did, his fingertips touched the wood beads of the necklace. It felt heavy and tight around his neck and the sardonyx stone was uncomfortably warm.

Take it off.

Yes, he could just take it off and grab her and bring her in, she wouldn't be heavy, cover her mouth and —

No!

The girl was looking at the path and back at him. She was going to grab it!

'Don't!' he called, but his voice sounded so thin he could have been on a distant hilltop.

If I can't stop walking, he thought, *I'll run.* He jolted his legs into a sudden sprint.

She knelt and picked up the dead bird.

BRING HER IN!

Nicholas stumbled. The voice was so low it set his teeth shaking; it seemed to convulse his organs and whip his blood. The animal gravity of the woods was as primal and strong as any need to sleep or eat or fuck. His crotch bulged with a new and thumping erection. The necklace was hot, burning. He couldn't breathe.

Then he heard them.

In the woods. A chittering. The rustle of a thousand unseen spiny legs on shadowed leaves. They were coming.

The girl stood rigid, staring at the dead bird in her hands, its head a ball of twigs and marked with blood. Thurisaz. Nicholas grabbed her by the arms.

Bring her —

'No!' he yelled, and picked her off her feet. He staggered – she felt as heavy as a man, as two men; too heavy. He swooped one hand under her thin legs. The tick-tick rustling was getting louder. He bent, shaking under the strain, and scooped up the dead bird talisman and shoved it into his pocket. He took a quaking step, then another, away from the woods.

The chittering of leaves gave way to a rustling in the grass behind him.

His legs were burning with effort, lactate already racing like bushfire through his thighs. He took another step, another, another . . . and ran.

Just as he stepped onto the path, he cast a look behind.

The grass was turning black. It was as if flood waters had instantly risen to halfway up their stalks. Only the tide was not dark water: Nicholas knew it was a rising wave of black and grey spiders.

He turned and ran like hell.

•

This was the last box. Pritam pulled it down from the shelf, dropped it unceremoniously on the floor, and began emptying its contents.

Rifling through the other archive boxes had yielded a hodgepodge of curiosities: photographs of a twenty-years-younger Reverend John Hird smiling with disabled children under the World Expo monorail; a yellowing folder containing John's papers discharging him from 3RAR; another envelope holding the location and number of his brother's crematorium plot. Pritam set these aside.

Other finds were not personal and less interesting. Tax receipts for repairs, three notepads containing bookings for the church hall, an audit of plants in the church grounds, receipt for a mimeograph machine.

Pritam had spent the day trawling through the boxes, occasionally answering a telephoning well-wisher or a knock at the door, confirming in a cracked and tired voice that, indeed, the Reverend John Hird had passed away last night; that, yes, he went peacefully, and agreeing that, indeed, he had been unwell a long while. John certainly was a very strong spirit, an inspiration. He was, most surely, with his Lord now. Yes, there would be a service.

And so to the last box.

If the previous cartons had been pedestrian in content, this was numbingly dull. Old bus timetables. Ticket stubs for bus travel. Suggestion-box notes held together with a rusted bulldog clip. A large envelope marked 'Fundraising'. Within this last were four smaller envelopes labelled by decade, the topmost reading '1970–80'. Pritam opened it.

Inside were a few copies of a flyer printed in purple ink – he was pleased the mimeograph got used. They advertised a fête: 'Fun for the Family!', 'Sack races!' and 'Home-baked cakes!'. Handwritten lists of helpers and their duties ('R. Burgess, set up trestle tables & remove rubbish'). Faded Polaroid photographs of the big day: ladies shyly holding their iced cakes and smiling. Children with long hair and flared pants were lashed together at the ankles, running and laughing. A wide-tied man wagging his finger at the camera while eating a pie. A woman staring, unsmiling, at the camera.

Pritam's breath stopped in his throat.

The woman staring at the camera was Eleanor Bretherton.

He flipped the photograph. In pencil, written in a fine copperplate hand: 'Mrs L. Quill. Contributed $60 to fête fund 17 May 1975'.

Pritam sat back.

He felt small again, a thin-limbed boy in his grandmother's cottage before his parents took him from India, listening after dinner as Nani told the story of a small village in Uttar Pradesh where every child was cut open, alive and screaming, to save the village from the wrath of Kali. That tale had terrified him as a child; not just his imagining being one of those utterly helpless children not even able to turn to their parents who themselves wielded knives . . . but imagining how terrible must be the face of Kali to drive loving parents to commit bloody murder.

Eleanor Bretherton. Mrs L. Quill.

Now things go bad, he thought.

At that moment, someone pounded on the rectory door.

•

The girl sat in one of the old club chairs, staring into space with slack eyes. She blinked occasionally and breathed slow and deep, but hadn't shifted or spoken a word in the twenty minutes since she'd arrived at the presbytery.

'"Hannah Gerlic, 5D",' read Pritam. His voice shook. He replaced the exercise book into the girl's school bag.

He looked up to the other club chair opposite. In it sat Nicholas Close, who nodded acknowledgment. In the middle of the cleared chessboard lay the dead plover talisman. One of its claw horns had been lost, but even to look at it made Pritam's skin prickle.

This is not hypothetical evil, he thought. *Not the evil of lust, nor the evil of hate. This is fundamental evil, as old as the world itself. This is the devil's handiwork.*

The thought was electric and terrifying, as if the veneer covering the world had peeled at one corner, affording a glimpse of dark and yawning depths below.

'I'm sorry,' whispered Nicholas.

He sat slumped in his chair, staring at the dead bird. For an unsettling moment, Pritam thought he was talking to the tiny corpse. Then he slid his eyes to Pritam and smiled.

He's peered into the depths, too, thought Pritam. *And he looks ready to fall into them.*

He shook his head. After finding that photograph of Quill, he'd been shocked to open the presbytery door to stare right into the face of the man who'd brought her to his attention. Pritam had been ready to dismiss him, tell him John Hird was dead and to come back another time – better yet, don't come back at all! – when he saw the girl standing dumbly behind Nicholas, holding his hand and staring into space. His first impression struck him like a fist: *she's been raped.* Then Nicholas said a word that was the second blow to finish the one-two: 'Quill.'

Pritam had let them in, put the girl in the chair, listened as Nicholas briefly recounted the story about finding her outside the woods, finishing by pulling that horrible, disfigured bird from his pocket.

Now Pritam knew the girl's name.

'They'll want to know,' he said.

Nicholas cocked his head – who?

'Her parents. They'll want to know why you grabbed their daughter while she was walking home.'

'I told you —'

'*I* believe you,' said Pritam. The words surprised him. But they were true; he did believe. Every poisonous bit. That abomination of a bird verified it all: so unnaturally dead, so *alien*. It looked like a lightning rod for evil.

'I believe you, but I don't think her mother will,' he continued. 'I don't think the police will. Not so soon after the Thomas boy. Nicholas, I think you're looking down the barrel of some serious questions.'

Nicholas didn't seem to care. He was watching Hannah Gerlic, and the concern in his eyes for her was real.

She stared into space, her expression blank as glass. Pritam had seen black and white footage of World War I soldiers in hospital wards, automatons staring at infinity. Shell shock.

'I suppose I am,' agreed Nicholas quietly. He looked at Pritam. 'They won't believe the truth.'

The men regarded one another.

'I won't lie for you,' said Pritam.

Nicholas frowned. 'Who asked you to?'

There was a rustling from Hannah's chair and they looked at her. She was staring, wide-eyed, at the dead bird. Suddenly, she sucked in a surprised breath, gagged, coughed up some briny yellow spittle, and started crying.

•

Andrew and Louise Gerlic were the happiest parents in the world.

Mrs Gerlic hugged Hannah tightly, tears running quicksilver paths down her red cheeks. 'Silly girl. Silly girl. Silly girl . . .' She rocked her daughter in her arms. Mr Gerlic had his arms around them both, his eyes shut, nodding to himself.

On the drive to the Gerlics' house, Pritam and Nicholas had worked out a story set in the awkward middle ground between lies and truth. Nicholas had been reading the development sign when Hannah appeared. She was distraught and wouldn't respond to his queries. Uncomfortable with the idea of going through a young girl's bag unaccompanied, he drove her immediately to his friend, the local reverend, where they discovered together the girl's identity. Why was she so traumatised? They didn't know. Had Nicholas seen anything unusual? No.

Police arrived at the Gerlic residence. The sight of a clergyman set the room at ease. Nicholas and Pritam were thanked together and questioned separately. One female officer was questioning Hannah without success: Hannah simply screwed up her eyes and shook her head. Another female officer spoke quietly to Mrs Gerlic, who listened a while then nodded consent. The women took Hannah to the girl's bedroom. They emerged a few minutes later and Nicholas saw the female officer catch the eye of another uniformed officer – she shook her head. No signs of physical interference. The police began to wrap things up.

Nicholas drifted to join Pritam. 'I don't know if she'll be safe,' he whispered.

Pritam looked at him.

'We have a great deal to discuss.'

Nicholas dropped Pritam back to the presbytery, and the men made arrangements to catch up there later that evening. Nicholas then kept driving, back to Lambeth Street.

•

Dinner was awkwardly silent, considering how loud it had been to prepare.

Nicholas had sat at the kitchen bench, watching Katharine chop vegetables, water chestnuts, onion, chicken. Every time he'd started to speak, she'd whacked some ingredient into submission or ground spices in her large granite mortar.

'Want a hand?' he'd yelled.

'No, no,' she'd yelled back brightly, then began throwing diced things into the wok where they shrieked loudly in the sizzling oil.

When they both sat to eat, the silence was so severe that Nicholas didn't think he had profound enough words to break it. Katharine didn't seem to feel compelled to; she chewed quietly, shooting the occasional cool smile to him.

'Delicious,' he said finally.

'It's nothing,' she replied. They were quiet for a long moment, then she added, 'I bought a tajine.'

'Oh? Tall, pointy thing?'

'Yes. Haven't used it yet.'

'Wow. Exotic.'

They ate without speaking again until their plates were clean. It was only when Nicholas made to stand and clear the table that Katharine broke the silence.

'Sit. Please.'

He remained on his chair. Katharine licked her lips, lifted her chin and looked at him.

'What's going on?' she asked.

Nicholas had been wondering when she would ask. He'd practised a careful, oleaginous answer that slipped neatly around issues that he knew his mother wouldn't accept – ghosts, witchcraft, child sacrifices – while still keeping alive the notion that this had become a bit of an iffy suburb and maybe moving might not be a bad idea. However, his mother's bright eyes seemed to burn away all his clever duplicity and he found himself simply saying, 'What?'

Katharine tilted her head – her don't-take-me-for-a-fool look.

'Your sister came up from Sydney,' she said, her words coming brisk and clipped hard. 'You two huddle together like twitty schoolgirls. Gavin Boye shoots himself outside my front door. *You* duck away and find yourself a flat without so much as a thank you. She flies back to Sydney so fast you'd think they were giving away harbourside houses. She calls up today, la-di-dah as if nothing's happened, and then suggests I sell this house and move down to Neutral Bay.'

Nicholas shrugged and inspected the tablecloth. 'Neutral Bay is nice.'

He felt her gaze on his face, drawing at his thoughts like a poultice.

'What can I tell you, Mum? Jeez.'

She took a long breath. Then she nodded to herself and pulled his empty plate towards her. Nicholas could see an opportunity was passing. He tightened his jaw.

'Kids are getting murdered here, Mum.'

Katharine's hands fussed around the plates. She looked up at him.

'A child died,' she agreed. 'A terrible thing.'

'A lot of kids. Over the years.'

He watched for her reaction.

'Well, I'm no spring chicken. I'm not likely to become a victim.'

'Adults, too. That Guyatt chap who killed the Thomas boy. He was from Myrtle Street.'

'He died in prison.'

'Yes. So did Winston Teale, remember? He was a local, too. Wasn't he?'

Katharine's fingers stopped moving. 'Yes. From over the hill in Kadoomba Road.'

They looked at each other for a long moment.

'And Gavin Boye. There's something wrong with this suburb, Mum.'

He could see her eyes narrow. But she didn't disagree. When she spoke, her tone was even and reasonable.

'If I thought it was safe enough for you to stay here after that terrible business with Tristram Boye all those years ago, why on earth shouldn't it be safe enough for me now?'

Nicholas wanted to say, *Because of the ghosts. Because Quill isn't dead, she's alive and living in the woods. She's murdering again.* He clenched his jaw. He couldn't say any of this to her.

'Or do you blame me for what happened to you down there?' she asked.

Nicholas blinked. 'No. Why would I?'

'Because I didn't keep you safe. Because I was . . . I don't know . . . I was a bad mother. Because I didn't move when your fa—'

Her eyes widened ever so slightly and she bit down the last word.

'Dad? Dad wanted you to move?'

Katharine stood noisily, picked up the plates and carried them to the sink.

'Donald wanted lots of silly things. That just happened to be one of his rare good ideas.'

Nicholas frowned. His father wanted his family to move? Why? Because Owen Liddy went missing in 1964? Or was there more he knew?

'When?'

'Nicholas! I don't know.'

'Before he started drinking?'

'A long, long time ago. When we were happy and there was no good reason to move. Okay?' She scraped the plates off with a harsh clatter.

'But there must have been a reason!'

Before he could press the point, the telephone rang in the hallway. Katharine clip-clopped out of the room to answer it. Nicholas sighed, and watched her listening as the caller spoke. Then she held the receiver out to him.

'For you.'

He took the phone. It was Laine Boye.

'Sorry to disturb your evening, Mr Close.' Her voice was so crackly it could have been cast from Mars.

Katharine slipped into the bathroom and started the shower. There would be no more talking about Donald Close and Tallong tonight.

'That's fine,' replied Nicholas. 'Is there . . . Can I help you?'

'This might sound odd, Mr Close,' said Laine. 'But I need to ask you about a dead bird.'

21

The rain thundered down so heavily that Pritam could imagine that space itself was made of water, and was now pouring through rents in the sky's tired fabric.

The three of them sat in the presbytery's leather club chairs, finishing coffee. The mood was odd. Three very different people, each effectively a stranger to the other two. They had next to nothing in common. A neatly dressed Christian clergyman. A reserved, elegant woman recently widowed. And that long-limbed scarecrow of a man Nicholas Close. Would they ever have gathered were it not for these unusual circumstances? He didn't think so. Yet they were surprisingly comfortable together. None had a loved one waiting at home for them. All had lost someone close to them recently. Sad, strange events had brought them together, yet there was something warming about each other's company. Something easy and right, but very fragile — a fine rope across a wide chasm. Each felt it; the silence while they sipped was delicate and none wanted to break it.

After returning from the Gerlics' house, Pritam had set himself busy to fill the time until Nicholas arrived. He'd mopped out John's room, cleaned his ensuite, found a hundred small excuses not to go into the main church. When he heard a knock at the presbytery door, he had been surprised to find not Nicholas, but Laine Boye. She explained that Nicholas had invited her. Not long later, Nicholas himself arrived. Pritam made coffee, they exchanged small talk, and a silence settled that each recognised as a cue: it was time for serious talk.

'Okay,' Nicholas began. 'I've told Pritam some of this, but not everything. Not by a long shot. Laine, you said Gavin mentioned a bird?'

Pritam felt the last word suddenly flutter in his gut like a real bird, nervous and ready to flee. He watched Nicholas walk over to the small bar fridge; he pulled out the plastic bag and untied it on the coffee table. Pritam's heart beat faster as he saw again that violated little body, that disquieting woven ball for a head. He looked over to see Laine's reaction to the mutilated bird, but her grey eyes were utterly inscrutable.

'I first saw a bird like this four days before Gavin's brother was murdered,' Nicholas said, starting in 1982 with finding the dead bird and showing his best friend, Tristram. Then there was Winston Teale chasing them both into the woods, and watching Tris and his broken wrist disappear under the old water pipe through a tunnel full of spiders. How Tris's drained body had been found miles away under tin and timber. Teale's confession and suicide. Years later, Cate's death. His fall on the stairs outside the flat in Ealing. The ghost of the screwdriver-wielding boy. Then more ghosts; sad, trapped ghosts. Cate's ghost. Returning from London on a rainy night like this when Dylan Thomas disappeared. Elliot Guyatt's confession and suicide, so eerily like Teale's. Gavin's dawn message punctuated by two sharp cracks of his rifle on which Thurisaz was scored: the rune that kept reappearing and seemed inextricable from death. Pursuing the Thomas boy's ghost into the woods. The strawberries. The *Wynard*. The old woman and her dog Garnock that was no dog. The nauseating hand job. The archived flyers and news articles: so many missing children, so many dead men. Eleanor Bretherton, grim patron of this church, the spitting image of Mrs Quill the dressmaker. Her shop, now a health food store, with a rune marked into its door. Garnock attacking Suzette and wrenching out her hair, and Nicholas's nephew falling ill the next morning. The odd power of the sardonyx and elder-wood necklace. And earlier today: a development sign erected, another bird talisman found, and a girl nearly snatched with Nicholas himself darkly urged to deliver her into the gloomy woods on Carmichael Road.

His story finished. The room fell silent under the cold gaze of Eleanor Bretherton, staring belligerently out from monochromatic 1888.

Pritam was exhausted, as if he'd just finished watching a disturbing horror feature that he knew couldn't be real, but still made him want to avoid the shadows. He looked over to Laine Boye. She was watching him intently, as if gauging his reaction.

'And, of course,' said Nicholas, 'a credible witness who could have confirmed that Quill and Bretherton were, forgive the pun, birds of a feather is dead. John Hird.'

'True,' said Pritam, and was surprised how quiet his voice was. 'But there is this.'

He went to his desk drawer and returned with the photo of Mrs Quill at the church fête thirty-two years ago. Nicholas put out his hand, but Pritam stepped past him and handed it to Laine.

When Laine saw it, her lips tightened but her face betrayed no emotion. She stood and went to the hanging photograph of Eleanor Bretherton and compared the two for a full minute.

'Could Quill be her grand-daughter?' she finally asked.

'Yes,' replied Nicholas. 'But there was no record of Eleanor Bretherton marrying or having children. She was a spinster.'

'You tell me, Mrs Boye,' said Pritam. 'Are they the same person?'

Laine held the photographs side by side, comparing Quill's and Bretherton's scowls, their chins, their frosty alarm at being photographed. After a long minute, she returned the photograph to Pritam.

'Similar,' she said.

The rain outside roared.

'So?' asked Nicholas, looking from Pritam to Laine.

Laine looked at Pritam. He nodded – you speak first.

'So,' said Laine, 'we have two photographs a hundred years apart with two women who look alike, but that means nothing of itself. A list of deaths and murders, but they were all explained away or confessed to. As for the bird, you could have mutilated it. We only have your word, Mr Close, that you found it. But . . .'

'But?'

'But you say you can see ghosts.'

Laine kept her cool gaze on Nicholas. For a long moment, he was silent. Then he spoke quietly.

'True. The only thing it doesn't explain is why your husband was talking in his sleep about a dead bird before he left your bed and shot himself.'

Pritam saw a shiver of something behind Laine's eyes. Was it fear? Anger? It was gone so quickly, he wondered if he'd seen it at all.

Nicholas turned and looked at him. 'Well, Reverend, what do you think? A coincidence with Bretherton and Quill? Secret relatives?' He smiled grimly. 'And what about me? Crazy guy who thinks he sees ghosts?'

Pritam could see that Nicholas was fighting to seem contained, but was ready to snap.

'My religion,' he answered slowly, 'says that one of the three aspects of my God is a ghost.'

Nicholas smiled grimly. 'However?'

'However, I need to ask . . . Are you afraid of spiders?'

Nicholas blinked, suddenly caught off guard. 'Yes, I'm afraid of spiders.'

'Were you always?'

'What are you, a psychiatrist?'

Pritam took a breath. He could feel Laine's eyes on him, appraising his line of questioning.

'Is it possible that the trauma of losing your best friend as a child, and the trauma of losing your wife as an adult, and the trauma of seeing Laine's husband take his life in front of you just recently . . .' Pritam shrugged and raised his palms. 'You see where I'm going?'

Nicholas looked at Laine. She watched back. Her grey eyes missed nothing.

'Sure,' agreed Nicholas, standing. 'And my sister's nuts, too, and we both like imagining that little white dogs are big nasty spiders because our daddy died and we never got enough cuddles.'

'Your father died?' asked Laine. 'When?'

'Who cares?'

Pritam sighed. 'You must see this from our point of —'

'I'd love to!' snapped Nicholas. 'I'd love to see it from your point of view, because mine's not that much fun! It's insane! It's insane that I see dead people, Pritam! It's insane that this,' he flicked out the sardonyx necklace, 'stopped me kidnapping a little girl!'

'That's what you believe,' said Pritam carefully.

'*That's* what I fucking believe!' Nicholas stabbed his finger through the air at the dead bird talisman lying slack on the coffee table.

Pritam's jaw tightened. 'Please don't swear in my church.'

'IT'S *HER* CHURCH!!' Nicholas snatched up the photo of Mrs Quill and threw it at the photograph of Eleanor Bretherton. 'She paid for it! She owns this place! Do you know why? I don't, but I think it's pretty fucking fishy! And why do you think, despite all those people that *died*, all we have is this crappy pile of *speculation*!' He was spitting out the words. 'Because she's *smart*! She watches and she waits and she takes and she gets away with it because it's insane to think otherwise!'

The air in the presbytery was as sharp and fragile as crystal. Pritam felt as incensed as the first time Nicholas Close was in here. What was it about the man that infuriated him so?

It's because he has no respect for God.

Pritam licked his lips and said softly, 'I think perhaps we should continue this another night when you're a little calmer.'

Nicholas glared at him, then jerked his gaze to Laine.

She looked back evenly, her hands in her lap, expression indecipherable.

'Jesus Christ,' he whispered.

'And don't blaspheme, please,' Pritam said curtly.

Nicholas stood and opened the front door. The roar of rain filled the room.

'I'm sorry. I don't expect you to put aside the real world for this stuff. I'd give my right arm to not believe it.' He looked at Pritam. 'But if you're going to be offended by a couple of words, I don't think you're up for what this is all about. This is murder and black magic. You don't believe in magic? That's fine. I didn't until a few days ago. But if you two have any sense, don't take the risk. Get out of here.'

He closed the door behind him, and the room again fell almost silent.

•

Anyone outside the church would have seen a tall man striding to his car, not caring that his unruly hair was slicked down by the heavy rain, throwing open his car door and angrily wrenching the engine alive. As the car drove away, its tinny burble faded, leaving only the hot skittle spatter of rain on the road. And a small, careful slide of footsteps from the pitch black eaves of the cold stone church.

Were there anyone to see, they'd have watched a small, hunched form step into the rain and look behind itself. Were they close enough, they'd have heard a dry whisper that defied the downpour.

'Go.'

A small white thing the size of a cat stepped from the same shadows with movement too fluid, too wily, for its squat form, before hurrying silently away through the rain.

Anyone watching would have seen the dark, stooped figure stare at the presbytery for a long, long moment, before she turned and hurried away in the direction of Carmichael Road.

Only no one was there to see, and she knew that well.

•

Pritam could hear the ticking of the mantel clock. He settled in his chair with a sigh. 'I shouldn't have let him go.'

Apart from rising to inspect the photograph of Eleanor Bretherton, Laine Boye had hardly moved since she first arrived. Her back was straight, her hands neatly folded in her lap. She watched Pritam.

'Do you believe in magic, Reverend?'

Pritam nodded over at his desk. It was, of course, very tidy: his laptop folded away, his pens capped and sitting in a Daylesford Singers Festival '04 mug. Beside his diary were his Bibles. 'In Act

Eight, Philip goes to the city of Samaria,' he said, 'where a man named Simon was supposedly using sorcery and bewitching the city folk. So, my faith acknowledges magic.'

Laine shrugged. 'No offence, Reverend —'

'Pritam, please.'

'No offence, Pritam, but reading something in the Bible isn't the same as seeing it with your own eyes.'

Quite right. Gavin Boye hadn't married a fool.

'I left India when I was nine,' he said. 'So I don't remember that much about my early years. But my most vivid memory happened, oh, about six months before we left. We'd gone to visit my uncle and aunt in their village near Kirvati. When we got there, the men of the village were holding down a screaming old man and pulling out his teeth with pliers. So much blood. He was a tantric, the old man. A mystic. He had charged five hundred rupee – about fifteen dollars – to advise a young man to kidnap a girl and sacrifice her to the Goddess Durga, who would show him where treasure was secretly buried. The girl was twelve. He cut off her hands, feet and breasts. She bled to death. The young man never found his treasure and went back to the tantric to complain. The police caught him, thank God. But then the villagers tracked down the tantric and pulled out his teeth so he couldn't summon the gods again.'

'That's human violence, not magic,' said Laine. 'All those deaths Nicholas mentioned – more human violence. Even that . . .' She nodded at the headless plover on the table. For the first time, Pritam saw a clear emotion in her eyes: revulsion. '. . . Even that is just an act of human violence.'

She stood and held out her hand. He rose and took it. Her skin was dry and smooth.

'I know your faith mentions ghosts and magic, Pritam. But I'm afraid I just can't believe in either of them. If you speak with Mr Close again, wish him luck. I think he needs it. Good night.'

She collected her umbrella from the stand beside the door, and a moment later she was gone.

•

The rain continued through the night. Storm-water drains in the inner suburbs choked with branches and rubbish and mud, and flooding waters rose. A low-lying commercial block in Stones Corner was inundated: a carpet wholesaler and a car yard both went underwater, and Persian rugs and Mitsubishi Colts bobbed in the rising brown tide.

Birds in trees curled their heads under their wings and clung to branches for dear life. On the river, the last ferry services were cancelled. In expensive houses with private docks, owners old enough to remember the flood of '74 lay in their beds biting their lips and resisting the urge to check their insurance policies.

Pritam set his jaw and unlocked the internal door that led into the church proper. He flicked a switch and the long, vaulting room flickered unhappily into half-light. He fought the need to glance overhead and check that the Green Man wasn't staring back at him through dark, unblinking eyes. Instead, he kept his gaze level and sat in the foremost pew in front of the image of Christ crucified before a strangely lush, tree-studded backdrop, bowed his head and prayed for the souls of lost children. Without knowing when, he slipped from prayer into fitful dreaming.

He was on Calvary, but the hill was devoid of crosses and peppered instead with incongrous trees. One was cleaved through the trunk. He was caught in the crush of it, broken and dying. Eleanor Bretherton was directing a regretful John Hird to saw off Pritam's feet, hands, head. 'It's for Mother Kali, you loafing black tit,' said Hird cheerfully. No one heard Pritam cry out in his sleep, his whimpers echoing down the nave to be quashed by the dispassionate rumble of rain.

•

Laine lay awake, staring at the ceiling, a pillow over her head to block the sound of Mrs Boye berating her dead husband. Although the screech-glass words filtered through, Laine found her mind drifting away from Airlie Crescent, flying on stiffly animated wings to the cold stone church and that dead bird on the coffee table.

When she'd received the call from the police that her husband was dead and she was required to confirm it was his body, she'd refused to identify him by simply looking at the CCTV image of his wedding ring on his cheating fingers. No; she'd insisted on going into that cold room and seeing his face. They'd cleaned him up, removed the blood. But his face was broken and split. Bat-like. Horrible; all trace of his handsomeness sucked away by those bullets. It occurred to her now, as his mother ranted against the rain, that Gavin and the bird he'd muttered about had both lost their heads. Both looked pathetic and hideous in death. Both looked somehow *used*. She fought a surge of bile and rolled over.

•

In his tiny flat, Nicholas sat on his bed staring out the rain-smeared window down Bymar Street at the yawning darkness at the end that was the woods, imagining a million spiders marching silently through the deluge.

22

Hannah Gerlic was dreaming of wings.

In the dream, she was trapped in a cage – a strange, spherical cage made of hard twisted wood, or maybe of bone. She was screaming, but no human noise came out of her mouth. Instead, the sound from her throat was the panicked batting of wings, of terrified birds flapping madly to escape. But the *wap-wap* cry was drowned by the wretched scratchings of a hundred real birds scrambling around her, all squawking and beating, trying to escape the cage. Their claws scratched her neck and face and hands; their beaks drove into the soft flesh of her ears, her thighs, her eyelids; their wings beat her. She screamed and cowered and tugged fruitlessly at the wood-or-bone cage. Suddenly, the beating and scratching and spearing ceased. The birds fell still, electric and listening, claws hooked onto the cage or into Hannah's flesh or hair. Another noise. A tick-tick. A crackling. What was it? It sounded like heating metal, or rain on tin, or . . .

Suddenly, she screamed and the birds took wild wing.

Hannah's eyes flew open.

She was instantly wide awake, and the dream of wings and bones disappeared like a stone dropped in deep water . . . all except the noise. The tick-tick sound. A gentle tapping. Testing.

Hannah was in her bed, and her room was dark. Her Emily the Strange alarm clock said it was 2.13 a.m. (the letters stood for *ante meridiem*). It was raining outside; raining hard. And yet, over the rain, she heard the tick-tick noise. The scratching, tapping, testing sound. She rolled over and looked at the window.

Her stomach did a roller-coaster lurch.

There were spiders on the sill. Hundreds of spiders. Their stiff, black bristles glistening with rain. Each was at least the size of Hannah's hand. They were piled on one another, five or six deep, and they were scratching at the glass and poking their legs into the thin gaps around the frame. Hundreds of bristled black legs were poking, prodding, scratching . . . trying to get in.

Hannah's window was what Mum called double-hung sashes and what Dad called a pain in the arse to paint: two wooden-framed windows, one inside and below the other; the top was fixed, but the bottom one could lift vertically and be held open by hinged supports in the frame. The windows locked with a swivelling brass catch.

The catch was almost undone.

The swivel was barely caught on its stay plate. Just a tap would loosen it and the window would be free to rise. As Hannah watched, a spider pressed against the glass and slipped one long, spiny and graceful leg up between the window frames and patted the catch with its hooked foot.

Without thinking, she leapt from the bed and slammed the catch hard shut, slicing off the spider's leg. Her stomach threatened to gush itself empty over the carpet as she stumbled back to her bed. *Get them! Get Mum and Dad!!* She opened her mouth to shriek.

But before she could, her eyes widened and the scream died in her dry throat.

Something was crawling over the scuttling mass of spiders, shoving them out of its way. It was itself a spider, but a size Hannah thought impossible. It was large as a cat. It shuffled aside its tiny cousins to crouch on the sill. Its ugly nest of unblinking eyes – like enormous drops of glistening black oil sitting in a dense carpet of bristles – seemed to fix on Hannah. The creature's legs were as thick as carrots.

Hannah stared, shaking. *It's huge it's huge it's huge!* It was big enough to simply smash the window in.

As she watched, frozen solid, the huge spider brought one leg before its head and raised its horny foot vertically in front of its curved fangs. The breathing holes beneath its abdomen let out an audible *hiss*.

Oh my God, thought Hannah. *It's shushing me to stay quiet.*

The large spider began scooping the smaller spiders away. The hundreds of legs withdrew from probing the gaps around her window and the spiders fell away. As they did, the giant, feline spider gracefully and silently stepped back and down and out of sight. In just a few seconds, all the spiders were gone. It was as if they'd never been there; as if they'd been a wakeful extension to her nightmare in the cage. Except she could see on the inside sill the hairy section of leg she'd sliced with the catch, lying like a bit of black pipe cleaner. Her bed was shaking. She realised it was her heart pounding.

They were coming to get her. She knew it. Just as she knew that the horrible thing she'd picked up that afternoon – the dead bird that someone had cut up and *changed* – had been left for her and no one else. Her urge was to throw the covers over her head and crawl into a ball.

That won't help! she told herself. This was like those movies on the TV where the idiots did nothing instead of doing *something*, like locking the door or driving away or calling the cops.

Where had the spiders gone? Hannah swung her legs over the bed and padded to the door. There was a brass latch under the handle. She turned it and tried the handle. Locked. Good. But there was a two-centimetre gap under the door. More than enough for the smaller spiders to crawl through.

Then she heard a sound that made the soles of her feet tingle.

A long, low squeak.

The back door was swinging open. They were coming.

She had to wake Mum and Dad and Miriam! Hannah opened her mouth and drew back a deep breath —

No! You yell, and the spiders will have to kill them. They're here for you!

Hannah's eyes began to sting and her vision softened with tears. What should she do?! She looked around for something to shove under the door.

There was a framed picture on the wall; it was a poster of Hermione Granger (whose real name was Emma) and she'd begged and begged her parents for it and agreed to pay it off with her pocket money. The frame was thick plasticky stuff cast and coloured to look like wood; it was as thick as her thumb. She ran to it and took its bottom edge. It was heavy. She strained and lifted. The picture came off its hook suddenly and its weight tipped her backwards. She threw back one foot and dropped her arms, gaining control just before she overbalanced. She turned and staggered to the door.

Black spindly legs were probing through the gap. A row of spiders was hunched there, low on their bellies, starting to crawl under.

Hannah dropped Hermione's picture face down on the carpet, expecting the crash of breaking glass. But it just thudded. *It's Perspex*, she realised gratefully. She slid the painting towards the door. *It won't fit!* she thought wildly. *It's too big! It'll jam on the frame and they'll just crawl right over it and get me and bite me and drag me out the back door and through the rain and down . . .*

. . . to the woods.

The thought of the Carmichael Road woods suddenly drenched her with more terror than the sight of the searching, testing, hairy legs. They were nearly in. She aimed the picture frame square at the door and shoved.

It squashed the spiders back and slid neatly between the jambs with just a couple of millimetres to spare each side. A nearly perfect fit.

Hannah knelt on the floor, eyes wide, breathing hard, suddenly wanting badly to go to the toilet. Rain rumbled on the roof.

Then the picture frame moved.

It slid back into the room a centimetre. Then another. The spiders were pushing it back.

Hannah scampered forward and sat all her weight on the frame.

For a moment, nothing happened. Then, a scratching at the door, and the handle began to slowly twist. First one way. Then the other. Then it jiggled – click, click, click. She could imagine monstrous, thorny feet on the other side pressed hard against the door.

She realised her lip was trembling. She was going to cry.

Stop it. *Stop it.*

The scratching stopped. The door knob ceased moving.

Quiet, except the hushed hiss of rain.

They've gone, she thought. Relief as sweet as cordial flooded through her. *They've gone.*

Then she heard another slow, sly noise down the hall.

The door to Miriam's bedroom was creaking open.

23

Nicholas woke with a splitting headache. He blinked blearily and checked his watch. It was quarter to nine. How had he slept so late? Then he remembered how frustratingly last night had gone. What a fractured quorum he'd convened: an Indian Christian minister, a recent widow arcane as a sphinx, a white witch forced a thousand kilometres away . . . and himself.

Well, it was like the old saying: if you want something fucked up properly, form a committee. That's what he'd done. Who knew how much later into the night Pritam Anand and Laine Boye had kept arguing about whether Quill was alive or dead, whether the murders were connected or coincidence. Nicholas felt a fool for telling them so much.

Fuck them both.

He believed more than ever what he'd said last night: Quill was *smart*. She knew no one in their right mind could believe a woman could live so long, could hide in the middle of a crowded suburb, could get away with so many murders.

He showered swiftly, dressed, slipped on the elder-wood necklace. There was a pay phone outside the shops on Myrtle Street. He needed to see how Suzette was doing.

The world outside felt waterlogged. The torrential rain last night had swelled the gutters to fast-running freshets. The footpaths were wet, and the grass strips flanking them leaked water onto contiguous driveways. Grey clouds massed overhead, pressing down like monstrous fists and threatening to finish work left undone.

Nicholas jingled his pocket – a few coins, enough to phone Sydney and see if Nelson was improving. What if he wasn't? What if he got worse? What if he died? He felt a slow wheel of fear tighten straps in his gut. *Then it will be your fault.*

A car slowed behind him. Then another vehicle slowed and stopped a few steps ahead of him. Police cars. Four doors opened and four officers stepped around him.

'Mr Close?'

Nicholas recognised two of the officers: they'd visited his mother's house the evening the Thomas boy went missing. He smiled without an ounce of fondness.

'Silverback and Fossey. Don't you guys miss Rwanda?'

The officers were unamused.

'Sir, we need to ask you some questions.'

•

Pritam had been up since six.

He'd awoken sore and cold on the pew, and the sight that greeted his eyes was of Christ suddenly sideways, as if God had decided crucifixion was, in fact, a poor fate for his only begotten son and so had uprooted the cross.

Pritam stood, shambled to the presbytery, boiled the kettle. He felt as if he'd had no sleep at all. Sipping tea, he unplugged the telephone, plugged in the modem and switched on the church laptop.

Laine Boye had been right. If one dismissed Nicholas Close's theories, boiled away all the speculation and happenstance, all that was left was one simple coincidence: Eleanor Bretherton looked uncannily like Mrs L. Quill. Pritam wished he could dismiss that as a fluke, but he'd seen John staring at Bretherton's photo and turning pale. That was enough to warrant a bit of effort. He opened Google and started typing.

'Eleanor Bretherton 1880s'.

The search revealed only one unhelpful curiosity: Macmillan had published a book by Mary Ward entitled *Miss Bretherton* in 1885.

He dug deeper. He logged onto and searched the Anglican database. Then he rifled electronically through records at the Registry of Births, Deaths and Marriages. He emailed the Department of Immigration for information on how to secure lists of free settlers from the city's founding in 1859. He searched the State Archives for shipping manifests, cargo allocations, passenger lists.

By a quarter to nine, he had found absolutely nothing.

More tea. A quick piss. Back to it.

'L. Quill, Tallong'. *Search*. Several Quills in several different states. Back to Births, Deaths and Marriages. He guessed a birth year, around 1910, her death around 1995. Several L. Quills, but none the right age, the right gender, the right place. This, he told himself, was not unreasonable: Quill could have been born interstate and died far from home. To search every state's and territory's records could take days. Weeks. It was hopeless.

Nicholas would say that she meant it to be hopeless, he thought.

He made toast, chewed slowly, debated stealing a quick nap. Rain pattered again on the roof and tapped through the trees. *English weather*, he thought. He stopped chewing. An idea crystallised in his mind. English. If Quill *was* as old as Nicholas thought, surely she came from Britain, one way or another. Either freely or . . .

He typed: 'Convict Ships to Moreton Bay'. *Search*.

Three ships. One arrived twice; one three times; one just once. The *Elphinstone*, the *Bangalore*, the *County Durham*. All left Spithead, all docked Moreton Bay.

Pritam clicked *County Durham*. Master: William Huxley. She arrived 2 October 1850, having sailed 144 days. Convicts embarked: male – 154, female – 34; disembarked: male – 147, female – 30.

He clicked the hyperlink and the female convicts' names appeared.

Eighth on the list was 'Quill, Rowena'. 'Trial place: Trim, Meath County. Crime/s: Fraud. Prostitution. Term: Life. Comments: Pardoned 1859.'

Pritam sat back in his chair. He was stunned. A quotation by Flavius Josephus crawled in his skull: 'Now when Noah had lived three hundred and fifty years after the Flood, and that all that time happily, he died, having lived the number of nine hundred and fifty years . . .'

Pritam.

His eyes stung from staring at the screen, but his heart beat excitedly. The printer – he had to find the printer. Nicholas and Laine would need to see this —

Pritam?

He looked up. Was someone calling him? He listened. Only the steady tocking of the clock, the whisper of drizzle. No.

Anyway, the printer. He'd seen it in the storeroom and —

'Pritam?'

He froze. There was someone calling him from outside. He went to the sidelights and peered out. He could see no one. However, the church was on a corner block, so the visitor could be round the front.

'Pritam!' came the voice again. A man's voice, and his tone was urgent. Pritam fetched an umbrella from the hatstand.

'Pritam Anand!'

'Coming!' he called. He struggled to free the umbrella, accidentally pressed its button and it popped open, one rib jabbed him in the shin. *That's bad luck, that.*

'Pritam!'

Who is *that? So familiar . . .*

He opened the door and hurried outside. The rain spat on the umbrella. He walked carefully along the slick path beside tall hibiscus bushes. The voice had come from the road fronting the church. There! He could see a figure on the opposite footpath. The man held an umbrella and leaned on a cane; his shadowed face was unclear through the drizzle.

'Pritam?'

Pritam squinted. The man's stoop was familiar. But it couldn't be . . .

'John?'

Reverend John Hird stood on the other side of the road. He waved the walking cane he held. Beside him was a small suitcase.

'They released me from the hospital! I've been trying to phone, but it's been engaged all morning. Have you been downloading porn, you dirty black reprobate?'

Pritam smiled and frowned simultaneously.

'But, John, you . . . I saw you . . .' Had he dreamed Hird's death? He was so tired, he wasn't sure . . . was this a dream?

'Here!' John waved him over. 'Give me a hand.'

'Okay,' said Pritam, stepping onto the road. 'But I don't —'

The car hit him with a dull and meaty thud, and hurled him up the road. The driver slammed the brakes too hard and the car slid . . . one locked wheel snagged Pritam's leg and ground flesh and bone into the tarmac. Car and victim finally stopped. The rain fell blindly.

The old woman watching from across the road hobbled quickly away.

•

The kitchen smelled sharply of herbs and oils. In small, clean bowls were blue borage flowers, dandelion flowers, plucked waxy ivy leaves. In a glass bowl was maidenhair. In a mortar was a handful of poplar bulbs. Suzette lifted the heavy pestle and started pounding them into a tart, scented paste.

'What are you making?'

Suzette looked up. Quincy was in the doorway.

'I thought you were playing with Daddy?'

Quincy shrugged. 'He fell asleep.'

Suzette nodded. Both she and Bryan were exhausted. They took turns watching over Nelson; neither was game to fall asleep unless the other was awake and watching the rise and fall of his chest. Nelson's colour had improved, and his eyes flickered open from time to time, but he quickly slipped back into a hot, herky-jerky sleep. She and Bryan had made a quiet pact the day Nelson fell ill that they would not worry Quincy. Suzette knew the hex would pass and Nelson would revive, so there was no point making Quincy fearful.

'So, what are you making?' repeated Quincy.

'Elephant paint. To paint elephants with.'

Quincy rolled her eyes. 'It's not elephant paint. We don't have an elephant.'

Suzette smiled. 'Do you want an elephant?'

Quincy thought about it. 'Yes.'

'It would have to sleep in your room,' said Suzette.

'Can't it sleep in yours and Daddy's room? It's bigger.'

Quince, thought Suzette, would make a fine stockbroker. Practical mind.

'No, Daddy's allergic to elephants. It would have to be in your room and your bed.'

Quincy wrinkled her nose.

'No elephants,' she decided.

Suzette nodded – wise decision. She mixed the other ingredients in with the poplar paste. She had woken from her short sleep exhausted and furious with Nicholas, who still hadn't called. Did he give a rat's about his nephew? She'd decided to turn her bright indignation into action, and started this healing mix. Now, how was it applied? She seemed to think it was pasted over the heart and bandaged. Or was it on the temples?

'Pass me that book, sweetie?' She nodded at her kitchen dresser, its shelves loaded with books on herbs, spells and charms; a book on healing herbs was open on the dresser top.

Quincy skipped over, delivered the book, and skipped back to the shelves. She'd never shown the slightest interest in her mother's hobby, but today she was perusing the spines with interest.

'Want me to put on *Dora the Explorer*?' asked Suzette.

Quincy pursed her lips and shook her head. She reached up and pulled out an old book. Suzette watched from the corner of one eye as Quincy opened it. She was a good reader for her age, but this book would be full of words she wouldn't know; it was one of Suzette's father's aged volumes: *Herbs of Old Europe*. It wasn't surprising that it attracted Quincy's eye: its fading cover was dotted with stars and mystic symbols, a fantastical image that belied the utilitarian descriptions inside. It was so dull, in fact, that Suzette had never got more than a quarter way through it.

'Can we have a Pan?' asked Quincy.

'I beg your pardon, hon?'

Quincy turned and said, 'I don't want an elephant. But can we have a Pan?'

Suzette could see she was holding a scrap of paper in her hand. 'Show me?'

Quincy brought the scrap over and handed it up to her mother. Suzette wiped her hand on her apron and took it.

It was half of a page torn from a book that looked like it had gone out of print eighty years ago. In the centre of the page was an etching of a satyr under a night sky, rubbing his hands and capering beside nymphs in a water pond. Suzette blinked – he sported a raging erection. Beneath the picture, most of the caption had been torn away, leaving only 'Pan: Greek god, son of Hermes . . .'

'Can we get one?' asked Quincy again.

Suzette didn't answer. In a small patch of yellowing page between the etching and the torn edge were drawn in ballpoint pen: '???' She had no way of knowing, but she was sure the handwriting was her father's.

'I don't think so,' she said softly.

She folded the paper away and slipped it into her apron pocket. Pan? It must mean nothing, surely; just something that caught his eye and he kept it. But the etching felt so oddly discomfiting. Why did he keep it?

And why did he leave it for us?

'Why not?' asked Quincy. 'They look funny. He's got no pants!'

'I don't think you'd want one, honey biscuit.' She put on a bright smile. 'Come on. Let's put this on your brother.'

24

'Tristram Hamilton Boye! Come in here this *minute!*'

Laine's eyes flew open.

'Where is your brother?' shrieked Mrs Boye. She was in the kitchen, and slammed down a saucepan lid like a cymbal. 'Your father will be home shortly and the carport has *not* been swept!'

Laine rolled slowly out of bed. The double ensemble was one of the few new things in the house – a concession to physical comfort she'd been intractable about when the prospect of moving in with Gavin's mother moved from possible to probable some six months after Mr Boye succumbed to cancer. But now, even the new bed felt tainted. It was an inner-sprung monument to lies, a Petri dish of mendacity she had shared with her faithless husband, and shared now with creeping dreams that flew from light but left harsh scratches and diseased, black feathers. Laine promised herself that, as soon as she could, she would rid herself of this house, this bed, her clothes, her jewellery – everything but the flesh she lived in. She would scrub herself clean and flee to start a new life whose first and only commandment would be: Never let thyself be lied to again.

She sat on the edge of the bed, wondering how much of yesterday – strange yesterday – she had dreamt. The almost ridiculously neat young minister Pritam Anand. The haunted, angry, oddly attractive Nicholas Close. The dead bird. The photographs. A shadowed haberdashery where an ageless woman once kept shop and watched and spun plans . . .

And where now a pretty young woman sold health food, she reminded herself.

My dead husband was one of her customers.

That was exactly the kind of coincidence she'd poured scorn on last night. She pulled back her hair and went to face the crazed force that was her mother-in-law.

She tended to Mrs Boye, gently steering her away from unfocused rage to eat, to bathe, to sit while Laine picked up the telephone and sifted through the bones of a diminishing list of potential live-in carers. Two encouraging interviews were set for the afternoon, and Laine felt satisfied enough to shower, dress, and step into the misty drizzle and walk towards Myrtle Street. It was stupid, it was childish, but she needed to see for herself this young woman from whom Gavin – Gavin, of all people, for fuck's sake – had started buying health food.

The fine rain was cold and held the world closely in a gauzy veil. She tried to avoid the puddles on the footpaths, but her shoes soon squelched and her feet turned icy. A pair of crows huddled on the branches of a tall gum let out a half-hearted protest at her passing. The birds brought back the memory of the miserable dead thing Nicholas Close had placed on the young reverend's coffee table, its limp wings flopping around that bizarre fist of a head.

Laine had been very proud of herself last night. Nicholas Close had talked about ghosts and magic, and woven a bit of a spell himself. He'd sounded so convincing, so logical, so *sad*, that she'd found herself wanting to believe him. But testing prods at his argument had made him angry, and long years with Gavin had taught her that angry, defensive people shared the lousy habit of being wrong.

Ahead, she heard water dripping a monotonous tattoo in some downpipe and the jut-jaw awning of the shop appeared out of the misty drizzle. Closer, she could see the wire frames outside holding the banners for women's magazines and newspapers. One headline read: 'Health Minister Under Fire'. This was the real world. What room was there for magic when Syrian rockets and Israeli smart bombs could snuff a hundred lives in a moment? An overflowing council bin, a nearby car with a flat tyre, dog shit on the nature strip, a ludicrously yellow chip packet that seemed to leap out in the water gloom. Even the shopfront was frank and wonted: Plough

& Vine Health Foods written in a hokey rustic font and flanking a logo of a rustic hand plough and a rustic trellis that combined to give an effect that was, let's face it, rustically ham-fisted and artless. A less magical façade was hard to imagine.

For two long minutes, Laine stood in the drizzle and debated turning around and sloshing home. But the prospect of returning to the twilit house where Mrs Boye shouted at ghosts was a strong disincentive. So, she stepped under the awning to the door of the health food store and went inside.

•

The shop was pleasantly warm, and smelled delicious. Warm pools of light fell on jars of bush honey, open sacks of coffee beans, tantalisingly spiced joss sticks, wooden boxes of fragrant tea leaves. Every step brought an appetising new aroma, a tempting and sapid morsel.

Why haven't I been here before? Laine asked herself. *This is lovely!*

'Are you looking for something in particular?'

She turned to the voice.

Two downlights over the counter flicked on. A slender young woman stepped out from the back room and flipped a switch on the side of the electric till; it beeped and its zeros lit green.

So this is her, thought Laine. The young woman was pretty, but naturally so. She carried herself more like a country girl, pleased with her looks but they didn't factor on her top ten issues of the day.

'Just getting out of the rain, really,' answered Laine.

The woman nodded and smiled warmly. 'You're welcome to browse as long as you like.'

'Thanks,' said Laine. From the corner of her eye she saw the other woman open the till and stock its drawer with notes from a cash bag.

Laine drifted along the shelves, sniffing the lotions, rolling small hessian sacks of beans in her hands, plucking a leaf of rosemary from a sheaf and lifting it to her nose and savouring its autumnal spice. Then she saw the pumpkin seeds.

'They're pretty popular. Have you tried them?' said the woman, shutting the till.

Laine shook her head. 'Just opening?'

'Yeah, late start. I had to . . .' The woman wiped her hands on her jeans and wrinkled her nose. 'Mammogram.' She smiled and shrugged – what can you do?

Laine nodded. 'All okay?'

'Yes, thank God. It's a stress. My mother, she had a double full mastectomy. I don't know how she coped. I guess you just do.'

'Yes.'

'I don't know how I would . . .' She trailed off, then laughed. 'I kind of like mine!'

Laine found herself smiling. 'I hear you.'

This girl is nice, she thought. *She's no husband-stealer.* And as for the old seamstress who Nicholas said had nested here . . . this place was so inviting, so pleasant, it was impossible to imagine.

The woman opened a box of tea tree shampoos and began marking the bottles. 'I mean, it's not like I'm going to have kids, but you never —'

She bit off her last words. Laine watched. Embarrassment bloomed in the other woman's pale cheeks.

'Pardon?' asked Laine. She could see the girl's jaw was tight.

'Nothing.'

Christ, she had some other kind of sickness? Cervical cancer? That would be so cruel, a girl this attractive and young unable to have kids. She touched her shoulder.

'Are you okay? Jesus, I'm sorry. It's none of my business. But is it serious?'

'No, nothing like that. No.'

She gently took Laine's wrist and lifted her hand off her shoulder. Laine found her skin on the underside of her wrist tingling. *How long has it been since anyone touched me there?* The girl kept her eyes on the floor. 'It's a preference thing.'

Laine's eyes widened just a little as she understood. 'Oh.'

The girl nodded and smiled.

Laine kicked herself. Gavin might have tried to crack on to this woman, but it certainly didn't happen the other way round.

'I didn't . . . I wasn't trying to pry,' she said.

'That's okay.'

'Does your . . . your partner must have been relieved your tests were clear.'

The girl put her hands in her pockets. Her blush deepened, then she frowned and laughed. 'I'm . . . I'm not . . . I'm single right now.'

Laine held up her hand – I understand.

'The joys of being out there, huh?'

'Yeah.' She laughed and rolled her eyes in mock despair.

Laine smiled. The girl's eyes were dark brown, the beautiful colour of polished rosewood. 'But, hey,' said Laine, 'this must work as a way to meet people.' She waved at the shop surrounds.

'You'd be surprised how bad, actually.' She laughed again. 'I mean, if I was into threesomes with very hairy vegan couples, this would be paradise. But I like . . . I prefer, you know, more sophisticated women.'

She held her gaze on Laine. Her expression was frank. *Women like you*, it said. But the moment Laine thought she read that, the other woman looked away and got back to her work.

Laine found her heart thudding harder. Was she afraid? She'd never had a woman try to pick her up. Was *she trying to pick me up? Is she just being nice? How do I say no?*

Do *I say no?*

Laine blinked, shocked at her own thoughts, and knocked a packet of caraway seeds onto the floor.

'Sorry!' she said, and stooped to pick it up.

'Don't be silly.' The girl knelt, too. As they stooped, their foreheads tunked together.

'Ow!'

'Oh!'

The girl threw back her head and laughed. Laine smiled wider, rubbing her head. *She's attractive. She has beautiful skin. Beautiful lips. How long since you were kissed? How long since anyone traced their fingers over your belly? Looked at you like* you *were beautiful?*

Laine inhaled through her nostrils. The girl's hair smelled like sandalwood. Exotic. Different. Clean and exciting. And her eyes. Dark brown and deep . . . Laine shook her head as if to clear it. What was she thinking? She'd never found other women attractive. This was ridiculous: the young woman was simply doing her job, being pleasant. *And me? I'm just tired. And yeah, maybe a bit lonely.*

'What's your name?' the girl asked, watching her.

'Laine.'

'Laine.' She said the name slowly, her tongue flicking behind her white teeth, as if tasting it.

Laine felt a small shudder below her navel.

She's seducing me, she thought. *I don't want this.*

Are you sure?

'And yours?' Laine asked.

'Rowena.' She stared at Laine's face, her skin, her eyes. Appraising. Approving. 'Here.' She reached up and gently swept aside the stray hairs over Laine's eyes, pushed them back and swooped them behind Laine's ear. Laine sucked in a breath at the touch of another's fingertips on her temple, her ear, her neck. Laine half-turned her head. *I shouldn't like this. Not from a girl.*

'How's that bump?' Rowena whispered.

She softly took Laine's face in both hands. Her palms were dry and cool. She tilted Laine's face to her own. Her mouth opened slightly and she leaned forward.

'Looks just fine,' she whispered softly, and dropped her eyes to look right into Laine's.

Those eyes, thought Laine. *Beautiful eyes. I could do this. I think I'd like to do this.*

Rowena smiled. Lips apart. White teeth. Red lips.

'Good,' whispered Laine. She leaned forward.

The ringing of her mobile phone was as shrill and sudden as a steam whistle. Laine rocked back in surprise. Rowena's fingers slid on her skin, and one nail caught on her jaw, slicing into the flesh, drawing blood.

'Oh, God!' cried Rowena. 'I'm so sorry.'

Laine jerked back. *What am I doing?!* She felt the burning of the deep scratch on her jaw.

The phone trilled again, insistent. She fumbled into her bag.

'It's fine. Fine.'

'You're bleeding.'

Laine blinked, and raised her fingers to her cheek. They came away lightly dotted with red. Rowena stood and hurried to reach under the counter.

'I'm fine, it's nothing.'

Was I going to kiss *her? What was I thinking?*

Rowena returned with a tissue. 'Here . . .'

She gently reached for Laine's cheek. Laine fought the urge to shrink back from her. Rowena pressed the tissue onto Laine's skin. The scratch pulsed in new pain.

I'm sorry, she mouthed.

Laine forced a smile – forget it – and finally grabbed her phone and hit the green button. 'Hello?'

'Mrs Laine Boye?'

'Ms Boye, yes.'

'Ms Boye. Okay. This is Detective Sergeant Kaye Waller from Police Headquarters. I need to ask you a couple of questions. Is now a good time?'

Rowena frowned as she pulled away the tissue. A flecked line of blood on the white gauze.

'One second.' Laine covered the phone with her hand. 'I'm sorry, I have to go outside and . . .'

Rowena nodded. 'Sure. But come back in and I'll put some pawpaw ointment on that. I'm so sorry . . .'

Laine stepped outside. The door shut behind her. Rain tattled on the awning overhead.

'Sorry. Go ahead.'

'Ms Boye, can I ask you about your movements last night?'

'What's going on?'

'If you could please tell me what you did last night, and the times.'

Laine's heart started thudding again. She turned around.

In the back of the store, Rowena was frowning, hands busily tidying.

'Ms Boye?'

'I went to the Anglican – what do you call it? Parsonage? – here in Tallong about eight or so and was there with Reverend Anand till, I guess, ten?'

The detective asked a few questions to confirm the times, to confirm she drove straight there and back, to confirm what make of car she owned.

'And I have a Nicholas Close here,' said Detective Waller. 'He wants to talk to you.'

Laine looked into the shop. Rowena was out of sight.

'Sure.'

She took the opportunity to slip away into the rain.

•

Nicholas leaned against the cold black granite of the Police Headquarters building, wanting desperately to sit.

Rain was hitting Roma Street so heavily that he wouldn't have been surprised to see the tarmac. Only by pressing himself against the building could he get any cover from the high, clipped-wing awnings. The metal bench seats out front were all exposed to the rain and rang dully as the heavy drops struck them. Nicholas shut his eyes, figuring anyone passing would take him for a swaying vagrant too pitiful to charge.

For the last half-hour, he'd been trying not to watch a middle-aged man on the footpath in front of him reel under a barrage of invisible punches, fall to the ground, heave and jerk as he was struck by unseen kicks to his kidneys, his groin, his head. The man's face was white and wide with terror and, under the steady bombardment of ethereal steel-tipped toes, caved in and bloodied. His eyes came out. His jaw snapped. His fingers bent and their bones broke through skin. Gradually, he stopped his voiceless wailing, spasmed briefly, and was still. Then there was a silent edit in the spool of his death and he was suddenly swaying whole and seemingly drunk beside the steel bench in front of Nicholas, his ghostly clothes dry despite the downpour . . . and the grisly replay of his murder began again.

Nicholas was too exhausted to lift his feet and find another spot to wait. It was now well after eleven. His hour and a half in the police building had been almost solid questioning, punctuated with short breaks when the detectives left him alone. He supposed the pauses were designed to allow him to panic and consider confessing. Instead, they gave him time to divine from the questions what might have happened to Hannah Gerlic's sister, Miriam.

Detective Waller and a male detective had tag-teamed the interview. Each asked slow, deliberate sets of questions: some were repeated over and over; some were rephrased or amalgamated with others; some came out of the blue to catch him off guard. Nicholas's favourite had been: 'Why did she take your cigarettes?' He'd chewed over the cleverness of that while he leaned against the ice-cold wall, recalling how carefully Waller had watched his response. 'I never saw her,' he'd replied truthfully. He supposed Waller had been hoping for 'I don't smoke' or better yet, 'I don't know, but the little bitch has still got 'em'.

'When you picked up Hannah Gerlic, was she alone?' Waller had asked.

'Yes.'

Nicholas guessed that this was unusual and Hannah habitually walked home with Miriam.

'What were the two girls arguing about?' asked Waller.

'Hannah never spoke to me.'

The girls were having a fight. That explained their separation.

'Was Miriam still in her school uniform when you dropped Hannah home?'

'I never saw Miriam.'

Miriam had made it home after school, but she'd gone missing afterwards – sometime through the night.

'You say you were at the presbytery with Reverend Anand and Laine Boye. Till when?'

'I don't know. Ten or so.'

'Did you drive straight home?'

'Yes.'

'Did you stop at any shops? Petrol station? Parks?'

'No.'

He was left alone in the room then for a quarter of an hour, before Waller came in again, as friendly as if they'd never laid eyes on one another.

'You're free to go, sir. There's a taxi rank in the Transit Centre across the road.'

Without realising why, he'd asked her to phone Laine Boye.

And so now he was hugging the police building's front wall, trying to stay dry. He lifted his fingers to his neck. The wooden beads felt warm. His back against the stone felt frozen.

Eventually, to his surprise, Laine arrived.

•

The car's tyres hissed on the road. Nicholas slumped in the passenger seat. They drove in silence for a long while. He looked at Laine. Her eyes were as grey as the sky.

'How do you feel?' he asked.

Laine glanced at him. A flash of . . . what? Self-consciousness?

'What do you mean?' she replied.

'I mean, how do you feel?'

The rainy-day traffic was stop-start and the cars inched ahead like cattle towards a crush. She didn't answer, so he spoke again.

'There are nights I still dream that Cate is lying beside me. And then I wake up. And at that moment when I . . . remember . . . I feel like I feel now. Heavy.' He watched the rainy world sliding idly by. 'Like if you laid me on the ground I'd just sink into the earth.'

Laine drove, grim-faced.

'I used to feel like that,' she said. 'Then Gavin killed himself.'

He looked back at her. Her profile was strong and fine. Hers was a face out of antiquity, anachronistic. She should have been born in a city of Renaissance sculptors, or the daughter of some Pharaoh, not today when culture was a thousand hits on YouTube. No wonder she was always angry.

As if feeling his gaze, she turned suddenly to face him. 'Did you love her?' she asked. 'Cate?'

Nicholas nodded. 'Very much.'

Laine lifted her chin. 'You said last night that you can see . . .' She hesitated. 'That you see ghosts. Did you ever see her? Cate? After she died?'

Nicholas was quiet. For some reason, this seemed deeply personal, like a new lover's questions about past partners. He didn't want to answer. But his tongue betrayed him. 'Yes.'

Laine drew a long breath through her nostrils. 'You must be so sad.'

He thought about that. 'I'm not sad. I'm angry.'

Laine smiled. 'I was angry. Now I'm sad.' She flicked on the indicator. 'Aren't we a pair?'

The car turned onto Coronation Drive, and their speed picked up.

'Where am I taking you?' she asked.

Before he could think why, he answered, 'The church.'

She nodded, checked her mirrors and changed lanes. As she turned, Nicholas saw a small cut on her cheek.

'What happened to your face?' he asked, and guessed: 'Mrs Boye?'

'Yes.'

Her tone said the talking, for now, was over.

●

Outside the church, a group of middle-aged and elderly men and women huddled under umbrellas, hardly moving, heads turning this way and that. To Nicholas they looked like a team of mallard ducks – dignified and vulnerable. Their heads all followed Laine's car as it slowed and stopped. He would have been unsurprised if they'd sprouted wings and fled, honking forlornly. He wound down his window. 'Hi. The rectory's around the side.'

An old man with a long face and wide, hairy nostrils looked down at him. 'We do know.'

Nicholas shook his head – then why . . . ?

'The reverend is dead, and his replacement is in hospital.'

'Who?' asked Nicholas. 'Pritam? Reverend Anand's in hospital?'

An old woman with sagging wattles looked at him as if he were a fool. 'Do you know any other replacement? We're discussing what to do.'

Nicholas looked at Laine.

At that moment, Laine's grey eyes rolled back in her head and she sank into her seat.

25

Hannah Gerlic sat in her beanbag stroking Swizzle. The cat's girth was growing in direct proportion to his unwillingness to go outside. Hannah liked his warmth on her lap. If she thought about nothing but the immediate task of scratching behind Swizzle's ears and keeping the rumbly motor inside him purring, things were okay.

Her bottom hurt where her father had hit her for lying. Just thinking of how his face had been a twisted fist at once so angry and terrified made her want to start crying all over again.

She had been dragged up from the depths of ugly sleep by motion, sliding. She'd opened her eyes and looked right up into the pale, angry, scared face of her father – a man whose soft features were usually buried in a book or newspaper or smiling over his wife's shoulder while they danced in their pyjamas – a sight that made their daughters roll their eyes. This morning her father took a moment to process the empty bed, the picture frame on the floor, his youngest daughter blinking sleepily on it, before whispering, 'Where's your sister?' The memory of the spiders tumbled back as heavily and hard as stones off a tip truck, and Hannah started to bawl. Her father asked her again and again until Hannah finally stuttered through sobs, 'The spiders took her.'

Before she could explain that she'd had no choice, that if she'd let them in she'd be dead too, or if she'd screamed he and Mum would be, her father smacked her. Hard. And stalked out of the room.

Hannah hung around in a distant orbit as her parents set fire to the morning with raging phone calls, storming to the car and screeching away, storming back, standing at the door and yelling for Miriam. The fire died and became something quiet and tight-lipped. When Hannah heard her name mentioned, it was quickly snapped up by her father hissing something about 'ridiculous dreams'.

It *was* ridiculous that a black, silent army of spiders would come in the dead of night to steal one girl and, bested, would take her older sister. But it was true. So Hannah sat in the beanbag, nursing Swizzle and her still-stinging bum, trying not to think about what had happened to Miriam after the spiders got her. She was still in her beanbag when the police came. When the lady police officer came over and asked Hannah if she'd heard any funny noises in the night, Hannah knew she would be a fool to say anything but 'No'.

Miriam was dead. Hannah searched inside herself for the smallest feeling that disagreed, but found none. Miriam was gone. And if it hadn't been Miriam, it would have been her. The fact that she was so relieved not to have been taken by the spiders and cocooned up alive and screaming to be bitten and poisoned and sucked dry or whatever else spiders did made her feel guilty and even glummer. Something had tried to get her yesterday, leaving the horrible dead bird disguised as a crystal unicorn. It had failed, and instead had taken Miriam to the woods.

As Hannah sat, her lap warmed by Swizzle and her buttocks by the hot sting of a hard slap, surrounded by a buzz of men and women in blue and her parents clenching each other's hands, she realised what she had to do.

She couldn't bring Miriam back. But she could kill whatever had taken her.

26

Nicholas sat on the toilet. He thought if he could sit there long enough, he could get back enough composure to find his way out. Then his stomach heaved again. He rolled onto his knees just in time and a thin stream of amber bile gushed into the bowl. He gripped the stainless-steel rail beside the pedestal as he vomited.

'Fuck it,' he whispered.

Time to go out.

He didn't want to go. It was horrible. But he knew he had to.

He got to his feet, wiped his mouth with some paper towel, and unlocked the toilet door.

Dead floated by like bodies on the sea after a tsunami. They rolled by on invisible gurneys, some thrashing wildly, some almost motionless; some choked silently, arched like fragile bridges, some sobbed with pain. They rolled to and fro between the curtained bed bays of the Emergency ward.

Nicholas felt his knees threaten to give way.

'Help you, mate?' asked a harried male nurse.

'Lai—' Nicholas swallowed back a stubborn mouthful of gorge. 'Laine Boye?'

'Bed twelve.'

Nicholas nodded thanks. An old woman suddenly lurched in front of him, pulling on catheter lines in her arm that had been binned who knew how many years. She fell gracelessly to the floor, looking up at Nicholas, before unseen hands scooped under her thin shoulders and dragged her into a nearby cubicle, depositing her on a small, shifting sea of overlapping ghosts. In their midst, an unshaved patient chewed thoughtfully as he read a newspaper. Feeling Nicholas's eyes on him, he peered over the paper's edge.

'You right?'

Nicholas nodded stiffly and hurried away.

Laine lay on the trolley bed in bay twelve. A saline drip line snaked into her arm. Monitor leads were attached like lampreys to her upper chest. A red-glowing plastic thing was attached to one long-fingered hand like some electrified leech. About her drifted a fog of overlapping ghostly bodies.

Nicholas fought the electric urge in his legs to flee.

'Yes, sir?'

A round, black African nurse bowled into the bay, not looking at Nicholas as she quickly grabbed Laine's chart, scanned it, then went to check the rate on the drip.

'I brought her in,' he replied.

'You her husban'?'

Laine's face was placid, unmindful of the misty sea of death floating around her. Again, Nicholas was struck by the classical lines of her cheeks, her eyes. *This is how Orpheus must have found Eurydice, asleep beneath a shifting veil of spirits . . .* but perhaps without the blurts of rough laughter from the medicos' fishbowl office in the middle of the ward. Again, he noticed the fingernail-fine scratch on her cheek.

What happened to your face? Mrs Boye?

Yes.

She'd lied. Quill had done this. But how? When?

'No,' he answered.

'Relative?'

Nicholas shook his head.

'Uh-huh,' said the nurse, suspicious.

An idea occurred to Nicholas. He reached to his neck and unclasped the elder-wood and sardonyx necklace.

'She wanted this. Can I put it on her?'

'No.'

'It means a lot to her,' he said.

'Then why in' she wearing it already?' The nurse glanced at the rough necklace, then fixed Nicholas with a humourless, don't-waste-my-time arch.

'Fine. Can you give it to her for me?' he asked.

The nurse watched him for a moment, sighed far too loudly, then held out her hand.

He dropped the necklace onto her light brown palm. As its touch left his skin, the world suddenly lurched and he staggered. He heard a rustling in his ear, a high-pitched squeal like a million cicadas trying to burrow into his skull. The bay and the nurse swam out of focus.

'Sir?'

'Feeling . . .'

The nurse pressed the necklace back into Nicholas's palm and shut his fingers over the wood and stone. The world steadied, leaving only the aching weariness.

The nurse was watching him anxiously with careful eyes. 'I think you need it much as her.'

She looked away and wouldn't meet his eyes again.

'Nurse?'

She hesitated beside the bay's front curtain, anxious to be gone.

'Can you tell me where Intensive Care is?' he asked.

'Take the lifts to five,' she said, and lifted her meaty arms to wave him out of the ward as if he were an evil smell.

•

Pritam was in a closed ward sealed with glass. An oxygen tube fed under his nose. A neck brace held his face rigid, and a web of stainless-steel frames hovered over his body. To Nicholas, he was a rock in a squally sea, lying motionless as men and women surged around him silently: jerking, vomiting, dying, lapping into one another like morbid smoke. There were so many that they were a blur, but through the thrashing haze Nicholas saw their eyes – dozens of eyes – watching him.

His heart beat fast and his neck grew hot.

I'm going to faint, he thought.

Just go. Pritam won't know.

The duty nurse walked past and Nicholas asked her in a voice that, he hoped, sounded more upset than selfishly miserable how Reverend Anand was doing. She explained that the operation to repair a split renal artery had been successful, and he would be in theatre again tomorrow morning to set his pelvis, left leg and two breaks in his clavicle. A CT scan had revealed a minor swelling of the brain that was being monitored.

The nurse left, and Nicholas fixed his gaze on a spot in the corner where no dead seemed to accrete. He stared at it, thinking.

Quill. She's done this without raising a sweat. As Suzette said, she's divided us. And divided, and divided. What a joke. What a fool I was to think we could do anything.

And Miriam Gerlic was dead; he was grimly certain of it.

Pritam opened his eyes and blearily looked around.

Nicholas called a nurse. Through the glass, he watched her enter Pritam's small room and speak with him, asking basic questions. Can you tell me your name? Do you know where you are? Do you know what day of the week this is? Do you remember what happened? Pritam's eyes wandered across the trelliswork of steel supporting him, over the ceiling, down to the glass and finally found Nicholas. His mouth moved, and the nurse pursed her lips. She reluctantly waved Nicholas inside.

He didn't want to go, but his legs shuffled him in.

'You can stay for a minute,' said the nurse, stumping out. 'The doctor's on his way.'

Nicholas looked down at Pritam. The young reverend's normally brown face was as pale as milk. He raised his eyebrows.

'Lazy bastard,' said Nicholas. 'Hell of a way to get out of Sunday service.'

Pritam smiled. His eyes stayed on Nicholas. They twinkled like night stars under the shifting layers of heaving, gasping, weightless dead.

'It was John,' he whispered. 'But it wasn't John.'

Nicholas shook his head slowly – I don't understand.

'John called me over the road,' croaked Pritam. 'But John's dead. It was Quill.'

The name hit Nicholas like a wave of frosted air.

'Laine's in here, too,' he whispered.

Pritam's eyes closed and he took a rattling breath. 'How?'

Nicholas shook his head again, and shrugged. 'And Hannah Gerlic's sister is missing.'

Pritam's eyes rolled up to the ceiling. *Is he talking to God?* Nicholas wondered. *Begging? Interceding?* The reverend's eyes slid back to Nicholas; Pritam was fighting to stay awake.

'Key under . . .'

'I can't hear you, Pritam.'

'. . . key under the mat,' he whispered.

Nicholas understood. At the presbytery. 'Oh, that's clever.'

Pritam gave a weak smile.

'Computer. Last search.' He licked his dry lips. ''kay?'

Nicholas nodded.

Pritam's eyes folded shut. He sank back under his shroud of writhing ghosts.

Nicholas watched the steady rhythm of the coloured lines on the monitor. He departed as fast as he could.

•

It took the taxi driver three-quarters of an hour to negotiate the rain-worried traffic and get to the Tallong Anglican Church. On the way, Nicholas dozed.

'We're here,' said the cabbie.

Nicholas paid with a credit card. As the cab drove away, he looked at the road where Pritam had been hit this morning. There wasn't the tiniest sign anything had happened. *And that is how she works. Accidents and scapegoats. Even her murders are neatly explained and easily forgotten.*

The presbytery key was, indeed, under the rubber and coir mat. Nicholas entered. A half-cup of cold tea rested beside the computer; the screensaver scrolled shots of sunsets, mist over placid ponds, light streaming through trees, silhouettes of praiseful people on cliff tops arching to the heavens. He touched the mouse. 'Connection timed out' read a message box. He shut it and clicked the 'refresh' arrow. The modem whistled.

He stared as the page updated.

The manifest from the *County Durham*. Female convicts. Eighth on the list was Rowena Quill.

Nicholas sat heavily and for a long while did nothing.

'Rowena,' he whispered to himself.

What a fool. As much a fool as Gavin Boye. As Elliot Guyatt. Sucked in and played like a fiddle. A pretty smile and a laugh and he'd been chumped.

He unplugged the modem and rang Suzette.

•

Suzette made sure Quincy wasn't in the room before she hissed, 'Are you sure you don't want to fucking wait a few more days and call back then?'

Her brother astonished her with an apology.

Then he stunned her into aching silence with his news. He told her about finding Hannah Gerlic outside the woods. About the plover with the rune head. The meeting with Pritam and Laine. His detainment by police. Discovering Pritam was shattered like a hated toy in hospital, and Laine collapsing into a slumber like Nelson's.

Suzette realised she could see the pulse in her wrist hammering like a tiny creature trapped under her skin.

'A cut on her cheek?' she asked. 'How, do you think?'

Then he told her what he'd found on Pritam's computer. That in 1850 a female convict transported from Trim, Meath County, arrived here, and her name was Rowena Quill.

'Rowena,' said Nicholas quietly. 'The name of the young girl in the health food store is Rowena.'

Suzette sat down heavily. 'Oh,' she whispered.

Neither said anything for a moment.

'How's Nelson?' Nicholas asked.

'Okay. Still sick, still . . .' Her voice sounded as dry as paper. 'I don't know, Nicky. I think she's keeping the pressure on.'

'Will he be okay?'

She nodded, then realised he couldn't see that. 'I think so. Hey, are you wearing your necklace?'

'Yes.'

'Then keep it on. Keep it on and catch a cab to the airport and fly down here. A strategic retreat. Fly down and we'll make a plan. We'll figure out a way to get Mum down, too.'

'I'll think about it,' he said.

'Nicky —'

But she was left listening to electric space. He'd hung up.

27

The walk to the Myrtle Street shops was the most exhausting of Nicholas's life. Every step felt nightmarishly slow, as if he were wading through tar. By the time he was near, all he wanted was to collapse and fold into a black sleep.

The thought that *she* was in there kept him moving.

The rain had slowed, but oyster-coloured clouds still mumbled darkly and low, and the hills in the west were hidden by a grim curtain of heavier rain approaching.

Muddy ruts cut by the postman's motorcycle ran through the grass of the footpath. As Nicholas's eyes wandered over the hacked, intersecting tracks, his leaden feet slowed and stopped. At one point the wheel marks diverged from the deeper track and ran out in a V to a letterbox and back. A line flanked with an arrow. Thurisaz.

Distant screams made him look to the sky.

A flock of birds turned overhead, their wings winking black topsides and grey undersides at him as they wheeled, so they were one moment a cloud of almost invisible grey flecks, the next a dark flash of black in the sky. There and gone. Visible, invisible. Dark, light.

Without thinking, Nicholas knelt and pushed his index and middle fingers into the mud. It was cold. With his left hand he lifted his jumper, exposing his white chest to the chill. With his muddy fingers, he drew on his chest a vertical line and then a truncated diamond off its side.

He looked at the sky. The birds flew over the green and red tin rooftops and away. He lowered his shirt, washed his fingers in the gurgling gutter, and stepped under the heavy-lidded awning of the Myrtle Street shops.

•

'Hi,' he said.

Rowena looked up from a vitamins catalogue. She wore a plain shirt and jeans. She smiled. 'Hi, yourself.'

Nicholas nodded, wiped his feet on the mat, shut the door, and slid the catch that locked the deadbolt. He turned back to Rowena.

She frowned, the smile still caught on her face like an afterglow. 'What are you —'

'*County Durham*,' he said.

She watched him for a long moment. Then she lifted her shoulders in a curt shrug. The change was subtle and horrifyingly fast. The sunny innocence that lit her pretty face was suddenly switched off as if its power cable had been severed. An invisible mantle fell over her pretty features, making them somehow sharper, more feline. More sleek and womanly and knowing. She stood up. Her brown eyes seemed to grow wider, darker. She smiled.

'That was a long time ago,' she said. An accent, now: an Irish lilt.

Nicholas looked around. 'Where's Garnock?'

Rowena smiled wider. She wasn't just pretty. She was beautiful. Pale and long and slender and beautiful.

'Away,' she replied. 'Your friend was here this morning. She's attractive. Less so now, but cuts heal.'

'Tell Dylan Thomas that. Tell Tristram Boye that.'

Rowena cocked her head and watched him.

Nicholas suddenly wondered what the hell he was going to do. He felt vulnerable, and wondered if locking the door wasn't a mistake.

'I'm surprised you're here,' she said, and stepped around the counter to lean on it. 'And pleased.' She uncrossed her ankles and placed her feet a hand width apart. Her legs were long and her jeans were tight. He looked into her eyes. They sparkled like polished chestnut.

'You've done some work on me,' he said. 'On my nephew. On Pritam Anand.'

Rowena raised her eyebrows coyly, a compliment taken. She reached to the shelf behind the counter, her arms lifting her shirt high so it revealed a section of tight belly and pressed the thin cotton against her breasts. He could see she wore no bra. He felt himself hardening. She found what she wanted and straightened; in her hand was a small wooden box. She opened it, but its lid disguised its contents from his view. She smiled at him over the box and his breath caught. Earlier today he'd thought Laine's profile was classical, but Rowena's smile sent a jolt through him, starting behind his eyes and travelling like warm fire down to his groin. It was a smile that promised a knowledge of flesh, of deep shiftings. He understood now how Helen's face had launched a thousand ships.

Rowena dipped her finger in the little casket and withdrew it – wet and sparkling.

'Did you think I didn't know you'd be back?' she whispered.

She brought her glistening finger to her mouth. Eyes narrowing with pleasure, she watched Nicholas as her tongue slipped, pink and wet, from between her white teeth and slid up the length of her finger to its tip. There, it lingered, the fingertip nestled on the fold of her tongue . . .

'I was counting on it,' she murmured.

Then she pursed her red lips and blew towards Nicholas.

Instantly, the weariness left him. His muscles flooded with warmth. His heart thudded. His penis swelled hard as steel.

'I enjoyed you following me the other evening,' she crooned. 'Walking, knowing you were behind me. Feeling your eyes on my neck, my back, my legs.'

She smiled around her finger, returned the box to its shelf. Her shirt rose to reveal the cream skin of her waist.

'I didn't much like the charade of catching the bus.' She smiled, turning back. 'But it was fun to play the part.'

She slid her feet just a little wider apart.

'Have you asked yourself, Nicholas,' she whispered, 'why you're not in hospital, too?'

Nicholas was shaking. His body was vibrating, fully alive. He wanted to stride over to her, rip down her jeans, rip off her shirt.

No.

'I needed your help with the little girl's sister, and you didn't help me . . .' She smiled, mildly censuring. Her fingers reached for the buttons of her shirt. She undid the bottom one, the next, the next, exposing a triangle of perfect, pale flesh.

'Naughty, unhelpful man.'

She undid the second to top, and then the last button.

Nicholas took a step forward. His legs were shuddering. His cock hurt, straining against his pants. Her fingers idled up to her lapels, then slid the shirt off. Her breasts were full and high, nipples brown and hard. Her mouth opened. Her neck was long.

'Take off your necklace,' she whispered.

'No.' But his hands went up behind his neck. 'No,' he repeated more weakly. His fingers undid the clasp. The wood and stone necklace clacked as it hit the floor.

Get out! he shouted in his head. His muscles jerked. One foot took another step towards Rowena. He needed her. He needed to be inside her young, tight flesh.

Rowena smiled, and ran her hands across her shoulders, over her breasts, down her flat belly, down her jeans. She slipped off one boot, then the other. Her eyes were locked on his.

'You don't see what the others see, Nicholas. When you were a little boy, you found the wee bauble I left for you. Not how I wanted you to see it, but as it was.' She shrugged, and he watched her breasts shift. 'But you showed it to your friend, so . . .'

She licked her teeth and lifted her fingers slowly to undo the top button of her jeans.

'. . . so, when your mother came in to have your school badges sewn on, I asked her about her boy. And found out your birthday. Your special birthday.'

She undid the second and last button of her jeans.

Every tendon in Nicholas's body was taut and singing like bridge cables. His foot shuffled closer. He throbbed.

'That's when I chose you,' she whispered.

She slid her jeans down. Her thighs were pale and slender, her skin tight and unblemished, a tightly cropped nest of blonde on her pubic mound. She stepped out of the jeans and leaned back, placing her palms on the counter. She looked at Nicholas.

'Now,' she said.

He stepped to her.

Her hands flew like clever birds and unclasped his belt. Her chin raised and her eyes, wide and dark and hungry, ate his. Her lips were wet. She released him from his pants, hard and straight. She looked at his length: it pulsed with his racing heart.

'Aaah,' she hissed, and lifted her face to his.

Nicholas leaned in, to consume her, to fill her. His lips touched hers.

That instant, a torrent of revulsion tumbled through his veins – from his lips to his neck down his arm down his spine down his legs into his fingers into his penis. His eyes flew open.

She was hideous.

The skin of her face was grey and flecked with liver spots, heavily wrinkled and scarred. Her breasts were two flaccid sacks hanging over a puckered belly that looped on itself, pale and fishlike and splotched. Her legs were deeply creased twigs, bowed and knobby. Her skin hung off her shoulder bones like diseased hide hung over horns. Her eyes were shut in ecstasy, mouth wide and gums wet.

Nicholas gagged. And then saw the sly movement: she waved her gaunt fingers in a swift, dismissive gesture.

A spider as large as a saucer unfolded itself from its hiding place on her drooping mons veneris. It slunk around her slack waist to crouch patiently on the countertop. She spread her legs wider.

'GOD!' cried Nicholas, and hurled himself backwards.

Rowena Quill jumped, her baggy eyes flying open.

Nicholas retched and stumbled back again. His body shook. His erection fell like a dropped handkerchief.

'Nicholas?' she croaked, confused.

He groped for the deadlock.

Understanding dawned in the old hag's eyes.

'You fecker,' she hissed, and took a shambling step forward. Her clawed feet caught on her pooled jeans and she stumbled.

His fingers were wet with cold sweat and slipped on the chrome of the lock. Once. Twice. *Come on!*

Quill righted herself and walked towards him.

'You sneaky little feck,' she said, her accent thick and her voice as dry as ash. 'You refuse me and you will rue it!'

His thumb slid over the nub of the latch. She stepped closer, and the spider eased down off the counter and stole up behind her, climbing the spotted skin of her spindly legs to perch on her shoulder. She paid it no mind; her eyes were dark with hate and fixed on Nicholas.

'I've had your mickey in me hand and I'll have it where I please!' she croaked.

He could see every one of her hundred and eighty-odd years hanging off her like vapid curses.

'You get it in me, or your friendly widow will fess to the wee girl's killin'!'

She moved fast, her hand whipping up like a snake. It grabbed his shirt and tore it open. She saw the mud rune there and let out a furious, animal gurgle.

'Garnock!' she shrieked.

Nicholas whipped his head up.

From around the corner of the storeroom, a long, unlikely leg thick with dark bristled hairs stepped. Then another. Garnock eased itself noiselessly into the room. Its eight round, black eyes, alien and rimmed with bristle, all seemed locked on Nicholas. The smaller spider leapt from Quill's shoulder and jumped around Garnock like a puppy.

Nicholas looked down at the crone. Her eyes were dark and round and as inhuman as the spider's.

'Open that door, boy, and there'll be all Christ to pay.'

Nicholas changed hands and undid the lock – he fell outside. He slammed the door shut.

'AUUUGH!!' Her cry of fury tore the air like plates breaking. 'Garnock-lob!'

Nicholas stumbled and ran, cock flapping in the cold air. He looked over his shoulder. The door flung open and the giant spider landed deftly on the tiles under the awning. It crouched, turned, and locked its orb eyes on Nicholas. Its fangs slid out and up, large as butter knives, as the chelicerae that bore them engorged: a horrifying, twin parody of Nicholas's own recent erection. The horn-black fangs were moist. Garnock hunched to pounce.

A thin stream of piss slid out of Nicholas. The edges of his vision swirled silver.

Don't faint. You only get one shot.

He steadied his left foot, and drew his right back . . .

The spider leapt. So fast!

Nicholas twisted and kicked.

His boot connected with the hard, hairy plate of Garnock's underbelly. Pain rocketed through Nicholas's leg as a muscle over-stretched to tearing. But the hideous spider flew up and over the rail under the awning. With a meaty *thack* it landed on its back, and scraped its legs like a dropped goat, scrambling painfully to right itself.

Nicholas turned and ran like hell.

•

Dusk settled like a darkening fog over Tallong. The pleasant, narrow streets emptied of playing children; the evening was too brisk for games. Streetlights winked on, cheerful baubles along avenues that huddled down in comfortable, lazy nests of old trees and old houses. A jogger in shorts and a sloppy joe pounded up the undulating streets, his breath pistoning in and out in small, steamy puffs that were tugged from his billowing cheeks by a stiffening breeze. Men and women in warm jackets walked smiling dogs.

The sight of the old woman walking along Ithaca Lane was unremarkable except for two things. She kept her chin high despite the chilly evening air, walking proudly, aware that she'd once been a lovely thing and perhaps willing that prettiness to linger through her poise. The other was that, where others walked their dogs on leashes, she carried her tiny white terrier in her arms. Which of these two things caught the eye of the driver, we'll never know. But whichever it was, he slowed and stopped in front of her.

'Excuse me?' he said. His name was Miles Kindste. He would be dead in just a few hours. A bachelor, he would be missed most of all by the proprietor of the local video store where he was a regular patron.

The old woman looked over, feigning with great skill a little flutter of alarm at being spoken to by a strange gentleman.

'It's okay,' said Miles Kindste. 'Your dog. Did it get hit or something?'

The old lady blinked.

'Yes,' she replied. 'I didn't see it, but I heard the car drive off, and . . .'

Miles Kindste was certain she was crying, but the evening was now becoming dark and it was hard to tell. He suspected the dog was this lady's sole companion, and he was right to an extent.

'Well, can I give you a lift? To the vet? Or home?'

'Oh, dear man,' said the old lady. 'That would be wonderful.'

Miles Kindste smiled, perhaps feeling a small wave of warmth at the goodness of the deed he was about to do. He opened his car door on his last evening on earth.

28

Getting her out proved disturbingly easy.

Nicholas gave the cabbie a fifty and asked him to wait in the hospital carriageway, then he hurried inside. He simply took hold of one of several wheelchairs sitting idle in the corridors, and went to Laine's ward. He loitered out front until the duty nurse stepped from sight, then wheeled the chair to Laine's bedside.

Her face, normally light olive, was pale. Her eyes were closed and her breaths were shallow and slow. Nicholas went to the trolley at the far wall and hunted through its plastic drawers for adhesive tape, then withdrew the drip in Laine's arm. He was about to bandage over the pinhole the needle left, but was arrested by the large, ruby red drop that swelled out of the wound. A sphere: round and perfect and thick. A certainty appeared in his mind, whole and clear. He knew what to do.

He lifted Laine gently and slid her gown over her shoulders and down her chest, exposing her breastbone, stopping just above her small breasts. He dipped his fingertip into the large drop of blood on her arm and drew on the skin of her sternum a vertical line with a half-diamond attached. He looked at it critically, then used the little bit of blood remaining to tidy up the lines, making them equally thick. Satisfied, he tidied her gown and put the sticking plaster over the puncture on her bruised forearm.

She was surprisingly light. He placed her in the chair, put her feet on the rests, wrapped a blanket around her torso and wheeled her out. The cab was still waiting. It had taken less than ten minutes to kidnap an unconscious woman from a busy ward of a public hospital. *Something for the résumé,* he thought glumly, and asked the cabbie to take them to Lambeth Street, Tallong.

•

Night.

Spiders were busy spinning webs between pepper trees and devil's apples.

Overhead, rain was brewing. A few scout drops fell on the shingled roof of the old cottage and rolled down to the edge to perch precariously above a rambling herb garden: rich thickets of hops, chickweed, lovage, tonka beans, high john, marigold and coltsfoot.

Inside the cottage, a naked man lay on his back near a flickering fire. Miles Kindste's eyes were open and daft, staring at nothing. His breath eased in and out in a slow, opiated rhythm. His erection was thick. Blood oozed from a neat, deep cut in the webbed flesh between the big toe of his right foot and its neighbour. His eyes couldn't see or his mind couldn't register that a spider the size of a possum sat on a blanket in the corner of the dark room.

A figure stepped out of the cottage, stooped but spry. She wrapped a scarf around her head against the cold rain, and started along the flagstone path through the herb garden. Though the clouds were snuffing the last light from the night sky, were anyone close enough they'd see that her expression was as hard as flint.

The path she took meandered through stands of hawthorn and blackberry towards a ring of trees: twenty-four weeping lilly pilly planted in a wide circle, tall and beautiful. Carved low in the trunk of each was a different arcane symbol. The old woman stepped off the flagstones and around the outside of the circular grove till she found the tree she sought. She stroked its trunk with tenderness. Then she reached to her belt and, with a whisper, unsheathed a sharp stiletto. She cut a finger-thick branch off the tree, then stepped into the circle.

The ring was some ten metres wide. Its surface was sandy dirt kept meticulously clear of weeds. Within the ring were many things, but four were significant: three were posts forming a triangle; the fourth was in the triangle's centre. It was a low column, thigh high and the same wide, made of vertically set branches held fast by woven twigs. On this basket-like pillar sat a sphere, or a globe, or a cage. It, too, was made of woven branches and twigs, but also of bone. It was bound tightly with vines and tough stems and hair.

In the cage was a thin girl. Even Mr and Mrs Gerlic would have had trouble recognising their elder daughter; Miriam's eyes were red and puffed from terrified crying. Her naked skin was alive with welts: a thousand spider bites. Her arms and legs were tied fast to the ribs of the globe, strung by wrist and ankle. When she saw the old woman approach, a pitiful stream of urine trickled from between her legs. Her throat was raw from hours of fruitless screaming, and only a ragged sigh came out.

'Time to go,' the old woman said cheerfully.

She caressed the little ladder rising to the odd cage with the branch, then ascended, softly speaking old, old words. She held her sparkling knife to the blind eyes of the trees, and reached down to the girl.

29

Nicholas watched his mother.

Katharine Close sat in a chair beside the bed Laine was lying in, watching the younger woman breathe. Laine's jaw twitched, and a light frown danced on her forehead. The scratch mark on her face was healing fast. Katharine held the back of her hand to Laine's forehead and cheeks, and nodded to herself.

'It's an improvement,' she said and looked up at her son indicating that they should leave Laine to sleep in peace a while.

They walked softly down the hall towards the kitchen.

'I rang your sister,' Katharine said. 'Nelson's ill.'

'Yeah.'

'Nothing serious. She wanted you to know that she's "keeping it up". That you'd understand. Do you know what that means?'

Katharine went to the sink and filled the kettle.

'Yes,' replied Nicholas, and waited for his mother to ask him to elucidate. She silently fetched the teapot and leaves, and he realised the question wasn't coming.

He went to the fridge and grabbed the milk. They both sat. Katharine poured the tea. It smelled strong and good.

'She still wants me to move down there. And she said you were thinking of going?' Katharine asked lightly. She looked at Nicholas over the rim of her cup.

Nicholas stirred sugar into his tea. 'No.'

They sipped in silence a while.

'So much rain,' said Katharine. 'Too much.'

Nicholas wondered how he looked. When was the last time he'd eaten? Or shaved? He must look like the wild-eyed derelict that every mother fears her daughter might bed or her son might become. He watched his mother. She bore dark circles under her eyes, and her skin seemed so thin he could almost see the worried skull beneath. She folded her hands together on the table and returned his gaze. He knew this pose of old: he remembered it as the same patient expression she'd worn when she'd caught him masturbating in his bedroom when he was thirteen. 'Do it in the shower,' she'd said. 'I have enough washing to deal with.'

He shifted and waited for the lecture to start.

'Your father,' began Katharine, frowning and uncomfortable, 'thought that Mrs Quill was an evil woman.'

Nicholas was so surprised, it took him a few seconds to realise that he was holding his breath.

Katharine kept her eyes on him.

'Don told me not to go to her with our mendings,' she said. 'I used to do them all myself – God knows we didn't have a brass razoo spare to pay a dressmaker.' She shrugged and pulled her cardigan tighter around her shoulders, and smiled fondly. 'He was such a fool like that, your father. Had he said nothing, I'd have done nothing. But it made me so *angry*, Don supposing he could tell me what to do and where to go and who was fit to mend my babies' clothes and who wasn't. So, I started taking bits and bobs there. To Quill.'

Nicholas felt suddenly very small. The house around them seemed thin and unsubstantial. A frail shell of wood. Vulnerable.

'When was this?' he asked.

Katharine topped up her tea; steam rose from the amber stream, making her face look dreamier and younger.

'Oh, you were maybe . . . three? Suzette hadn't turned one. Your father drank perhaps a beer a week after mowing the lawn.' She smiled sadly at Nicholas. 'And he hated rum.'

Nicholas remembered shadowy images of his long-limbed father lurching down the hallway followed closely by a sickly sweet smell of sweat and alcohol. Rum had been all his father drank.

'That changed.'

'Yes.' She stared into space, remembering something. Nicholas was quiet, unwilling to disrupt this strangely unfolding conversation. Finally, Katharine roused herself and sipped from her cup.

'Don was not a practical man. A lovely, funny man, yes. That's why I married him. But infuriating. Implacable. You look more and more like him. How much did I tell you?'

Nicholas cocked his head. 'About what?'

'About your father's death.'

'Enough to stop me asking any more.'

Katharine licked her lips. Nodded.

'He took a job at Biloela and went away for a few weeks. Do you remember that?'

Nicholas shook his head.

'Well, I wasn't too happy about him going and leaving me with you two,' continued Katharine. 'Maybe it was spite, maybe it was because a bit of extra money was coming into the house, but I began taking the odd garment to Mrs Quill.'

Nicholas watched his mother. Her hands burrowed into one another nervously.

'Anyway, he came back all jolly and full of yarns. I'd been tending a toddler and a baby, and was exhausted. Full of spit and fury. I told him all the things I'd done without him, how good we were without him. I told him how I'd taken torn pants and shirts without buttons to Mrs Quill – I don't even know how that came up. But it did. And he suddenly —'

She looked at him. He saw her lower lip was trembling.

'He looked like you look now. Pale and haunted.'

Nicholas blinked. He hadn't heard this much about his father . . . well, ever. And never without a bitten-back curse word thrown in.

'And?' he asked.

'And he went to see her.'

Katharine held his gaze for a long moment, then looked down at the tea cosy.

'What happened?'

'I don't know,' she replied, picking up the teaspoon and wiping it on the tablecloth. 'I really don't. He came back. His face was red, angry red. He went to his garage and started hammering at something.' She shrugged.

'But . . . ?' urged Nicholas quietly, knowing what came next.

Katharine sighed. 'But. He started drinking. Maybe a week or so later, he brought home a bottle of Bundaberg. Yes. I asked him to move out, oh, six weeks later.'

Nicholas remembered the few times he'd seen his father after he'd left their home – iceberg moments: cold, sharp tips with enormous unhappiness hidden below. Banging on the door at eleven at night. Meeting him and Suzette after school. Each time thinner, until it seemed impossible there was man left to waste.

'And then the crash,' he said quietly.

'And then the crash.'

He could see her eyes were welling with tears. The tea was cooling and there was no more steam to fog away her wrinkles. She'd passed middle age and was becoming elderly. Smaller. His insides felt hollow and cold; if he could plunge into his mind and retrieve his thoughts, they'd come away frozen and hard. Quill had killed his father. He was sure of it.

'Did you ever connect the two?' he asked. 'Dad's visit to Quill and his drinking?'

'Of course not,' Katharine snapped. She clattered the spoon back on her saucer, then swiftly straightened it as if that might erase the recent noise.

'Did you wonder why he went to her?'

She looked at him. And as she did, he saw something flick behind her eyes.

Christ, he thought. *She's terrified.*

'I didn't have to. He told me. He said he was going to warn that witch off his children.'

Nicholas opened his mouth, but nothing came out.

Water tinked in the downpipe outside; a lonely, cavernous sound.

'She stayed there, Mrs Quill, in her shop for another fifteen years or more. Then I thought she moved to Ballina. Mrs Ferguson thought her sister won the Casket and bought her a house in Hobart.' Katharine shook her head and shifted in her chair. 'Then a large lady opened some sort of Celtic shop, selling – oh – tartan cloth, Scottish gifts, tea towels, tinned haggis and trinkets from Edinburgh. Did you ever see her? Family crests. I don't know how she turned a dollar, but she was there till a couple of years ago. Then a pool shop. And now this new young lady with her health food.' She sneered out the last two words.

Nicholas stared at his tea. It was brown and inscrutable as river water. Dark.

'And still,' whispered Katharine. Nicholas wondered if she was reading his thoughts, until she said, 'Still this business goes on.'

She looked at him. Her eyes were hard. 'It's her again, isn't it? Down there now?'

He felt a shiver of panic race down his spine to his bowels.

'Don't you go down there, Mum,' he said.

'Nor should you,' she replied quietly. 'I think you should pack your things and hurry down to your sister. Or farther, if you can.'

She seemed to realise her eyes were wet. She plucked a tissue from her sleeve and dried them. She stood and took her teacup to the sink.

'I'm sorry I never said too many good things about your father. But no woman likes to come second to a bottle.'

Nicholas watched her put her cup on the drainer. She smoothed the front of her cardigan.

'I'll check our guest and then be off to bed,' she said.

As she passed Nicholas, her hand drifted over his shoulder and squeezed it, then left as lightly as a startled swallow taking flight.

30

Tony Barisi stood on his balcony finishing a Dunhill Superior Mild, watching sheets of rain blow like impossibly tall sails across the half-lit office buildings of the city across the river.

He stubbed the smoke out and dropped it in a cast bronze vessel filled with damp sand held between the paws of a sculpted Asiatic lion. Tony didn't feel fifty-one. Tonight he felt thirty-one! Fuck it, *twenty*-one! He didn't want to sleep, because sleep would hasten the rising of tomorrow's sun, and he didn't want to miss a minute, not now. Business was beautiful. The city was beautiful. Life was beautiful. He turned to the tall, frameless glass door and went back into his penthouse.

The boy was asleep on the couch. Tony smiled. He was a gorgeous one, Dan: just gone thirty but tight and tough as a teenager. And he was *different*. Dan had stayed with Tony right through the court case, even when everyone – Tony's solicitor included – was sure that all was lost. Dan was the only one who knew – *knew!* – they'd settle out of court. And he was right. Dan's confidence was infectious and Tony loved him for it.

Loved him.

Admitting that sent a thrill into his stomach. He smiled, watching Dan sleep. Yes, it was love. And being in love was divine. Dan was a keeper. Tony watched his lover slumbering where he'd drifted off after their *many* celebratory drinks, and decided not to wake him. He padded silently to the bedroom.

As he undressed, a delicious weariness crept over him and the bed suddenly looked inviting. *Screw it, I won't even clean my teeth.*

Sleep when you're tired, eat when you're hungry; the rest of the time was for hard work and hard play. He stripped off his boxer shorts and pulled back the covers to curl onto the delicious four-hundred-thread-count Egyptian cotton sheets.

Life was beautiful. Life was perfect.

Tick, ticketty-tack-tacktacktack . . .

Tony sat up.

The echoing sound had come from the ensuite bathroom. Something had fallen into the sink. He felt his face grow hot. That was a seven-thousand-dollar Villeroy & Boch vanity – the thought of some badly installed light globe chipping the enamel made him instantly angry. He threw back the covers and stomped naked through the walk-in robe, past his bespoke suits and shoes, Zegna ties and Duarte jeans, into the ensuite.

The bathroom was as wide as a garage, tiled in icy white with a cathedral ceiling that had made Dan gasp (a delightfully erotic sound) when Tony first showed it to him. One wall was a single pane of one-way glass, affording an unimpeded view of the city and allowing the glow of its buildings' lights to illuminate the room. A set of three large hopper windows rose above the wide white vanity: the first was head height, the second rose to three metres off the floor, the third rose to the ceiling five metres up. These huge windows were usually kept closed – it could blow a gale here on the apartment building's top floor, and even up this high the noise of human traffic on the boulevard below could be disturbing. But he'd left the middle hopper open a crack, and something dark was hunched on top of the pane. A bird? A mouse?

Tony crept closer, wondering what he could use to shoo away the pest. And then he stopped. His stomach gave a slow gurgle as if suddenly filled with spoiled milk.

The creature perched on the middle window frame was a spider. One as big as the barking spiders that used to crawl the sides of his father's tractor shed in Innisfail. Motherfucker. Tony was just about to creep backwards, to run to the kitchen and get the insect spray, when he noticed . . .

It's holding something.

The creature held in its jaws – fangs? mouth? – a tiny white pebble. As he watched, the spider carefully balanced itself, took a sly half-step forward and dropped the pebble.

It fell through the air and landed neatly – tick, tack, tacktacktack – in the vanity basin.

Tony stared with wide eyes. Then something even more incredible happened. The spider threw itself into space and fell away. Just a moment later, another spider of the same size but of a different genus stepped delicately from the side of the building onto the middle pane. It, too, held a white pebble, and carried it to the centre of the pane. Then it stopped, motionless and waiting.

Waiting for me.

Tony took a reluctant step forward, his eyes locked on the spider. And another, until he was standing at the vanity, staring up at it.

The creature leaned forward and dropped its hard little parcel.

Tony caught the stone, and watched the spider throw itself backwards, slide down the glass and fall away into darkness.

No others came to take its place.

He was about to call out to Dan, but glanced down at the pebble in his palm. There were two others like it in the basin. The stones were the size of large ball bearings, smooth and white and slightly ovoid, like tiny eyeballs. The one in his palm was translucent, like quartz, and cold. On its flattest part a mark was scratched. It was a line with two angled hooks, one each end:

$$\mathcal{N}$$

The mark had been stained with something rusty red.

Tony looked into the basin. The other two stones bore the same symbol. There was something about it. Something sad. Something depressing. Something familiar.

Papa's cheek. The mark looks just like the deep lines in my father's cheek. The lines that grew deep as chasms as he got sicker and sicker . . .

A wave of unhappy nostalgia flowed over Tony like a noxious wind. He recalled his father lying in the hospital bed, his cheeks bristled white and deeply furrowed, panting like a dog. And his eyes, Papa's blue eyes. Papa's body was thin and dying, lungs wasted with emphysema, but his eyes were blue as flames. His glands were swollen and his voice was reed thin, but not so thin as to hide the hate as he whispered to Tony in a voice dry as cane stubble, '*Finocchio.*'

Tony leaned on the vanity and looked into the mirror. *That's me*, he thought. *That's me. A big, fat-bellied faggot.*

He ran his fingers over his scalp. The hair was thin. When had it been thick? Before the divorce. 'You're going to look after Gabrielle,' Karan had said. Gabrielle. Oh, the poor kid. Did her classmates know she had a big fat wog faggot for a father? His face grew warm. Of course they knew. Kids found out everything. Did Gab ask for that? For a father who liked the feel of cock in his arse? And what was her reward for the schoolyard taunts? He'd nearly lost it all – a hair's breadth from bankruptcy.

Tony's heart started thumping. I could lose it all again! *He was one signature away from committing everything to the Tallong block development. What a fool!*

He hurried to the bedroom, picked up the phone and dialled.

'Hello?' The woman's voice on the other end was sleep-fuddled.

'Ellen, it's Tony.'

'Mr Barisi? It's . . . is there something —'

'Stop the Tallong development. First thing in the morning. Ring Koopers and tell them it's off. I'm not ratifying.'

'Mr Barisi, are you —'

'It's off.'

Tony disconnected. He dropped the phone. What a waste. He could hear Ellen's disgust, having to talk to such a filthy, pathetic *finocchio*. Tears welled in his eyes. What did he *really* own? A mountain of debt, a fag brothel of an apartment with a filthy little fuck monkey faggot asleep on his couch dribbling cum out of his dirty faggot arse.

'Oh, God!' he whispered. Papa was right. So right. He wasn't fit to live.

Not fit to live.

The thought struck into him with the brightness of steel on steel.

He sat up. *Of course.* The realisation glowed like a spotlight in an auditorium: Gabrielle was beneficiary.

He walked stiffly to the bathroom and climbed up onto the vanity. The bottom hopper was easy to swing wide. Cold wind flooded through the room. Cold and sharp and cleansing.

'Yes,' he whispered.

He slid his legs out the window, then pushed himself out.

The thought in his head just before his skull split open like a dropped melon was of kissing his father's craggy dead cheek.

•

Just as passers-by were running to the shattered body of Tony Barisi, Sergeant Peter Lam was returning to the station's front desk, ripping off the top of a sugar sachet with his teeth and pouring it into his coffee mug that read '**de'caf** [dee-kaf] – *noun* useless brown warm water'. It was a quiet night. Two calls about some V8 thumping around the side streets doing donuts: he'd sent Erica and Mick to have a look. One call from Crazy Joan, who rang every night; this time she was complaining about an ad on TV she said was clearly made by the Mormons and *must* come off the air. Other than that, a lovely, quiet night. Then, movement in the CCTV monitor above the desk. A sedan was pulling into the front car park. It was commonplace for people to come in at all hours with queries about licence renewals, barking dogs, cars broken into.

Sergeant Lam sipped his coffee. A bit hot. He watched a man get out of the driver's side. He moved slow and easy, no signs of drunkenness. Lam relaxed just a little. Then he stiffened, suddenly alert.

The man went to the boot of his car, opened it.

Lam placed down his coffee. The guy could have anything in there: a cat he'd hit on the road, a box of God-knows-what that someone dumped on his footpath . . . The big worry was the folk who'd received speeding tickets that day and decided to try for some payback with a tyre iron. Lam's hand inched closer to the desk radio; Erica and Mick might need to come back in a hurry.

Then the guy in the car park straightened his back and turned towards the surveillance camera. In his arms was the limp body of a naked child.

'Oh, fuck,' whispered Lam. One hand grabbed the radio handset; his other slipped down to release the clip holding in his Glock.

The man outside – who would later be identified as a Miles Kindste from the neighbouring suburb of Tallong – placed the dead girl at his feet, reached into his pocket and produced a Stanley knife. Without a pause, he flicked out the blade and drew it across his own throat. He sat himself down to die.

•

The phosphorescent hands of Nicholas's watch glowed eldritch green. Nearly two thirty in the morning.

He sat in an armchair that had seemed huge when he was a boy, but now was small and uncomfortable. After the first few hours, he'd realised that moving didn't help, and so stayed as still as he could, trying to will himself to numbness.

Through the window over the bed where Laine slept, he'd watched the rain grow softer as hours passed, until it finally ceased an hour ago. The clouds were lit faintly from below by the orange tungsten glow of the sprawling city. Gradually, those clouds parted and dissipated like smoke. Stars winked faintly. Just ten minutes ago, the fingernail crescent of the moon had begun falling with aching slowness beyond the silhouetted leaves of the camphor laurel tree outside the window to light the figure on the bed a ghostly silver.

Laine shifted again. Around midnight, her finger had twitched. By one, she was moving her feet in her sleep. Now she was rolling over, pulling the blanket up around her chin. She opened her eyes. Nicholas was again struck by their colour: a slate that was almost black in this half-light. He'd never seen eyes that colour – smoky and sombre as storm clouds.

'We're at my house,' he said. 'We're okay.'

She nodded, closed her eyes, and fell instantly back to sleep.

He watched her for a long while. He reluctantly turned his eyes back to the moon.

He couldn't remember the colour of Cate's eyes. He was sure they were blue. Or were they hazel? Now he imagined them grey.

31

The room was so bright that Swizzle's eyes were matchstick slits. Hannah squinted.

She sat at the breakfast table, chair pushed out, with Swizzle on her lap. Her mother made coffee. Her father poured juice into glasses. The room was as silent as a classroom after a student has been sent to the principal. Eerily still.

The police had come late last night, and for hours afterwards Hannah had lain awake listening to her mother sob and her father speak quietly, his voice a bowling ball rumble of words she couldn't make out.

She had slept on and off, with a can of Mortein hidden under her pillow. She'd been awake to see the night turn from black to purple-blue to green and yellow. She'd heard her parents rise, voices low, reaching agreement that they 'had to tell Hannah'.

Like she didn't know. How stupid did they think she was?

They'd come in around seven and sat quietly on her bed, neither seeming to know what to say. So Hannah had said it for them.

'Miriam's dead.'

Her mother had jerked back as if slapped.

Her parents had looked at one another, and nodded. A man, they explained, had stolen Miriam from her room. He'd killed her. But the police had him now. There was no need to be scared. He'd be locked up. They dragged the words reluctantly from deep within themselves, like heavy hauls from a dismal sea.

Hannah watched while her father spoke. It was obvious he loved Miriam as much as Mum did – much more than Hannah had herself. She wondered if they'd be this upset if the spiders had got in here instead of Miriam's room? It seemed doubtful. Her father finished by explaining that the next few days and weeks would be very, very hard. They both hugged Hannah tight and told her they loved her, and made her promise that if she needed to talk about how she felt to come straight to them.

That's a joke, thought Hannah; she remembered all too well how much that slap on her buttocks had hurt. Maybe a man *had* killed Miriam; Hannah didn't think her parents were lying. But they sure didn't know everything.

They didn't believe her about the spiders? Fine. She'd watch the news stories about the guy who said he'd killed Miriam. She'd see if *he* said anything about spiders.

If he didn't, Hannah knew where she had to start looking.

The woods weren't far away.

•

Pritam watched ephemeral diamonds crawl across the ceiling of his ward: scintillating colander holes of morning sunlight reflecting off the river and darting like fireflies above his head. The light winked between the wires and rods that held him in his web, peeking here and there between the chromium and the tubing, delighting him, making him smile. He felt sure the relucent sparks were about to divulge the definitive answer to Thomas Aquinas's dilemma about how many angels could dance on a pin head . . . but whenever the answer was on the tip of his tongue, a dazzling flicker would steal it from his mind.

When he'd woken just before dawn, the pain had been extraordinary. His pelvis and the bones of his right leg felt filled with molten metal, and their white heat was pulsing from within, cooking his flesh. He was shaking so badly that he could hardly press the call button with his left hand – his right remained immobile, strapped across his chest. The nurse had arrived and showed him how to use the morphine demand button next to the call remote. Since that lesson, the morning had passed in a delightful fog, punctuated by occasional moments of brilliant clarity and modulated by a chorus of skittering ceiling fireworks.

Best of all, Pritam now knew what to do with Rowena Quill.

She was, most surely, a sinner, a murderer, a dancer with demons. But Pritam had felt the pain of martyrs now. He had tasted, at last, the physical agony of the saints who had died in the service of the Lord; perhaps even a sense of the pain that the Son Himself felt as His body was broken. And he had passed through. He was closer to the divine. And he was humbled. And what could be a greater display of his gratitude than to guide the most egregious of sinners to seek forgiveness?

He would find Rowena Quill and, filled with the power of the Holy Ghost, convince her to admit her sins, to accept Christ and receive His mercy.

Pritam smiled and pressed the morphine button again. Yes. This was so right.

A pretty nurse entered the room, carrying something. She was young and lovely: a delightful work by the Father in this morning brightness.

'Mr Anand?'

'Will you marry me?' He peered to read her name tag. 'Joanna?'

The nurse smiled. 'No, Mr Anand. But I will hold the phone up to your ear. You have a call.'

She held the mobile handset against Pritam's left ear.

'God be with you this Heaven-sent morning!' said Pritam brightly, pleased that his words slurred hardly at all.

'Cheers,' replied Nicholas.

'Nicholas!'

Nicholas was sitting on the back steps of his mother's house, looking out over her vegetable garden. It was ludicrously green after the rains: an impossibly emerald world of vigorous growth. To counteract the salubrious sight, he lit the last of Gavin Boye's cigarettes and inhaled deeply.

'Hole in one. How are you?'

'Blessed. How am I, Joanna?'

'You're doing well, Mr Anand.'

'Joanna's going to marry me,' explained Pritam.

'Are you . . . Are you high, Pritam?'

'No! Well, I have a morphine button.'

'Okay.' Nicholas got to his feet. 'I'll call you back —'

'No! I have been thinking about Rowena Quill.'

'So have we. Laine's here with me.'

'Good. Now, listen. Have you read Luke?' asked Pritam excitedly. 'Read Luke!'

Nicholas screwed the cigarette butt into the doorframe. 'Pritam, you're fucking high. I'm going to call back.'

'Shh, listen! Luke fifteen something. Woman loses a coin. She has ten but loses one. And she finds it and she's so happy!'

'Goodbye, Pritam —'

'Wait! That's how the angels feel when a sinner repents!'

Nicholas squinted against the sunlight. The cigarette had made him feel nauseated.

'Like they just found twenty cents?'

'No! You're not listening!' Pritam rolled his eyes in mock exasperation. The nurse smiled and took the telephone with her other hand so she could check his catheter bag.

'I don't feel like repenting right now,' said Nicholas.

'Not you; her! Quill! I'm going to help Quill!'

Nicholas watched a butcher bird land on the Hills Hoist. It had a grasshopper in its beak, and the insect kicked, kicked, kicked. It occurred to him that he'd never seen the ghost of a bird or a dog or a grasshopper. Did they not have souls? Or did they never die before their time? Or did only haunted birds and dogs and insects see the ghosts of their own kind? Despite the nausea, he wished for another smoke.

'Pritam? Hannah Gerlic's sister was murdered. The guy who killed her – supposedly killed her – killed himself at the cop shop.'

Pritam's bright mood faded slightly. 'Oh.'

'And remember I told you a developer put a sign up at the Carmichael Road woods? Barisi Developments. A Tony Barisi committed suicide last night.'

'Oh,' repeated Pritam. He pressed the morphine button, but nothing happened; he'd reached his limit for the moment. A last facet of sunlight on the ceiling flickered and vanished. Another nurse, older with short brown hair, appeared in the doorway. Joanna waved at her – can you do this? The brown-haired nurse shrugged and took hold of the phone. Joanna whispered in her ear, smiled at Pritam, and hurried from the room. Pritam glanced down at the new nurse's badge: Helen Muir.

'I think Quill killed my father,' said Nicholas simply. The words left his mouth without fanfare or footprints.

Pritam felt the pain start twisting again in his broken hip, his shattered leg: some sharp-mawed worm stirring in its uneasy sleep.

'Nothing's changed, has it?'

'No,' replied Nicholas. 'But at least we know. We're going to go into the woods.'

'You and Laine?'

'Yeah. Listen, just be careful, okay?'

'I can't run too fast right now.'

'You know what I mean,' said Nicholas.

'Watch out for white dogs?'

'That kind of thing, yeah.'

'Okay.' Pritam was feeling tired. Maybe a nap now. 'Nicholas?'

'Yeah?'

'I did mean that, even though I didn't know it was you. God be with you, this Heaven-sent morning.'

Nicholas watched the butcher bird swallow the still-kicking grasshopper. 'And also with you.'

They said their goodbyes, and Pritam nodded at the brown-haired nurse. She pressed the 'end call' button on the handset and reached behind him to adjust his pillow.

'Thank you, Helen,' Pritam said.

'You're welcome, Mr Anand. But it's not Helen,' she added, smiling at his mistake. She tapped her name badge.

Pritam blinked, and a wave of ice water rolled up through him. The badge read 'Rowena Quill'.

He grabbed for the call button – but his fingers were as slow as old creek water. She easily pulled the button away, and smiled again. Pritam could see that she had Eleanor Bretherton's eyes: hard and shining.

'Are you going to call out?' she asked pleasantly.

A lilt, he thought. *Her accent. After all these years . . .*

'No,' he replied. His throat was tight. Fear.

She nodded, as if pleased with an obedient child.

'You know who I am?'

'Show me,' he said.

She raised her eyebrows and smiled, and looked to the door. No one was there. She looked back at Pritam and winked. And suddenly, right in front of him was John Hird.

'Will this make it easier, you useless black fucker?' the older reverend asked brightly.

Pritam reeled. Here she was. Just a few minutes ago he'd been ablaze with the idea of bringing her to her knees with the Glory of the Host, penitent and humbled. But now he was cold inside, doused ash.

John's friendly, wrinkled face vanished in a blink, replaced by the young nurse, Joanna. 'Or her?'

Joanna's face was gone, seamlessly replaced with Pritam's mother's. 'Or her, my little *chinnanna?*'

'Stop,' he whispered. His mouth was as dry as cardboard.

'Or me?' His mother's loving face vanished, replaced by a woman who looked older than time. Withered and wrinkled and hard as wood, with eyes that were bright blue sparks in folds of nut-brown flesh. 'I heard you at the door,' she whispered. Her breath was foul and smelled of decayed flesh and the mouldy misshapen things that grew in damp shadows. 'You want to save my soul, boy?'

Pritam felt the last of his strength drain from him. The room was still light, but there was no longer warmth in it. *This is the room I die in*, he realised. He looked at the crone. She smiled, showing two rotten grey stumps that looked like snapped-off sparrow bones.

'Christ can forgive you,' he whispered, though he didn't believe it. There wasn't a hint of compassion in those ice-blue eyes.

'That's grand,' she said.

Her features became again those of the pleasant, brown-haired nurse. She smiled, pulled out the pillow behind his head and covered his face.

•

After Nicholas hung up the phone, he watched his mother carry buckets and garden tools across the couch grass towards a bed that would, come spring, be as brightly ablaze as tropical coral with colourful arctotis, impatiens and petunias. Katharine dug with hard, chopping strokes, pulling out wandering jew and oxalis, tossing the uprooted weeds into a black pot beside her. *The garden will be beautiful*, he thought. *But how do the weeds feel about it? Sacrifices must be made.*

Blood is the only sacrifice that pleases the Lord.

He needed to ask Laine something. He went inside.

The bed in Suzette's room was empty. Laine was awake and up somewhere. He stepped back into the hall. Through the dimpled glass of the front door, he could make out the hunch of someone sitting on the front steps. He took a breath and went outside.

Laine wore his tracksuit pants and a woollen jumper that swallowed her. She didn't look up as he shut the door behind him. A westerly wind troubled the trees in the street. The sky was cloudless. The sun gave no warmth. He looked around, and spotted what he was looking for. Gavin was walking up the footpath towards them.

'Will you sit?' she asked.

Nicholas watched Gavin reach the front gate.

'I don't think so.'

But he needed to talk to Laine, and so reluctantly sat beside her.

'What happened?' she asked.

'You passed out in the car. I took you to hospital. Then I took you out of hospital.'

She stared out at a blue, wind-streaked sky that seemed impossibly vast above the ruby and emerald tile and tin rooftops.

'I dreamed,' she said.

He waited.

'I was in a ship, a wooden ship. It was crammed full. A woman beside me had a baby. So much blood. It was stillborn. She cried and cried and held the dead baby and the crying seemed to last all night. The only way for it to stop was for me to bring her another baby. And I would have. I would have, only I was held down. Pinned down. By this weight, this warm weight on my chest. But I would have done anything to get her another child and stop that awful, awful crying.'

Nicholas watched her profile. She raised her hand to the cut on her cheek. 'It was my blood. She used it.'

Nicholas nodded.

'And you drew on me,' she said.

He looked at the ground and nodded again.

As if remembering the rune on her chest, she closed her arms across her breasts.

'How's Mrs Boye?' he asked.

'There's a carer from St Luke's with her. For the moment.'

She shrugged, and finally looked at Nicholas.

'Is he here?' Her voice was steady and matter-of-fact until the last syllable, which trembled.

Nicholas looked up. Gavin was on the stairs. He stepped through Laine to stand behind her.

'Yeah.'

'What's he doing?'

He could just see Gavin's mouth moving. In his hand was the black plastic bag. He reached into it.

'You know.'

Laine curled her arms around her knees. 'I didn't feel him. I can't feel him. You'd think . . .'

She stared up at the sky, perhaps to keep the tears in.

'Laine, did Gavin have more than one gun?'

She looked at him. And the instant she did, Gavin fell through her in a crumpled heap, his jaw flapping, his skull topped by a macabre, broken crown.

Nicholas closed his eyes for a moment. When he opened them, Gavin was once more halfway down the street, walking towards them.

'Yes,' she said. 'Locked under the house. He was very firm about obeying those kinds of rules.' She smiled coolly.

Nicholas watched Gavin approach the front gate. The dead man's face was tight and confused. *God, don't let him be stuck in there,* thought Nicholas. *Let this just be a picture. Don't let him be stuck in that loop.*

'The locker key's on my key ring,' said Laine. 'When do you want to do this?'

'Tomorrow,' he said. 'I want to go back to the library this arvo.' *And please let that be the last lie I have to tell her.*

Laine nodded. She was quiet a long moment. She watched the sky with those grey eyes.

'We could leave, you know,' she said.

I can't tell what she's thinking. But he found that was a good thought. He'd had enough of life's mysteries exposed for his eyes; the idea of kept secrets pleased him. What did she mean by 'we'? Separately? Together? As friends? As fellow victims? Lovers? He didn't know.

'We could,' he agreed. The wind picked up and sent a small wave of brown leaves hissing up the street. 'I have a little money.'

'I have a lot,' she said.

They sat, her hugging her chest, him his knees. He looked at her and smiled. To his surprise, she smiled back.

'You should get some more sleep,' he said, and stood. He went inside before Gavin could fall again.

32

Nicholas walked silently under the Airlie Crescent house. He and Tristram had run and ridden bikes under here like madmen, but now he had to stoop slightly to avoid the low bearers overhead. The fine dirt underfoot let out puffs of powder, and he was pleased that his footsteps were silent.

He could hear a bath running overhead, and the muffled sounds of a nurse coaxing Mrs Boye.

Near a trellis that separated the under house from the backyard was a workbench. The vice and hacksaw were covered with tiny mothwings of dragon's blood powder: the police scientific team must have come for fingerprints after Gavin's suicide.

Beside the bench was a relatively new concrete slab with a solid-looking steel cabinet bolted to it. Nicholas softly placed down the duffel bag he carried, and carefully inserted the key Laine had given him. He listened: overhead, the bath stopped running. There was a shout: 'Why should I?' Then the soothing voice of the St Luke's nurse.

Nicholas twisted the cabinet handle. Inside was a shelf stacked with boxes of rounds and a hard plastic case for a telescopic sight. Below were vertical racks for four guns. Two rifles were there, both dappled with dusky fingerprint whorls. One was a Miroku under-over shotgun. The other was a Number 1 Ruger; Nicholas recognised it because Cate's father had owned one exactly like it: a hunting rifle with a scope but no magazine because it took only one bullet at a time. He lifted out the Miroku, figuring that its two shots made it . . . well, twice as appealing.

He slipped the shotgun into the open throat of the duffel bag; its stock rattled against the four cans of insect spray and two bug bombs. Also in the bag were rubber dishwashing gloves and a cricket stump to clear web, a bottle of kerosene, and the purchase Nicholas was most proud of: imitation Zippo lighters, *Fabriqué en Chine*. He dropped in a box of twelve-gauge shells and relocked the cabinet.

He stepped carefully out from under the house and onto the drive. It was after two in the afternoon. He'd spent hours getting his bits and pieces together, and had rung Suzette and told her what had happened with Miriam Gerlic and Pritam and Laine, and how the rune painted on Laine's chest seemed to have done some good. He looked up; the sun was just over its high hurdle and arcing down to the west. He hefted the duffel bag over one shoulder. It was as if he was again ten years old and he and Tristram were preparing to fight the Japs at Wewak or the Jerries at El Alamein . . . only this time the gun was real.

'Tommy guns?' he asked the boy who'd been gone a long, long time. 'Of course,' he answered, and strode to his car.

•

Nothing moved under the shadowed brow of the Myrtle Street shops.

Nicholas walked towards Plough & Vine Health Foods with one wrist in the duffel bag and his hand on the shotgun grip. It occurred to him there was no good way for this to finish: at best, he'd go to gaol for the murder of an unidentified old woman; at worst . . . well, there were thirty-one flavours of worst. One of the least unappealing was emulating Gavin before Garnock's extended family had a chance to do a thorough job on him.

The shop's door was locked. A sign hung in the glass: 'Closed due to sickness. Sorry!'

He shielded his eyes and pressed against the window. The shop within was dark and still. He let out a slow breath, guiltily relieved. He could move to Plan B.

There was hope now: he could take the fight into a remoter place where, perhaps, no one would hear the shotgun blasts. The downside was that it would be *her* place. The woods.

Movement caught his eye.

A house spider jumped from its hiding place atop a wooden rafter of the awning. It abseiled down on the silk it spun out behind, and landed soundlessly on the ground. It scurried around the corner and started down the footpath towards Carmichael Road.

Nicholas was about to chase after it and squash it, but stopped himself. *Let her know*, he thought. *Let her know something's after her. Even if she gets me – and God forbid, Laine and Pritam and Suze – at least she'll get a taste of being hunted. She'll realise that things can turn. It doesn't always go her way. Not any more.*

He got in the car and steered it towards Carmichael Road.

•

Suzette watched her son carefully. Her heart was racing.

Nicholas's call that morning had made her feel sick; after he'd rung, she'd gone to the bathroom and lost all her breakfast. But then the excitement of his one piece of good news had carried her into Nelson's bedroom on swift feet.

Her fingers had been shaking when she drew the paring knife over the skin of his thumb – she didn't want to hurt her boy. But he didn't so much as wince as the steel bit in and red droplets rose around the blade. She quickly opened his pyjama top, dipped her index finger in the blood, and painted that ugly symbol above his heart.

That had been two hours ago. Now, he was sitting in front of the television, hungrily chewing toast as he played *Need for Speed*.

She and Bryan exchanged glances.

'You know what I think,' said Bryan. She could tell he was unhappy: his voice dropped an octave and his words were clipped.

'I have to go.'

'You don't.'

She shrugged. 'I can't leave him up there.'

'Then let's all go —'

'No!' she said loudly. Nelson looked up from the Xbox game. Suzette waved him back – it's fine. 'No way in hell,' she continued. 'You keep them here.'

'Suze . . .' began Bryan.

But she was already on her feet and reaching for the phone book.

33

The trees seemed to hiss like harpies at his intrusion. The wind harassed their high tops, making the gum leaves and pine needles whisper harshly. But the wind seemed far away on the rainforest floor. Here the air was still and smelled strongly of sap and sweet decay and wet earth. It was gloomy; vines and trees wound around themselves like snakes carved of something at once frozen and moving, living and dead. Everything was green: green with growth or green with moss or green with rot; even the blackest shadow was a dark jade. Fallen trunks covered with dark vine lay like scuttled and rotting submarines at the bottom of a dim, glaucous sea.

Nicholas gripped the shotgun with his right hand and cradled its lower barrel over his left forearm; the rope of the duffel bag dug painfully into his shoulder. He was a long way from the sporadic traffic of Carmichael Road, so the risk of being seen was minimal. *Zero, in fact*, he corrected himself.

As he stepped over thick roots and under low, damp branches, he realised that, even as a child exploring in here with Tristram, he'd never seen other children playing here, nor teenagers smoking, nor retirees bird-watching. Other parks in other cities were havens for teenagers and derelicts, but Nicholas had never found a beer can or a milk carton in these woods. This was a haunted place. People knew it in their hearts, even if they never thought it in their heads, and stayed away.

For a while, he followed the eerie, backwards-flying form of a dark-haired boy dressed in long shorts that were popular in the sixties. He'd recognised the child from the Tallong yearbook: Owen

Liddy. But the sight of Liddy's terror-split face was too horrible to watch, so he tacked right far enough to avoid the ghost.

He groaned as he saw another.

A small, raven-haired girl emerged from behind the wide, fluted trunk of a fig to slide herself over one tall, finlike root. Pale skin, thin limbs. Nicholas blinked. It was Miriam Gerlic.

His eyes narrowed.

The girl wasn't being dragged away; she wasn't wailing in silent dread. She was frowning and picking her way carefully over the obstructing root. And she was carrying her school bag. It wasn't Miriam at all.

'Hannah?'

Hannah turned at the sound of his voice, then fell suddenly from sight.

•

'Your Aunty Vee's here, puffin.'

Hannah's father stood in the doorway of her bedroom. Grey bags like oysters sagged under his eyes and stubble roamed carelessly on his cheeks.

'Okay, Dad.'

He nodded and stepped away down the hallway. To Hannah, he had turned into an old man overnight: hunched and mumbling and pale.

She listened. Her Aunt Vee's usually loud and husky voice wrestled with her parents' exhausted pleasantries. The screen door hissed and slammed shut. Hannah sat up on her bed and set aside her Elizabeth Honey paperback. Mum and Dad were going out. They weren't telling where, but when Hannah was told she couldn't come, she figured that they were going to: a) the police station; b) the morgue (which was where dead people were stored); or c) the gravestone shop. Aunty Vee would mind her during their absence.

Aunty Vee was Mum's younger sister. She was pleasantly round and smoked and swore and was Catholic and kept wondering aloud why Mum wasn't Catholic any more. The subject of Mother Mary's

Undying Love would come up later; for now it would be hugs, tears and food.

A short while later, Hannah was standing on the front patio with Vee's hirsute sausage arms wrapped around her, waving as Mum and Dad backed out of the driveway, speaking low and unheard words to one another. When Hannah looked up at Vee, her aunty smiled but her eyes were red and wet. 'Let's eat!' she said.

While Vee busied herself preparing a lunch fit for a circus troupe, Hannah quietly went to the laundry to filch the items on the mental list she'd been compiling all night. Fly spray. Matches. The local newspaper. She looked for anything marked 'Inflammable' (which apparently meant the same as flammable, only more flammable) and found a half full plastic bottle of methylated spirits. Then she crept softly through the kitchen for two more items. Vee was near the sink, buttering bread and farting like a Clydesdale, and so didn't see or hear Hannah float past.

At lunch, Hannah ate sparingly. When Vee quizzed her about why she wasn't eating, she tried her first gambit. 'I'm a bit upset,' she said softly. It worked like a charm. Vee bit her lip and hugged her. 'Of course you are, of course,' she said.

Hannah pushed her luck. 'I didn't sleep much last night,' she said. 'Is it okay if I have a lie-down?'

Vee looked relieved. 'Absolutely, hon!'

Hannah lay on her bed and read for exactly half an hour, then sneaked into the lounge room. Vee was asleep on the couch, thick ankles demurely crossed, snoring.

Hannah hurried back to her bedroom, filled her school backpack with the purloined bits and pieces, then rolled up her dressing gown and her tracksuit and shoved them in the bed so it would appear to the casual glance that she was still in it.

She slipped out the back door.

•

It took her less than five minutes to jog to Carmichael Road. She stopped on the footpath opposite the woods, more or less at the same spot where, two days ago, Nicholas Close had stood, reading the sign, watching her. That development sign was now covered in black plastic, and the shroud gave Hannah an odd, cold feeling.

She checked left and right, then crossed Carmichael Road to the strip of tall sword grass. The tall tree line loomed in front of her, waving at her, the wind shaking the leaves in delighted applause at her arrival. Or hissing a warning.

An adult would have hesitated. An adult would have wondered if she were about to undertake an errand of dangerous foolhardiness. She'd second-guess herself; after all, didn't the police have a confessed killer in custody? She'd wonder how she could possibly have seen a black wave of spiders at her window, working the locks with intelligence that arachnid entomology had never witnessed. She'd curse herself as a coward for doing nothing while her sister was stolen. But Hannah was young and her doubts were not adult but of adults. She knew what she'd seen was true. She knew that she hadn't imagined the crystal unicorn set to trap her. She was angry for being deceived. She knew things that no one else did, and there was no choice: she had to *do* something. She stepped between the trees, and light fell away.

•

Walking into the woods gave Hannah the feeling she was sinking underwater; the fiery crackle of wind in high leaves became more and more distant, as if she were dropping into the depths. Shadows became thick and liquid. Spears of sunlight as thin as fishing rods probed down from the high canopy. The only sounds that were sharp were the wet crushing steps of her slip-on shoes on damp leaves and soggy twigs, and her panting breaths that were coming faster and faster. This was hard work, climbing over moss-furred logs and under looping vines. To go ten metres forward, she had to wend and wind another ten around twisted, scoliotic trunks, over hunched roots, under needy, thorny branches. This was going to take a while.

After twenty minutes, she was slick with sweat and exhausted. She brushed wet leaves off a nearby log and sat. From her backpack she pulled a water bottle. As she sipped, she took inventory of her other goods: insect spray, a paring knife with its blade wrapped in Alfoil (so it wouldn't stab through the sides of the pack), the half-empty bottle of metho, newspaper, matches. Satisfied, she capped her water and slid the pack over her shoulders and pressed on.

She'd lain awake most of the previous night wondering how to kill the giant spider that had taken Miriam. Clearly, it was smart – or at least knew enough about little girls to set a beautiful, sparkling unicorn as bait. It was magical: it had put some sort of charm on the dead bird, and it commanded the smaller spiders. But there was the possibility that the big spider at the window wasn't in charge, that it was just another lieutenant in the spider army. There could be an even bigger spider – a giant spider like the one that Sam Gamgee fought in *The Lord of the Rings* – and that thought made her tummy tighten. Of course, whatever was in charge might be something else entirely; it might be a witch or a warlock or some sort of vampire that drank the blood of children. Considering these limitless possibilities, Hannah dismissed a dozen weapons, from arrows dipped in insect spray to crucifixes. The only weapon she knew of that killed *everything* was fire. A bomb would have been better, but she didn't know how to make a bomb. Fire would have to do.

•

She was tired.

From the outside, the woods appeared to gently roll towards the river, but within, the forest floor rose and fell sharply, and the going was hard. Small but sharply cut gullies wound between massive trunks. Rises were steep, made slippery by the dense carpet of wet leaves. Hannah's footfalls disturbed beetles, uncovered swollen white grubs, and sent crawling things to scatter for new, damp dark.

Her legs were too short to step easily over the big roots of old, old trees that hooked like enormous sly eyebrows out of the spongy dark ground. Her eyes probed ahead of each step to avoid rocks that lurked under thick caps of sodden leaves. And so she was most way up a steepish slope before she realised that a huge Moreton Bay fig was directly in her path. It was easily four metres wide, and each of its buttressed roots spanned out another six or seven from the trunk and was half a metre thick. The nearest rose high above her head. To move forward, she had either to scramble over one of these tall roots or backtrack. She checked her watch and a sharp twinge of panic raced through her tummy. It was already well after two – she didn't want to be caught in the woods after dark.

She followed one root away from the tree until it had diminished enough in size for her to get her arms over it. She crooked one elbow over the root. It was as cold and damp as a fish. She hoisted one leg up till she'd straddled it like a hobby horse. She rocked her weight from one hip to the other, and began her slide down the other side when she realised just in time that the ground below fell away sharply. She balanced awkwardly, wondering what to do next.

'Hannah?'

Her head jerked up at the voice. She caught a glimpse of the man from Carmichael Road, the man who had been there when she woke up in the church, then she overbalanced and fell.

One foot hit the steep, slick ground and slid instantly away. She tried to hold on to the root, but it was so slimy and broad that her fingers found no purchase; her shoulder wrenched sharply and she careened down the slope. Shrubs lashed at her as she tumbled, and her knees and elbows struck evil-edged schist hiding under the mulch. She turned twice before she hit a fallen beech trunk. Her head struck it with a thud. Were the log not decades fallen and soggy with rot, she'd have split her skull open. Even so, the pain was sharp and her elbows and knees were badly grazed.

The throbbing in her head and the hurt in her limbs hit her all at once . . . and she started to cry. She tried not to, but the sobbing wouldn't stop. She heard the man crunching through the leaves, and a moment later saw him through a fog of tears leaning over her.

'Huh . . . huh,' she stuttered, snuffling wetly.

'Let me have a look.' He placed the shotgun down beside him and gently took her head in his hands and examined her scalp. *A gun!* The sight of it arced across Hannah's flash flood of tears and a thrill of excitement raced through her. *He's hunting, too!*

The man seemed hugely relieved that she was whole and largely unhurt. Then he sniffed the air. 'What's that smell? Is it . . .'

Hannah realised that her knapsack was underneath her. Her back felt wet and cold and she smelled the antiseptic tang.

'Oh *no!*'

She wrenched around and shrugged off the pack, zipped it open. The bottle of methylated spirits had split. Her backpack smelled like the doctor's surgery.

'Bum!' she swore, and started pulling out the other items. The newspaper was soggy, which wasn't a bad thing, but the matchbox fell apart in her fingers.

'Yeah, bum,' muttered the man, frowning as he watched her produce the knife and the can of insect spray. She gave it a test squirt – it still worked.

'Well, that's something,' she said quietly. She looked up at the man. 'Are you here for the spiders, too?'

He blinked.

'Spiders?'

•

Nicholas's first instinct was to lie. 'What spiders?'

Hannah pursed her lips, annoyed.

'Okay, for whatever *sends* the spiders then?'

Nicholas felt another gust of unreality. Of all the people he could use beside him, the fates had sent him a ten-year-old girl.

'You should go home, Hannah. You don't know —'

She stared at him. He hadn't seen much of her eyes two days ago: she'd been unconscious for most of the time in the car and at the church, and she'd been puking and sobbing for the rest. This was a different girl. Her tears over the fall had dried suddenly, and she was shaking her head, watching him through eyes that were a strange, dark blue as hard as sapphire.

'I'm not going home,' she said flatly.

'You don't know what you're getting into.'

'So, tell me. Spiders took my sister two nights ago and now she's dead. Whatever got her wanted to kill me. They said the man on the TV news did it, but I don't think it was him. Not really.' She seemed to remember something. 'I know it tried to get me the other day on the path. And it would have, if you hadn't . . .'

Her voice trailed off. She looked at the ground and then stuck out her right hand.

'I'm Hannah Gerlic. Thank you for saving me the other day.'

For the third time in two minutes, Nicholas was amazed by this tiny person. He took her hand.

'I'm Nicholas Close.'

'Were you there by accident or on purpose?' Hannah asked. The civility that had been in her voice was gone. This was short, sharp interrogation. He no longer felt the need to lie.

'You found a bird. A dead bird,' he said.

'I *thought* I found a unicorn,' she corrected. 'But then it turned out to be a bird.'

Nicholas stared away into the gloom of green and brown.

Hannah watched him.

'Mr Close?'

He nodded to himself. 'What a fucking bitch,' he said.

Hannah blushed. 'You shouldn't swear.'

'People swear, Hannah, get over it.' He stood and brushed clean his knees. 'I found a bird just like you did when I was a kid. And she nearly got me. She got my best friend instead. You said spiders?'

She nodded. 'They came for me, but I wouldn't let them in the room. They got Miriam though.'

Nicholas stared at the girl. *What sort of a kid sees what she's seen and then comes after it?*

'You're some kind of a freak, are you?' he asked.

She stared at him coolly with those dark eyes. 'You're rude. I don't think I like you.'

'Yeah, that's going around.' Nicholas picked up the shotgun. 'Go home, Hannah.'

He began climbing back up the slope. Hannah quickly stuffed the pungent wet things back into her pack and hurried after him.

Nicholas looked down at her. This kid was brave.

Like Tristram.

'This old woman. She kills children.'

'I know. It got my sister, *remember?*'

'It's a she. And she's . . .' He shrugged. 'She's been around a long time. She's dangerous, Hannah. You really gotta go home.'

'I have to go home.'

'Yep,' he agreed, relieved to be finally getting through to her. 'Yes.'

But she kept following him. Then the penny dropped.

'Are you correcting me?' he asked.

'Yes. You don't speak well,' Hannah replied, shouldering her backpack. 'I don't want to go home. But since I don't have anything to *burn* her with any more —'

'Good.'

'— I'll help you.'

She struggled to keep up with him. Trickles of blood ran down her thin legs from cuts on her knees and shins. He checked his watch. It was nearly three. If he took her back, it would be after four by the time he returned, leaving less than ninety minutes of light – if you could call this murky gloom light. He stopped and took her by the shoulders and knelt to look her straight in the eye.

'She cuts their throats, Hannah. I don't know if I can protect you. She's probably expecting me. I have a shot, but I don't honestly like my chances. I can't be responsible for you, too. You should go home, and put your energy into convincing your parents to move somewhere safe and dull. Suggest Canberra.'

He rose, turned and started walking again.

A moment later, he heard her footsteps behind him.

•

A quarter of an hour later, the water pipe loomed above them like a glacial wave of rust red. Nicholas realised the steel flanks were the exact colour of dried and crusted blood. Rainwater flowed out of the twin tunnels below the pipe; the forest floor was still weeping out the heavy rainfall. They had followed the creek up the gully to the pipe, but it had been Hannah who'd pointed at the water.

'Look.'

Small creatures floundered in the cold, tea-coloured stream. Spiders. Spindly, fat-bodied orb weavers; squat jumpers; spiny, coal-black widows; platforms; broad huntsmen; chunky imperials – all scrambled to escape the cold, mumbling waters, clutching at twigs or knotted in groups to crawl over each other. Some floated with their crablike bellies in the air, curled like dead fists, drowned.

'This could be bad,' said Nicholas.

It was.

The tunnels under the water pipe were so thick with web that there were no circles of light at their far ends. The mass of silk was so dense that it overflowed the pipe and the water carried it like an obscene caul some three metres downstream. Thousands of spiders made the silk shimmer darkly.

Hannah turned away and vomited up her lunch.

Nicholas watched, not sure whether to help her or leave her. He shifted awkwardly. 'You all right?'

She nodded and wiped her mouth.

'I think she knows we're coming,' he said.

Hannah dragged her eyes to the tunnels. 'You went through there?' she whispered.

'It wasn't as . . . bad as this.'

She looked at him, as if appraising him afresh.

Nicholas checked his watch and a fresh ripple of fear fluttered up his spine. The day was vanishing fast. He'd planned to repeat his trick, throwing another bug bomb into the pipe and this time lighting the gas. But the web plugged the tunnels so solidly that he wouldn't be able to get the can more than an arm's length in.

'We need a ladder. We need two ladders,' he mumbled. He looked over at Hannah. She was frowning, deep in thought.

'What?' he asked.

'How does she get through?'

Nicholas shook his head. 'I don't understand.'

'How does Quill get through?' asked Hannah. 'You said she makes herself look like a girl and works in the shops on Myrtle Street. If her cottage is on the other side, she must come through somehow, right? Unless she can fly.' She looked at him, clearly worried. 'Can she fly?'

Nicholas shook his head. He felt a fool. Of course Quill would have another way through.

'There must be a break in the pipe.'

Hannah shrugged as if that was obvious.

If there was a break in the pipe, it could be anywhere half a kilometre in either direction. It might take hours to find, and, knowing Quill, it would be disguised. Nicholas checked his watch again. It was three thirty. The temperature was already starting to fall.

'I don't know where to start,' he said hopelessly. 'Hacking our way through this bush is going to take hours —'

'Lift me up.'

'What?'

'Lift me up,' repeated Hannah. 'I can walk along the top and look from up there. And I can go fast. My balance is good, see?' She stood on one foot.

Any other time, Nicholas would have said they should turn back, that it wasn't worth risking her neck. But he was sure that if he didn't deal with Quill before nightfall, he would be the next to die. And if he didn't kill Quill, she would kill again. And again, and again.

'All right. I'll get down, you stand on my shoulders, then I'll grab your feet and push up. Okay?'

'Okay.'

He knelt. She put her hands on the flanks of the pipe and carefully stepped up onto one shoulder, then the other. When she was ready, he slowly stood, and realised for the thousandth time that he really should exercise more – his thighs burned.

'Yeah?'

'Go!'

He grabbed both her feet and lifted. Hannah sprawled over the top of the pipe and swung her legs clear. She stood. 'I'm up!' She grinned and looked around. 'Which way?'

Logic wasn't going to help here. Nicholas tried to clear his mind, to forget the ticking clock, and found himself pointing.

'That way.'

Hannah nodded down at him, and started off, arms spread wide like a tightrope walker. In just a few seconds, the tightly packed trees had obscured her from view. Her light footsteps echoed faintly through the metal, then they, too, faded and were gone.

Nicholas was alone.

The minutes seemed to stretch into hours. He could almost feel the hidden sun falling faster and faster into the west. A light mist began to rise from the lush undergrowth like the earth's own disturbed ghost. Where was she? Nicholas had terrible imaginings of her slipping on the damp pipe, scrabbling and falling, landing headfirst with the sickening bony crack that haunted his dreams of Cate. He shouldn't have let the kid go. What was he thinking —

'Mr Close?'

Light footsteps grew louder, then Hannah's pale face appeared high on the pipe.

'Did you find it?'

She was frowning. 'I don't know. It's weird. This way.'

She waved him on. He followed from below, straining through dense thickets of native holly and blackthorn.

'Not far,' she urged.

'Easy for you . . .'

He struggled to lift aside a chaotic tangle of wait-a-while vine and the spiny stem grabbed at his sleeves and the duffel bag. Then he was through. He looked up.

Hannah was pointing. 'There.'

He followed her finger.

Had he not been looking for it, he'd never have seen it. But sure enough, a narrow track almost devoid of undergrowth struck out perpendicularly from the pipe. He bent to inspect it closer. It was only two hand spans wide, but the ferns and saplings were compacted by years of passage into a distinct but well-hidden path. Whoever walked it was careful to stick to the same route every time. The weird thing was, it terminated right at the pipe.

'Does it go on the other side?'

Hannah disappeared from view for a moment, then reappeared overhead. 'No.'

Nicholas suddenly realised what Quill had done.

'Clever bitch . . .' he muttered.

He stood close to the pipe and started running his fingers over its surface. They found the neatly disguised crack. He traced it – it made a rough rectangle a metre or so high in the side of the pipe.

'It's a door,' he said.

'A door?'

'A hatch.'

He pressed against the curved rectangle. A slight give inward. He pressed harder and a loud 'clack' echoed within the pipe. When he released his pressure, the steel hatchway opened outward on oiled hinges.

'Wow,' she said. 'Catch me.'

Before Nicholas could argue, she'd slid down the side of the pipe into his arms. She wriggled to the ground and pulled the hatch wide, poking her head inside.

'Wow,' she repeated, and the word echoed away into pitch darkness: wow-wow-wowwww . . . She climbed up inside the pipe. 'Did you bring a torch-orch-orch . . . ?'

'No. But . . .' He reached into his duffel bag and pulled out one of the Zippo knock-offs. 'This will do.'

'Here,' said Hannah, 'you hold that and give me the gun.'

Nicholas pulled her out of the hatch.

'I'll keep the lighter and the gun. You follow me.'

•

It was easy to decide which way to go inside the pipe. One direction was thick with dust and littered with insect carcasses. The other was almost spotlessly clean.

By the flickering flame of the lighter, they walked through the darkness, saying nothing, listening to their footfalls dance to and fro like ripples in some subterranean lake. The barrel of the Miroku occasionally ticked off the curved metal walls, the sharp sound chased away by a long, lonely echo.

'How will we know when to get out?' whispered Hannah.

'We'll know,' replied Nicholas.

And they did.

After what felt like hours, but was less than three minutes, two faint slits of light hovered in the darkness. As they got closer, it was clear they were the top and bottom cracks of another hatchway. When they reached it, light trickled in all four sides of the rectangle. Inside was welded a grab handle. Nicholas wondered what poor sucker Quill had seduced into doing this steelwork and what rotten fate had befallen him.

He looked around at Hannah. 'Not too late to go back.'

She shook her head.

He nodded, extinguished the lighter, hefted his gun and pushed open the hatch.

At their feet was a wider, clearer path through the trees. Nicholas recognised it as the track he'd found the day he ate those strawberries. Clearly, Quill wasn't concerned about hiding her presence on this side of the pipe.

He turned and helped Hannah out of the hatch.

'Okay?'

She nodded.

He checked his watch. It was nearly four. There was less than an hour and a half of daylight left.

'Then let's go.'

34

Achill wind blew hard as the sun inched closer to the hills in the west. It sucked away moisture, leaving her skin dry and her eyes raw.

Katharine Close's arms were so tired that they burned, yet she kept hacking at the soil of her garden bed as if it were a beast that needed violent subduing. What else was there to do? Her hands were blistered inside the gardening gloves. She had spent the last few hours digging, pulling weeds, clipping stems, trying not to think.

But she did think.

Maybe it was time to go. Maybe enough years had passed that she could admit she'd won. She'd laughed at Don, to his face and to his memory, waving a nasty blowtorch over the hidden things he'd believed. What room was there for bone-pointing and curses and witchery for children born in the time of rocket ships and global warming? How could lines on stone or wood have potency when real power lines crisscrossed the skies on poles, breathing useful life into computers and LCD televisions? What fear was there of spells when corpses, hands bound and heads shot, were being pulled daily from the Tigris?

At nights, though, Katharine shivered. She remembered how she'd marched, fair-faced, into Mrs Quill's store, handed the old woman her children's clothes and blessed her with kind words and smiles. She'd shouted down that impotent voice inside her that agreed with Don. What else was a modern, single mother to do? Curl away and make the sign of the evil eye each time the old crone passed?

And yet that's exactly what she did do. She remembered a cold winter's night, as empty and still as the inside of a bell jar. Suzette and Nicholas tiny and asleep in their beds, and Don six years in the grave. She had been ready to go to bed herself when she heard a soft *clip clip* of footsteps on the street. She had crept in darkness to the front room and peered between the venetian blinds. Looking up at the house was the dot of the old woman, her face a black shadow. And yet Katharine had imagined her eyes, bright and sparkling, dancing and ravening, looking back. Hungrily. As if knowing there were two ripe young children within. In the pragmatic daylight of the next morning, Katharine had ridiculed herself for her fears – the old dressmaker was perhaps a little senile and lost, or just wanted some friendly company but hadn't the courage to knock on the door.

But two days later, Tristram Boye was pulled dead from under a woodpile two suburbs away, his little throat cut wide to the world.

Katharine put down her trowel. Maybe it was time to admit not that she'd won, but that she'd lost. She should sell this empty house. Listen to her daughter and buy an apartment near her.

A flicker of white jigged in the corner of her eye.

She turned, wincing at the tight pain in her punished neck and shoulders. A small white terrier trotted cheerily along the path at the side of the house. It sparked a memory, something she and Suzette had discussed just a few days ago. Hadn't Quill owned a little white dog?

'Shoo! Go home, you naughty . . .'

The words died in her mouth.

The dog stopped at her call. It turned and regarded her with black pebble eyes.

Katharine had grown up on a property and animals had been an everyday part of her childhood, but only once before had she seen a creature regard her with this cold contempt. It had been spring, and a nesting magpie had begun swooping on anyone who neared her tree beside the utility shed. It was the weekend, and Katharine had been helping her father make a new chook house. He was working on the coop roof, and asked young Katharine to go to the tool shed and fetch tinsnips. She had stridden to the shed, and in her last few steps heard the dry swoop of wings on air. She put up her hands just as a flash of black and white feathers rocketed past her, blowing her fine hair around her ears. Fired by her suddenly tripping heart, she sprinted through the open door into the black, cave-like shed. Deep in the cool dark, she turned. Through the doorway she watched the bird land in the square of squintingly bright sunlight. The magpie hopped to the edge of the doorframe, and stopped, peering into the darkness of the shed. Its eyes were black as stones, shiny and cold. They found her. The bird watched her, calculating whether or not to attack. And young Katharine knew that if it did, it would attack without reservation, biting and spearing with every cell in its body focused on the task of hurting her. The bird held her captive in the shed until her father found her an hour later, tears rolling down her cheeks.

The little white dog watched Katharine now with the same look of icy appraisal, its round coal eyes scrutinising her, deciding whether or not to attack.

Katharine realised her skin felt frozen hard. She was terrified. Terrified by a small dog that stared at her in a way no dog had. Then a realisation struck her: its ribcage hadn't moved. It wasn't breathing.

Because it's not a dog, said a voice in her head.

Then the creature turned and trotted up the stairs to the back door. Katharine watched it rise with eerie fluidity to its hind legs, turn one paw, hook and swing open the screen door, and slip inside the house.

'Laine!'

She climbed to her feet, ignoring the jagged pains in her hips and back, and ran.

35

The *Wynard* was wretched. The boat lay on her side like the mummified body of a long-dead elephant, her grey hull beginning to cave and collapse as moisture and unseen insects completed their rotting work; her timbers were faded and bleached like cow bones. Far overhead, wind roared like fire in the treetops, an invisible wave endlessly crashing.

Nicholas shifted the shotgun to one hand and checked his watch. It was nearly four. The winter sun remained hidden by a million leaves, but he could feel its distant warmth vanishing from the day with greedy speed. The air here in the deep green shadows was frigid and still. Hannah shivered beside him.

'Which way?' she asked.

He looked around the hunching curtains of green and black. At the boat, the track had petered out.

'I don't remember.'

The last time he'd left here, he'd been carried unconscious on eight thousand spindle legs, Garnock riding on his chest like a stygian cavalier.

The ground ahead, thick with vine and root and trunk, seemed to rise. The air that way had a slightly sour tang. Nicholas reasoned that the river couldn't be far away, its salty mud banks thick with mangroves and rancid with the droppings of flying foxes. He nodded that direction, and he and Hannah started again uphill.

As they crawled between the ancient trees, picking their way through the dense shadows over mossy flood-felled trunks and under incestuous, noose-like vines, Nicholas told Hannah everything he knew about Rowena Quill. About the woman's arrival a century and a half ago. Her pseudonyms. Her faces, hiding carefully behind spinster smiles in the cool dark shops on Myrtle Street. Her killings. Her spiders.

When he'd finished, Hannah was silent for a moment.

'She must be very lonely,' she said.

Nicholas looked at her. She shrugged.

'Maybe that's why she's so mean,' she continued. 'Because she's sad. Everyone she loved is dead and left behind.'

Nicholas stopped. The trees around them now were more shadow than substance. Even Hannah's face was a grey mask, as featureless as the sandy bottom of a deep pond.

'I think we have to turn back.'

Hannah blinked. 'We can't. If we don't get her today . . .' Her voice trailed off with a shudder.

Nicholas nodded.

'Hannah . . . ?' A voice as thin as smoke wended from the dark belt of trees up ahead. Nicholas watched Hannah's eyes widen and her face tighten like a fist. His own heart began to gallop.

'Haaaannahhh?' A girl's voice. A pained voice.

Hannah's eyes darted between the woods and Nicholas.

'It's Miriam,' she whispered.

Nicholas saw goose bumps on his arm. He shook his head. 'It's not.'

'It is! She's not dead! They were wrong!'

She started forward. Nicholas snatched her arm and wheeled her round. He grabbed her chin and made her focus her wild eyes on him.

'It's not your sister, Hannah. Think about it.'

Hannah blinked. She nodded.

'Okay,' he said. 'Stay here.'

He looked around to orientate himself, then cocked the shotgun and stepped into the deeper gloom.

'Haaannnahhh? Help me, Hannaaaahhh!'

The voice was a keening tapestry of pain and sorrow. It made Nicholas's skin crawl. What was it doing to Hannah?

He moved as quickly as he could, but the trees were wide and old and huddled tight as conspirators. The spaces between them were filled with even older stumps that rose from the rustling ground like the broken teeth of titans. It was growing so dark. Nicholas suddenly realised what a stupid thing he'd done. He'd left Hannah alone.

'Hannah?' The voice was no longer scared; it was relieved and cheerful. A shadow shifted between the gloomy trees ahead of Nicholas.

'Miriam?' he asked, carefully swinging the gun barrel up towards the movement.

'Hannah!' replied the voice delightedly. And suddenly the shadow jolted forward.

It was a spider at least the size of Garnock, a widow with gloss black and hairless legs, each as long and thick as a cricket stump. They moved a shelled body as big as a water-filled black balloon. Yet the spider jumped from tree to tree with amazing speed; one moment swaying like a ready boxer, the next leaping and landing with eerie silence, so fast that Nicholas barely had time to thumb the hammer back.

'HHHaaaaaa!'

The voice changed from human to something utterly alien as the spider's fangs lifted and it pounced. Nicholas pulled the trigger. The blast was loud but was squashed instantly by the disapproving trees. The spider jerked, but its momentum carried it right at him – he scrambled sideways and the spider hit the tree behind him with the wet crack of a giant egg smashing. It slid lifeless to the dark leaves, its long finger-bone legs quivering in death palsies.

Nicholas turned and ran.

'Hannah!'

He sprinted downhill, dodging between trunks and jumping over spiny branches, sliding and falling and rising and running. Ahead, he heard Hannah scream in terror.

'Hold on, Hannah!'

He thumbed back the shotgun's other hammer and jumped over the last log into the clearing.

Hannah stood shaking, eyes locked on something hidden from Nicholas's sight by a wide trunk.

'What is it?' he asked.

She pointed, and he stepped closer to see what she faced.

He felt his own legs turn light as dust.

If the last spider had been big, this one was huge. Its body was the size of a sheepdog, squat and dense, bristling with sandy brown hairs. It was reared up on six legs; its front two pawed the air, tasting it. A cluster of red eyes stared out from a nest of ugly grey hair. Its fangs shuffled noiselessly.

'Kill it, Nicholas.'

He raised the gun, and squeezed the trigger.

And as he did, he noticed the straps tucked in the folds where the spider's tubelike legs met its thorax. Hannah's knapsack! As the hammer fell, he jerked the gun aside. The blast shook a sudden hole in the bush beside the spider, which jerked in silent pain. As it moved, its horrible appearance melted away, becoming Hannah on her knees, her hands tied behind her back, and a tiny red circle of a single shotgun pellet hole in her calf. Her mouth was gagged with rags.

Nicholas whirled, nauseated that he'd been so stupid.

The other Hannah stood behind him, grinning. She stepped forward lightly and Nicholas felt a sting in his arm. He dropped the gun and blinked. The smiling Hannah held a syringe in her hand and, as she stepped back, her limbs lengthened and her hair grew. Rowena Quill, young and blonde and beautiful, stood in front of him, smiling as only one truly pleased with herself can.

'Hello, my pretty man.'

36

Gavin was explaining why he'd cheated on her.

'It's not because I don't love you,' he said, smiling his charming, lopsided, I-can't-help-being-me grin. 'What attracts me to them is what attracts me to you. It's not a choice thing, angel. It's just what happens. It's what happened when I first saw you. When I still see you. I want to stop it, I do. But I'm just afraid that if I stop being attracted to other women, I'll stop being attracted to you, too.'

Behind him, in an airport lounge, sat a group of long-haired, long-legged women, speaking quietly amongst themselves with the sweet whistling of trapped birds. As Gavin fell silent, they all turned to look at Laine. And they all smiled the same pretty, sympathetic smile. Gavin smiled, too, and offered her a pumpkin seed.

'Laine?' called one of the pretty sing-song women.

'What?' she snapped. She'd intended the word to sound steely and tough, but it came out small and wounded.

'Laine!'

No; it wasn't any of the women calling. It was someone else. Someone farther away . . . yet strangely closer. Then she heard the screen door bump shut.

Laine sat suddenly upright in the bed.

The bedroom door was silently swinging open. And into the room stepped one long, bristled leg, placing its hooked foot stealthily on the floor. Then another followed it, moving with completely inhuman fluidity. The legs belonged to a squat, solid spider as large as a fox.

Laine felt her exhaling breath flute down to a whisper as her throat tightened with terror.

At the sound, the spider hunched and adjusted itself with unbelievable speed to face her. Two large, black hemispherical eyes were orbited by six smaller ones, all sitting on a grey-haired bump of a head that would feel, Laine knew, as hard and alien as a bristled watermelon. Between the spider's two front legs was a pair of fangs, sharply pointed and hard as polished ebony. The fangs curled in, wet themselves on the glands tucked under its crablike mouth, then extended again, glistening wet with poison.

'Hello, Garnock,' said Laine with a forced pleasantness that defied her nearness to the cliff edge of total panic.

Her left hand was farthest from the spider, and it crept out from under the bedsheets, hunting for a weapon.

The spider, low to the ground, took an incredibly slow, very careful step forward. It raised itself slightly on its legs and Laine heard a faint hiss from under its thorax as air was sucked into its lungs there. The spider then released it in a whisper that set the hairs on the back of her neck hard.

'Aaiiide.'

Oh God, she thought madly. *It's trying to say my name.*

Her sneaking fingers found the alarm clock. Useless – she could grab it but every chance was that the cord plugged into the wall would stop her swinging it. She kept hunting for the other object she knew was there.

The spider steadied itself on its feet, tensing its legs and reminding Laine deliriously of how a golfer wiggled his feet and hips, positioning himself for a clean swing. Again, she heard air drawn in and released in a controlled hiss: 'Maaaie maaaiee.'

She understood the bastardised words: *Bye bye*.

Her fingers finally touched what she wanted: the smooth, round steel of a spray can. But as she grabbed, her sweaty fingers slipped and the can clattered across the floor and rolled impotently into the corner.

Laine's eyes widened.

Garnock's mandibles parted. A smile. Then it leapt.

But the spider only moved a fraction before it was slammed back down to the floor with a hard ring of steel on wood. Two tines of a pitchfork had speared through its bony shell and pinned it to the pine floorboards.

Katharine turned and retched.

The impaled creature let out a horrible hissing wail, and its horned feet scrabbled against the floor, gouging the polish. Its fangs pistoned up and down like thresher blades. It was pulling the fork out of the floor.

Katharine stepped carefully behind the skewered spider and leaned more weight on the pitchfork handle. Her stomach convulsed and she strained to keep from gagging.

'It was a dog. It looked like a dog when I stabbed it . . .'

Laine padded quickly across the floor and scooped up the pressure can of insecticide. She glanced over to Garnock.

It was wheezing and straining against the tines. The hairy armour of its exoskeleton was starting to tear, and a puddle of blue haemolymph spread beneath it.

'I think it's going to pull itself free,' said Katharine quickly.

It was true. Though it would kill itself doing it, Garnock was aiming to pull its flesh right through the pinning tines. Laine popped the lid off the spray can. She stood in front of the giant spider and watched its fangs swoon up and down.

'Bye bye, indeed,' she whispered, and sprayed insecticide right into the nest of its eyes.

The spider let out a piercing whistle that bubbled in the blue liquid leaking from below it. Its legs pounded a sloshing tattoo on the boards. Laine kept the spray going, saturating the spider's head, covering the creature in a pungent chemical fog.

'Come on,' she whispered, grabbing Katharine's arm as she slipped past Garnock. It twisted on its impalement and Laine saw its fangs stab the air as she passed. The women hurried down the hall.

'We should leave that for a while,' suggested Laine.

'Yes,' agreed Katharine. 'I'll boil the kettle.'

•

They were in the kitchen, Laine helping Katharine make tea. Outside, daylight was fading from the sky.

'When did Nicholas say he'd be back?' asked Laine as lightly as she could.

Katharine frowned and checked the wall clock.

'He didn't.'

The telephone rang. Katharine and Laine glanced at one another. Katharine picked up the phone.

'Hello?' she said. As she listened, her eyes stayed on Laine. 'When?' She nodded. 'Is anyone there going to . . . ? Okay. Thank you.' She cradled the receiver. 'Reverend Pritam Anand died today. Heart failure.'

Laine set down the crockery as a shiver of understanding went through her. Pritam was dead. Garnock had come for her.

Quill would be after Nicholas.

He must know that.

'The fool,' she whispered. 'He's in the woods.'

37

Small, shifting gems of woad winked through the high, wind-harried leaves. Evening's fast fingers were drawing velvet across the sky.

Nicholas came awake, slowly and painfully, as if being thawed from a block of black and acidulous ice. At first, he thought he was on fire, and the flickering yellow lights at the corners of his eyes were his limbs aflame. But as he worked blood into his fingers and limbs, he realised the pain was just the agony of pins and needles.

A faint whistling. An old tune, bittersweet, mournful and thin, was barely audible above the wind troubling the eaves.

Nicholas lay on the floor. He could just see out a clear window: trees almost black with approaching night masked all but the tiniest glimpses of bruised evening sky. Everything shifted, in and out of sharpness. His stomach felt ready to let go its contents, and he swallowed back salty bile. He tried to sit, but sharp pain in his wrists and ankles stopped him spreading. He was well tied with ropes.

He rolled a few degrees, wincing at the bright potsherds of pain in the bigger muscles of his legs and arms.

Quill sat on an old oak rocking chair before a small iron stove, staring at the flames flickering behind the black-toothed grin of the stove door, whistling through her grey prune lips. As the firelight shimmered, so did her appearance. One moment her skin was ancient and sagging, pale and deeply scored as drought-cracked earth, but when the flames rose and shadows played across her, Nicholas saw the clear skin and gold hair of young Rowena Quill. Young, ancient; haggard, beautiful. Dark brown eyes, now black, now brown, reflecting red, locked on the flames. Quill's tune was soft and came from far away and long ago. She seemed to feel Nicholas's eyes on her and her whistle fell to a sigh.

'Awake?' she asked.

Nicholas rolled a little more. He lay on clean wooden floorboards that smelled of pine oil. The room was a cosy mouthful of shadows: it was panelled in dark wood, but neat. A small cedar table stood on a rug with a single chair keeping company. A curtain to a toileting room was held back by an embroidered sash. A tall pine dresser as thin and stately as a butler held some painted dishes and glazed figurines. Another curtain, this one of lace that reminded him too much of spider web, hid all but the shyest glimpse of a trimly made brass bed with a floral counterpane. At the far end of the room he lay in, the floorboards were cut away in a circle. The ring was lined with neatly mortared stones: a fire pit in which coals glowed dully. On the far side of the pit, a folded blanket, kneaded and pressed by the weight of a pet – Garnock, he guessed – but there was no sign of the monster.

'Yes,' he replied, barely recognising the dry rattle of his own voice.

Quill nodded, and looked at him.

Again, Nicholas had a vertiginous feeling of seeing her through idling water, or of a hologram viewed in passing: her features swam in the fickle firelight, vacillating between old and young, hideous and beauteous. Only her expression remained fixed and cold.

He flexed an arm. The rope bit into his wrist.

'Where is Hannah?' he asked.

Quill rocked. 'Hush.'

As she moved to and fro, in and out of shadows, her twin selves waxed and waned. Behind her, through the window, the last of the day's colour bled from the sky.

'You can't —'

'I said, HUSH!' she commanded, and her voice seemed to rouse the flames behind the stove grate. The room danced. She half-rose from her chair, and the young Rowena Quill, pale and blonde and terrifyingly beautiful, leaned forward, rage sparkling in her dark eyes. Then she caught and reeled in her anger and sat back down – her

337

skin rippled again into leathery furrows. She folded her hands together, watching him.

'You think you know,' she whispered, 'but you can't know.'

She looked back at the flames. As she rocked, Nicholas noticed something on the wall behind her. It was a calendar of sorts, but made of wood, with moveable squared pegs plugged into holes like a board game belonging to some Victorian-era child. But the pegs were marked with strange symbols: stylised seasons, runes, phases of the moon. The board had an elaborately carved frame; at its top, staring through hooded eyes as black as wells from a face of oak leaves, was the Green Man.

'I have so much to tell. So much,' Quill whispered. 'So many stories. So many years.' She spoke so quietly, her lips hardly moving, that Nicholas wondered if he was dreaming her voice in his still-swimming head. 'Can you imagine my delight when I learned from your mother that you were a Samhain child?' She pronounced the word as Suzette had: *sah-wen*. A word lush and full. Quill turned her eyes again to Nicholas. 'A special child. A child with the sight. And you *do* have the sight. I can see it in your eyes. A gravedigger's eyes. A stomach full of sadness to match mine.'

The old woman was suddenly gone and the young Rowena Quill sat in the same dress, its collar loose enough around her pale shoulders to show the curve of her breasts below. Her lips were red as blood. Then a log cracked in the fire, and the old woman was back in the chair.

Nicholas stared. 'Then why did you try to kill me?'

Quill watched him for a long moment. 'Oh. I never did.'

'You set a bird for me,' he said. It was hard to talk, his own weight pressing on his ribs. 'As you did for Hannah. And God knows how many other children.'

Anger flared freshly in her eyes, but was hidden away just as fast.

'But never for you. The one you found was for your friend, and it found him sure as sure. With your help, in fact. I had Gavin Boye tell you a wee fib, to entice you here.' She winked – a wrinkled sphincter. 'You saw it for what it was, not the trinket I wanted seen. You saw a dead bird. Your blond gossip saw a lovely tin hussar. But it was never for you, Nicholas Close. I wanted you full grown.' She looked back at the warmth of the fire. 'That's why I asked Him to send you back.'

Nicholas suddenly felt his heart beat harder. Its thudding pumps shook him on the floor.

'What do you mean?'

She smiled, perfect white teeth alternated with rust red, almost toothless gums.

'England was too far away. Too, too far. So I asked Him to bring you home,' she said. 'And here you are.'

Nicholas felt his vision sparkle and the blood drain from his face. And memories of flashing green; the thrum of a motorcycle; the glimpse of an inhuman face among the black tangles of an oak grove; Cate's neck bent too far back over the white porcelain edge of the bath, her open eyes dulled by a fine patina of plaster dust.

'What did you do?' he whispered.

She let free a laugh that was at once as clear and pretty as fine bells and gravelled and moss-thick as a blocked drain. Her eyes watched him fondly.

'My pretty man. I did what I had to. I want us to be together.'

●

The smell was familiar.

There wasn't a hint of goodness about it. It was the sour scent of rot and wet shadow; the smell of bad earth and failed flesh. Hannah recalled it, or something like it, from when she had accompanied her father under the house, crawling low between stumps, over damp earth where sunlight never shone, until they found the dead possum. Its grey bones poked from beneath a pungent shroud of fur, green stuff and wriggling white. Maggots. The smell of death had made her gag and skitter back to fresher air. Now she had no such luxury.

She was upright, but couldn't move or see. Her legs were swaddled fast together and her arms were bound tight and crooked against her body. Her eyes were shut and she couldn't open them: a second skin had her wrapped from head to foot, with only a little space left under her nostrils. Fine strands like baby's hair tickled her nose when she inhaled the stale, soiled air.

But she knew what it was holding her. She was trussed up just as she imagined Miriam had been: spun tight in spider web, alive and waiting to be fed upon by scuttling things with sharp fangs and unblinking eyes.

A hot wave of panic swept through her, and she fought for control of her bowels. *Idiot*, she thought for the thousandth time since she'd watched Nicholas – at least, she'd thought it was Nicholas – return from chasing Miriam's voice. He'd smiled and said, 'Just the wind.' Then he pointed, 'But what the hell is that?' She'd turned to follow his outstretched arm, realising as she twisted that she had fallen for the oldest trick since 'smell the cheese'. Something hard had come down fast on the crown of her skull, and minutes suddenly disappeared. She'd woken on the ground with her arms tied behind her back and her knees lashed together and rags shoved in her mouth. Then, like looking into a bewitched forest mirror, she saw herself standing in the darkening glade, smiling back at her. The hairs on her arms and neck turned to wire, and her twin called in her own voice: 'Nicholas!'

The real Nicholas – *the one with a gun, dummy!* – had rushed back, looked at Hannah, and his eyes had widened. He'd raised the gun and, just when she thought she was dead for sure, swung the barrel away. Then, *blammo!*, and a sting ten times worse than any bee's had rammed like a hot darning needle into her left calf muscle, which now ached like hell. Tears had rolled down her face as she watched her twin self pull out a syringe and stick it into Nicholas. He folded like a dropped doll, and then her twin came over to her. 'Sleep tight,' the other Hannah had said, and stuck the needle into her arm. About ten minutes ago she'd woken from a black sleep to here, a fly stuck in the spider's parlour.

Hannah realised she was crying. Fat lot of good that would do. 'Help!' she called.

Her voice was muffled and sucked up by the blackness; it was like yelling from inside a wardrobe full of clothes. The dead sound

340

and the spoilt butter smell of rancid earth confirmed she was underground. It was as if she was dead already.

Hannah expected this to make her sob even more, but instead she found her tears drying up and her tummy growing warm. How dare they? How dare they do this to little *girls*! She understood why her parents got so angry when they saw the results of bombers in the white hot streets of the Middle East, why men and women wailed in anger as well as grief when they lifted the limp bodies of children from the rubble. How *dare* they? No. She wasn't going to die like this, wrapped up like some helpless baby.

She concentrated, trying to picture herself. There was no weight on her feet. She was vertical. Her heels, back and shoulders were pressed against something hard and cold – the earth wall. She was hung like a side of lamb. She sent a testing kick of her twinned legs against the wall behind her, and heard a small shower of earth trickle and a faint rattling like glass. She kicked again. Another small fall of soil, another rattle like glasses on a shelf. If only she could *see*. There was only one way that was going to happen.

She strained and forced open her mouth, and stuck her tongue between her teeth. It touched a fibrous skin that made her wet flesh instantly recoil and her stomach jumble. *Come on*, she told herself, *there's no other way.* She opened her mouth again, wider. She felt the binding silk around her jaw stretch. She closed and opened again, wider, the muscles in her neck straining hard. *Come on!!* She closed and opened one more time . . . and felt the horrible fabric tear a little.

She put her tongue out and felt the raw edges of the torn silk. She looped her tongue around them and drew them into her mouth. *Just a little bit*, she thought. *That's all I need to free my eyelids.* She pulled the tasteless web between her teeth and ground, pulling her jaw down in a grimace – it felt as if she was eating the very skin off her face. But the silk over her eyelids shifted. She opened her mouth and gagged, her stomach heaved and finally let go, and a warm gush of acidic mush jetted out. She spat and sniffed up snot. Her eyes opened a crack.

It was impossible to judge the room's size because it was almost completely dark. The inkiness was broken by three weak slices of light that shone down onto a set of ascending stairs made of old bricks. The far wall was swallowed by the darkness – it could be three metres away, or three hundred for all she could see. She twisted her head to the right. From the corner of her eye, she could just make out the wall she was hung from; into its earth were cut rows of horizontal shelves, and on them were jars and jars and jars. So that's what was rattling. She twisted her head left, and bit back a scream.

The skull looking back at her had its mouth open. The spider webs that bound the mummified child had long turned grey, and now sagged morosely. The child's skin was the black of old book leather. Curled black hair poked dully between the smoky silk around its skull. Its eye sockets had been built over with fresher webs.

She looked away, heart cascading. How long had she been here? How long would she need to hang here until she was too weak to do anything and met the same fate? How much time did she have? A fresh wave of tears built up inside her, threatening to burst out. How much time?

Time.

T-i-m-e. T-I-M-E. T-I . . .

If she screamed now that she'd spat the gag, the witch would surely hear her. She closed her eyes, focused on the letters. *T-I-M-E. T-I-M-E. Tick tock. Tick tock goes the clock. Hickory dickory dock, the mouse ran up the clock . . .* Her breaths came more evenly as she ran the children's rhyme through her mind. *The bird looked at the clock. The dog barked at the clock. The bear slept by the clock . . .* Her heartbeat slowed. Before she realised what she was doing, she moved her legs left, just a little, then let them drop back. As she swung down, she lifted her legs right. And drop. Tick tock. She began a rhythm, a human pendulum, swaying on the wall. She didn't ask herself why; she knew it felt *right*. With each drop and swoop up, she strained, getting higher and higher. She felt her back, her bottom, her elbows, her heels, scrape on the dirt, grinding through the silk. *That's it! Scrape! Tick! Scrape! Tock!* She swung herself, straining left, straining right; swing-scrape, swing-scrape. The tightness around her chest eased just slightly. Her strapped ankles grew slightly freer. She felt wet, cold earth trickle into her shirt, down her back. Left-swing-scrape . . . Right-swing-scrape . . . a little higher, a little higher . . . She could flex her arms, just a little, but that little bought her room to swell and contract as she swung. *A couple more!* She could hold her legs a few centimetres apart. Her shoulders could shrug. She could slide her hands across her belly. *Yes! One more!* She swung . . .

And felt a line of fire draw across her shoulder blades. She yelped. Her body scraping across the raw earth had exposed a sharp rock, and it dug deep into her flesh as she slid across it. It felt like a line of boiling oil had been dribbled from shoulder to shoulder. Hot tears poured from her eyes and she bit her bottom lip hard to stop the scream from coming out. She stopped swinging.

And, despite the tears, grinned in triumph. Her feet were on the floor.

•

Laine watched the very last of the day's colour leach from the sky. A thin slip of cobalt blue kissing the western hills was being subsumed by the black arch of night.

She turned to Katharine. They'd hesitated and delayed, both hoping Nicholas would walk through the door, but as each minute passed it confirmed what they suspected: that he'd never gone to the library, instead had slipped into the woods to deal with Quill himself.

'He's in trouble,' said Katharine.

Laine nodded.

Then they heard a key in the front door.

'Nicholas?' called Katharine.

'Mum?' called Suzette.

She was halfway down the hall when she must have glanced into her bedroom and seen what was pinned to the floor with a pitchfork – she let out a shriek. Katharine and Laine ran to her.

Introductions were quick, but Laine felt a warmth when Suzette took her hand. She liked these Close women.

They explained to Suzette that Nicholas had not come home.

'The fucking twit,' said Suzette.

'Well,' said Laine. 'Let's go get him.'

The three women looked at one another, and smiled.

'Yes,' said Katharine. 'We'll need some things.'

Laine found it hard to suppress nervous, insane giggles as she watched Katharine rock the pitchfork free of the mass that had been Garnock. The massive spider's flesh was rotting at a rate that reminded her of time-lapse clips where flowers sprang forth, bloomed, wilted and died in seconds. As Katharine yanked the fork out, the corpse fell apart into a grey, pungent soup that made both women retch, and which – ironically, it seemed to Laine – buzzed with flies.

Suzette hurried across the twilit back lawn to the garden shed, where she found two spades with blades polished silver and sharp by being driven into unwelcoming shaly soil.

From under the kitchen sink, Katharine produced a torch, spare batteries and another can of insect spray.

Stars were opening their eyes in the black sky when they shut the front door behind them. Katharine checked it was locked, and the three women hurried down towards Carmichael Road.

•

Nicholas watched Quill rise from her chair and walk to the fire pit.

Her calves – squat and blue and veined, then slender and pale and taut – passed before his face. She knelt at the larger fire and began stoking its coals. Glowing orange sparks rose in a syrupy fountain of dying stars.

Outside, the wind grew stronger. It batted at the window, setting it knocking in its frame, and whistled sorrowfully in the flue. The fire behind the grate grew brighter as if jealous of its increscent neighbour.

Nicholas felt his mind eat its way back, like a snake through its burrow, to the Ealing flat's bathroom where he sat watching Cate hear her mobile phone, climb down the ladder, slip and fall – sudden as a snapped branch – to strike the icy white of the bath edge, to lie still. She'd never have fallen if he hadn't phoned. He'd never have phoned if he hadn't dropped the bike. He wouldn't have dropped the bike if he hadn't seen the face between the dark trees in Walpole Park. And he wouldn't have seen the face if Quill hadn't asked for him to see it.

She'd summoned the Green Man.

'You killed my wife,' he whispered.

Quill drew a hooked poker through the coals as if she hadn't heard him, and blew gently through pursed lips. Flame burst alive, and, as reward, her profile grew young and perfect, a sculpture cruel and lovely.

'I asked. The Green Man arranged. But *you* killed her,' she corrected.

The flames in the fire pit licked higher.

'You selfish bitch,' he whispered. 'Cate. Me. Tristram. All those children.'

Quill looked sideways at him. 'You haven't asked why,' she said.

Nicholas saw she wore a thin belt under her cardigan. On it was slung a sheath, narrow as a letter opener, from which protruded a bone handle.

'I know why.'

She arched her eyebrows.

'You bought yourself a longer life with theirs,' he said.

She watched him for a while, long enough for him to hear the hungry crackle of flames and the eerie moan of high, cold wind – the scene was so rustic, they could be a hundred miles away and a hundred years ago. Then she shook her head and laughed. For just a moment, it was a pretty, girlish laugh without poison or hate. Then it soured and died. She gritted her teeth.

'I did *nothing* for me, Nicholas Close,' she tutted. 'I thought you were wiser than that.'

He watched her: an ancient woman with a ghostly flicker of youth haunting her features, tending a fire in an old cottage in the middle of woods that should have been bulldozed and built over long ago.

'For the woods?'

She gave the fire a last prod. Satisfied, she rose painfully to her feet.

'Everything I've done was done for these woods.'

She sat again, and fussed her fingers over the wooden calendar, then leaned to look out the window. As she did, moonlight struck her skin, washing away the years and bringing the young Rowena Quill full into life. She stayed that way – youthful and perfect – as she spoke, staring at the moon.

'My mam had skill. She taught me. Her mam taught her. We were women of the woods for as long as long. There was respect once, for women with knowledge. Who knew how to heal. How to divine this and that. How to help sway luck. Respect and fear. But the world . . . the world moved on . . .' Rowena cocked an eye at him. 'Bought life, ya say? Do you know what was considered an *old* woman when I was born? Forty years.' She hissed the words, disgusted. '*Forty years* was old age. We were a dozen folk a cabin in our clachan. Our land was long in the hands of the English. Cromwell did his work well and thorough. My folk were cottiers, pretty low folk. We grew lumpers, 'taters. We all grew lumpers . . .' She nodded to herself. 'I was jes' a girl, not twelve, when the 'tater leaves started turnin' black and rottin'.' As she spoke, her lilt grew thicker, her gaze farther away. 'You've smelled dead t'ings. But nothin' stenches like a t'ousand fields of a million wet, rottin' lumpers. No 'taters. So they sold us corn. Peel's brimstone. It rips ya up inside and does nothin' good for ya. Useless. We were payin' ta die. We started starvin'. My beautiful mam . . .'

Rowena's skin was the cold blue-white of marble in the moonlight. She might have been carved of milkstone, but for the flicker of her dark eyes.

'She, all of us, we all starved thin. So we all stole. And we all whored. Only I picked poorly. The man I whored for wanted what

I wouldn't give him. He wanted a wife and a sprig.' She frowned. 'Sweet words and fancies. I thought about it, I truly did. But the shame of an English husband was too much. Too much.' Her small nose wrinkled with distaste. 'He got violent, this Englishman. Got to hittin' hard, takin' for free t'only thing I had to sell. So I stabbed him. But I were no good at that, neither. Three days he took to perish. Plenty of time for him to tell who done it and for the coats to find me and gaol me up. And try me. Hangin', they gave me.'

She swiped the fire lazily with the poker, and turned her eyes to Nicholas.

'But we had a calf, a skinny ragged t'ing. But the most valuable t'ing me mam owned. Mam took it to the woods on Mabon, when we say thanks for the harvest. Not much ta thank for. But she took it and cut it and asked Him to save me from swingin'.' Rowena nodded her head at the carved image of the Green Man. 'The next week, m' sentence was commuted to transportation. Mam waved me off from Youghal. She walked all the way, poor pinched t'ing, and as we were marched to the pier, she ran up and told me how she bought my life. What He did for her. She made me promise, wherever I ended up, to show m' thanks by lookin' after His woods.

'He saved me.'

She stared at Nicholas, chin high.

The fire ticked uneasily.

Nicholas held her eyes.

'And who is here to save the children from you?'

Quill didn't move a muscle. She seemed frozen in light and time, an ice statue that could stare implacably for a thousand years. She spoke at last.

'Blood is the only sacrifice that pleases the Lord.'

•

There was nothing left in Hannah's stomach to sick up. As she'd struggled to ease her hands out of the silk, the clinging strands had stuck between her fingers and under her nails. Finally, she'd freed her fingers enough to rip a hole through which she could shove her forearm. She cleared her eyes and mouth, but the feel of the persistent, sticky web pulling at her face and hair made her choke. What she removed from her hair stuck to her fingertips. After a while, the sense of it clinging and grasping sent her into a panic, and she danced about, trying to fling it from herself; as she whirled, she collided with the mummified black boy in his cocoon, sending him rattling dryly. Her stomach gave itself up in a long retching fit.

It was while she was on her hands and knees, ropy spit hanging from her mouth and nose, that she spotted something curled in the corner of the cellar. She wiped her mouth and hurried to it. Her backpack!

She carried it to the brick stairs and, under the three slivers of moonlight, opened it, heart thumping excitedly. Inside were sodden newspapers, still tangy with the smell of alcohol. Loose matches scattered like tiny bones. She dug, and found what she was looking for: the paring knife, its blade still wrapped in crinkled aluminium foil. Just holding its plastic handle in her fingers made her feel better. A weapon.

She climbed the stairs and pressed on one of the wooden doors. It was heavy, but as she strained, it lifted the barest amount . . . then the solid clack of metal on metal marked the limit of its travel. A barrel bolt on the upper side of the doors was locking her in.

She was trapped.

38

Wind from the west whipped the treetops into a breathy susurrus, driving the women faster.

Suzette felt pushed, urged by dry fingers to a place and fate that was pregnant and black and waiting. She wondered again, as she had since her mother told her about Pritam's death, if this was just another part of Quill's plan.

'What a trio we make,' said Katharine as they strode side by side. Three women: one stern-eyed and pretty, one lean and quite beautiful, the other sliding into attractive late middle age, all with hair pulled back sensibly as they trotted with a fork or spade in hand and grim purpose on their faces.

Laine smiled. 'Are we mad?'

Katharine slid a sure eye back. 'Oh, yes. It's good, isn't it?'

Suzette recalled Nicholas's words from days ago – days that felt like weeks. *I thought you just liked gardening*, he'd said. *That was . . . what? Hemlock and mandrake and double-double-toil-and-trouble shit?*

'Fire burn, and cauldron bubble,' said Suzette. She looked at her mother. Katharine held her gaze and gave a small nod. It made Suzette smile.

'That's us,' said Katharine. 'Three witches armed by Bunnings.'

Laine let out a small laugh, but her smile soon evaporated.

The word 'witch' seemed to scare them all. They were silent, perhaps sharing the same thoughts. Where was Nicholas? Still in the woods? Had he found Quill? Had she found *him*?

The night was young but cold, and something was shifting on the air. Suzette noticed Katharine watching the sky, and followed

349

her mother's gaze upwards. Clouds, heavy as slate and swollen like the underbellies of diseased beasts, were rolling across the sky. Rain was coming. Heavy rain.

'Do you feel small?' asked Katharine. 'I feel very small.'

•

By the time they reached Carmichael Road, their faces were toneless shadows.

'What are those cars parked there?'

Suzette and Katharine followed Laine's grey eyes.

On the dark strip of grass bordering the black trees were several cars.

'I don't know —'

Red and blue lights flashed on, dazzling the women, and a siren *hoo-hooed* once in warning.

'Ladies?' called a man's voice. 'Please step over here.'

39

After Rowena Quill had told her story, she'd fallen silent, tending her fire.

Nicholas had tried to turn away, to close his eyes, to think, to plan how to escape and kill her . . . but then he had started watching her fingers.

The fire was fully birthed and breathing on its own, and Quill put down the poker and tongs so her hands were free. They began to weave the air above the flames, seeming to pull shadows and firelight through each other, drawing symbols in the shimmering, sparking air above the fire pit.

Nicholas stared, mesmerised. Her voice was a singsong of words he didn't understand, but their tone was clear. Invoking. Inviting. Imploring. *Please. Please* . . .

He was startled from the spell by the thudding of the first heavy drops of rain on the shingles above him. It was a short entrée; in just moments, drenching rain stampeded down. Rain to deter the searchers. Rain to buy Quill time enough to kill Hannah Gerlic and move her body to be found kilometres away.

Nicholas rolled onto his back. The ropes dug painfully, pinching the skin of his wrists and cutting most of the blood to his feet, making them cold and numb.

'Let the girl go, Rowena.'

For a while Quill said nothing, but cocked her head and listened to the tapdance on the roof.

'She can't go back,' she said. 'She will bring *them* here.'

'You killed her sister, her parents are already —'

'She won't suffer,' snapped Quill. She rose quickly to her feet and hobbled across the room. No sign of the young, svelte Rowena now.

He'd seen the terror on dead Dylan Thomas's face as he was hauled, again and again, to a violent death that occurred somewhere near here. A death, Nicholas was sure, he would see tonight.

'They suffer,' he said.

She sent an angry glance at him, ready to bite again.

'It's an honour. They don't know it, but they give of themselves so that others live.'

'Trees,' whispered Nicholas.

'Yes, trees!' snarled Quill. Orange light danced under her chin and eyes, so she seemed to rise like a fiery djinni. 'And more than trees. There are secrets in live wood.' She turned her full face to him and, as her passion rose, she again grew younger, so chillingly beautiful that Nicholas could only stare. 'The woods ruled once, and men were tiny in them – tiny an' afraid. The woods fed us an' taught us an' shared their secrets with those that listened to Him. Oh, how terrified they were when we learned fire! Fire an' steel. Fire an' steel, an' the scales swung. Then we grew more plentiful than the trees. We became the blight on 'em, like that cursed fungus on our lumpers. Poisonous, infecting everythin'. One of them,' she pointed out the window at the black panorama of hidden forest, 'can grow five hundred years. Do you know how many people can breed from two humans in five hundred years? A *million!* A million mouths an' bodies needin' more fire, more wood, more food, more space.'

She shook her head and her long, blonde hair sparkled like silk. Her eyes probed his, desperate.

'We're the disease,' she whispered. 'What odds if a few young ones must die? There's always more. Trust me on that.'

She lifted her head, her throat was long and slender and white. On the skin that plunged down from her neck to the curving tops of her breasts glistened delicate gems of perspiration. Nicholas found his skin growing hot, and looked away, angry with his body. The rain swelled on the roof. Rowena and he could have been the only people in a hundred kilometres, a thousand kilometres. Despite his fury, despite his disgust, his body wanted her.

'It's a lie,' he whispered. 'You're a lie.'

She rose from her chair, lithe and light as air, and crouched over him. Her eyes sparkled.

'This hair's a lie?'

Her face hovered over his and her hair fell like gold curtains around them. Her teeth were perfect pearls behind thick, soft lips. She lowered her mouth till her lower lip grazed his forehead.

'This skin?' she murmured.

Her touch was electric. His blood throbbed and his groin ached.

'It is fleeting now, yes,' she purred. 'But it needn't be. I have only to ask. I have never asked for anything for me, just for me.' Her head crept forward until her white throat was over his face, and her breath blew over his chin, his neck, his chest. Her breasts swung loose and full, tantalising centimetres from his eyes, his mouth. 'We can be young together.' She prowled backwards till her lips were above his.

Nicholas felt his heart thumping in his chest, so hard it shook him on the floor. He felt the pulsing rain outside was driving his blood, falling hard and alive, desperate to sink into the ground, to rise through roots and trunks, to explode in lush, bright leaves.

But Hannah . . .

'And what will that cost?' he whispered.

The corners of her perfect lips curled upwards in a gentle smile. 'She'll not suffer long,' she whispered back, a breath as young as saplings.

He could feel her heat. Smell her sweet sweat. The skin above him was so white and perfect that there was nothing else to the world – she could be his sky, his bed, his food. He gritted his teeth. *It's a lie*, he thought. *It's all a lie. Her excuses, her double life, her names. Pretending to be part of a town that she fed off, that she bled, which she plucked children from as carelessly as weeds from a herb garden.*

'Your church was a lie, too,' he hissed. 'A church to one God, but meant for another.'

She hovered over him, her lips so close to his the air tingled as if lightning were ready to leap between them. She smiled.

'What makes you think they are not one and the same?'

Nicholas blinked. Did Pritam once say that, too? It was so hard to think. His groin throbbed painfully, ravenously. His chest hammered. His mouth felt at once wet and dry. What was she saying? Church of Christ? Church of the Green Man?

Her tongue danced behind her white teeth. Her eyes were wide, her pupils dark and large with excitement, her breath was sweet and lightly spiced.

'He has gone by many names in many ages. But His story is the same,' she said. 'He dies so we can live. Each year He dies for us, and then is reborn for us. And all He asks in return is humility,' her lips touched his, 'and a little sacrifice.'

It seemed so simple now. *Stay*. All he had to do was stay. Wasn't this what people dreamed of? An idyll, a singing nest of trees in which to live a life so long he would be like the trees themselves: deep-rooted and protected and safe. A woman who understood him, who knew his gift, who wanted him enough to kill for him, who was achingly beautiful and raised his flesh like a drug. Time would lose its weight. Life would be perfect.

Rowena smiled at him, as if reading his thoughts. Her fingertips ran down his throat – her lips gentled the air above his own. His mouth was wet with the need to taste her flesh. Her body was so close its heat poured down with the erotic rhythm of the rain. *Yes*, she said without words. *Life would be perfect.*

Except . . .

'Except for the ghosts,' whispered Nicholas.

He spat in her face.

As she shrieked, the mask of youth ripped apart like smoke in a sudden gust and the old hag Quill reared over him, wrinkled and rotting. She slapped his face so hard that white stars joined the orange sparks in the air.

•

Rain clouds rolled overhead and what little light the night sky had given was vanished. Where moonlight had sliced three white knives through the gaps between the heavy timbers of the cellar doors, raindrops now leaked, accreting into globs of cold water as big as marbles that fell and spattered on the brick stairs.

Hannah was soaking wet and sobbing. Her fingers were frustrating millimetres too thick to slip between the boards of the trap doors and reach the bolt. So, she crouched on the stairs on the underside of the doors, reaching between the heavy timbers with the paring knife, trying to snick and persuade the barrel bolt to move . . . but it was fruitless. The bolt needed to twist ninety degrees before its loop would clear the guide and it could be slid aside. The blade found no purchase on the round steel.

Hannah could feel her heart trotting faster. She didn't know how long she'd been down here, but it had certainly been hours. She remembered that it had rained this heavily the night Miriam had been taken. Time surely was running out. She was going to die.

She slid on her bottom back down the stairs into the inky gloom. She had to find *something* to move the barrel bolt, but what? *Such an idiot!* If only she'd worn her sneakers instead of the slip-ons, she would have had shoelaces! She could picture slipping the lace over the bolt, pulling down hard on both ends, and gently rolling the bolt free. *If wishes were horses, beggars would ride*, Vee would say.

As soon as she moved away from the miserable glow admitted by the door cracks, the room was almost pitch black and she could only make out the vaguest forms. Her fingers probed the dark: hunting, feeling. Shelves were cut into the walls of the cellar like catacombs. Jars of all sizes. She pulled one out and shook it. A faint rattle. She unscrewed the lid, and tipped the contents into her hand, and guided her fingertips over it. The object became so instantly and horribly familiar that she let out a yelp. A tooth, long pronged roots still attached. She dropped it to the floor and went to the next jar, rattled it. A faint sloshing inside. The next felt empty, and when she opened it, a small piece of furry paper fell onto her palm. As she felt the patch, her stomach twisted. It was a piece of dried skin, short hairs still attached. Her heart raced faster, and she kept going through the jars. One after another, their contents were equally repulsive and useless to her. *Useless, useless, useless!*

She felt tears start to salt her eyes, and blinked hard. This was no time for crying. There had to be *something*. There were four walls, that was clear. One wall was hewn shelves full of jars. One had the stairs. The next was blank. The last was where she herself had hung, and where the mummified black boy still slumped in his cobweb cocoon. This wall was the last one to search.

Hannah put her arms out in front of her and gingerly stepped towards the last wall. Her fingers touched silky threads and jerked back involuntarily. *Okay*, she thought. *That's him. What's beside him?* Her fingers delicately slid past the wispy strands until they again touched the wall. Nothing, nothing . . . cold earth and the mute heads of rocks. Then her fingers slipped into space. Another shelf?

She used both hands to map the hole.

Where the excavated shelves were perhaps twenty centimetres or so high, this was taller; so high that she couldn't reach its top, and it was at least a metre wide. She put her hand into it, then pulled back sharply. *What if there are spiders in there?*

Vee's voice came back at her, at once cheerful and serious: *There'll be spiders in here soon enough, girlie, so get a wriggle on.*

Hannah stood on tiptoe and reached into the hole . . .

Her fingers touched something hard and flat and cold. Steel. She probed, and her hand closed around a looped iron handle. It was a box.

Or a coffin.

'Shush,' she hissed at herself.

She gripped the handle and pulled. The box chuckled unhappily, steel scraping on rock. It was heavy, but it moved. *Well,* she thought, *if it's a coffin, it's empty*. She pulled more and the end of the box cleared the wall. It still rested flat in its hole. She pulled and took a step backward, then another. How long was this thing? And when should she put up her other hand to stop it overbalancing? But just as she asked herself, the far end of the chest cleared the wall and it fell fast and hard. One sharp metal corner pounded into her cheek, then the box slammed sharply on the damp ground with a booming clang. Hannah lost her grip on it completely and the metal box tottered forward and fell, scraping skin from her shin on its downward arc.

Tears sprang out of her eyes and she bit her lip to stop herself howling at the bright pain.

At least it's down.

Hannah knelt. She seemed to be hurting everywhere, worst of all her hot-and-cold throbbing shin. She gritted her teeth and made her fingers feel the chest. It had fallen onto its lid. She gripped the cold corners of folded steel and lifted. The chest rolled slowly and, as it did, its lid opened: its catch must have broken loose. Stuff spilled out over her hands and forearms.

Papers. Lots and lots of papers. Small pieces of paper – thousands of small rectangles.

Oh, wow, she realised. *This is . . .*

She picked up a handful and sloshed over to the dull grey light leaking in from the trapdoors. The golden yellow plastic of contemporary fifty-dollar notes. The red paper of old twenties. A grey-green note printed '£100'. Hannah blinked. There was a fortune.

But it won't buy your way out of here, she thought acidly.

She felt her way back over to the chest and started sifting through the money. *Please, please, please*, she thought, *please let there be something in here. Something . . .* She shovelled the notes aside, feeling, probing, digging . . .

Then her fingers closed on a roll of larger sheets. She followed the dry cylinder along its length. *The roll's held together, but with what?*

Then a smile appeared on her face.

The roll was tied with a leather thong.

40

Nicholas's head ached sharply. He'd spat in Quill's face, and she had slapped him – slapped him *hard*.

Then she had risen, passing the fire pit and muttering to herself. She bent to the dresser and he heard through the ringing in his ear the clinking of glass and the tick of tin and the shush of things unscrewing. Rain mumbled heavily all the while.

His hatred for her was now as solid as the boards he lay on, as the stones ringing the fire pit. But despite it, he hadn't come up with anything approximating a half-baked plan, let alone anything that promised a whiff of success. He was her prisoner, and Hannah was shortly to die.

'I'll stay if you let Hannah go.'

She kept her back to him. Her silence was terrifying.

'I said —'

'You will stay,' said Quill, cutting him short. 'And the cuttie will surely go.'

She turned her body and Nicholas saw what she held. A jar. It was open and in its bottom ran a small amount of greyish, once-white fluid. In her other hand, she held a silver cone on a rod. It looked like a candle snuffer; God knows he'd found plenty of those over his years of scrounging. But this metal cone was larger and curved like a horn, writhing with symbols and darkly stained with soot. Quill reached for her belt and, with a motion as swift and practised as a torero with a banderilla, produced the small, wickedly sharp knife. She drew the blade over her thumb and a red ruby of blood sprouted there. She let a thimbleful of thick crimson liquid drop into the silver cone. Her wrinkled oyster of a mouth mumbled words Nicholas couldn't make out. Then she closed the wound, licked it, and poured the semen from the jar into the crucible. Without hesitating, she set the empty jar aside and held the cone by its stained silver handle over the flames.

Nicholas felt his limbs instantly blaze with pain, as if she were holding not the silver horn but *him* over the flames. Then, just as suddenly, fall slack and dumb. His heart stopped beating. He felt his breath sigh out of his lungs.

Oh God, she's killed me!

Then his chest began thumping again, a deliberate, slow-paced tattoo that was dislocated and inhuman. As the blood swept from his heart through his veins, he seemed able to feel its passage. *It's not mine*, he thought. *It doesn't feel like my blood any more! It feels like . . .*

'Stiff, now,' said Quill.

Nicholas felt his throat tighten and his arms, legs, chest, harden, every muscle closing like a thousand fists, till his body was straight and rigid as wood. His eyes watered with the pain of exertion, yet his sight remained his. He rolled his eyes.

Quill was watching him from a face that was all shadow bar two bright orbs that shone orange and owlish in the firelight. And she was smiling.

She got to her feet and scuttled over to him. With her neat knife, she sliced the ropes around his wrists and ankles and knees. Again, she was kneeling over his face, but instead of ripe young breasts and a long white throat, poised above him now was wattled grey flesh and rags. Her wet gums shone like the insides of dying clams.

'Not for long, my pretty man.'

She let a string of spittle fall from her mouth into his, and giggled.

'Stand.'

His legs swept under him and his arms gracefully pushed. He was on his feet. She watched him for a moment. Her eyes slid down his chest to his groin, and he could see the corner of her mouth grin upwards as she debated if she had time to play. Instead, she put the little knife in his fingers.

'Take it,' she said.

As his fingers closed around the bone handle, Nicholas suddenly understood what he would be forced to do. *No!* he yelled, but his mouth would not work a word of protest.

'Follow me,' said Quill. She pulled a scarf from a peg beside the window and tied it over her white hair, then opened the grey wood door and stepped into the rain.

Nicholas found himself following her, fluid as smoke.

•

He glided after her on legs that moved of another's accord, as if transported in a body borrowed.

He followed as she hobbled along the neat, rain-soaked flagstones beside the cottage. He could feel his feet step carefully on the wet path, his breaths ease wet air in and out, his fingers on the cool bone of the knife . . . but had no control of any of them. He ordered his feet to stop, but they kept walking; he tried to scream, but his breath continued in and out in a steady rhythm; he tried to throw the knife, but his fingers held it fast. He was going to cut Hannah Gerlic's throat.

As if hearing the thought, Quill turned to him and stopped. The rain pulled her ashen hair down over her limp skin, and her clothes lumped with sodden heaviness. She lifted her chin. For the first time, he could see without her sortilege past the old flesh and shrinking bone to the woman she had been. She nodded around at the tall, ancient trees.

'It's easy. You'll see.'

A flash of white and pink flickered at the edge of the clearing, and streaked towards them. When it grew closer, Nicholas felt the regular rhythm of his breaths catch. The figure was a child, arm outstretched, heels bouncing on the ground as she was hauled by invisible hands. The girl in the forties' sundress. As she passed, her wide eyes swung to Nicholas, pleading and resigned. He felt his stomach lurch. The girl screamed silently and flew backwards into the circular grove of trees behind them.

Quill continued her rocking hobble towards the rear of the cottage. She hadn't seen the ghost.

How does that help me? wondered Nicholas.

She rounded the corner, and he followed close behind. They saw the same sight at once. The flat cellar door lay open on the sodden ground, rain spattering the descending steps.

Quill stared for a long moment, her eyes wide and her jaw tight – then whipped her eyes around to Nicholas. She trembled from head to foot. Anger poured off her in waves. Nicholas felt a thrill of excitement rise through him. *Hannah must have escaped!* As Quill glared, her mouth opened wide and she let out a screech that was alien and shrill, neither animal nor birdlike, but a sound much older and deeply unsettling.

The ground itself seemed to shimmer darkly. It rippled like the surface of a dark pond disturbed by something great and unseen below. And an insect-like ticking crisped the air under the rain. Nicholas strained, and rolled his eyes to the surrounding forest. The dark wave grew closer and closer until he could see what it was: the ground was alive with spiders. Thousands and thousands of spiders. Tens of thousands. *Hundreds* of thousands. Some were as small as rice grains, some as large as plates; smooth and hard; bristled and grey. A million round, black eyes collected around the old woman on a sea of shifting, spiny legs and round, swollen abdomens.

Nicholas felt a cold wave of primal terror swirl through his gut and fountain up his back.

The spiders watched Quill, waiting.

She was shaking. Angry. Pale.

And scared, he realised.

Quill looked over the mass of spiders. They coated bushes and her neat hedges. They piled on one another. Poised and listening. Her mouth worked. She glanced at Nicholas, unsure. Her fingers vibrated. Her jowls trembled. Then she spoke.

'Find the girl,' she whispered in a voice that sounded more suited to a beak than to human lips. 'Find her. Kill her. And take her far, far, far!'

The spiders moved. Like a wave receding from the sand back into the sea, the mass drew away off the gardens and the path and the ground and shrank back into the trees.

Quill turned to Nicholas. Her eyes were wet, and not with rain. She stepped up to him. A smile crept onto her face, but it crumbled away. With one hand she wiped the briny spill off his chin. With the other, she gently took the knife from his fingers.

'My poor man,' she whispered. 'Come.'

She started towards the circular grove, and he followed.

He knew what would happen. She was going to kill him instead.

41

Branches tore at Hannah's face, and the sharp hooks of thick vines raked her wrists and tangled her feet. She was exhausted. Her frantic scramble slowed from a run to a walk. Her leg throbbed where the shotgun pellet had lodged in her calf, and the limb felt like a load she had to carry. The rain had eased, but heavy drops fell like cold pebbles from high, hidden leaves onto her neck and scalp. The paring knife was wet and threatened to slip from her grasp. Her breath came in hurting, inadequate blasts – deep, greedy sucks of air. She knew she had to stop before she stumbled and hurt herself even worse, but the memory of the dead black child in his ancient grey cocoon spurred her on.

The dark was thick, but her hours of peering in the cellar had allowed her pupils to widen to their fullest and she could at least make out the barest outlines of trunks and logs. She saw a fallen tree a few steps ahead, and sank, gasping, onto it, unmindful of the cold that clenched her buttocks as the wet soaked instantly through.

It felt both long hours and mere minutes since she had threaded the leather thong up the gap between the doors, watching it fold and flop over the barrel bolt. The moments she'd spent carefully pulling down on both ends of the thong – slightly more tension on one end than the other – had been the most stressful of her life. Each time the bolt slipped too far under the wet leather and clacked, her heart had hammered as she waited for the door to fling wide and something petrifying to grab her. But, finally, she'd found the balance, and turned the bolt upright, then carefully pulled to the side . . . and the bolt arm had cleared its stay.

The burning in her legs was fading at last and her breaths were coming easier. *What now?* she asked herself. Run home? Tell her parents, tell the police that were surely there? And then what? Lead them back in here? No, they wouldn't let her out of their sight. Her story was unbelievable. They'd see the pellet wound in her leg, hear that Nicholas shot her . . .

They'd come in hunting not Quill, but Nicholas.

And he'll be dead by then, if he isn't already.

But he wasn't. Hannah was sure of it. She could feel it: Nicholas was alive. But for how long?

She wiped the black plastic handle of the paring knife. Miriam was dead. Nicholas was going to die soon. And the old witch was going to get away with it. The spark of dull anger inside her flared.

Unless . . .

She took a deep breath, wiped the knife handle, and started back towards the cottage.

•

Laine sat in the back of the police car listening to the rain on the roof subside from a roar to a light drumming to a sporadic whisper. She glanced back to the other police sedan parked behind, and through the distorting swirls of water could vaguely make out the silhouette of Katharine's and Suzette's heads flanking a large male officer's in the vehicle's back seat.

Laine turned back to the two officers in the car with her. Both men sat in the front on the other side of a Perspex screen, one drinking tea from a thermos, the other staring glumly into the rain.

'I think you have to arrest me or let me go,' she said.

'Well,' replied the one with the tea, but then fell silent.

'We're just keeping you out of the rain,' said the other. 'We'll know soon.'

To Laine it felt like hours since the officers had summoned her, Suzette and Katharine over as they hurried towards the woods, shovels and forks in hand. Laine had been amazed by Katharine's quick lie that the three of them were part of a woodlands conservation group. She and Suzette had picked up the mistruth, explaining that a rare dwarf syzygium needed its mulch turned over or it would get root rot. The police had all but let them go when Katharine spoiled it all by answering truthfully when asked for her name. Clearly, 'Close' was on record as associated with the Gerlic children. And so the women had been divested of their makeshift weapons and split into separate cars, where streams of questions kept flowing until the rains drowned them out.

Laine had the temerity to ask several times why the police weren't out looking for Hannah Gerlic instead of harassing her, to which the thundering rain gave its own answer.

'I think I need to talk with my solicitor,' she said finally.

The police officers looked at one another. A car door opened and closed behind them. 'Wait here.' The officers opened their own doors and went out into the drizzle.

Laine watched them meet another four officers in a huddle. Arms pointed at the car in which Katharine sat, and fingers gestured towards Laine, towards the sky, towards the woods. Heads nodded. Torches flicked on. Men walked towards the dark tree line.

A minibus pulled up on the verge and a file of shadowed men and women in orange State Emergency Service overalls disembarked.

The front door of Laine's car opened and a police officer slid back in. He turned to her.

'Fancy a cup of tea?'

42

The walk from the open cellar door, back past Quill's cottage, and into the circular grove was as slow and silent as a dream.

Nicholas lifted his eyes to look at the sky. The rain had all but finished, and clouds were easing apart like rotten lace in a stiff wind; behind them, stars blinked cold, faint light. Ahead, a round wall of trees glistened and their wet leaves whispered to one another with sly drip-drips. There were two dozen or so trees in a circle twenty metres wide.

As Quill walked between two trees, she touched fondly the trunk nearest. She didn't look back at him.

Nicholas knew what was happening. Hannah was gone. Quill needed a miracle. To summon one, she had to have blood. She would use his.

A figure slid through him, and his eyes widened with surprise, but his body allowed no other shock. Miriam Gerlic screamed without sound, wrists bound together behind her, legs kicking at air as she was carried by unseen hands between the trees. As she slipped out of sight, her ghost eyes fell on Nicholas . . . then were obscured by sable branches.

Nicholas let out his own silent scream as his body carried him into the circle.

The ground underfoot was wet, sandy dirt, raked clean. In the centre of the unnatural grove was a pedestal of stilted legs a metre high holding aloft a spherical cage made of woven branches and bone.

Quill hobbled to stand beside the cage. Within it was a shifting cloud of moving shadows. As Nicholas grew closer, he understood:

inside the cage, five or six children half-knelt, half-hung, their ghostly skins melding with one another's. Each was suspended by the wrists, which were lashed to the curved branch bars above them. A half-dozen children. A half-dozen ghosts. Their faces were an overlapping blur. But as each bobbed or struggled, he or she would drift apart from the others and Nicholas could see their singular terror. Little Owen Liddy in his long shorts, his face pale with disbelieving fright. The girl in the forties' sundress, her bare feet torn and bleeding. Another boy, younger than the others and with red hair, had his eyes screwed tight above wet cheeks. Miriam Gerlic's eyes were impossibly wide and without hope. Dylan Thomas, head bowed and bawling. And Tristram Boye.

Nicholas felt the rhythm of his breathing break, and he sucked in cool air.

He knew that Tristram had died here in the woods, but to see him, his friend, his hero, at the edge of his pitiful murder filled Nicholas with such an awful sadness that he wanted simply to fall to the ground. Tristram's jaw was tight, one wrist crooked at a strange angle. *Broken.* Nicholas's tongue flicked the roof of his mouth as he tried to form his name – *Tris* . . . – but no noise came out.

The dead children struggled: Miriam screamed; Dylan sobbed; Owen Liddy nodded like a savant. Suddenly, the red-haired boy's head jerked upwards. His face grew brighter, and his throat opened up as if an invisible zipper dragged wide. The little boy's eyes flashed open and went dull. His small body spasmed and stiffened . . . then he vanished.

Nicholas felt sick.

'Hurry, hurry,' whispered Quill, gesturing to Nicholas and glancing to the sky. She climbed the short stick ladder that rose to the sphere behind the ghostly children. Feet on the highest rung, she unlatched a hatch made of the same grisly bone and twisted wood, and swung it wide before scuttling down to the ground.

Nicholas saw her for what she was. A spider. A spider herself: bloated and old and thirsty, scuttling to do dark work at the centre of her ancient web of dark trees . . .

'Up,' she whispered. 'In.'

A wind was born, and it tickled the ring of trees, setting them awhisper like excited spectators at a night coliseum. Nicholas's hands grasped bone and branch, and his feet climbed the makeshift ladder. The dead children squirmed in desperate terror before him. *God, no*, he thought. *Don't make me go in there* . . . But his legs stepped into the hatchway, and his body slid in after, slipping him into the ghosts of the stunned, wailing, weeping, lost children.

Cold, he thought. *This is how death feels.*

'Kneel,' she said.

He knelt. He was aware of the pain as the hard wood dug into his kneecaps, but could not so much as flinch against it.

'Reach.'

His hands rose willingly; where the dead children strained against invisible bonds, his agreeable hands grasped the cold stick and bone lightly. As he took hold, the hair of the girl in the forties' sundress stood on end and her neck jerked long. She tried to twist her head from side to side, knowing she was going to die and fighting. Her skin grew suddenly silvery and pale, as if a spectral spotlight were turned on it, and the skin of her neck opened up, revealing darker, wet flesh in the deep cut. Her small body arched, then slowly slackened . . . and she vanished.

'Wait,' said Quill. She was behind him, out of sight, a lurking presence.

Nicholas was larger than the ghosts of the children. His arms were longer. Where they half-crouched, he squatted on his heels and so sat behind the four-folded children and could see the backs of their entwined heads. Their faces interwove and became as hard to discern as ripples in a stream's crosscurrent.

He willed himself to scream and fight and flee . . . but he sat immobile as a monk. He heard Quill's careful footsteps on the ladder behind him. She sniffed back mucus.

Then Miriam's hair grew brighter and the skin of her arms glowed. Nicholas realised what this ghostly light was: the echo of moonlight from several nights ago. Suddenly, her hair jerked straight, wrenched upward by an invisible hand. Her eyes threw wide. Nicholas saw the edge of her throat split open in a new, deep wound, severed by a keen, invisible blade. Her tiny body strained in a last animal panic; her muscles wrenched tight . . . then she swooned. The hair fell down like a final curtain. Her body sagged, then winked out, leaving the ghosts of three boys struggling in front of him.

Oh God, thought Nicholas. *Like a slaughtered lamb, simple as that.*

'Why so hard? Why so hard?' Quill's voice was ragged, broken by a tight throat. 'All these years, and what?' She was talking to herself as she settled on the ladder behind him.

Nicholas watched ghostly moonlight fall on Owen Liddy. The child's hair was gathered in an invisible hand, wrenched up, and his throat eased apart like a hidden mouth opening. He jolted a few moments, then sagged low and was gone, leaving two ghost boys. Nicholas's heart pumped peacefully in his chest, a lie to the horror.

The moon. The moon came out just before she cut their throats.

He rolled his eyes upwards, but could not see the moon. *Move!* he commanded his head. *Back!*

'You brought him and now you take him,' muttered Quill accusingly. Her voice was wet and bitter. 'What choice?'

Nicholas saw the hair of one of the boys grow bright. Dylan Thomas's. His scalp and skin glowed silver as the forgotten light of a ghost moon fell on him. A moment later, his short hair twisted cruelly upward, yanking his head high and his neck straight. Then the skin of his neck slid apart in a neat cut, deep, exposing arteries and tendons.

Only he and Tristram were left.

But now Nicholas knew. *She'll cut my throat when the moon comes out. I have to see the moon!* He closed his eyes and strained his head back. *Move!* His mind became a sharpening funnel. Every ounce of strength, every bit of anger, every breath he wanted to take before he died, was concentrated into a single thought: *Move!*

His head tilted back a degree.

'Not fair,' hissed Quill. She was crying. 'Not fair.'

Again! Move!

His head tilted back another tiny arc.

Tristram was turning. Someone was behind him. His lips moved, grim. Shaking with fear, but not crying. Not grovelling. Brave. *Oh, Tris . . .*

The ladder creaked behind Nicholas and he heard the tick of the knife touching old bone.

Back! His head tilted another degree. Tristram's skin grew bright as moonlight touched it. Nicholas could not watch his friend die; he rolled his eyes high to the sky.

The clouds overhead were grey waves, breaking. A glow indicated the moon at the edge of the moving cloud. It would be out in a moment.

His eyes rolled down just as Tristram's white throat opened. Nicholas's heart skipped from its metronome beat. *You fucking bitch.* Tristram stiffened and fell.

'Nicholas,' whispered Quill.

Tristram was gone. He was alone.

Moonlight opened from behind the racing cloud, touching the distant trees and turning them silver, sprinting closer, closer, closer.

'Goodbye, pretty man.'

The moonlight kissed his skin. His heart thudded hard as a storm, the blood building inside him like a swollen dam, ready to burst.

Somewhere in the dark, a curlew sounded like a girl's scream.

Nicholas felt a gnarled hand grab his hair, and the corner of his eye caught the wink of shining steel. His head jerked up.

BACK! he yelled at every muscle in his body. He let the dam inside him break, and threw himself backwards.

It wasn't dramatic, just a lurch.

The cage rocked back a fraction. Quill had a poor grip on his wet hair and it slipped through her bony fingers. The knife blade nicked his chin, and he heard a creak behind him as Quill went off balance.

'Oh,' she said simply.

He heard her fingers fly through the air, clutching for something to grab. And, suddenly, a thrill rippled through his body, as if a wave of warm water struck him inside. He moved his fingers. *She's distracted*, he thought wildly. *She's let me slip.* He told his hands to let go – they released their grip on bone and wood.

'No . . .' hissed Quill. 'No!'

Back! Nicholas threw himself backwards and this time he slammed against the side of the cage. It rocked violently on its low tower.

Quill scrambled to grab the cage. The knife slipped from her fingers and clattered against wood and bone. The cage teetered . . . Quill finally grabbed hold with her free hand, but her extra weight on the side of the sphere was too much . . . the cage groaned, the low tower leaned, and the cage began to fall.

'NO!' she screamed.

The cage toppled, carrying Nicholas within and Quill beneath it, and hit the ground with a loud and sickly splintering crash.

43

Wind tugged at Hannah's hair and slapped her face cold.

She concentrated on placing one foot in front of the other, not knowing if she was heading the right way . . . yet strangely certain that she was.

She crawled blindly over roots and under branches, hurting everywhere, guided by sound. Between gusts and the timpani rush of black leaves, she heard snatches of a woman's voice, a sad and lilting speech to someone or no one, carried away covetously by the fast air. She blundered between the dark trees, arms outstretched, falling and rising, ignoring the nauseating throb in her leg. This was right. This all was meant to be.

She was nearly there, perhaps fifty metres from the cottage. Nicholas was still alive – Hannah felt it in her heart – but things were about to turn.

Just then, the wind grew.

The clouds rolling high above the unhappy trees thinned.

The woman's voice skipped on the air like a black pebble on silver water.

The moon peeked out of hiding and the trees seemed to spring from darkness.

Hannah stopped.

The ground around her seemed to shimmer. But not just the ground: the trunks of trees, the hanging leaves on hanging vines, the mossed fur of logs, all crept and trembled.

Hannah felt her heart gulp blood. Was it . . . ?

As the clouds parted further, cold silver dropped down between the leaves, lighting everything in front of her – and her breath caught in her throat.

A million spiders watched her. Small and squat, large and bristled: all took a sly, feline step towards her on their alien, skeletal legs. The moonlight winked off their eight million eyes, an evil forest sprinkled with pernicious diamonds. She felt their stare. She felt their surprise at finding her. She felt the tiny sparks flying through their tiny brains, taking her picture, tasting it, conferring.

It's her. She watched a hungry shimmer run through them. *It's her.*

The edges of her eyes prickled brightly, and her head felt like an emptying balloon. Her body seemed to know that she would be better unconscious for the horrible fate that came next. Her legs started to fold.

NO! she yelled in her head. *Don't faint!* She pricked the point of the paring knife into her thigh and brilliant new pain chased away the swoon. What good would one knife do against a sea of needle-sharp fangs?

Hannah felt them watch her, see her, know her. The forest seemed to shift as the carpet of spiders, with its spiny, bristled legs and wicked little fangs and clusters of cold black pebble eyes, crouched.

She turned and ran.

And got one step before her right foot caught on a root.

She fell.

An instant later, the wave of spiders swept over her.

Hannah curled into a shrieking ball, waiting for the pain of a million stings . . .

But it didn't come.

The spiders seemed frozen. Their hooked feet grew rigid, snipping gently into her skin, her lips, her ears. All of them – large as breakfast bowls, small as match heads – were motionless. Listening.

Then they fell away.

They dropped off her and began scuttling over one another. Some wandered in confused circles. Some burrowed for cover. Some sprang away into the darkness. Some hunkered down stupidly to hide in her hair.

She sat up and brushed the few remainders away. Whatever had been guiding them was gone. The spell was broken.

And Hannah heard a splintering crash from the direction of the cottage.

She got to her feet and ran towards the sound.

•

Nicholas was on his back. The cage had rolled as it fell, and had struck the firm, wet ground with a sharp crack. He had instinctively tried to shield his head from the hard branch and bone and so had left his torso exposed; when the cage crunched into the ground, knurled branches and knobbled bones thudded into his exposed kidneys and ribcage. He was winded. Of all the fights he'd lost in high school, the worst was to a Scottish boy named Murray who had hammered his freckled fist deep into Nicholas's solar plexus, not only knocking every scrap of air out of him, but seeming to switch off his lungs so they wouldn't draw back in. Nicholas was left humiliated, gasping, desperate for air. This was worse – he was drowning in pain.

He curled on his side, mouth wide, frantically willing a scrap of air to draw into his burning lungs. His diaphragm finally jittered alive and he sucked in a throaty gasp.

His eyes rolled, hunting for Quill.

The old woman was on the ground. She had clung to the cage as it fell, but it had rolled as it collapsed; only one leg had been caught beneath it, and now she strained to pull it from the splintery grid of spiny wood.

'Feck ya!' she hissed, but Nicholas didn't know if she was cursing him, herself, or someone else. Her hands patted the earth, crawling like grey crabs, hunting.

For the knife, he thought. *Where is it?*

'Where is it?' she whispered, echoing him.

Nicholas in the cage, Quill on the wet, sandy ground. Both rolled to their knees. Both scoured with eyes and fingers for the knife.

'You fucking bitch,' whispered Nicholas.

'Feck you,' she hissed again, this time surely to him.

'You cut their throats!' he spat, fingers crawling under the hard, gnarled branches and into the damp soil.

'For Him!'

'For yourself, you greedy whore!'

'Feck you,' she repeated quietly. 'Where is it?!'

Nicholas painfully rocked back on his haunches. His shadow was a black smudge inside the half-collapsed sphere. The cold moonlight made the bones in the cage as white as the ribs of undersea things. A wink of silver! His eyes jerked to the shine off the keen edge of the knife. The weapon lay just outside the bars. Near to him. Far from Quill.

'Yes,' he whispered, and reached between the branches.

'No!' snapped Quill. She scrambled.

Nicholas grabbed the knife.

And a small figure shrieked from the shadows and drove its own knife down at Quill.

•

As Hannah crept into the ring of trees, her eyes widened. On the ground was the cage she'd dreamt of, the cage of bone and branch, the round prison where she'd dreamt that spiders had bound her ready to die. It had collapsed on the ground, and Nicholas was inside it, on his back, heaving like a landed fish. An old woman was nearby, clawing at the ground like a blind thing. Hannah didn't hesitate. She ran.

'Horrible!' she yelled as she pounced on the old woman.

But Quill saw Hannah's shadow before she heard her voice, and rolled aside. Hannah's paring knife whisked down and through Quill's cardigan, nicking her withered breast and driving into the sandy dirt.

'Hannah!' yelled Nicholas.

'You little brasser!' cried Quill, and her voice trembled – not with anger, but with delight.

'Hannah, run!' shouted Nicholas. He scrambled backwards for the hatch, but his feet fouled on the branches and his clothes snagged on the snapped bars. 'Run!!'

Hannah scooted back, eyes locked on her paring knife driven blade-first in the ground.

Quill whirled on her, grinning brightly.

Nicholas fumbled with the cage hatch. But the frame had distorted as the cage landed and the hatch was firmly stuck.

Hannah eyed off the distance to the knife. Quill watched her, and the grey skin around her eyes wrinkled. 'Are ya quick, girlie?'

Hannah stared. *I can make it. I can get it. She's old. She's slow.*

'Quicker than ya sister, I hope,' taunted Quill in a singsong.

Hannah's jaw clenched.

'No, Hannah! Get out of here!' cried Nicholas. He bashed at the hatch. It didn't move.

Hannah dived.

Fast as a crow beak, Quill swung out. Her arm struck Hannah mid-flight, knocking the girl face first into the dirt. Hannah's outstretched hand grabbed nothing but wet, dark sand. Quill rolled, snatched up the knife, and drove her free hand down on the back of Hannah's neck.

Hannah yelped, but the cry was cut short as Quill pushed her face hard into the cold, wet dirt.

'Get off her!' yelled Nicholas.

'He is cruel and kind, isn't He?' twittered Quill. 'Eh, pretty man? Sends her back, whole and ready, out of His woods to me!' She laughed. Wind tickled the trees, and their leaves whispered approvingly. She straddled Hannah's back.

Nicholas stopped beating at the hatch. In his left hand was Quill's wicked little knife, but it was as useless as a burnt match with him trapped inside.

Hannah kicked and struggled, but Quill had her pinned. She tested the paring knife's blade with her thumb, and nodded. Overhead, the moon sailed high in clearing skies. Pleased, Quill looked over at Nicholas. Her mouth creaked open in a dark smile. 'Let's send her on her way, then,' she whispered, 'so that you and I can be.'

Hannah tried to scream, but Quill pressed her mouth deeper into the sandy ground.

'Don't, Quill. Don't do it,' whispered Nicholas.

Quill looked at him, as a mother looks at a child.

'She'll not feel much. Blood is the only sacrifice that pleases the Lord.'

Hannah's one eye above the dirt stared at Nicholas, wide with terror.

The moon rode high and easy overhead.

The sharp paring knife glinted.

And, suddenly, Nicholas knew what to do.

The idea arrived as clear and bright as the moonlight had, casting everything sharp and lucid.

There was a choice. He took it.

'Rowena,' he said softly.

She didn't hear him, and put the knife in her right hand and took a handful of Hannah's hair.

'Rowena,' he repeated. He was surprised at how calm he felt.

Quill looked over.

He lifted her little knife to his wrist.

The old woman's face fell. 'No . . .' she whispered.

Nicholas plunged the blade in. The pain was as clean as glass. He dragged the blade through tendons and veins. Blood, dark like syrup, gushed out.

He watched his blood flow between the branch bars onto the sand, soaking away. His calmness felt beautiful. *Now, how do I start?* he wondered. *What do I say?*

But the words came of their own accord.

'With my blood I call on you. I call on the Green Man.'

'No,' repeated Quill, more loudly.

Blood pulsed out, slapping delicately into a growing puddle. Nicholas watched it, fascinated.

'I give you my blood and I ask you —'

'No!' Panic.

'— to remove Rowena Quill from these woods —'

'NO!' Her voice was sprung tight with terror.

Nicholas felt his head grow hot, then cold. His vision danced.

'— forever.'

'Noooooo!!' Rowena Quill's last word became a scream.

Her shriek brought back to Nicholas a memory two decades old. He'd been employed to lay out a brochure for an abattoir in Kent. The manager had given him a courtesy tour, and he'd been shown the killing floor. The sound Quill now made was the exact cry of animal fear the cattle screamed when they rounded the narrow chute and saw ahead the crush and, beyond it, the corpses of their cousins that had gone before. Terror in the face of certain death.

Quill's eyes were wide and rimmed with white. Her head swivelled as she scanned the trees. She dropped the knife. She scrambled to her feet. And ran.

Nicholas watched the little sharp blade fall from his grasp. He put his right hand over the deep cut in his left wrist. *I'm going to faint now.*

He looked at Hannah. She lay on the ground, her eyes shut. His vision seemed to blacken at the edges, like paper charring. *Not yet!* He strained to focus.

He saw Hannah's back rise and fall so slightly. She was breathing.

He nodded, relieved.

'Okay,' he whispered, and his vision silvered. His spine seemed to turn to water and he fell inside the cage.

The wind stopped. The trees grew still.

The world looked far away – even the moonlit cage of bone and branches around him seemed small and distant, like viewing a room through the wrong end of a telescope.

Take off your shirt. Bind your wrist.

But there was so much blood . . .

He struggled to remove his jumper, but weariness crept up inside him like the pleasant, drowning waters of Lethe.

I can't.

Then roll over, he told himself.

With numb fingers, he lifted his jumper and shirt, pressed his pumping wrist against the skin of his belly, and rolled onto it.

Enough, he thought. *Sleep now.*

He was too weary even to close his eyes, so he stared out at a world far away and ringed with inviting gloom. The woods were eerily quiet. The circle of trees stood silent, their still leaves as green as frozen sea-water in the icy moonlight, black as pitch in shadow. They were hushed. Anticipating. The only movement was the gentle rising and falling of Hannah's tiny back.

Sleep.

Nicholas closed his eyes, wondered what the wetness on his belly was, then nodded as he remembered. He was dying.

Don't worry. Sleep now.

Cate would be waiting.

He smiled.

But a smell shivered him awake.

It was a scent as old as the world. It was a hundred aromas of a thousand places. It was the tang of pine needles. It was the musk of sex. It was the muscular rot of mushrooms. It was the spice of oak. The meaty redolence of soil and bark and herb. It was bats and husks and burrows and moss. It was solid and alive – so alive! And it was close.

The vapours invaded Nicholas's nostrils and his hairs rose on their roots. His eyes were as heavy as manhole covers, but he opened them. Through the dying calm inside him snaked a tremble of fear.

The trees themselves seemed tense, waiting. The moonlight was as hard as shell, sharp and ready to be struck and to ring like steel.

A shadow moved.

It poured like oil from between the tall trees, and flowed across the dark, sandy dirt, lengthening into the middle of the ring. The trees seemed to bend towards it, spellbound. A long, long shadow . . .

Then, a hoof. As large as a bucket and dark as stone, grey-splotched with moss; layered and peeling like ancient horn. Above the hoof: a massive leg. Feathered. Or furred. Or dense with leaves. A dark green-grey cast blue as gunmetal by the glacial moonlight.

Muscular and long. Its knee bent backwards like a horse's hind leg's, but thrice the size and powerful. Another hoof, another enormous leg. A torso dense as an ape's, but so much larger, as dark as the shadows between the roots of ancient trees. Arms like a man's: knotted with ropy muscle but thick as tree trunks, their topsides shimmering with fungal grey fur or leaves or vestigial feathers, their undersides creviced as old bark. A bull neck, corded like worn rock. Shoulders, shifting with a frost of green, wide as boulders. Antlers like oak branches, webbed with vines and moss, and huge. And a face in shadow.

Nicholas stared. *I am dreaming. I am dead.*

The creature's head turned to him. Its face was rimmed with skin like leaves, or made of leaves. The jaw was massive and oxlike, dripping with tendrils like curling roots. Great tusks the shape of oak leaves thrust from the corners of its wide, leathery lips. Huge nostrils flared. And eyes as dark as wells of deep, distant water reflected the moonlight; eyes at once human and yet so inhuman – inscrutable as winter sky, hungry as an eagle's. And old. So old.

It was the face he'd seen in Walpole Park. The face he'd seen carved in wood and stone in Bretherton's church.

The Green Man.

Nicholas's body was rigid with electric panic, white terror, delirium . . . His flesh knew what the creature before him was; it knew at some fundamental, cellular level what it smelled and faced, and would have begun digging through the ground itself to hide were it not locked tight in bright horror.

The Green Man stopped halfway between Nicholas and Hannah. He was taller than the trees. He lifted his head and his nostrils splayed. The air shifted. The trees shimmered with pleasure, opening their moist leaves with dark delight. Then the Green Man's head turned in the direction that Quill had fled . . . towards her cottage.

A tiny sound. Hannah groaned softly.

She rolled. Her eyes flickered open and found Nicholas.

He opened his mouth to speak, but only a hiss of air escaped his lips.

Hannah looked up.

The Green Man loomed over her, dwarfing her small as a kitten. He shifted his hoofs, and snorted a blast of warm air as pungent as the forest floor.

Hannah smiled, and her eyes closed.

The Green Man stooped and picked her up.

'Hannah . . .' whispered Nicholas.

The Green Man turned at the sound. In an instant he stamped towards the cage, three enormous steps, a colossal wave about to crash, his wide, dark face right before Nicholas's.

His scent was overwhelming: erotic and wildly horrible; hunger and rot and age and lust. His green leafy lips parted, showing teeth as large as bricks and hard as ivory, goatlike and sharp.

Nicholas stared into the eyes. Eyes as large as saucers, without whites: huge dark stones that glittered with intelligence and violence.

And the Green Man chuckled.

The warm, foetid air from his mouth washed over Nicholas, strong and whipping as a storm wind through ripe brambles.

Nicholas's eyes rolled back in his head, and the night world became as black as the centre of the earth.

44

Hannah enjoyed this beautiful feeling. Of gently drifting above the ground. Of flying.

She felt the cool air on her face, the warm leaves under her legs, her back. Overhead, she could see that the clouds were moving again, rolling in a steady dark wave towards the moon. *More rain*, she thought idly, and snuggled back into her warm cot of ferns.

But the trip did not last long. She sailed past the roof of the old woman's cottage, watching as the shadows of clouds raced over it, casting it into bleak shadow. Then she was being lowered. She was placed on her feet.

'Oh,' she half-complained.

But the hands were wise. The earth was good. And – oh! – the smell. The smell was divine! A delicious brew of vanilla, of newborn puppy, of jasmine, of sweet sweat and His skin. He had put her down, and that was good. Because there was a task to do.

Of course!

Hannah stood beside the closed barn doors of the cellar. How long had it been since she was locked in there? An hour? A year? It was a dream lost in waking. But down there now was something that needed attention.

Some*one*.

She turned to look at the one who carried her, to ask —

But His firm, large hands held her head gently, preventing her turn, silencing her question. And then she saw . . .

Oh! How clever!

On the ground was Nicholas's duffel bag.

I shall do this right, thought Hannah, secretly thrilled, knowing that He would watch her work. *To please Him, I will do it well.*

She reached into the warm, dark bag and her fingers probed gently. Ah! They found what she knew would be there.

A cigarette lighter. And a bottle of kerosene.

'The doors are heavy,' she said. She kept her voice light and breezy, not wanting to betray how her skin tingled knowing His eyes were watching her.

His large hand reached, and opened one of the wood doors as easily as lifting a magazine.

Moonlight poured into the cellar. Curled in one corner was a ragged figure, barely visible in the deep shadows. Quill was sobbing.

'Please . . . please . . .'

Hannah smiled. She knew what to do.

There was so much money on the floor. *I put it there*, she thought, pleased with herself. Some of the pile of bills had been wet by the rain that had dripped between the doors, but most was still dry. She unscrewed the lid of the kerosene bottle and poured its contents down the stairs. The oily smell was harsh, and she frowned – she didn't want to mask so much as an atom of His charged, musky aroma.

'Now?' she asked.

She felt the cool air swirl as His huge head swooped down through the air, down behind her, till His mouth was right next to the nape of her neck. Her skin prickled in delight and her heart pounded.

'Now,' He said with a voice as warm as sunlight on old stone or the sea-water of a summer rock pool. Delicious and old and deep.

Hannah opened the lid of the lighter and flicked the flint wheel.

'Please!' begged the huddled old shape cowering below.

The flame sparked brightly, and Hannah felt Him slyly retreat behind her. It made her sad. She threw the lighter down into the cellar and heard the sucking *fwoompf* as the kerosene caught.

'MY LORD!!' cried Quill, but her last word was smothered by a solid *bang!* as the cellar door shut again.

Hannah scurried neatly to where the doors joined and slid the barrel bolt shut. *Done!*

She looked up, beaming, ready for His praise.

Beneath her, the screaming started.

•

He was ten again. Tristram had been carried past him on a floating carpet of eighty-thousand legs. Now, he, too, was dead, and being borne away to be hidden clumsily, ready to be found exsanguinated and white amid broken wood and discarded things.

The night slid past him, weeping, its tears as cold as the far sky. *It's all right*, he wanted to say to the sighing trees and the lowing clouds. *Don't cry. I'm glad.*

He was going back now. Back to him, whom he'd loved as a boy, and to her, whom he'd loved as a man. This last cool passage could not end too quickly.

Pleased with death, Nicholas opened his eyes.

The woods moved. The trees strode by him, waving in the cold wind, shaking off their doleful rains. Nicholas was surprised. He wasn't on his back, drifting over the forest floor on a shifting bed of scuttling spiny legs, but cradled in an arm as great as a tree bough, aphotic and smelling of soil and worm and pungent stag musk. He wearily rolled his head.

The girl lay near him. Her name was lost just now. She slept, as he so dearly wanted to, and her lips were curled contentedly in her sleep. She could have been a dreaming sprite nestled deep between the loving roots of ancient trees.

Sleep. A faery dream.

Nicholas closed his eyes, and the rain fell on them, growing heavier.

45

That night, the river swelled. Rain hammered down as if determined to dissolve the earth.

The police recalled the State Emergency Service volunteers searching the Carmichael Road woods for Hannah Gerlic; the forest was simply too wild and treacherous in the rain at night . . . and this rain was violent. Tethered to powerful spotlight beams, the drenched men and women in orange overalls stumped back from the tree line and headed towards the parked minibus they'd arrived in. They tramped up the chequer-plate steps, stamping hard to shake off the water, switching off torches, tutting to their neighbours about how they wished they could keep looking, but all secretly glad they didn't have to continue battling through the wild turns of blackthorn and cunjevoi and lantana while this incredible rain smashed down on their skulls.

Veterinarian assistant Katy Rhydderch was the second last to climb the bus stairs. She just happened to glance down at a flicker of movement before she entered the vehicle. An orb weaver spider was straining across the grass on its matchstick legs, slipping as it headed for cover. Katy, notorious among her friends for hating to hurt any living thing (excluding, perhaps, the ticks she occasionally had to pull off matt-furred dogs) was afraid the spider would be crushed under the minibus tyres. She knelt to let the creature crawl onto her torch handle so she could move it out of harm's way. As the spider tentatively stepped onto the flashlight, Katy saw there was a shadowed bundle under the bus.

It was a little girl. She was curled like a comma under the drive shaft, fast asleep.

∙

Twenty minutes later, Hannah Gerlic lay dozing on a stretcher in the back of an ambulance parked just metres from where the minibus had sat. The cabin roared as if the Pacific were crashing on its roof, but Hannah's parents didn't seem to mind the deafening noise: each held one of Hannah's hands. Hannah had woken long enough to yawn, ask to go home, and confess she couldn't remember one thing that had happened after eating Vee's enormous lunch.

Police in raincoats paced outside the ambulance, waiting to be released from the scene. Constable Brian Wenn was counting the minutes to the end of his shift – his girlfriend, Eva, had returned from a week-long conference today and was no doubt lying naked in his bed. Even more pressing, his bladder was full to bursting. Wenn checked his watch, cursed his soaking wet feet, and hurried through the tall grass towards the tree line, unzipping his fly as he went. As his waters mixed with the rain, he glanced idly to his left.

And so the second happenstance discovery of the night was made.

A man lay unconscious in the tall, dark grass, his head not two steps away from Wenn's stream of warm urine.

46

The rain stormed down for three days, never stopping, a seemingly endless disgorgement on roofs and roads and car hoods and gardens.

Residents who just weeks ago had complained bitterly at the council's water restrictions turned their ire to the ceaseless rain. Elation at the filling of the distant dams that fed the city turned to apprehension as inner-city storm-water drains failed to cope with the torrents. Streets closed. Mains burst. The wide, brown river rose . . . and kept rising. Landscape suppliers sold out their stocks of yard bags and sand. Schools closed. Birds too wet to feed and too weary to cling fell dead out of trees.

Five people drowned.

Three were in a car trying to cross a floodway from their five-acre property on the city's western outskirts, swept away in waters that ran far faster than the driver had guessed. The fourth was a Chinese-born shop owner in Fortitude Valley, whose import warehouse had flooded. He had been working with his wife trying to raise the cardboard boxes of teapots, calendars, woks and – incongruously – vibrators off the flooding warehouse floor when a sodden carton at the bottom of one precarious stack slumped and gave way, and a whole mountain of cardboard, ceramic, steel and soft-to-the-touch silicone came down, trapping the man until the waters covered his face. The fifth death was an elderly man whose inquisitive foxhound crept too close to racing creek waters and was swept away. The pensioner, desperate to save his only companion, stepped calmly in after the tiny creature, which witnesses said, screamed like a child until it went under. Its owner drowned without a sound.

While the river eventually broke its banks in many places, the first flood was over a lobe of land at Tallong, which the waters normally circumvented in a lazy loop. Now, the river was travelling at twenty knots and decided no longer to take the slow way round. The waters rose four, five, eight, ten metres, and then poured across the hundreds of hectares of thickly wooded land – land that had been slated for clearing and construction until the developer withdrew his plans and subsequently suicided. The fast brown waters smashed through trees, uprooted the smallest shrubs, picked up surface boulders, and strained against gums and figs and muttonwood and wild quince.

No one but the spiders perched high in rain-lashed branches were there to see a wave of brown water gush between the bristling trunks to drown a garden of fragrant herbs and smash against a tiny cottage. An hour later, the insistent, powerful tide sent a floating trunk like a battering ram into the cottage: the collision swept one wall clean away. With the structure breached, the waters soon took the other three walls, and the cottage washed away. A cellar beside the cottage filled first with water and then with mud, burying forever a steel box surrounded by wet ash, the mummified remains of an Aboriginal boy named Billy Fry who went missing from the Our Lady of the Rosary Orphanage in 1916, and the charred body of an impossibly old woman. One door to the cellar was carried off by the swirling waters and ended up punching a hole in the hull of a catamaran moored fifteen kilometres downstream. The other door, like the cellar itself, was drowned in black mud.

A sagging cage of wood and bone within a ring of trees floated away and broke up gradually, tossed among the living branches of yellow wood and spotted gum. Two small knives were lost forever.

One early morning revelation to the residents of the city was the reappearance of the ferry *Wynard*. A dizzy Lazarus, the ferry floated with her hull upturned to the thundery skies, like a turtle emerging from long hibernation. Her grey timbers threatened at every moment to sink forever, yet she bobbed downstream with the grace of a retired soprano convinced to make one final curtain call.

She passed the rain-washed glass towers of the city proper, and finally was caught by enterprising young men from the Kangaroo Point Abseiling Club, who appropriated one unpopular member's old ropes, attached a makeshift grapple and snagged the *Wynard* from the shore. They sold her carcass on eBay for almost three thousand dollars.

•

As the flood waters ploughed through the woods, Nicholas Close slept in his hospital bed.

He was tended in shifts by three women: firstly by Laine Boye, then by his mother, then by his sister. Suzette would wait for the nurses to leave the ward and then trace strange symbols with fragrant water on Nicholas's forehead and over his heart. Neither Katharine nor Laine protested, just nodded and watched.

The doctors informed all three women that there was nothing gravely wrong with Nicholas's body: it had recovered surprisingly well, although the reattached tendons would never again close a full fist of his left hand. He had, however, lost a lot of blood and lasting risk was to his brain, which had been starved of good blood flow for a long while. Unfortunately, any damage to his brain would only be apparent if and when he woke again.

The three women watched and waited.

•

Two policemen visited twice.

The first time, they ignored Katharine as if she were invisible gas instead of a mother beside her unconscious son's bed, and spoke only to Nicholas's doctor. The second time, they marched straight up to her, and informed her matter-of-factly that the Department of Public Prosecutions would not be pursuing any charges against

Nicholas Close for firearm offences, including the shooting of Hannah Gerlic.

Katharine followed the pair all the way to their unmarked car, quizzing them relentlessly, until the younger of the two finally admitted that the Gerlic child insisted that Nicholas did *not* shoot her, and had no recollection of how the lead pellet had got into her calf.

'And where's the gun?' asked Katharine.

The policemen sent warning looks to one another and drove away.

Katharine guessed the answer. There was no gun. The floods had taken it.

Nicholas slept.

47

He opened one eye at 2.13 a.m., just as the last of the flooding rain fell on the city and the clouds pulled close their coats to scurry out to sea.

He was certain he was dead. He was certain that he was lying in Quill's cottage, waiting to enact again and again the trudge to the cellar, the walk to the ring of trees, the incarceration in the cage of bone, and the cutting of his throat. So much blood. So wearying. But then he remembered . . . it was not his throat that had been cut, and not Quill who did the cutting.

Nicholas opened his other eye. He wasn't in the cottage. His fingers inched to his left wrist and felt the hard sleeve of plaster there. He rolled his head one way, towards the window.

Stars trembled above the subsiding river.

He rolled the other way, and saw her.

Laine was in a cot bed beside his, her face pale and lean and grimly tight, even in sleep.

He watched her a long time. Missing Cate. Exploring Laine's face. Wondering if he was glad he was alive.

He rolled back to stare at the ceiling. There were things to be remembered. Incredible things. The sight of something awesome and terrible. But as he mined the thought, ready to expose its shape, sleep dragged at him like insistent imps. He would sleep now, and remember tomorrow . . .

But by dawn, his memory of the Green Man had vanished as completely as had the rain.

The doctors conducted cognisance tests, assayed his blood, examined his urine, and decided there was no reason for him not to be discharged.

Laine helped Nicholas pack. She told him carefully about Pritam's death – but he simply nodded. She explained his mother had killed Garnock, and how she and Suzette and Katharine had been thwarted by the police. Again, he nodded. The silence between them wasn't uncomfortable: it was small and warm and as sad as reading the headstone of a stranger's child.

She took him home.

As he walked from the road to the front gate and then to the front porch, his head turned this way and that. He refused to go inside, and sat on the front steps, watching the street. Laine realised he was searching for Gavin's ghost, so left him alone.

Nicholas waited on the porch outside 68 Lambeth Street for a full hour, watching workmen with shovels follow a truck up the road, scooping the gutters clear of debris.

Gavin's ghost never showed.

Nicholas held his jaw tight, and went inside to have tea with the three women.

He sat for long hours looking out his childhood bedroom window at the streets of Tallong, trying to remember. His mother, his sister and Laine all asked him in their different ways what had happened the night that Hannah Gerlic had slipped away from home, and had been found under an SES minibus hours later.

He couldn't remember.

Nicholas sent his gaze over denuded trees, over eroded streets half-closed with orange emergency barriers, over energy company crews rising in cherrypickers to repair power lines. That was not entirely true: there were two memories.

The first was a clear picture in his mind – solid and smooth as marble – of following Hannah's pointing finger to the rippling waters of the gully creek, and seeing rafts of small, moving things struggling to escape the dark water. But the instant he recognised the shifting masses as arachnids, the tape inside his brain ran out, and his next recollection was of waking in the hospital and seeing stars over the flooded night river.

And there was another, fragmented memory. It hardly deserved to be called that: it was more a wisp, a faint scent on the fickle air of recollection. A dream.

It was of moving. Of being carried through the woods. The air had smelled wet and thick and vivid with greenery. And a voice was speaking to him, not in words, but in a vibration that carried through his body and into his mind. What it said was unclear, but it was as primal and lustful as the thunder of the ocean . . . but also deathly sad and doomed. A dream.

He watched as the energy company crew lowered the boom with its cage and the truck drove away.

•

Nicholas asked Suzette to walk with him to the woods.

They spoke little on the way down, batting between them recollections of schoolteachers and the venial sins of childhood. They stopped at Carmichael Road, and looked across at the woods. Neither said a word for a long while.

The trees had been given new life by the recent downpours. The sun winked on their leaves, which shimmered with green lustre, and their lightly laughing tops rolling up the gentle hills to the river. They were still dark and dense, but there was no foreboding any more. No sense of things lurking. No gravity to draw you in, no ill shiver to send you hurrying. The woods were plain, and vulnerable.

'It's gone,' said Suzette.

'Yes.'

'*She's* gone.'

'Yes.'

Suzette nodded, took his arm, and brother and sister walked home.

EPILOGUE

Hannah waited and waited for him to come.

Eventually, the telephone rang, and she ran to the lounge room to answer – but her mother beat her to it.

Mrs Gerlic was speaking with him. Her voice was snipped and severe, warning him not to call, that Hannah was fine, thank you, but to please stay *away*. She hung up.

But Hannah knew he would come. He was a good man, a fine man. A brave man. A little misguided, though.

Her leg was healing nicely. She felt quite good, and told her parents so. She went to Miriam's funeral, and cried at all the right spots.

The police asked her questions about the night that she and Nicholas went into the woods, but she said all she could remember was finding a shotgun on the path, and touching it even though she *knew* she shouldn't, and dropping it and it going off with a very scary bang. Everything else was . . . Well, that was all she could remember.

She said she was sorry for sneaking out, and everyone believed her.

But she did remember. She remembered everything.

Including *His* promise.

She was angry that Nicholas hadn't come, but that was okay. Things would work out in time.

In weeks and months, after her parents were lulled by normalcy and their tears were done and they'd grown bored with watching out for Hannah, she would be allowed again to walk to school and back.

Then she could go back into the woods.
She could build a new place.
Replant the garden. Tend her trees.
And get back her pretty man.